THE CUT *of the* MOON

ALSO BY CYNTHIA ELLINGSEN

Marriage Matters

The Whole Package

The Lighthouse Keeper (a Starlight Cove novel)

The Winemaker's Secret (a Starlight Cove novel)

A Bittersweet Surprise (a Starlight Cove novel)

The Choice I Made

When We Were Sisters

A Play for Revenge (a Starlight Cove novel)

The Lost Letters of Aisling

THE CUT *of the* MOON

A NOVEL

CYNTHIA ELLINGSEN

LAKE UNION
PUBLISHING

This is a work of fiction. Names, characters, organizations, places, events, and incidents are either products of the author's imagination or are used fictitiously.

Published by Lake Union Publishing, Seattle

www.apub.com

EU product safety contact:
Amazon Media EU S. à r.l.
38, avenue John F. Kennedy, L-1855 Luxembourg
amazonpublishing-gpsr@amazon.com

ISBN-13: 9781662529399 (paperback)
ISBN-13: 9781662529382 (digital)

Cover design by Caroline Teagle Johnson
Cover image: © Jan Hakan Dahlstrom / Getty; © Eyesblink

Printed in the United States of America

To Hudson, Hazel, and Ryan. With love, always.

Chapter One

Upstate New York, 1925

There were too many secrets. Delicious. Dangerous. Ruby drank them in from beneath the parlor table as the jazz band kept time with the misdeeds of the glittery guests. The nub of her pencil was tight in her hand as she jotted it all into her journal.

> *Miss A. took two chocolates when no one was looking.*
> *Indira has been grabbed by Brad three times, even while trying to carry a tray of drinks. Father better not notice or Brad will be lashed.*
> *The diamond women laugh with Uncle Peter but will whisper about him when he walks away. They know he's no good.*

Ruby settled on her heels, the sharp leather of the boot cutting into her flesh as she reread that last one.

Keep, or cross it out? Keep it. Uncle Peter deserved every word. Besides, no one cared about the scribblings of a foolish girl; isn't that what he always said? Certainly, no one paid attention to her now.

Setting down her pencil, Ruby watched Uncle Peter follow a servant out of the room with his uneven gait. Most likely to hit her across the face for spilling water. His smile was stoic but his jaw tense, not a good sign.

Uncle Peter had lived with their family ever since the war. He'd come for a visit, and he'd never left. In the past few years, though, he'd been too brazen, arguing with her father at the dinner table over business matters. Two nights before, he'd slammed his fists against the table so hard her sister's wine spilled onto her dress. Glenn and her brother were the only men invited to the library for drinks and smoking after dinner that evening, while Uncle Peter stood in the dark by the river, the tip of his cigar glowing in the night.

Ruby didn't want him here—no one wanted him here—but he was her father's brother, so he owned half the house and half the business. Her mother said he was as integrated into their family as a tail on an animal, and there was nothing they could do about it.

Ruby bit down on her pencil, wondering what the guests would say if they knew the truth about what went on at Wind Thorne. Especially since it seemed so idyllic, with the smell of woodsmoke and decorative pine boughs filling the room in preparation for her sister's winter wedding. Outside, the cattle fields stretched to the forest along the river, the hidden distilleries further cloaked in snow.

Ruby took a gulp of hot cider and returned to her notebook.

Father Aaron poured wine when he thought no one was watching. Funny, since he's the one who says God is always watching.

The music picked up. Like the second hand of a clock, the bassist swung his foot, as if accounting for each lost moment. Some guests danced the Charleston, everyone drank, and no one knew Elizabeth's wedding was about to be called off.

Ruby was surprised her parents hadn't made the announcement yet. Perhaps they couldn't bear to send away the guests who had traveled for the wedding week or waste the trays of oysters that sat on ice in rows down in the kitchen. It would be a shock to them all when her father stepped into the room in his tailored suit, clinked his glass, and proclaimed that his daughter would remain at Wind Thorne for good, leaving Glenn of the slick black hair and plump lips searching for a new bride.

Everyone thought Glenn was so dapper, like a silent-movie star, but now that Ruby knew the truth about marriage, she could barely look at him. He stood over by the musicians, keeping time against his thigh. One of his well-dressed friends slapped him on the back, and he grimaced with a glance toward the stairs before launching into some story that made everyone around him laugh.

Ruby couldn't wait to see his face when he heard Elizabeth wouldn't marry him after all, not after the way he'd acted when she'd lost the ring. It would probably mirror Ruby's face the night she'd learned her sister planned to leave their home to be with him.

"Why wouldn't she live here?" Ruby had demanded when her mother had first explained it. *"Why?"*

Ruby had just assumed Glenn would move into Wind Thorne. The rooms stretched endlessly along the upper hall, fifteen of them at least, all with stone fireplaces and sitting areas. He could manage the workers on the farm and supervise the fermentation of the mash, and it would have been perfect. Glenn had once been fun to be around. He'd brought her presents, little candies, and books, like he was courting her and not her sister.

Well, she didn't have to worry about that anymore. Now that he'd shouted at Elizabeth, that was that. Her sobs had echoed through the upper hall all afternoon. They became more insistent with each report that the ring had not yet been found and that the servants would be questioned. The whole thing made Ruby's stomach hurt, but it had been worth it.

If Elizabeth had married—had left—Ruby's heartache would've been endless. She'd have no one to let her win at Lost Heir or arrange flowers in the spring or steal warm rolls from the kitchen to eat down by the river while searching for deer tracks. She'd be invisible for real, and not because she wanted to be.

The wooden table she sat beneath jostled, bumping her on the head, and a whirlwind of perfume and shimmery beads slid under the table. Elizabeth. Ruby drew back, surprised to see her sister at the party.

"What are you doing under here, you little dish?" Her sister crawled in next to her, draping the fringe of her dress over to the side like a veil. "Oh, I see." She poked at Ruby's notebook. "Spying."

Elizabeth's dark eyes were bright, lips as ripe as the inside of an olive, and she smiled so much her dimple showed. No tears. In fact, she seemed ready to celebrate.

Ruby fidgeted with the strand of pearls around her neck, the chill of the marble-like orbs cold as bone.

"What are you doing here?" she asked. "I thought you'd stay upstairs."

"Yes, I took forever, I know." Elizabeth's diamond earrings flashed. "Worth the wait, yet now I'm on the floor, risking this dress just to be with you." She took a sip of Ruby's cider. "This is delicious. This whole party is delicious." She beamed. "Can you believe it's finally here?"

"I . . ." Ruby stared at Elizabeth's finger.

Still empty. So why was her sister pretending everything was all right?

"You ready to dance?" Elizabeth adjusted the black headband that held her waved hair in place. Outside the safety of the table, the party thundered on. "Come on out."

"No." Ruby's cheeks burned. "Father will make the announcement soon. He'll tell them the wedding is off."

Elizabeth lifted her perfectly painted-on brows. "Huh?"

"The fight." Ruby could barely speak. "The ring."

Sympathy crossed Elizabeth's face. "Dear heart, is that what you thought?"

The trumpet player hit a note like a long wail.

Her sister pulled Ruby close against the scratchy beads of her dress. Ruby breathed in the scent of her sister's lavender body talc and the deep musk of her hair cream, wishing to stay in the moment forever.

"The ring will turn up." Elizabeth shrugged. "I can't believe I was so careless to lose it, but the wedding will happen either way. The ring is a thing. Love, it's until the end of time." She lowered her voice. "Besides, it was costume. Father told me. He swapped it during the appraisal and kept the real one in the safe."

Ruby's mouth dropped open. "What?"

"Yes, it was quite a relief to hear it." Elizabeth shrugged a thin shoulder. "Glenn was about to put the screws on everyone, you know."

"You shouldn't marry him," Ruby insisted. "He was awful to you."

"He was upset." Her sister waved her hand. "He's a doll."

Uncle Peter walked back in, the heavy hood of his gaze sweeping the room. Ruby considered Uncle Peter's mean face. She'd disliked but never feared him because she'd always had the protection of her older sister. The nights Uncle Peter stormed through the halls, ranting about this or that, Elizabeth would climb into Ruby's bed in her dressing gown and hold her tight. What would it be like to face that alone?

"Let me come with you," Ruby said. "I can't stay here. Not with him."

Her sister, who had started to crawl out from beneath the table, stopped. She followed Ruby's gaze. "He's bothered you?"

Their father walked into the main room then, looking angry. His face was flushed, and half the women in the room clawed at his arm, trying to pull him to dance. Their mother sat in the corner, sipping her drink, whispering to Gram behind her crystal glass.

Ruby was about to answer when shiny black shoes appeared next to the table. Glenn crouched down, his face lit with a mischievous grin. "There you are, my love. How improper of you."

Like always, her sister forgot all about Ruby as her fiancé swept her into a kiss. Guests surrounded them, sharing well-wishes.

"I cannot wait to spend every second of my life with this woman," Glenn proclaimed, lifting Elizabeth's hand. The black beads of her dress sparkled in the low light.

Ruby held tight to her pencil. Carefully, she wrote Glenn's name in her journal. Then, with the hardest stroke possible, she crossed it out.

The hours of the engagement party passed with toasts and tears.

Brined hens lined the table for the dinner, along with a feast of roasted vegetables, potatoes, and rolls. Ruby sat in silence, picking at her food and ignoring the chatter of the Mensley boys. Their father owned the house and the land next door, but they were farmhands and had dirt under their nails.

It annoyed her that out of an entire roomful of people, she was stuck sitting next to them. On top of that, word had spread about the missing engagement ring, and Chester Mensley wouldn't shut up about it. He was only a year older than she was, sixteen, and always up to something.

"The ring, it's here somewhere." His round, freckled face was lit with excitement. "I'm going to find it."

Elliot nodded. He was fourteen but practically the size of a grown man. He went along with anything Chester said.

"You think there'll be an award?" he asked.

"*Re*ward, dummy." Chester gulped some water. "Nope, but finding it is the right thing to do."

Ruby narrowed her eyes. Chester's father owned the house next door, so she'd known him her entire life. One of his favorite crimes was to put Elliot up to playing card games with the drivers, the ones who transported the biggest barrels of whiskey out on their trucks. The workers got a kick out of fleecing Elliot out of his pennies and had no clue Chester was busy glomming whole dollars from the cash envelopes in their trucks.

"Never enough to be noticed," he liked to brag on the days Ruby sipped lemonade with him outside the back kitchen. "I've got a lot of money now. I'm almost rich."

When Ruby's father had caught wind of Chester's antics, he laughed. "That's an enterprising young man. I'd better make sure he doesn't wait downriver for my barrels, planning to sell them out from underneath me."

The comment was made in jest, but Ruby's father was serious about his distilleries. Prohibition had complicated their family business, but so far, there hadn't been any trouble.

"Loyalty," her father liked to say. "That's the secret ingredient."

Everyone respected her father, and most people feared him. The one time a worker had tried to steal from their family, the whispers about what later happened to the man gave Ruby nightmares for weeks. She kept hoping he would be on the trucks the next round, that the stories weren't true, but she never saw him again.

"Hey." Chester's little brother jostled her arm, splashing cranberry compote on her dress. "How big's the diamond in the ring?"

Chester shot him a look. "Bigger than your brain." Handing Ruby a napkin, he lowered his voice. "Do you have any clues?"

The image of the ring gleamed in her mind. So stunning on her sister's slim finger. Ruby had spent hours staring at the solitaire, mesmerized by how it sparkled like the sun on the river. The gold band itself was a work of art, with detailed texture along the edge and ornate carvings on the band. When she'd tried it on, the deep yellow was so buttery that it dented beneath her fingernail.

It was frustrating to learn it was fake. Elizabeth should still be crying in her room, not center stage at the head table, letting her fiancé nibble her shoulder like he was some mink stole come to life. The glasses clinked, and their father stood to give a toast.

"Stop asking me about the ring," Ruby mumbled. "Besides, I don't know why you think you'd be the one to find it."

His dark eyes were vaguely amused. "Well, Ruby, because I'd do the right thing. Return it to the owner. You know I'm always looking to do what's right."

Sure, like he did last Christmas at church, when he'd spotted her gold coin. Ruby had received it in her stocking and brought it to the service in spite of her mother's warnings. She'd fiddled with it in her lap, the gold gleaming in the light from the nearby candles. The moment she noticed Chester watching from the next pew over, she tucked it away. That night, the coin was no longer in the pocket of her dress, and she never said a word about it to anyone.

Now she set the white napkin stained with compote on the table and gave him a small smile.

"I suspect it's in my grandmother's room," she admitted. "This morning, Gram gave Elizabeth a long talk about marriage. The ring came up missing right after that."

Chester looked around, but no one else was paying attention.

"Her room, huh?" he said.

"Yes, but . . ." She shook her head. "You can't go in there, Chester."

"No, no. I know." He tugged at the sleeves of his blazer. "I'm not stupid." He took a drink of wine, eyes darting all over the room.

Ruby picked up her fork and took a cheerful bite of carrots. Chester had no way of knowing that her grandmother retired immediately following each meal, regardless of the occasion. He'd sneak into her room like a raccoon, only to have Gram sit straight up in bed and ring that bell of hers like a fire alarm. Justice.

"I'm sure someone will find it soon." Ruby shrugged. "Good thing, too, because that diamond is extremely valuable."

Chester practically choked on his roll with delight.

Once the servants had cleared the table, Ruby expected he would sneak off immediately, but he was too smart for that. Instead, he focused on the sideboard, now filling up with foil-wrapped candies and chocolate cakes that draped the room in their dark, sweet scent.

Ruby took the opportunity to head up the back stairs on her own. The silence was thick, and she slipped into her father's room. The one time she'd dared search his belongings, a few months back, she'd found the key to his safe. One of the maids had walked in, and Ruby ducked down behind the coats in his closet. That's when she spotted the key, tucked back between a crack in one of the wooden shelves, so well concealed that only a mouse would find it.

Now Ruby grabbed it as fast as she could, then went downstairs to his office. Heart pounding louder than the bass of the music, she opened the safe and let out a breath. Stacks of money stared back at her, as well as gold coins and several pieces of her mother's jewelry. She ignored the impulse to study the deep, moody rubies and sapphires and instead found the diamond ring, slipping it deep into the secret pocket with the button in her dress.

Glenn would no longer trust their family when the real ring came up missing, too. She jumped at a sudden sound in the hallway and quickly locked the safe. Some of the servants were in the hallway when she peeked out, but no one paid any mind to her as she returned the key and headed back to the party.

The tempo of the music was slow while the servants threw open the windows and added more logs to the fires. Ruby stood by the drink table, waiting. Chester passed by, shoving another dessert into his mouth. He lingered for a moment too long at the bottom of the stairs, and Ruby raised her eyebrows at him.

With a grin, he went over to a group of mutual friends and started joking around with them. Ruby ducked back under the safety of her table, keeping close watch as the others returned to drinks and dancing. Chester meandered over to the stairs and, after a quick glance around, ran up. Moments later, Uncle Peter followed, thunder on his face.

Ruby almost went after them, but the memory of her stolen Christmas coin stopped her. Instead, she pulled her notebook out of the deep pocket she had sewn into each dress, and jotted down her thoughts. They had to be quick, because she didn't have time to write whole paragraphs tonight.

It's prettier than the other. I can't wait to study it in the light.

Chester's dad doesn't like Father. He kept talking during his speech at dinner.
Elizabeth keeps touching the finger where her ring used to be.
My brother seems happy about the wedding. Brad's always been mean to Elizabeth, so I'm surpr—

The scream was bone chilling. Ruby dropped her pencil, which rolled through the sudden silence. The music stopped and so did the guests, some standing stock-still in the middle of the dance floor.

Chester.

Horror rushed through her. It had been a fun joke to trick him, but that scream was far beyond what she'd meant to have happen. The guests looked frightened, and her brother rushed from the room. He was nodding when he returned, but his whole body looked tense.

"Start the music back up," Brad called. "Everything's fine."

The horn player let out a loud blast. Glenn set his drink on the sideboard and rushed to dip Elizabeth in the middle of the dance floor. Their feet flew with the rhythm of the bass. The guests chuckled, drunk enough to take the mood right back up again.

Ruby wasn't fooled. It had to have been Chester who screamed. She raced toward the back hall, determined to save him from a brutal beating. Her family could be so cruel, and Ruby didn't understand what evil part of herself had set him up like that. Chester made her laugh, in spite of his mischief. Breathing heavily, she rounded the corner and stopped.

Uncle Peter and two of the men who helped Father with the cattle were in the back hall, blocking her view. Ruby slipped into the shadows along the stairs. If she distracted them, gave a scream of her own, perhaps Chester could get away. Ruby took in a deep breath, a worker moved to the side, and the scream caught in her throat.

It wasn't Chester—it was Indira. The servant Ruby loved the most, the one her brother couldn't keep his hands off, lay in a crumpled heap at the bottom of the stairs. Her head was twisted at an angle and rested on a pillow of dark-red blood.

"Get her outside," ordered Uncle Peter.

The two men picked up Indira's limp body as if she were nothing more than a sack of grain. They took her out back, and Ruby watched from the door as they laid her on the snow-frosted ground. Uncle Peter knelt down and leaned his head in close to her chest. Ruby's father rushed into view, slipping on the snow, with Father Aaron by his side.

"What did you do?" her father cried.

Uncle Peter looked up, his eyes black and wild. He leaped to his feet and lunged for her father, punching him with a sickening thud. The two rolled across the ground, hitting and kicking each other. They skidded through the snow, each desperately fighting to gain ground. Uncle Peter was vicious, grabbing her father's face and forcing it into the ground, but her father was stronger, using his legs to flip him over before pinning him in the back with his knee. Ruby shrank back against the wall. Her brother rushed out of the house, followed by her mother.

Her mother came to a sudden stop and put a handkerchief to her mouth before heading straight back into the house. Father Aaron pulled her dad off Uncle Peter and separated the two. The men breathed out steam in the icy air, then lunged at each other once again.

Ruby came outside, taking tentative steps toward the body, careful to stay away from the fight. She knelt down in the snow. Indira was still alive. Her breathing was shallow as blood spilled from a gash on her head.

Ruby stared at her face. The full lips Ruby had always admired, the sharp cut of Indira's cheeks. Her hair was black, shining against the snow. Ruby wrapped her shawl tightly around Indira's head, trying to keep the blood in.

Indira's eyes fluttered and she tried to speak. Then she gave a loud gasp and fell still. It was as if Ruby's father and uncle had heard it through their grunts, because they stopped fighting and turned to stare.

Ruby's father rushed over, pushing her out of the way to cradle Indira close to his chest.

Ruby's breath was tight. She knew death in the animals. She'd seen it in the cattle, the ones lost overnight during the winter with ice across their noses, lifeless as bales of hay. But never people. She was glad her notebook was tucked away because this was more than she wanted to observe.

"Ruby," a voice whispered from the shadows.

Chester stood there, face pale. For once, he wasn't smiling.

"What's wrong with her?" he asked.

Ruby's mouth was almost too dry to speak. "What do you think?"

Chester slipped away the moment her father gave him five dollars to keep quiet. A police officer arrived soon after, the party still in full swing. It was her father's friend, the one who sometimes came to dinner.

Ruby sat in the back hall by the windows, wrapped in a blanket and shivering. She watched as the officer examined the body. He jotted something down in his notebook, then considered her father and Uncle Peter. Their faces were swollen, bruised, and bloodied. Her mother stood next to her father. For once, her face was beautiful in comparison.

Ruby moved to the back door, cracking it so she could hear. No one even looked her way.

"What happened?" the officer asked.

"Brother stuff," Uncle Peter mumbled.

"*Whisk*ey stuff." Her father chuckled, indicating a glass resting nearby on the ground.

The police officer glared at the glass. "Don't push me, Racine." There was a hint of warning in his voice, and for once, Ruby's father looked subdued.

Shoving his hands in his pockets, he said, "I apologize."

The officer let out a deep sigh. "This . . . it's difficult."

It occurred to Ruby that Indira must be freezing, there on the ground. Ruby edged outside, staring down. She tried to drape the blanket across the body, but her mother grabbed her so hard by the arm that she winced.

"Where was the fall?" the officer asked.

Her mother stepped forward. "The stairs. She was careless. Dropped a tray."

Ruby rubbed her arm. "There wasn't a tray at the bottom of the stairs."

Everyone stared at her in chilling silence.

"Did you see it happen?" the officer asked.

Ruby's father stepped forward. "None of us did. Pete found her."

The officer made a note.

"When was the child due?" he asked, glancing up.

Ruby's father gave an anguished cry. Uncle Peter pushed his hands deeply into the pockets of the suit Ruby's father had paid for, the one that caused problems between them because it was silk.

Her father ducked his head. "I did not know."

"Or we would have been searching for a replacement," her mother said, glaring at him.

Ruby's father picked up the glass of whiskey resting in the snow and took a long drink, right there in front of the officer.

It was a surprise to hear that Indira was pregnant. It made Ruby feel even sadder because eventually, there would have been another child to play with, one she could have looked after. One who might have been as pretty as Indira.

The whole thing was confusing. Ruby had run up and down those stairs so many times. She'd never once worried that she could fall and get hurt, that something like this could happen. Her teeth began to chatter, but of course, no one noticed.

The officer let out a hearty sigh. "There will be an investigation." He closed his notebook. "It should move quickly. These workers are a dime a dozen. You did what you could to help her, right, Racine?"

Ruby's father gave a vigorous nod. "Nothing could be done."

"I'll take a look inside, but I'll stay out of the way of the party. No one needs to know."

Ruby's father shoved his hands deeper into his pockets. "I appreciate that."

Uncle Peter turned away, and the stiff arm of her mother led Ruby back inside. The house was warm and the music loud. It sounded as if the guests were still dancing in the next room, and Ruby wanted to scream in disbelief that they had no idea what was really going on.

Ruby's grandmother was awake and downstairs when they walked in. She sat in a chair by the fire, a drink in hand. A tray of spilled cheeses was scattered across the floor.

"How did . . . ?" Ruby started to say, but her mother pushed her past it all, up the stairs.

There, a group of men stood together at the end of the hallway, laughing from the drinks and smoking. The servants were clustered together a few feet away, whispering in low tones. Her mother snapped her fingers, and they stared.

"See to it she's put to bed," she said, then headed back down.

Ruby ducked her head and went to her room.

One of the servants came in with wide eyes, her face pale. The moment she shut the bedroom door, she said, "Please, miss. What's happened?"

Ruby was not required to speak to the servants. She stared straight ahead, body shaking as she was changed into her nightgown. That scream echoed in the back of her mind with the same steady rhythm as the band downstairs. It was impossible to think over its relentless pulse of terror, to come to an answer to that question—what *had* happened?

Something more than an accidental fall down the stairs. The cheese tray had not been there. No, it had not. It had been put there after her mother mentioned it to the police, which meant her mother had lied to them. You don't lie unless you have something to hide.

The warm wool of Ruby's nightgown was placed over her head, and she shivered as it slid over her head and down her arms. It did little to help against the chill. Her mother was protecting someone, making it look like the fall had been Indira's fault. She would only do that if something else had happened, something terrible. Ruby didn't dare let herself imagine what, as those thoughts would settle into her chest so heavily that she, too, would no longer be able to breathe.

The servant dressed her and then seemed to wait. When Ruby didn't speak, she let out a small sigh. "Will that be all?"

"I liked her," Ruby said.

Ruby allowed in the other thoughts of Indira instead. The many times Indira had sneaked her extra biscuits from the kitchen, held Ruby tight as she cried after Uncle Peter had thrown her favorite book into the fire, and insisted Ruby read to her from her notebook, praising her observations. Indira had made her feel important. Indira had made her feel loved.

The servant paused. "Where is she? Please?"

Ruby hesitated, then led the girl to the back window and pointed.

Father Aaron was alone with Indira's body. He sat with her, praying, right there in the snow.

The servant put her hand to her mouth. "Dead?"

The word nearly made Ruby let out a scream of her own. Someone here had done this.

She climbed into bed and pulled the blanket tight up against her chin, wrapping her arms tightly around her body, but unable to stop the shaking.

"Miss?"

It wouldn't do to cry. Tears would do nothing to heal this pain in her chest, or quiet the echo of that scream.

Turning to the wall, she said, "There's a mess in the back hall. It needs to be cleaned up."

The servant took one last look out the window, then left the room.

Chapter Two

Upstate New York, present day

Lindsey was awake right at six but tried to be a good houseguest by not pacing the creaky wooden floors until six thirty. She read through *Bloomberg* and *The Times*, fired off ten work emails, and ate a plain yogurt for the probiotics, not the taste. Finally, she decided to drink her coffee on the screened-in front porch, the mug warm in her hands.

Through the early-morning mist and eastern hemlock trees, she caught a vague glimpse of Wind Thorne. She knew the exact break in the woods where the path would lead to the small footbridge to take her to the property. It would be interesting to walk over there now, to explore the grounds like she used to do with her mother, but she didn't have time. Her aunt would be ready to head over to the antique show any minute.

Lindsey stepped outside and dumped the rest of her coffee over the edge of the porch. Everything was quiet in that country way, completely different from life back in the city. The gentle call of birds, a rustle in the brush. The sun had cast its golden hue through the trees, but the air was already thick with humidity.

"You ready?" Aunt Petra asked as she bustled out. She wore a brown linen suit coupled with a white silk shirt, her gray hair neatly held back with a tortoiseshell clip.

"We're twins," Lindsey said, indicating her rust-colored linen suit. The girl at the boutique had said it brought out the warmth in her auburn hair. "Glad to see I dressed appropriately. Working from home means I own one suit jacket and fifty pajama pants."

Aunt Petra laughed. "Then this will be a treat."

Sliding on a pair of sunglasses, Lindsey followed her aunt to the Land Rover.

"I'm pleased you agreed to work the antique show," Aunt Petra said, sliding into the driver's seat. "It's our biggest fundraiser, so I really need your help, but I've also been excited for you to see Wind Thorne."

"I'm so happy to have the chance," Lindsey lied.

It had been a shock to the entire family when Lindsey's grandmother died and handed the Wind Thorne estate down to her aunt. Mainly because Lindsey's grandmother had never once mentioned that she happened to own the crumbling mansion that had captivated their family's imagination for decades. Instead, she quietly paid the taxes and funded the necessary repairs, leaving only an apology, the deed, and the keys.

It was startling, but on top of that, Lindsey's mother had passed away unexpectedly only six months before Lindsey's grandmother. It only compounded everyone's grief to learn she would have been a co-owner of Wind Thorne with her sister, if she'd lived. It took nearly a decade for Aunt Petra to accept the situation, but once she did, she squared her shoulders and brought Wind Thorne back to life. She'd spent the past several years restoring the estate to its former glory.

"I'm excited for you to see it," Aunt Petra said now, navigating the long drive that led down from her house through the woods to the main road. "Your mother would have loved it."

"I'm impressed you got it done. It needed a lot."

A rabbit darted in front of them, and Aunt Petra expertly dodged it.

"Turning it into a museum certainly helped the cause," she said as leaves from the nearby trees brushed against the windows. "It paved the way for several grants. I also pushed for every nonprofit opportunity I could find to cut costs and ended up with a hodgepodge of local helpers on top of that. It took about three years to remodel once the money was there. Given the shape it was in, that was actually pretty fast." Her aunt gave her a wistful smile. "Wind Thorne's a special place. People come from miles around to see it, and the antique show is a great opportunity for that. It should be well attended. So well attended, in fact, that I've already received texts that the parking lot is nearly full, so we'll go around the back, into the staff parking."

"I still can't believe Grandma never said a word about it," Lindsey admitted. "Every time we came to visit, it was obvious we were fascinated by Wind Thorne." She spotted the grove of trees to the side of the road where she and her cousin Barrett had spent practically a whole summer building an elaborate fort.

"I know." Aunt Petra adjusted her sunglasses. "I was angry with her for a long time. But in her letter, she said that her mother, Annabelle, refused to return to Wind Thorne after the murders. Her mother used to work as a servant for the Thornhill family, you see."

Lindsey tried to imagine what that would be like. Glamorous, maybe, but more likely difficult.

"It's such a fascinating story," Aunt Petra said. "Annabelle married so far above her station, but also, her husband ended up owning Wind Thorne. They didn't spend any time there, though. Their marriage must have been a scandal, because they left town for nearly twenty years. When they returned, Annabelle was a recluse. No one ever saw her."

Lindsey was surprised she wouldn't want to live there. To finally be the lady of the manor.

"I think the murder of the family must have been hard for her." Aunt Petra adjusted her sunglasses. "She worked there for years, so she would have known them quite well. That said, I don't think the servants were treated well, which might explain her reluctance to return."

"But why would that affect Grandma?" Lindsey wondered. "Once her mother had passed?"

"Because she saw how much suffering Wind Thorne had caused my grandmother," Aunt Petra said. "She felt it would be disrespectful to claim it as her own."

"Why didn't she just sell it?" Lindsey asked.

"Same reason. She didn't want to profit from a place that had caused her mother so much pain." Aunt Petra shrugged a thin shoulder. "However, I do think that, once she realized how intrigued your mother and I were with Wind Thorne, the idea of surprising us with its inheritance seemed like a good idea. She must have imagined it would give us something to feel good about after her death. I can only guess how much that decision impacted her once your mother passed away. I do wish she would have talked to me about it then. Your mother would not have wanted her to feel any additional grief, and I could have told her that."

Aunt Petra set her jaw, blinking rapidly. In the many moments Lindsey mourned the loss of her mother, it was easy to forget her aunt had lost a sister.

"It's not your fault." Lindsey touched her hand. "My mother would want you to make the most of it. For her."

"Yes." Her aunt gave a firm nod. "There's no changing the past."

Lindsey cracked the window to let in a breeze. "Wind Thorne always fascinated me, too. Even though it was falling apart back when we were around."

"You know, when your mother and I were growing up, we rarely went over there. My parents wouldn't allow it because it was an abandoned property and probably wasn't safe. I think that was part of what made it so intriguing, especially to your mother. She loved anything beautiful and mysterious."

That made sense. Lindsey's mother had started Lindsey's obsession with the property. They'd go on long walks together through the fields, and Lindsey would listen to her mother speak about the grandeur of the home, the artistic touches that painted every corner of the architecture, and, of course, the legends of the people who had lived there.

The Thornhill family had a booming whiskey business, a cattle farm, and a reputation as pillars of the community. What her mother didn't tell her—until much later in life—was that at one point, the entire family was violently murdered by someone they had wronged.

"My mother used to make Wind Thorne sound like this otherworldly existence," Lindsey said. "Did you know she took me to the library once and pulled up the microfiche of all the pictures in the local paper from the balls they had at the house? She studied their dresses, their style . . ." She felt a pang at the memory of her mother talking up a storm and then suddenly going silent. It was what her mother did when she spotted something she considered beautiful, to give her brain a minute to file it away. "Maybe you should pull up some of those pictures. Have them printed and hung up in the house."

Aunt Petra gave her a triumphant smile. "I already did."

Lindsey smiled back. "That will be fun to see."

"Fun" wasn't the right word. "Painful" jumped to mind, actually. But it had been long enough since her mother's death that Lindsey felt that she should have been able to handle the memories. To transition from the heartache into understanding that death was a part of life, but that was easier said than done. Besides, in a setting like this, where some of her favorite moments with her mother flitted past her memories like butterflies, it brought up more emotion than Lindsey wanted to entertain.

Aunt Petra reached over and patted Lindsey's knee. "It's good you came. I admit I've been worried about you, without any family around, always working."

"I love to work," Lindsey said.

Her aunt gave her a skeptical look.

"Seriously," she said. "I do."

Lindsey's job as a corporate data analyst was challenging but fun. She spent most days in her apartment with three screens of numbers and a coffee warmer running at all times. Plus, she had lunch with friends most days of the week, so it wasn't like she was alone all the time.

"I just wish your father would . . ."

Lindsey waited. "What?" she pressed.

Aunt Petra pursed her lips. "Nothing."

Lindsey toyed with the clasp on her purse. There had been some sort of rift between Aunt Petra and her father, but Lindsey still had no idea what it was all about. "I'd like to know what the issue was between you two."

"And I'd love to tell you." Her aunt slowed the car and turned on the blinker. "But you need to ask your father. Sooner rather than later."

That didn't sound appealing. Her father was bold and direct, and he often seemed irritated with Lindsey's precise manner. She felt much more comfortable around her aunt. Besides, Aunt Petra actually remembered her birthday and was prompt about returning phone calls. She also encouraged Lindsey to have a voice.

I know what it's like to be a woman in your family, Aunt Petra sometimes said. *We have to talk a little louder to be heard.*

Now Aunt Petra pulled onto the main road and did an immediate sharp right into a paved drive. The large stone entryway, followed by a dramatic canopy of greenery, made Lindsey sit up a little straighter. She leaned forward and watched as they pulled past the main gate that led into Wind Thorne.

The house had a strong base of worn brick that stretched up into several uniform gable roofs so regal and pointed that they could have been standing at attention. It reminded her of a fortress, complete with carved stone around the front casement windows and a solid oak front door. Stained glass above the entryway gleamed with the bright green of emeralds and deep, sapphire blues.

"I can already tell the difference," she breathed.

Back when she had explored the property with her brother and cousin, parts of the structure had been completely boarded off. Jack and Barrett were two years older than she was—both turned forty this year—and they frequently left her behind to squeeze through the boarded-up windows. They would drink, smoke, and meet up with the girls from down the road. Fine, because that gave Lindsey the freedom to explore the property on her own.

Her mother had told her endless stories about Wind Thorne, but the one that especially piqued her interest was about a lost diamond, so valuable that a woman had died for it. Lindsey had searched through the abandoned distilleries, scattered wildflowers, and riverbanks, quietly determined to find it embedded somewhere in the soil. Of course, she never did.

Instead, she collected countless other treasures and squirreled them away in a secret spot beneath her grandparents' porch. Her favorites had been a smooth amber glass bottle with old whiskey in it, a rough piece of raw turquoise, and a small diary with musings that seemed boring back then but would most likely interest her now. It might be fun to revisit those items, if she had time.

"It's stunning, isn't it?" Aunt Petra pulled around the drive and slid into a spot near the back entrance. "In spite of it all. Shall we head in?"

Lindsey stepped from the air-conditioned car into the humidity, following her aunt in through the back entrance. The hall was so vast that she had to actually stop walking to take it all in. Two grand staircases framed a large space that led to the front of the house, decorated with a row of stone pillars. They lined the path like a row of butlers, frozen in time, leading beneath the bridge of the staircases and to the main room at the front of the house.

The main room was nearly a football field wide, with polished mahogany floors, cream-colored walls, and dramatic floor-length curtains. Three enormous chandeliers hung up above, showcasing the facets of hundreds of crystals that must have been hand cut.

"This is gorgeous." Lindsey clasped her hands. "Aunt Petra, you've outdone yourself."

"No, it was already like this," she said. "It just had to be put back together."

They walked past the dark and moody landscape portraits. Several of the appraisers were already seated at the antique tables that filled the room, and Lindsey tried to assess whether she would fit in. Most of them seemed to be closer to her aunt's age, but a few were younger. Lindsey spotted a dazzling necklace on one of the women at a nearby table and knew she'd find an excuse to talk to her at some point to get a better look at it.

"Would you like to do a tour now or at lunch?" Aunt Petra asked.

Lindsey glanced at her watch. She wanted to do the tour now, but the doors would open soon. Besides, her aunt probably had several responsibilities for the show.

"Lunch," Lindsey decided. "So that there's more time."

"Sounds good." Her aunt led her to her table, which was to the right of the grand room. A guy about her age was stationed at the other half of the table. Her seat had a bottle of water, some pens, and a small placard that read *Lindsey McKenna, Fine Jewelry and Metals.*

"This is you, Lindsey McKenna."

Her aunt sounded proud. Lindsey was a bit embarrassed, considering it had been ages since she'd had anything at all to do with fine jewelry and metals. Her aunt loved her simply for her existence: something only family could do.

Something family *should* do.

Lindsey smoothed her hair. These thoughts were unproductive. This visit was meant to be an escape, not bring up feelings she wasn't ready to deal with.

Aunt Petra glanced at her watch. "The people in the green vests are the helpers, if you have questions or need anything. You're more than welcome to take breaks." She waved at an older woman, then added, "I'll be all over the place, but for now, I'll be in the back, helping with the food."

"Where can I find you for lunch?" Lindsey asked.

Her aunt smoothed her jacket. "Upstairs in the main office." She waved at another helper and gave Lindsey a quick nod. "Have fun this morning."

Lindsey took a seat. Her tablemate was deep in concentration, poring over the paperwork he had spread out over the table. Noticing her, he mumbled an apology and tried to move his papers out of the way, but in the process, he knocked them all to the floor.

"Oh, gosh. Let me help you," Lindsey said, dropping to the floor with him. The papers were business spreadsheets, and even though she did her best not to read anything, a quick glance showed some big numbers.

Once they had everything, he gave her a rueful look. "I guess I'm not the guy you should ask to hold a Fabergé egg."

She laughed. "Guess not. I'm Lindsey."

"Otis Allen."

Otis had a charming smile, and he wore a blue baseball cap and tortoiseshell-framed glasses. His clothes were rumpled, but she wasn't fooled. It cost a lot of money to appear that disheveled.

Brushing off her knees, she took a glance around. "Did we get everything?"

"Hope so." He took a seat and shoved the paperwork into a folder, in no particular order.

The idea of all those numbers crumpled up into a mess made her cringe. Numbers were sacred to her. Predictable. She wondered what he'd do if she grabbed the folder and quickly organized the papers, smoothing them out and putting them in order.

Instead, she adjusted her ring. "So, you're a . . ." She peered at his placard. "Gemologist? That's interesting."

Gemologists typically appraised the quality and value of gems. Given the numbers she'd seen, the spreadsheets were most likely for a jewelry store or one of their suppliers.

"Thanks," Otis said. "You'll have to tell that to my parents. They still don't know what to think about my career choices."

Lindsey nodded but didn't know what to say next. Making small talk was one of those skills her brother and father had in spades, but she'd always struggled. Her mother noticed, once, that Lindsey was hanging back at a neighborhood gathering back home and said, "Don't worry, honey. Friendships aren't built in ten minutes at a party. I pretend everyone is the same person with a different face. Because until you know their heart, they may as well be."

Her mother's advice stayed with her and, later in life, became handy for work parties, chatting up baristas, and the occasional dreaded dinner party.

Otis took a sip from a portable coffee mug. "So, you do fine jewelry and metals? Who do you work for?"

Lindsey's cheeks colored. "I have a background in fine jewelry, art history, and all that. My aunt just thought this would be a fun thing for me to do." She held up her hands. "I do actually know what I'm talking about, I just . . ."

"No judgment." His eyes fell on her ring. "Hey, is that a Stella Aiman?"

The sound of her mother's pseudonym made her heart skip a beat. "It is."

"May I see it?" he asked.

Lindsey held out her hand, and Otis took off his glasses before peering at it through his jeweler's loupe. He leaned in closer, and she flushed at how good he smelled, like hazelnut coffee and expensive aftershave. Notes of sandalwood and mint.

"I've never seen this one before." He glanced up, and without his glasses, she noticed his eyes were a bright blue. "It's not in her catalog of work."

"No, it's not," she said.

He seemed to study the flat-gold border that framed the delicate aquamarine. The frame was her mother's signature, the clean-lined, perfectly angled design. He lowered the loupe and gave her a curious look.

"Where did you find that?" he said. "It's really unique."

Lindsey hesitated, half wishing she'd thought it out before wearing the ring to a place with a bunch of jewelry experts. "It was a gift."

Lindsey's fifteenth birthday was one of those perfect memories she kept tucked away like a leftover candy bar, to pull out when she really needed it.

The morning had started with the smell of a German chocolate cake baking in the oven and her mother at the stove instead of in her studio, cooking her an omelet with garlic and cheese, Lindsey's latest obsession. Her mother had sat at the kitchen table drinking tea, and when it was time to go to school, she'd laughed and said, *You get the school of life today, my girl.*

They'd spent the afternoon in the studio together, Lindsey watching as her mother crafted the final details of the ring. That night, Jack and her father made a point to be home to grill steaks and eat dinner. The weather was nice, the backyard expansive and filled with laughter, and Lindsey marveled at the wonder and ease of becoming a grown-up.

That perfect day made her think of those memes, the ones that said *Who's gonna tell her?* because three weeks later, her mother had a heart attack on a walk through the woods. It was such an abrupt turn that, nearly a lifetime later, Lindsey always felt just a bit uncomfortable when things went too well.

Still, she wore the ring. No matter how painful losing her mother had been, she would have wanted Lindsey to remember the good. To focus on that, instead of the inevitability of heartbreak.

Otis put his glasses back on. "I studied all of her work in detail for a research project, in college. I live in the city, but my parents live nearby, so I was always interested in the idea that she had ties here. She grew up in the house next to Wind Thorne, the one that was the next farm over. She did a lot of her work in a studio there."

"Yeah. That is interesting." Lindsey fidgeted. "So, how about you? How did you get into gems?"

"Well . . ." He took off his baseball cap and ran his hand through shaggy blond hair. "My parents love estate sales. One weekend, back when I was still in college and home to do laundry or something, they dragged me along. I found a box of gems in a back room. Rubies, sapphires, and there was even a diamond in there. No one was paying a bit of attention to any of it, because the gems were in raw form. It turned out the guy who had lived there was a geologist. I bought the box for something like four hundred dollars."

Lindsey's mouth dropped open. "Stop it."

"I know." Otis gave her a sheepish smile. "I even told the person running the auction, 'Hey, these are real gems,' because I didn't want to rob the place. He shrugged it off, saying they didn't have any real value."

Lindsey couldn't even imagine watching something like that walk out the door. An entire boxful, ready to be polished and cut? The person running the estate sale had made a big mistake.

"You lucked out," she said.

"I don't believe in luck." He grinned. "But I did get to drop out of school a few weeks later." He cleaned his glasses on his worn, gray T-shirt, sending the scent of fresh soap and sandalwood her way. "My parents wanted me to do something real with my life, but that little box of gems gave me a good start and an even better origin story."

Lindsey's father had also insisted she do something "practical" with her life, which was how she ended up in finance instead of design. It had been a good decision, one she didn't regret. That said, she would have preferred to have been allowed to be the one to make it.

The woman with the necklace walked past, and Lindsey finally got a glimpse of it. Most likely from the 1940s, it was a wreath of gilded porcelain flowers in a variety of colors with sapphire centers. Lindsey would have done it a little differently, relying on metalwork to give the essence of flowers with only a slight hint of color, for a subtle elegance.

A man in a black polo shirt and khakis approached their table. "We're getting started." He had a forgettable face but a large presence. No green vest, but he stood behind their table with his arms crossed.

There was security at the front door to check bags, but Lindsey hadn't realized they'd be at the tables, too. Some serious items might actually come through. She hoped she wouldn't embarrass herself.

Lindsey lined up her water bottle and ink pens in a neat row. "I'm starting to get nervous," she admitted. "I've never done this."

"You seem smart, so you'll be fine." It hit her that his voice was attractive. It was deep and a little rough, like a guy who liked to sing around campfires. "Teach them something. Even if their item isn't worth anything, they still walk away with some bonus knowledge." His dimple clued her in that he didn't take himself or anything that seriously.

"Doors are open," the organizer called.

Everyone sat up a little straighter, and a flood of people started to rush in. To her surprise, several headed right for them. She braced herself, but most formed a line to talk to Otis, who turned out to be an articulate expert on the value and history of precious gemstones.

Through brief glimpses of his conversations, she learned he owned a gem distribution company that was an internet and local staple. People had traveled from Vermont and Pennsylvania to get his opinion. The quality of the stones that passed through his hands in a matter of minutes was startling.

"Hey, look at this." Otis showed her a large stone the color of red wine, so deeply hued that it nearly looked like it was made of plastic. Turning back to the woman who had brought it, he said, "This is a gorgeous stone. It's red beryl, which comes from the Southwest. I'd guess it's from the Wah Wah Mountains, given the fact that it's gem-grade. The structure of the crystals is beautiful."

Lindsey fidgeted. She hadn't heard anyone talk this way in years, back when her mother's friends used to hang around. So much time had passed. It really wasn't logical to miss her this much.

The woman at his table put on a pair of red reading glasses and squinted at the stone. "How interesting. You know, my late father is from Utah. He liked science and had a pretty large but boring rock collection. This was part of it."

Otis grinned. "Well, good thing that boring collection didn't make it to the trash. This little gem, once cleaned up, could be worth quite a bit. Get it appraised and insured."

Lindsey wanted to hear more, but a small line had started to form at her table. Squaring her shoulders, she greeted her first customer with a big smile. "What a wonderful art deco piece."

The room filled up pretty quickly, the buzz of conversation intense, and some interesting jewelry passed through her hands. Several costume pieces, lots of art nouveau. Many pieces caught her eye, especially the ones heavy on design and detail, but she didn't find anything of great historical or financial significance.

The line in front of Otis never let up. Every time she looked over, he was deep in conversation with a patron or studying a gem through an LED-lit magnifying loupe. Once, she could tell he'd found something good, because he discreetly signed an appraisal letter, and the security guard escorted the man back to his car. She looked forward to asking him about it later.

It was nearly eleven before Lindsey had a window to grab an espresso. She had just stood up to go on the hunt when a dark-haired older woman clutching a large leather bag approached her table.

Lindsey rested her hand on the table, willing to wait if the woman had something interesting to share. The woman didn't walk up to her, though. She just stood there, toying with the strap of the bag.

"Hi," Lindsey called. "Do you have something for me?"

The woman suddenly looked near tears.

"Is everything all right?" Lindsey asked, half rising from her chair.

"No." The woman had a slight accent. Broad cheeks, a wide nose. She looked over her shoulder as if worried that someone was watching the exchange.

The security guard strode to the front of the table. "Ma'am? How can I help?"

The woman took a step back, clutching the bag close to her chest.

"Ma'am, I apologize, but there's a rule that all objects must be visible." The guard spread his hands in apology. "Could you show me what's in the bag?"

The crowd near their table began to go quiet. The silence seemed to travel, and suddenly, several people were watching. The woman's face turned red.

"Ma'am?" the security guard repeated. "Can I see what's in the bag?"

She gestured at Lindsey. "I need to talk to her."

Lindsey felt the first prickle of anxiety. She had kept her bio ambiguous, but it wouldn't take much of an internet search to find out the truth.

The security guard held up his hands. "I understand. First, though, we need to—"

"Let me by," the woman insisted, then shoved a hand into the bag.

"Drop it," the security guard shouted.

Otis pulled Lindsey down behind the table, banging her knee against it, and the woman ran for the front door.

Someone shouted, and a group of people blocked the exit. The guards in the front, along with the guard from their table, surrounded the woman. Ducking her head, she handed over her bag.

No one in the room seemed to move. The guard opened it. He hesitated, then gave a nod and handed it back, and she practically ran out the front door.

There was silence. Then the crowd started murmuring in excitement, recapping what they'd seen.

"What on earth?" Lindsey said, brushing herself off.

"You okay?" Otis slid on his glasses, which had fallen to the floor. He helped her up and gave her a sheepish grin. "Sorry I pulled you to the floor. My mind clicks into 'Save yourself!' I'm sure you're thrilled I decided to save you, too."

To be honest, it had been a while since Lindsey had been on the floor with any man, especially one as engaging as Otis.

When the security guard returned, she couldn't help but ask, "What was in the bag?"

"Papers and an old book." He shrugged. "Sorry if you wanted to speak to her, but items have to be visible. It's a safety issue."

Lindsey rested her hand against the table. Papers and books didn't have anything to do with fine jewelry and metals. It was possible the items were somehow related to her mother, since the woman had made a point to seek out Lindsey.

Otis was watching her. "Why would she bring that to you? Any theories?"

Lindsey shrugged. "I have a few."

Maybe it had nothing to do with anything. Maybe the woman struggled with anxiety, and it had taken some serious self-encouragement just to be here. There could be a language barrier, or she worried her object wouldn't be as valuable as she'd hoped, or that it was more valuable than she'd dreamed. There were a million possibilities.

Otis glanced at her ring, then back up at her.

"I think we should take a break," he said, signaling to a line helper. "I bet she's still out in the parking lot."

Lindsey didn't hesitate. "Let's get some fresh air."

Chapter Three

Upstate New York, 1925

Breakfast was a bustling affair. The guests had no idea there had been trouble, and they arrived slowly, with much laughter about their headaches and the need for a salty breakfast. The servants rushed around, refilling the buffet again and again with pancakes, eggs, and bacon. The smell of maple syrup and hot coffee seasoned the air.

Ruby's stomach felt too sour to eat. She'd tossed and turned all through the night, seeing Indira's twisted body at the bottom of the stairs. Indira had been the only person other than Ruby's sister who had ever told her that she mattered. Who would do that now? Her sister was leaving. Indira was . . . Ruby winced, reliving the sound of that scream. It had haunted her all night, with each chime of the grandfather clock in the hallway.

Feeling ill, she left the breakfast table, moving past the early-morning buffet and out to the fresh air. The sun was so bright against the snow that it was blinding. The chill cut through her thick coat as she made her way across the front yard, stepping over the iced tracks from the motorcars. She should have worn a hat.

A figure streaked from the side of the house toward the trees. For a split second, she thought it was Indira. Her ghost. Then, Ruby spotted the dark brown of Chester's coat as he ducked into the pine trees.

"Chester!" she called.

What was he up to? It was too early for him to be lurking around. Surely, he hadn't come back in hopes of trying to find the ring. The idea seemed outrageous, considering everything that had happened in the past few hours, and she clenched her fists tight.

Pulling her coat close, she fought to keep her feet steady in the snow as she ran toward the woods to catch him. "Chester!"

There were squirrel tracks and the early-morning sound of birds, along with the eerie silence of snow on pine. Her breath came in quick gasps, and she slowed, the branches brushing against her like gnarled hands.

There. He was hunkered down, hiding beneath a pine tree. She stormed over, determined to let him have it.

"How dare you?" she demanded. "You think you can come to my house to take that ring? You think you can have whatever you want, and you can't. It's not yours!"

It felt good to scold him. It made her feel powerful after a night that had left her feeling anything but. Crouching down, she continued, "I'll tell my dad, and then you'll be—" She stopped.

His face was bruised and bloodied. Tears streamed from his eyes, one so swollen she could barely see it.

"Chester!" She scrambled under the tree with him, scooped up a handful of snow, and handed it over. He pressed it against his face, wincing.

"Who did this?" she demanded.

It couldn't have been his dad. He wasn't like Ruby's father, who had taught her brother a "lesson" more times than she cared to count. Had her father caught Chester sneaking into the house?

The cold, wet ground seeped through her tights, chilling her knees, as she waited for his answer. It took a moment to realize there wouldn't be one.

"You're freezing." She touched his shoulder. "Let's get you warmed up. Come back to the house. There's bacon."

He glanced around, the snow still tight against his face. "Only if we sneak in through the back."

Ruby shook her head. She couldn't go to the back stairs. Never again. There might still be blood, and she would see Indira lying there dying, she knew it.

"Come to the library." He started to protest, and she held up her hand. "No one will be in there, and there's a fire. I'll bring food."

"Bring extra," he said. "Bring a lot."

Chester peered out beneath the tree before crawling out. He got to his feet a bit unsteadily, as if searching for solid ground. Then he rushed to the house and slipped into the side door, a sack over his shoulders. She knew he'd take off his boots and carry them so as not to leave tracks. He knew how to not get caught.

When Ruby caught up to him in the library, carrying a plateful of food, the curtains were drawn as Chester knelt by the fire. He jumped when she shut the door. After turning the key in the lock, she set down the plate of breakfast in front of him.

It hurt him to chew, she could see that, but he still ate like he was preparing for a long journey. Ruby waited to talk, tracing her hand over the rug.

The patterns swirled in front of her, in pinks, greens, and yellow. If the light had been on, the room would've been bright and cheerful. For as sour as her mother was, you'd think every room would be ornamented in black, but instead, spaces were done in light blue and ivory, gold and pink, and yellow and green. Light, airy, and so different from the way Ruby felt inside.

She gestured at his face. "Who did this?"

"Look, Ruby," he said. "Elliot didn't come home last night. I didn't know until he didn't get up for chores."

"Maybe he fell asleep here." The last time she'd seen Elliot was after dinner, by the dessert table with Chester. He'd probably nodded off in a side room and would turn up any minute.

"No." Chester ran his hand through his hair, brushing out a few pine needles. Ruby winced, imagining him pushed to the ground during the attack that had left so many bruises on his face. "I checked. I came back here, and the servants looked everywhere. He wasn't in any of the rooms. I was searching the forest when I got beat up."

"Who did it?" she demanded.

If it was one of their guests, her father wouldn't send them away, but she could get back at them; they could be sure of that.

"I don't know. It was too dark. When I got back home, there was a note, from Elliot."

He pulled a page out of his pocket. It was from the Bible, folded. On the top, it read:

Leaving. Following tracks to city.

"My brother's scared. I've got to find him, Ruby." For once in his life, Chester didn't have that typical, sly expression on his freckled face.

"Do you think he saw it?" she whispered. "When she fell?"

Chester's jaw seemed to tense. "No. I . . . no."

She peered at him. "Did *you*?"

"No! I didn't see anything, okay?" He got to his feet and pulled a cloth napkin from his pocket. He wrapped it around what was left of the food and dropped it in his bag. A few biscuits, the orange.

"You did." Her stomach dropped. "You saw it."

His hands trembled, and he wouldn't look at her. "No. Don't be telling nobody that I did."

Tears were in his eyes again, and he pulled on his cap.

Ruby stared at an orange flame in the fireplace. She tugged at the sleeves of her wool sweater, suddenly too warm in the heat from the fire.

"Chester . . ." she said, slowly, "I . . ."

"Look, I've got to find Elliot. Besides, I can't stay here anymore. There'd be even bigger trouble if I did. I'll find my brother and be on my way."

Ruby didn't always like Chester. He'd taken her coin. Chased her with snakes when she didn't feel like running. Accidentally hit her with a rock. But in the summers, they caught fish in the river together. Looked at the stars and made up names for the constellations. Sure, he'd gotten her mad more times than she could count, but now he was going to leave her, too?

"What about your dad?" she demanded. "The farm? He can't do it alone."

"He'll be fine." His voice broke. "I have to find my brother."

Ruby held her arms close to her body, trying to fight back the panic welling inside. She couldn't be here alone. Not without him, her sister, and Indira. The memory of the blood on the ground, the way Indira had gone limp. It was all too much to face alone.

"Don't leave," she whispered.

"What?" Chester said.

Ruby considered what she'd need to gather. Food, candles, her notebook. Slowly, she eased open her eyes.

"I'm coming." Her resolve steadied. "I'll look for him with you."

"No." He paced the room. "No chance."

Ruby glared at him. "Elliot might be running because he knows what happened." She considered the scream, the trays on the ground. "I might know, too. Not yet, but . . ." She thought about the notes she'd taken after dinner. "I need to look at my notebook."

He moved toward the door.

"Chester." She held up the key that opened the door to the library. He couldn't go anywhere without it. "Please." He didn't answer, and her eyes pricked with tears. "I'm scared. I can't be here alone. Not after all that."

He glared at her. "You got money?"

"I thought you were rich," she shot back. "From all your card games and the money you steal from the trucks."

"I've got some but not enough to get far. Elliot went to the city," he said. "We went there once with my dad, but Elliot's not going to know how to survive on his own. I know you've got money. Someone here always does."

It was true. The top drawer of the dresser in her grandmother's room had plenty of gold coins. Ruby never would have thought to steal from her, but without it, they wouldn't survive. In this instance, stealing no longer mattered. Especially when . . .

The ring.

How could she forget? It was safely tucked away in the pocket inside her dress. She couldn't tell Chester she had it because he was still Chester. She didn't trust him, not completely, but the ring could serve as a safeguard, a way to get her own money if she needed it.

"There's lots of coins in my grandmother's room. I'll leave a note for my family, tell them that I'll return." Taking his hands, she said, "Please. I want to help. My family would understand that much. Let me help. I'm good at noticing things. I can write down the places we've looked, draw maps, keep watch."

There was a sound outside the door, and he jumped. "I have to go, Ruby. Now." Instead of trying to get her to unlock the door, he threw open the window and climbed out in a flash.

Ruby watched as he ran across the front yard, her heart aching. Her hands shook to think how close she'd come to leaving. It would have been a bad decision, brought shame upon her family and hurt Elizabeth. Still, she was scared at the idea of only having Brad around for company. He spent all his time working in the distilleries or in town with his friends, and never paid her a lick of attention. Maybe, she could convince her sister and Glenn to let her come live with them.

Off in the distance, the train's whistle sounded its approach. Chester would need money; she could do that much for him. He wouldn't survive without it.

Ruby crept out of the library and peeked into the dining hall. The brunch had ended, the servants were clearing the food, but her grandmother and several of the guests still sat at the table. Others had started to head to the drawing room, where games and entertainment were planned. She had time to sneak into her grandmother's room, but she'd need to be quick.

The piano struck a chord just as her feet touched the bottom step, and Ruby jumped, startled, nearly losing her balance. Gripping the railing, she flew up the stairs, listening outside the door before going in. The curtains were drawn and the room dark.

Ruby had her back to the door and had just grabbed a handful of coins when the door clicked shut behind her. She turned and let out a cry as Uncle Peter lunged for her, crooking his arm tight around her neck and pulling her in against his chest. His breath smelled like whiskey and something else, like gunpowder.

"You think you're so smart." His words were thick. "Watching everybody. Making your notes. I'm watching, too. What were you doing with the farm boy, huh?"

His lips brushed against her neck. She tried to scream, but his hand covered her mouth, so tight she couldn't breathe. His arm cut into her windpipe, and she clawed him hard, gasping when he finally swore and let her go.

Coins spilled from her hand to the ground, and Uncle Peter stumbled on his bad leg, a twisted laugh coming from his throat. "Pick 'em up. Go ahead."

Ruby's heart was full of fear and fury. This had happened too many times. Her mother had said to just push him away, but this time, she hadn't seen him coming. Her throat ached, and he started to move toward her again.

There were guests on this floor. Would she be the one to get into trouble if she screamed?

"Move back!" Her voice was hoarse. "I was putting these coins away."

"No, you were stealing." He swayed, an ugly grin on his face. "Don't worry. I won't tell." His face darkened, and he took another step toward her.

Ruby ducked underneath his arm, grabbing half the coins as she did and racing for the door. Light from the hallway blinded her, along with the heat of her tears, and she nearly tripped on the way to the step.

She gripped the coins tight, terrified she'd lose her balance and fall like Indira, but desperate to get away from Uncle Peter.

She tore past her mother and grandmother, who were on their way up. She was not about to tell them what had happened because her mother would find a way to blame her. The last time, her mother had demanded to know why she'd been alone with him at all, if she wasn't able to fight back.

"Ruby?" her mother called, but she kept running.

She grabbed her coat where she'd left it at the door, slipping on the snow and ice as she raced toward the woods, trying to outrun the stench of that breath, the feeling of his rough lips on her neck. Branches slapped her in the face, but she only ran faster.

The train was coming. She could see it in the distance, the puff of coal steam blackening the air above like a storm cloud. Chester was hunkered down behind a thick bush near the tracks.

"Chester," she screamed. "Wait!"

He turned and his mouth dropped open. "What are you doing?" he cried as she ran toward him, slipping through the snow.

"Uncle Peter . . ." She was crying so hard snot was frozen to her face. "I'm coming with you."

"You can't!" Chester pulled her down behind the bush, probably wanting to hide so the conductor wouldn't spot them through the front window. Ruby had never been a stowaway on a train, had never dared try it, but she'd heard some of the workers talking about a guy they knew who'd gotten thrown in jail just for bumming to the next town over.

The train was getting closer, the smoke puffing against the horizon. Chester squinted at it, as if calculating exactly when he'd have to jump on.

Ruby held out her hands, the coins shimmering in the sunlight. "I have to. They caught me."

Chester turned toward the train. It was close enough to see its front light now, and to feel the ground start to rumble. "It's not safe. You're a girl."

She pulled her hair up into her cap. "No one needs to know that. Give me a shirt and some trousers when we're on the train."

Chester looked down at the coins. The train let out a loud blast, like it always did as it approached the area with the main road.

"If we do this, we're family," he said. "From this point on. I give you my word I'll look out for you, but you can't be causing me trouble. There's too much that comes from all this."

"I promise." Ruby wiped at her face. "I won't be any trouble. I promise, Chester."

"The train's gonna slow," he said. "When it does, I'll jump on and you come right after me. We have to duck into the car quick, or the conductor could see us."

The train roared past them, the wind nearly taking her cap. The brakes squealed suddenly as it slowed for the road crossing, just like Chester had said. It was still fast, though—faster than Ruby had expected. Glimpses of the horizon flashed between each car, and her heart pounded. It was one thing to plan to jump on but quite another to actually do it. Was it hard? If she slipped, she didn't know what would happen.

You can't be causing me trouble.

Ruby could cause all sorts of trouble with her very first step.

"Ready?" Chester shouted. "Let's go!"

He tossed his bag into an open boxcar. Then he scrambled up like jumping a fence and held out his hand. Ruby hesitated, looking back toward the woods.

"Come on," he shouted. "Jump."

She ran until she could grab his hand, and he pulled her up on board.

Chapter Four

Upstate New York, present day

The lawn in front of Wind Thorne was striking, as bright green as an emerald and perfectly maintained, with structured back-and-forth patterns cut in by the lawn crew. Perfect white gravel made up the drive, which surrounded a large stone fountain. To the right was the paved parking lot for the museum, crowded with cars.

Lindsey spotted the woman sitting in an older-model sedan. "That's her."

Otis put on a pair of sunglasses. "I have to say, most people don't have your sense of adventure."

Lindsey laughed. "Oh, I'm far from adventurous." Her father and her brother were, though. They liked to ski, zip-line, and skydive, and had always seemed annoyed that she showed little interest in trying to keep up. "My father tells me I should give it a try, that I'd be more successful."

"Guess that depends on his definition of 'success,'" Otis said.

The definition was pretty clear in her family. Her father was partner at a law firm, with more work and money than he knew what to do with. Her brother owned an accounting business, which her father bragged about to anyone who would listen. It was a nice idea that success could be fluid, but, in her family, that idea would get laughed right out of the room.

The gravel crunched underfoot as they made their way to the woman's car. Close up, it was easy to see that the woman was older than Lindsey had thought, with deep wrinkles next to her eyes and her mouth. Strands of silver shimmered in her hair, but she looked strong and fit.

Otis gave her a half wave. "Sorry to bother you. I'm not quite sure what happened in there, but we didn't want you to leave the event with a bad taste in your mouth. Did you have something you wanted appraised?"

"I was looking for help." The woman spoke with a slight accent. "You see . . ." She fidgeted with an earring, a small white pearl nestled in gold. The set of her jaw was firm, her eye makeup stark but carefully applied. "Could we talk somewhere private?"

The parking lot was isolated, with only a few people walking to and from their cars. Lindsey glanced at Otis, and he frowned.

"I think we're good right here," he said.

"Please." The woman met her eyes. "Lindsey, I have something I'd like to share with you. It's something only you would appreciate."

The hairs on her arms prickled. "You do?"

In the past few years, Lindsey had hung on to the idea that there had to be some sort of final goodbye from her mother still out there. Lindsey had searched for meaning in the most random moments. Even though experience and logic told her that this woman in the parking lot could not possibly have ties to her mother, Lindsey was willing to find out.

"Can we chat over there?" she suggested, pointing at the small flower garden to the right of the main house. There was a trellis at the entrance covered in ivy, with some ornate iron tables scattered between the rose bushes and hydrangeas. Plus, the garden offered shade.

The three of them walked over together, the perfume of the flowers fragrant in the sultry humidity. Otis pulled out the cast-iron chairs for the two women, and they all took a seat. Lindsey considered the expansive view. They were to the side of the house, in a garden that allowed a view of the rolling hills in the back that led to the forest.

The woman set her leather bag on the tabletop and rested her hands on top of it.

"My name is Amrita," the woman said. "I live in New Jersey. My mother recently passed."

Lindsey bowed her head. "I'm so sorry to hear that."

"Thank you. She was quite old and lived a long life, but it's still hard to lose a mother," Amrita said. "It's a feeling that doesn't go away anytime soon."

"No, it doesn't." Lindsey met her gaze. "I lost my mother, too. When I was young."

"I'm sorry," Otis said.

Amrita nodded at her. "Then you understand. Before my mother died, I went through her paperwork and found several things that were tied to Wind Thorne."

"Did her connection go far back?" Otis asked.

"Well, my mother worked for the estate for several years, during the time when it was a working cattle farm. She started there when she was very young, only around fourteen years old." Amrita paused. "Do you know the history here?"

"Yes, absolutely," Lindsey said. "The website goes into it all, but basically, Wind Thorne was a cattle farm but started as a mining operation for sand back in the late 1800s. They sold the sand to New York City to make cement. Later on, during Prohibition, they sold whiskey. The tunnels from back in the day helped keep the illegal whiskey trade underground, so to speak."

Lindsey had been fascinated by the tunnels as a child. Her parents made it clear that the tunnels were completely off limits, so as a result, she had explored them more times than she could count.

Amrita nodded. "Wind Thorne was a big place, so they needed several workers to make it run smoothly, and it wasn't easy. My mother was a servant here until it all fell apart. She didn't have me until much later in life, so she didn't talk much about her experience here, but when she did, her memories were not fond." Amrita reached into her bag and handed Lindsey a folder. Inside was a neatly organized stack of pages. "When she died, I found several things from the estate with her papers. These seem to be from a ledger."

Lindsey flipped through. Dates and numbers for sales of cattle, barley, and corn. The data-loving portion of her brain was fascinated to see actual facts and figures from that time period.

"These papers are interesting," Lindsey said. "I can see how much the end of the war affected the numbers here. See how they went down?"

Otis took a look over her shoulder. "You'd think farms would do better, once all the people were back."

Lindsey nodded. Drawing on what she'd learned from a college economics class, she said, "Well, there was a massive decline because the prices changed. The government guaranteed a rate on things like wheat and pork during World War I, so the farmers did incredibly well. On top of that, Europe needed food, since their farmers were already fighting. So, the farmers here started working overtime. They would buy up more land, trying to produce as much as possible. Then . . ." She tapped the paper. "It stopped. The war ended. The money dried up. Farmers couldn't pay the banks back for the loans they'd taken to expand so rapidly. There were a lot of farms that struggled for nearly a decade before the actual Depression hit. Wind Thorne probably went into whiskey to make up for all the money they lost."

Otis looked impressed, which might have been her intent. Lindsey hadn't spent that time in economics classes for nothing.

"Racine Thornhill did very well," Amrita said. "The Thornhills were quite prosperous, until it all fell apart and the family was killed."

"Was your mother here then?" Lindsey asked.

"No. The workers left right before." The lines in Amrita's face became more pronounced as she squinted up at the house. "I have to wonder if they knew it was coming. Or . . ."

"If one of them did it," Otis said. "The murders were never solved, were they?"

Lindsey shook her head. "No."

"I wish I could ask my mother what she knew about it all." Amrita's eyes misted. "You know, I had the blessing of many years with my mother, but time doesn't matter much. I'm here now, and I do not have her with me to answer these things."

"I know what you mean," Lindsey admitted.

Amrita squeezed Lindsey's hand. "I do not know what happened that night," she said, "but I do know that my mother returned to the property once the tragedy was posted in the paper. To be honest, I think my mother went back—"

"Why?" Lindsey said.

The woman bowed her head. "To protect the family's personal items from poachers. To take what she could so that it did not end up in the wrong hands."

"Some would call that stealing," Otis pointed out.

Amrita shot him a look, before reaching into her bag and pulling out a small pale-blue leather-bound journal.

Lindsey's heart began to pound. "Is that . . . ?"

"It's a diary," Amrita said. "I've read it several times. It's interesting to learn what life was like here."

"Does it mention a diamond ring?" Lindsey asked. "There was a valuable ring that went missing and was never recovered."

"Oh, yes." Amrita smoothed her dark hair. "My mother spoke of it often. She was very interested in jewelry, probably because she couldn't afford to have any of her own."

Lindsey smiled. "My mother used to feel that way, too." Her mother often said in interviews that she had decided to start making jewelry after a school trip, when her class filed past the fancy stores on Fifth Avenue. That's where she first saw all the dazzling pieces that were just out of reach.

Otis slid on his sunglasses. "Whose diary was it?"

"The youngest sister," Amrita said. "Her name was Ruby. My mother said the servants always thought Ruby had something to do with the loss of the ring because she left town when it went missing. The diary mentions the ring several times, but nothing about where it went."

Tentatively, Lindsey reached for it. "May I . . . ?"

Amrita smiled. "Of course. That's why I brought it."

Lindsey had once found a diary in the tunnels at Wind Thorne that looked very similar to this one. It was possible it also had belonged to Ruby, because the author wrote in great detail about the ring. It was impossible to remember exactly what she'd said, but the journal included a description of the diamond gleaming like the face of the moon, glittering in a white so bright it was purple, gold, and green.

The diary was most likely still in its hiding spot beneath her aunt's porch. Lindsey had forgotten about it, over the years, but it was definitely something to share with Aunt Petra. It would also be fascinating to compare the two side by side.

Carefully, Lindsey opened its gilded pages. The handwriting was the same as she remembered—a tight, careful pen with several loops and embellishments to emphasize certain words. The entries were both full paragraphs and short, quick observations of life on the farm, sadness that the girl's older sister was getting married, and a big dose of dislike for certain family members.

"This is so cool," Lindsey said, slowly flipping through the pages. "I know my aunt would be interested in seeing this. Was your plan to give it back?"

In truth, there was a good chance the estate would insist upon its return. Amrita must have known that, because she held up her hand.

"I can make copies, but I can't allow anyone to just take it." She brushed away a bee that had landed on the sun-warmed table. "Right or wrong, this diary was something my mother held on to. I have to wonder why. She was quite neat and had few possessions."

"It was stolen, though," Otis pointed out. "Technically, it belongs to the estate."

"No." Amrita shook her finger. "*I* believe that she took it, but she never told me that. It could have been a gift."

"Maybe." Otis adjusted his hat.

"You said you're willing to make copies of the pages?" Lindsey asked.

Otis made fair points, but she didn't want him to scare Amrita away. When Amrita hesitated, Lindsey folded her hands in a pleading gesture.

"Oh, please say yes," she said. "You brought it here for a reason. There's an office upstairs. I could get my aunt to print them, and you could see the property in more detail."

"No, thank you." Amrita bowed her head. "It's hard to be here, to be honest. To think of all the work my mother had to do, with little rest and even less money, while the family threw big parties and feasted. Her life, her sacrifices, taught me to not let people take advantage of me. To take things for free. So, I cannot do that for free."

Lindsey drew back. "You want to sell it?"

Amrita raised her eyebrows. "Yes, I'd be open to that."

"Oh." Lindsey's cheeks burned to think this whole thing had been a sales pitch. "Then, why would you approach me?"

"Your bio said you have ties to the estate." Amrita lifted her hands. "I've tried to contact your aunt for months, but she keeps putting me off. Your picture looked kind, so I thought I'd try you."

To think she'd expected this woman to magically appear with some connection to her mother. Over twenty years living in the city, and Lindsey was still as naive as could be.

"I see." She got to her feet. "Otis, I think we should get back to the table."

People had been coming and going from the building for the last twenty minutes, so it had to be busy.

Otis also stood. "Thanks for talking to us."

"Wait." Amrita blinked. "You're leaving? I really thought these things might have meaning to you."

"Yes, it's great history." Lindsey looked up at the grand house, imagining it full of people. "I can't buy it from you, though. My aunt runs the estate. I don't have that type of power here."

Amrita handed her several pages from the ledger. "Fine. I can give you these. Show your aunt. Okay?"

The papers were an important piece of history for the property. It would be great to have the diary, too. It didn't make sense to completely write it off because Lindsey was embarrassed, or because Amrita had gone through the wrong channels.

"I'm sorry," Amrita insisted, as if reading her mind. "I truly did not mean to cause harm. I apologize if it seems that way." She looked to the parking lot, blinking as if to fight off tears.

"It's okay," Lindsey said. "Let me talk to my aunt. See what we can do?"

Amrita brightened. "Could we meet up this week? I'm free on Wednesday. We could have lunch, see where you're at."

Lindsey eyed the diary. She'd only planned to stay at her aunt's house for the weekend, but the city was brutal in the summer. She didn't have any major projects due until July, so it would be fine to work from her laptop instead of the three-screen setup back at home.

"Sure," Lindsey said, slowly. "I can stay a few more days."

Otis cleared his throat. "We really should get going."

Lindsey took Amrita's number, and Amrita then headed back to her car.

Otis was quiet as they returned to the entryway. The fragrance from the lavender bushes that lined the walkway was calming, and Lindsey hoped it wasn't too chaotic back inside.

Otis spoke first. "Your aunt owns Wind Thorne?"

"Yes," she admitted. "My great-grandmother worked there and married my great-grandfather, Elliot Mensley. He lived in the house next door, where my aunt lives now. Somehow, they ended up with the entire estate."

"The house by the river," Otis mused. "I don't mean to overstep, but—"

Otis was a smart guy. He knew her mother's history, so it was only logical he'd figure it out.

"Yes," Lindsey said. "It's where my mother grew up. Then, we all would spend summers here while my dad stayed in the city to work. Our family lived right outside of the city at the time, so it was so nice to have that time in the country. My brother and I slept on mattresses on the floor, and my mother would work out back in her studio. It was special." She glanced at him. "Sorry I didn't say anything earlier."

"I understand. But now that I know your connection, I have to tell you, her work is truly incredible." His eyes were as blue as the aquamarine in her ring. "I'd love to talk with you about it, sometime. Outside of here. If you'd like."

The opportunity to do a deep dive into her mother's craft with someone who knew jewelry was one of the best offers she'd had in years. It made her nervous, though, to open that door. Especially in a place where her mother's ghost lurked around every corner.

At times, Lindsey had believed her mother's last, unfinished collection had been based on Wind Thorne. The design of the house, the twisting of the trees, the forest, and the wildflowers. It was something she'd felt the moment she saw it, and part of the reason she'd stayed away from the estate for so long. She hadn't discussed her theory with anyone, but she might with Otis. He could speak her mother's language, point out the nuances in her work that Lindsey might have missed, and have a wealth of knowledge to contribute about each piece from his studies.

Of course, it was a leap. She'd known him for literally two hours. It was possible he had only perfunctory knowledge, and like always, she was looking for something that could connect her to her mother, something that wasn't really there.

The reality check made her shake her head.

"I don't really talk about her work."

He nodded, and they walked toward the front door in silence. She was mad at herself for being so closed off, but she barely knew him.

"So, what did you think of Amrita?" he asked. "Didn't expect her to be packing a diary."

"That was so infuriating," Lindsey admitted. "I can't believe that she's trying to get money for something her mother stole. That said, I'd pay to read it in a heartbeat."

Otis laughed. "Well, you made her sweat. I bet she's going to ask for a lot less money than she planned."

"I guess," Lindsey said. "I don't want to cheat her, and at least she gave me the papers from the ledger. Those will be good for the archives." She pulled them out and flipped through them as they walked, reading through the entries.

"How do you know that diary's legitimate?" Otis asked.

Lindsey lowered the papers. "You don't trust her?"

Otis shrugged. "I ask that a lot in my line of work. The true story typically isn't the shiny one."

"These seem authentic," she said, indicating the pages. "The number schemes are realistic, based on the size and scope of this place. And I know the diary's real."

"How can you tell?" Otis asked.

Lindsey hesitated, picturing the nearly identical one she'd hidden under the porch all those years ago. Perhaps he was right to doubt people, because Lindsey was the one holding things back.

She avoided his eyes. "Just a hunch."

It was nearly lunchtime. They were back in time to do about thirty more appraisals, but even as two exquisite enamel pieces in white and gold passed through her hands, Lindsey couldn't stop thinking about the invitation from Otis to talk about her mother's work and the fact that she'd turned him down. The moment the helpers shut down their section, she got to her feet.

Two lunch boxes had been dropped at their table, and the room smelled rich with chicken salad and the miso sauce on the glazed salmon. Several people were eating at their tables, since their half of the room had been roped off for the lunch break. Otis had a paperback tucked under his arm, one she'd read a few years back.

Lindsey had just decided to invite him to eat with her and her aunt when he held up the book. "I'm going outside to read. I always try to get some downtime at these things. It gets a little overwhelming, being around so many people."

Lindsey was interested to hear that. Otis had seemed like he relished the interactions, while she had slowly gotten a headache. The jewelry was fascinating, of course, but the small talk wore her down.

Sometimes, Lindsey wondered if she was the only one in the world who appreciated the part of the pandemic where she had to stay hidden in her apartment, with only books and data sheets for company. One of the legacies her mother had left was an apartment each for her and her brother in New York City. Jack had sold his, but Lindsey held fast to hers, and it had served as a place of comfort and solitude during that time.

"Well, enjoy your lunch," Lindsey told Otis. "And the solitude."

"Thanks. If you see a dessert tray come by, grab me something," Otis said. "I'm a cookie guy."

Lindsey nodded. "I'm more of an ice cream person."

"What flavor?" Otis asked.

"Lemon custard."

He grinned. "I'll have to try that sometime." For a second, she thought he was going to ask her to join him. Then he lifted his book and said, "See you."

Smiling, Lindsey made her way to the staircase and bypassed the burgundy ropes. On the second floor, a series of windows in the hallway stretched up nearly fifteen feet, affording an expansive view of the grounds. Every detail was so grand that she wondered what it had been like here at such a bustling estate in the twenties, with so many guests coming and going. Not to mention the incredible number of servants necessary to keep the tapestries dusted, the floors cleaned, and the crystal sconces shining. It was interesting to think that her great-grandmother had been one of them.

"There you are." Aunt Petra got to her feet when Lindsey walked in.

"This room is gorgeous, too," Lindsey said. "Will it ever stop?"

The office had likely once been a bedroom, with grand windows that overlooked the fields and forest, with a fireplace nestled into a back wall papered in burgundy and gold. She wondered who the room had belonged to, whether it had been the girl who had kept the diaries.

"There are so many fireplaces here," Lindsey said. "It must have smelled of firewood at all times." Back in New York, she lived down the block from several restaurants. One was a steak restaurant, and she loved the scent of the wood-burning stove. "So, remember that big commotion by the front door today?"

"What commotion?" her aunt asked. "I must have been up here or in the kitchen."

Lindsey filled her aunt in on the whole story, then slid the pages from the ledger across the table. Aunt Petra wiped her hands carefully before looking through them.

"This is fascinating." Her eyes lit up. "What a wonderful find."

"Well, there's more," Lindsey admitted. "The woman brought these pages to donate, but she also has a diary that she wants to sell."

Aunt Petra lifted her eyebrows. "Sell?"

"Yes, I know." Lindsey could practically feel her aunt's disdain. "I'm interested in seeing it. She wants to meet on Wednesday, so I'd like to stay with you for a few more days, if that works."

"You're always welcome to stay." Aunt Petra took a sip from her cup of tea. "I do have to say, I'm a bit disappointed to hear she wants to sell an artifact that should belong to the estate."

"I feel the same." Lindsey shrugged. "Especially considering her mother and great-grandmother Annabelle might have worked together. I'd think she'd be happy to share in the history, but no. She said her mother would want her to profit."

"I see." The worry line between Aunt Petra's eyes became more pronounced. "I don't know if I like the idea of you meeting with her alone."

"Why?" Lindsey opened her lunch box.

"Several reasons," her aunt said. "It concerns me that she caused a scene, instead of simply approaching your table. It concerns me that she's asking for money instead of offering to donate the diary. It also worries me that when I didn't respond to her queries, she found her way to you."

Lindsey frowned. "It's not like you to be so suspicious."

"I've seen too many wrong choices, even from the people I love. So, am I capable of believing that a stranger can be up to no good? Yes, in a heartbeat."

Lindsey suspected that her aunt was speaking of Lindsey's father once again, but she refused to take the bait. "There could be plenty of reasons for the way she acted. Besides, I think the paperwork is a wonderful thing for the estate."

"True." Aunt Petra sighed. "However, tread lightly. Don't promise her any money." Lifting a hand, she gestured at the room. "We have built such a wonderful reputation here and receive such incredible support from the community. I heard word from one of our guests today that Wind Thorne has been nominated for a substantial grant, and they've asked us to send in an application packet. So many of these things rely on public opinion that it makes me nervous to invite someone who may not be reliable into the fold, to share her version of a place that belongs to our family."

"I get that, especially when you're leaving," Lindsey said.

Her aunt was scheduled to depart in two days for a six-week cruise in Europe with a group of friends. The group often traveled, but this was the first break Aunt Petra had taken since starting the remodel, and Lindsey could tell she needed it.

"Exactly." Aunt Petra gave a cautious look around the room. "Now that the estate is remodeled, up and running, and there are no problems in sight, I'd be hesitant to talk to her until I get back."

Lindsey dipped a cracker into her chicken salad, thinking. The papers had been intriguing. Especially the diary.

"I can tell you're disappointed I'm not jumping on this," Aunt Petra said.

"What if . . ." Lindsey took another bite of her sandwich and thought for a minute. "What if I stayed here this summer? Help gather information for the grant?"

Every summer, Lindsey told herself that she would make an effort to get out of the city but typically ended up on some forced getaway with her friends and their young children. Staying at her aunt's house and exploring Wind Thorne, perhaps even giving herself the chance to learn more about her mother's last collection, sounded much more attractive.

Aunt Petra lifted her eyebrows. "I nearly asked you if you'd like to be the caretaker this summer. I didn't think you'd be available."

"Well, I do have a life and a job," Lindsey said, laughing. "But I never take vacation time. I don't have any big projects due, and I primarily work remotely, so what's the difference if I do it here or at home? I'd like to stay here and learn more about Wind Thorne. It's a special place."

"I love this idea." Aunt Petra added more hot water to her tea and dropped in a sugar cube. "I'd be delighted for you to compile information for the grant, but also, you could just enjoy being here." Her face brightened. "If I'm not wrong, your new friend Otis will also be in town, staying with his parents for the summer. They live down the road, you know."

Lindsey nearly choked. "I didn't know." She took a sip of cold water. "I doubt I'll see him."

Her aunt folded her napkin. "I can think of worse things."

Chapter Five

New York City, 1925

The number of people on the sidewalks left Ruby unsure where to look. Men dressed in tailored suits and overcoats, walking alongside women in finery. Black cars and horse-drawn carriages filled the streets.

There were so many windows—some squares, some oval, some arched. All inviting and uniform and beautiful. The lamps reminded her of the most elegant of the trees in the forest, the way they took their space on the street. There were clocks and towers and pieces of brass, porch landings and railings, and endless dimension, as if someone had taken the forest back home and multiplied it again and again. It was too much, and if she ever had the opportunity to write it all down in a notebook, she wouldn't know where to start.

Chester took her elbow and steered her beneath the awning on a building. "You scared? It's a lot bigger than Wind Thorne." For once, his face wasn't brimming with confidence.

"Not at all." Ruby drew her coat close. Her heart pounded from the thrill of being here, seeing the city. "I love it."

Chester stood up straighter. "Come on, then."

He started walking and Ruby followed, still taking it all in. The chill seeped through her bones, in spite of the shirt, cap, and trousers Chester had given her to wear when they were on the train. Her coat was utilitarian, so no one gave her a second glance with her hair tucked up. She pulled the cap low, delighted Chester was wrong—that here, she didn't feel afraid. A sense of calm filled her for the first time since seeing Indira dead.

"This is it." Chester stopped in front of a plain brown building. It stood three stories tall, with what looked like a mess hall on the bottom floor. "It's a boardinghouse," he said, off her questioning look. "We stayed here with my dad. I'll sign you in as my brother, so don't take that cap off."

Her stomach flipped. "Okay." They'd talked about this plan on the train, but she still didn't think anyone would actually believe her to be a boy.

Ruby stood out front while he went in, hands shoved in her coat pockets. Sharing a room with Chester would be so strange, but she couldn't stay by herself. Every time she closed her eyes to sleep, she saw blood spilling from Indira's head, or felt the horrific way Uncle Peter had pressed against her, calling her a thief. She wasn't scared of the city, but she was terrified of what would happen if she returned home.

It was starting to get dark, and Ruby watched as the ornate iron lamps flickered on like firelight, one by one. She wondered if her family knew yet that she was gone, and if her father would come after her. Probably not, once he'd heard she'd stolen gold coins to run off with a farmhand. The gold coins might be forgivable; leaving with Chester would not.

It was a comfort to feel the outline of the ring in her pocket. It was her safety net. Escape hatch. Even though she felt that Chester could be trusted, she could still survive without him.

The door to the building opened, and a boy with a busted face poked his head out. "Come on."

It took a second for Ruby to realize it was Chester. She'd gotten used to his swollen eye on the train, but now she wondered again who'd done it.

The dark hallway that led to the stairs smelled like sweat, and it was loud, with people talking and some shouting behind the doors. They passed several men along the way, and Ruby pulled her cap low.

Chester stopped at Room 213. "There's no one named Elliot here, according to the ledger, but that doesn't mean a thing." The key clinked in the lock. "He could be here under a different name. It's a big place, and he wouldn't know anywhere else to go."

Ruby swallowed hard at the sight of the two small beds. If Chester felt uncomfortable, he didn't mention it. Instead, he sat on one, the flimsy mattress sinking beneath his large form.

"Bathroom's down the hall." Chester took off his boots. The sight of his knit socks felt indecent, somehow, and Ruby looked away. "I did a full-board so we can be downstairs for each meal. We missed dinner, but we can get breakfast first thing."

"Then what?"

Chester squeezed his fists. "Keep looking for him. Once my face heals, we need to start searching for a position. With room and board, preferably. I paid us up for the week, but it was six dollars, so even with your coins, we won't last long."

Ruby's mouth dropped open. "Six?"

That was most of what she'd given Chester when they were on the train. She had the ring in her coat pocket, but she was not about to tell him that.

"Yeah." Chester studied her. "You really think you're going to stay?"

The idea seemed impossible. How would they survive? She didn't know how she'd find a way to go back home, but she hadn't been away for long. Maybe no one even knew she was missing. She cleared her throat to speak, then noticed her throat ached from where Uncle Peter had pressed his arm against it.

She yanked off her boots. "Of course I'll stay. I'm certainly not going back."

The next few days, Ruby and Chester searched endlessly for his brother until her feet ached with blisters. They finally spotted him through the dirt-encrusted window of a mess hall several streets over, but he noticed them and slipped out the back. Chester couldn't catch up. He kicked at a snowdrift and shouted himself hoarse with frustration, but Ruby could tell he was relieved Elliot was still alive.

Ruby waited until Chester was done shouting, then put her hand on his arm. "He was frightened. I bet he was happy to see you. To know you're here."

Chester turned to look out at the street, his shoulders shaking.

They spent every day after that near the boardinghouse where they had spotted him, waiting for him to come back. The dining hall was dark inside, and it smelled of something sour, mixed with the salty scent of pork and mashed potatoes. The food was good, though. Full baked potatoes, hearty plates of meat and vegetables, everything drowning in butter.

Ruby was relieved he'd found a place with decent food, that he hadn't been sitting somewhere starving, but she did wonder how he had money to pay for it. She fingered the two gold coins left in her pocket, grateful for the secret safety of the diamond ring.

On Wednesday, Chester and Ruby returned to the boardinghouse where they had first spotted Elliot. Since they were low on money and had already eaten, they waited under a tree outside, watching the front entrance. The morning dragged on into afternoon. There was a moment where the crowd had thinned out completely, but soon it was busy again with the shift change of a nearby factory, when the sun stretched long across the road.

Ruby started to doze, thinking of her sister and whether Elizabeth would ever forgive her for missing her wedding. A carriage clattered by, jolting her awake. She watched the dirt on its wheels and had the sudden sense her sister was walking down the aisle at that very moment.

Ruby was flooded with regret, but then she remembered. Uncle Peter, grabbing her. Indira, with blood gushing from her head. It wasn't as if she'd run for the fun of it.

"Look," Chester said, nudging her.

Elliot was across the street, walking down the sidewalk. He ducked in through the front door with another boy. Both clutched their caps, looking timid and more than ready for a meal.

Even if he was hungry, Elliot was still big. He was twice the size of Chester, always had been. She imagined his size was valuable to his father on the farm and hoped he was managing okay without his boys.

They crossed the street, and Chester hesitated at the front door. "Let's wait until he eats," he decided. "I don't want him to run without eating."

They stood outside and watched through the window. The panes were filthy, covered with soot and dirt. Once Elliot had his food, he found two open seats at a long table, his arm guarding his tray. He tore into the chicken, and when the kid he was with reached over as if to take something, Elliot shoved his arm away.

The moment he'd finished the last bite, Chester went in. He rushed up to Elliot's table and grabbed him by the scruff of his shirt. The friend scampered away.

"What are you thinking, running like that?" Chester demanded, shaking his brother. "Don't you know what could have happened to you?"

Elliot glared at him. Chester glared back, then finally pulled his brother in and held him tight. Everyone who had been watching went back to their food. For once, Ruby didn't want to spy, either.

She pushed open the glass door and stepped out into the street. She dug her hands into her coat pockets, taking in the noise and dust of the carriages, the cars and the people.

The scent of freshly baked bread wafted through the air, and Ruby pulled her coat tight. Four large horses clopped down the street, stunning with their dark, shining manes and white stars on their foreheads; they were saddled up and pulling a bus of some sort with glass windows. People sat inside the bus, staring at her. It was so cold that steam billowed from the horses' noses, their feet making a steady clip-clop in the slush of the street. The wheels splashed, and Ruby stepped back, not wanting to get anything on Chester's trousers.

Biting her nail, she looked through the window again. Elliot was talking, and Chester listened, his expression one of dismay. Elliot's face crumpled, and he put his head in his arms on the table.

Ruby hesitated, but her hands were freezing, so she walked back in and stood next to Chester.

"I didn't mean to do it," Elliot kept saying, shoulders shaking with tears. "I didn't mean to."

Chester turned to her. "Elliot enlisted," he said. "In the navy."

Ruby's heart dropped. *"What?"*

Ruby thought of Uncle Peter. Her mother said it was the problems caused by him going to war that had given him such hateful moments, such a hateful heart. She didn't want the same thing to happen to Elliot.

"No, he's too young," she insisted. "Chester, you need to tell them—"

"They'd put him in jail for lying about his age." Chester cracked his knuckles, thinking. "Unless . . ." He touched Elliot's shaking shoulder. "Did you use your real name?"

Elliot started crying harder. "Yes."

Chester let out a frustrated sound. He got up and paced around. The people at the nearby tables were half watching as they shoved food into their mouths.

"If you run, they'll find you." He turned to his brother and sat down, thinking. Finally, he said, "Look, I'll stay here until you ship out. Make sure nothing goes wrong. Okay?"

No one spoke. The only sound was Elliot's sobbing. Finally, he stared straight ahead, his eyes fixed on the street outside. He seemed desolate, and it hit her that he probably longed to be back in the woods, fishing and helping out at the farm.

Elliot wiped his eyes. "What about Eleanor?" he finally asked.

Chester's cheeks colored. "What about her?"

"She expects you to marry her."

That was an interesting tidbit, and surprising. Eleanor was one of the more attractive girls who had been in primer with them. She was older, and at boarding school. Her family owned a large farm two counties over, much larger than Chester's family farm, and she wasn't someone Ruby ever expected would agree to marry Chester.

"That's not for a few years," Chester said. "I'll write and explain the situation. I'm not leaving you here alone, Elliot. I'm not going to do that."

"Okay," Elliot said, sniffling like the child that he was.

Ruby took a seat. The streetlights were on, and they reflected against the spin of the snowflakes outside. The sight was enchanting, like nothing she'd ever seen.

"I'm staying, too," she reminded them.

"Ruby, no." Chester gave her an irritated look. "This isn't a place for you. It's not for any of us."

"It might be a good experience," she said. "You don't know yet."

"We'll get through it, okay?" Chester said. "We'll get through it. You and me."

She nodded, staring straight ahead.

In silence, they all walked back to the boardinghouse where Ruby and Chester were staying, and Chester gave her an apologetic look.

"Elliot's staying in our room," he said. "With us."

Snow had started to fall, blanketing the city and making the streets look pristine. Once they turned the corner, he said something to his brother, who nodded and stepped over to the edge of the sidewalk. Chester stopped walking and turned to her.

"Ruby, we need to talk," he said.

She looked at him, her hand tight around the ring in her pocket.

For once, Chester's expression was pleading instead of mischievous. His lashes were dark, his cheeks flushed from the cold. "You shouldn't be staying in a room with us," he said. "It's not right. What would your family say?"

Ruby's heart skipped. He was going to abandon her, right here on the street.

Trying to stay calm, she pulled her hands out of her pockets and blew warm air onto them. "I'm disowned, regardless. I ruined my sister's wedding."

"I'm sure she got married anyway," Chester said. "It wouldn't matter much that you weren't there."

Ruby took a step back. It felt like he'd knocked the wind out of her. Even the sting of the wind couldn't cool her burning cheeks.

Surprise crossed his face. "Hey, are you crying?"

Of course she was crying. What did he think she was going to do, when he'd just said that her family wouldn't even miss her? The worst part was that, in some ways, she wondered if he was right.

No one had looked at her twice since Elizabeth's engagement. Every moment, her mother and grandmother fawned over her sister like some prized calf that had won a husband at the county fair. Her father was so proud that Elizabeth had tied their family to Glenn's land farther up north that he spent all his time planning how to expand his whiskey trade, and stopped listening to a word Ruby said. It was very possible her family wouldn't miss her, but she would rather die than let Chester Mensley know that.

Ruby would have walked away from him right then, but she was not about to give him exactly what he wanted. He didn't deserve that kindness. Besides, she didn't have the first idea how to survive in New York on her own.

"Please don't cry," Chester said, looking flustered. "No one's gonna believe you're a boy, acting like that. I don't even know what's wrong with you."

"It *did* matter that I wasn't there!" Ruby swiped at her cheeks. "It would matter to Elizabeth. Why would you say it didn't?"

Chester pulled his hat off, looking annoyed. "I just meant everybody was already there for the wedding. They would have gotten on with it. Look, this isn't going to be easy if you spend the whole time acting like a girl."

Ruby wiped her nose. A horse-drawn carriage plodded past, and she stared at the spokes of the wheel.

"Fine, I'm sorry." Chester's voice was low. "I'm sure it was hard on you to leave your family to help me, to be stuck here. Let me help you get back home now, okay?"

"There's nothing for me at home."

"Ruby, I—" he started to say.

"No! You stop it right now." She shook her finger in his face. "You are not going to abandon me just because you found what you came here for. You promised we would take care of each other like family. Don't you dare go back on your word now, Chester Mensley. Don't you *dare.*"

He turned to Elliot, who kicked his foot against the snow.

"Fine." Chester's jaw was clenched, his expression thunderous. "Let's go."

More snow started to fall, and they walked in silence.

He stopped again and turned to her. "You're not what I expected, you know that?"

Ruby kept walking.

Chapter Six

Upstate New York, present day

Lindsey sat on the edge of the bed in the soft sheets with the blue flowers, staring out the window at the forest. The house had several bedrooms, but the guest room with the blue-and-white wallpaper that had been there for a hundred years had always been her favorite. It was hard to look out at the forest for too long, though, without remembering the day her mother died.

It was abrupt. Her mother had been working on her final collection, and Jack was angry about being up here for the summer instead of at a beach house with his group of friends. He'd spent a lot of time biking that summer, and he was off on a twenty-mile ride. Her grandmother was out at the farmers' market with her friends. Lindsey needed a break from working through the summer classics on her high school reading list, so she decided to visit her mom out in the barn. It was empty, and her mother's walking stick was gone, so Lindsey headed out to the forest to find her.

She closed her eyes tight now, not wanting to revisit the moment she'd spotted her mother crumpled in a heap on the ground, her head bleeding from where she'd hit it against a log when she fell. The doctor said later that it wasn't the fall that had killed her; it was when her heart stopped. Sometimes, Lindsey imagined her mother having a final moment to look up at the bright-blue sky with the trees stretched up high around her, as if the people she loved had gathered close one last time.

Lindsey's father had been devastated, of course. He loved her mother—there had never been a question of that—but he was always busy with work. That only intensified after her death. Lindsey's grandmother tried to convince her to stay, but Lindsey went back home. She spent the remainder of the summer alone in her room in New Jersey, while Jack went off with his friends, after all. Her father was always in Manhattan for work, rarely home, and when he was, he made a lot of speeches about self-reliance and moving forward. It was hard to look him in the face after that, but Lindsey never cried in front of him, not once.

Now Lindsey forced herself to push those thoughts aside, grateful that time in her life was over. That she'd moved forward, even if she sometimes looked back. Absently, she ran her thumb over the smooth stone of her pinkie ring.

It had surprised her when Otis identified it. Yes, her mother had been a household name after an intense reign in the seventies and eighties in the society set of metalwork jewelry, but few people of Lindsey's generation would recognize her work on sight. Yet Otis had spotted it right away.

It made her feel an immediate affection for him, and to be honest, she'd been disappointed to say goodbye to him earlier that afternoon, on the last day of the antique show.

Lindsey hoped he was staying here for the summer, like her aunt had suggested. She'd regretted not taking him up on the offer to talk about her mother's work, but to be fair, she hadn't given herself permission to think about it in some time.

The scent of sesame wafted in from the kitchen. It was nearly dinnertime, which brought a sense of relief. Time to move on.

Lindsey slid on a pair of cashmere socks and padded into the kitchen. Her aunt stood at the stove, pouring a cutting board's worth of chopped vegetables into a stainless steel wok. Lindsey watched the red peppers, onions, and celery hiss and pop as they cascaded in the oil. The bright colors reminded her of jewels and all the vibrant, polished stones that had passed through her mother's hands over the years.

"Smells good," she said. "How can I help?"

Aunt Petra glanced up over the rims of her readers. "You can open that bottle of wine on the sideboard. Thank you."

It was a pinot noir with fragrant notes of fruit and pepper. Lindsey poured two glasses, and her aunt gave her an apologetic look.

"Best make it three."

Lindsey hesitated. "Who . . . ?"

"Your favorite cousin, Barrett." She poured brown rice into a steaming pot. "He didn't want to intrude, but he's passing through on his way to Rochester for work and wanted to see me before the cruise. You, too, of course. Do you mind?"

Lindsey was surprised she'd even ask. "Of course I don't mind. I haven't seen him in ages."

"Good." Aunt Petra accepted the glass. "I wasn't sure if there were bad feelings between you since—"

"My father took him and my brother on a ski trip to the château that we always went to with my mother and never once thought to mention it or invite me?" Lindsey rested a hand on the white-tiled island in the kitchen. "Not his fault."

"I agree." Aunt Petra's expression showed her disapproval. "Yet how your father never once thought to mention it to you, to get your two cents, it's . . ." Her eyes misted, and quickly, she turned back to the stove. "There. The rice is nearly done. I hope Barrett's as close as he said he—"

There was a knock at the door, and Lindsey went to let him in. Her cousin stood in the doorway, the woods stretching up tall behind him. He wore a brown leather jacket, and his typically somber expression broke into a smile. "Linds. How are you?"

He smelled like fancy soap, and his shoulders were broad as she hugged him.

"I've been on the road all day," he said. "But I couldn't pass by without seeing you."

"There's my favorite son," Aunt Petra sang. She emerged from the kitchen wiping her hands on a blue-and-white-striped towel. "It's good to see you, love."

Lindsey couldn't help but feel a pang of envy at the ease with which Aunt Petra showed affection. Her mother had been like that, but her father was so different.

"Shall we eat?" Aunt Petra asked.

"Please," Barrett said. "It smells too good not to."

The three of them settled into the cozy nook of the dining room, a pretty view of the trees and the river outside the window.

Lindsey enjoyed catching up with her cousin. He worked in sales, often traveling to different territories several days a week, which meant that she got to see him in New York more than she ever saw her brother, who lived in Chicago, where her father also lived. She hadn't made time for Barrett once she'd found out about the ski trip, and she regretted that.

Barrett insisted on doing the dishes after they ate, so Aunt Petra and Lindsey settled in on the front porch.

"I'm glad you decided to stay here this summer." Aunt Petra had taken off her makeup, and she looked young in the faded yellow light of the porch. "This is such a special place, Lindsey. Your mother used to love it out here."

True. For as much as her mother worked when they visited for the summer, she also took time to focus on other things. For example, Lindsey's mother didn't cook much when they were back home, but here, she liked to bake. Lindsey and her mother had stood in this very kitchen countless times rolling out the dough for a pie, adding chocolate chips to an already-thick batch of cookies, and even trying intense recipes, like beef Wellington. They wore the aprons Lindsey's grandmother left hanging on a hook, and always listened to classical music. It was the time they talked the most about the things on Lindsey's mind, because her mother wasn't thinking about anything else.

"We used to take long walks," Lindsey told her aunt. "Next door to Wind Thorne. I bet my mother probably snuck in all the time. She was so curious."

Aunt Petra studied the wine in her glass. "Perhaps."

It was clear something was troubling her aunt, but before Lindsey could ask, Barrett walked in with a fresh glass of wine. He typically got tipsy after one drink, so she was surprised that he was already on number three.

Taking a seat, he gave his mother a pointed look. "How's it going? Have we talked about anything important?"

The sigh Aunt Petra gave was nothing short of frustrated. "Let me move at my own pace."

Barrett gave his mother a frank look. "If you don't tell her, I will."

Looking back and forth between the two of them, as her aunt pinched her lips together and Barrett gave her a steady stare, it hit her that his visit was not spontaneous. He'd come here for a reason, and the reason, apparently, was to discuss something she had been left in the dark about, once again.

"Another ski trip?" Her voice was wry.

"That was a rotten thing to do, wasn't it?" Barrett set down his wine and took her hand. "Look, I didn't know that you weren't coming until we were on the plane, and I threatened to turn back around at the airport. Your father hadn't thought it through. He was thinking of it as a guys' ski trip, and that's it."

"He would," she said.

"Seriously, Linds. I was furious." Barrett looked at his mother, and she nodded. "I know what those trips with Aunt Stella meant to you. He should, too."

No one spoke. The steady sound of the bugs outside chirped through the darkness, and Lindsey ached for the days when she could sit in solitude in her apartment. The stem of the glass was fragile in her hand, and she set it on the table.

"I wish he'd talked to you," Aunt Petra said. "The issue is that you weren't told."

Lindsey was done discussing it. "Let's leave it, okay?"

"Agreed."

Moths clustered around the light, and Aunt Petra got up to turn it off. The porch was suddenly shrouded in darkness, with the steady sleigh bell sound of the spring peepers. It was so peaceful, and Lindsey had just leaned back to relax when her aunt spoke again.

"Speaking of the things you have not been told . . . Lindsey, I asked Barrett to swing by today for the specific purpose of helping me to share some difficult news. I am perfectly fine," she said, when Lindsey leaned forward. "However, your father has done yet another thing that I find unspeakable, and I cannot sit in silence about it any longer."

Lindsey appreciated the fact that her aunt was looking out for her. On the other hand, Lindsey didn't care enough about her relationship with her father to keep finding things to be angry about with him. He didn't have to be a part of her life unless it was necessary. The rest didn't matter.

Picking up her wineglass, she said, "I'm sure that whatever it is, it won't shock me."

"Oh, my dear." Aunt Petra came and sat next to her on the couch and took her hand. "It will, because it's outrageous that he didn't give you a say in the matter."

Lindsey sighed. "What is it?"

"Your father is selling the rights to your mother's work," Barrett said. "The company he's talking to plans to license it for mass-market production."

The room suddenly went out of focus. That couldn't be right. Her mother had taken immense pride in the uniqueness of her pieces, that they were walking works of art. She never would have approved of that.

"He wouldn't do that," she whispered. "He can't make a decision like that without me and Jack."

"Oh, my darling." Aunt Petra's eyes filled with tears. "He already has."

Lindsey was unable to think, to move. Finally, she managed a stiff nod. "I cannot tell you how much I appreciate you for bringing it to my attention."

The words felt stiff and formal, but she was frozen inside. Barrett, who'd never had trouble showing his emotions, reached out his hand. He held hers with a firm grip.

"Listen," he said, "there has to be a way to change this. Your father is a decent person. He made a mistake. With family, you need to work through these things. Talk to him."

Her father wouldn't have any interest.

"I don't know how to do that," Lindsey said, frustrated. "Or how to even start that conversation."

"Come at it with love," Barrett insisted. "When you come from a place of love, it's possible to get through anything."

Chapter Seven

New York City, 1925

Ruby jolted to attention as Chester nudged her in the ribs. They'd waited in this hallway for at least thirty minutes, according to the grandfather clock ticking along with the beat of her heart. Ruby's feet ached, and trickles of nervous sweat dampened the back of her dress. She needed a glass of water, but the days of getting what she wanted when she wanted were gone. Especially now that she and Chester had reported to their first day of work at the Wellsley Manor, where Ruby would be working as a maid, and Chester a footman.

Ruby gave him a sidelong look. He looked clean cut, more like one of the doormen they had passed than a farm boy. Not too surprising, since Chester could adapt to any circumstance; she'd seen that back at home, whenever he was trying to get his hands on things that weren't his. She'd been surprised, though, to actually get a job as a maid that included room, board, and a wage, but it was time. Elliot was not scheduled to ship out for another three weeks, and Ruby could not have survived another moment of living in that tiny room with the Mensley brothers.

They had been kind and respectful. Some days, it was almost fun to be together, exploring the city and returning to the room for games of cards and charades. Still, melancholy hung over the brothers, most likely as they weighed the dangers that could come for Elliot, especially in the event of another war.

Steps clipped down the marble hallway, and Ruby stood up straight. She was excited to get out of the dingy boardinghouse and settle into this smart home. It was located next to Central Park—their employer had an incredibly high-up position at one of the textile companies and was always hosting elaborate parties.

Ruby had sent a letter to her parents the moment she was hired, weaving some story about working as a governess for a family who often traveled overseas. She apologized for leaving without permission and for missing Elizabeth's wedding, and she promised to write often with tales of her adventures. It didn't feel good to lie, but she figured it was a way for her parents to save face, especially since Ruby had no plans to return anytime soon.

Mr. Ward, the butler, entered. Well dressed, with a flat nose and a no-nonsense expression, he gestured at Chester. "Come with me." He glanced at Ruby. "Mrs. Roberts will be in for you shortly."

Chester raised his eyebrows as he left, and she shrugged. They had applied as brother and sister. They'd stay on different floors, Ruby on the fourth and Chester on the fifth, but the position was exactly what Chester had set his sights on for the two of them, other than the fact that neither of them had a clue how to do the jobs they'd been hired for, in spite of the fast talking Chester had done to get them hired.

Tugging at the stiff collar of her dress, Ruby considered the great hall. To the right of where she stood were three windows, each twice her height, bringing in so much light that she had to squint. The windows were covered in frost and overlooked the wide street, with its occasional motorcar and horse-drawn carriage, as well as Central Park, where the trees were covered in snow. Inside, the hall where she stood was papered in jade and gold, and the floral arrangement on the side table smelled of lemon and mint. It was a striking home, and she itched to write about it, and regretted not having the money to buy a notebook to replace the one back at home.

Upstairs, a door flew open, and a frazzled-looking woman in a maid's uniform rushed down the stairs. She carried a beautiful black-velvet cloak. When she saw Ruby, she stopped.

"Have you seen Mrs. Roberts, please?" Her voice was pinched with nerves. "My lady wants this cloak, and I have not yet had a moment to repair the button. I am not the lady's maid, but if she sees it hasn't been done yet . . ."

"Does it just need to be sewn?" Ruby had been fretting about all the things she didn't know how to do that might be expected of her. This, she could do. "Here, let me. I'm a strong seamstress."

Mother often complimented the size and uniformity of her stitches, no matter how dull she found sewing.

"I work here now," Ruby assured her. "Where is the sewing kit?"

"I'll fetch it for you." The maid looked near tears. "You're sure?"

Ruby nodded. "Give me ten minutes."

The maid returned quickly with the kit and the cloak. The black velvet of the cloak was the softest fabric Ruby had ever touched, and the bejeweled button of ruby and citrine was shaped like a flower. Its facets shimmered in the light from the window with every tack Ruby made as she practically speared herself in her haste to prove she could accomplish what she'd promised.

"There," she said, getting to her feet and then tying a knot.

The maid came down only moments later, and Ruby stood up straighter as she handed off the cloak.

"Is my car ready?" a sweet voice sang.

At the top of the stairs stood the most beautiful girl Ruby had ever seen. She flounced down the stairs and snatched the cloak without so much as a look. The butler appeared out of nowhere to open the front door, where a polished black car waited. A heavy trail of perfume followed her out.

The maid finally exhaled. "Thank you," she said. "I'm Millie. You just saved my life."

"Oh, good," Ruby said. "Because I can guarantee, you're going to have to save mine, too."

Ruby was exhausted each day by the time she climbed the steep steps up to her tiny room on the fourth floor. It was dim and barely had room for the bed, wooden chair, and dresser. A relentless draft came in from a small window next to the bed, but it was exciting that she could see out, like the porthole on a ship. Her breath came quickly as she changed out of her maid's dress and collapsed onto the bed.

The days got harder. Millie had either seen right away that Ruby didn't have a clue what she was doing, or she just figured Ruby could use the help, because she'd shown her how to do tasks the way their employers expected them to be done. Ruby's body ached from carrying buckets of hot water up and down the stairs, and at night, she fell into bed dreaming of her bedroom back home: the softness of the mattress, the weight of the blankets, and the richness of the room.

This mattress was thin and made her itch. The idea of returning home and sinking into the comfort of her bed was one that began to fill every waking thought, but then she'd remember the horror of what had happened to Indira and the fear of Uncle Peter's body behind her, and she forced herself to move forward.

Ruby was grateful for her friendship with Millie. The rest of the maids were sour, tired, and smelled of sweat as they worked. Ruby wondered if she smelled, too. The days were monotonous, and she did her best to stay positive, but she started to dream of returning home.

Chester, on the other hand, seemed content in this new life. He looked well when she saw him in the servants' hall for meals. Everyone seemed to admire him and listen to his suggestions.

Like one day when she was dusting the main room, Chester and three of the other men came in to move a couch that needed reupholstering. Chester made several suggestions, and when the men put them into action, he looked over at her. Their eyes met, and in the quickest moment, he winked.

That wink stayed with her every moment of the day when she scrubbed out the water closet, its stench turning her stomach. His wink helped her when she nearly slipped on the stairs while carrying a pail of water, and the panic that she would suffer the same fate as Indira made her entire body shake. Thinking of that wink kept her steady and strong, because it reminded her that they were imposters here. That one day, she would return to the place where she belonged.

That is, if her family could ever forgive her for running away.

I will find a way to bring Elizabeth back a perfume after all this is over. Chanel No. 5. I will bring it, and she will forgive me.

Ruby did not have pen or paper, but she had taken down each detail in her mind to one day share with her sister. The sophisticated way the house was decorated, the light. So bright through windows nearly as tall as the room. The smell of floor wax and the polished brass doorknobs, and the horses on the street below. The mother, dashing out to a luncheon followed by her girls. The makeup, the fashions. The flash and cut of jewels she had seen so often in the drawing rooms.

Elizabeth would like to hear about all of it.

The idea that she had wronged her sister did not catch up to her for quite some time. Then, one night, she had a dream where Elizabeth sat with her shoulders hunched over, crying in the corner. Her mother turned away to share a drink with her grandmother, and even Glenn came into the room with a sneer and dismissed her. Elizabeth looked up at Ruby's portrait with her big brown eyes, so sad and hollow that they turned into the long hallways of Wind Thorne.

Ruby woke up frightened and racked with guilt. She got out of bed and took the ring out of its hiding spot. She held it tight, like a cold hand, as she slept.

The weeks of working as a servant passed in a blur of pain, weariness, and a dreadful sense of boredom. Ruby often longed for her notebook and could picture exactly where she'd left it at home. She ached for the opportunity to write her observations, if only to feel like herself once again.

One of her favorite jobs was to pick up items at the store. The other servants didn't enjoy it because it was cold outside, so Ruby was quick to volunteer to go instead. It was refreshing to breathe in the cold, fresh air on the walk and admire the fine houses that lined the street, but the store itself was the highlight of the trip.

The bell jingled when she walked in. She'd already been here three times since she'd started working, picking up this or that for the house, and now, she gave a shy smile to the clerk. He nodded at her, tidying up his counter.

Ruby gathered up the candles her employer preferred for the gold-plated candlesticks at the table, as well as several other items on the list. She had just finished up when a notebook with a shimmering black cover caught her eye. She picked it up, relishing its thick cover and the scent of the fresh paper. It had been so long since she'd had the opportunity to write, to sit down and fill a page, that the lack left her with a physical ache.

The clerk eyed her over his glasses. "Do you need a pen? We just had some new ones come in."

"This one is lovely," Ruby breathed, removing one from the jar.

It was a pale-blue fountain pen with a white-and-gold embossment.

The clerk nodded. "Shall I add both this and the notebook to your account?"

The words rang out like an opportunity. It was wrong. She would be found out. Lose her job. Chester would lose his job. But if she did not leave with the notebook and pen, she very well might lose her mind.

Surely, the family would not notice. She could come back once she'd been paid. Before anyone discovered what she'd done.

"Yes." Her voice came out thick. "Please do so." Her body burned hot as she waited for him to wrap the items. She kept glancing at the door, worried someone would come in.

The clerk handed her the parcel with a nod. It was wrapped so neatly in brown paper, tied with a jaunty ribbon. Her hands shook at the deception, and she imagined Chester's shock if he learned she'd done such a thing. If anyone found out . . .

They won't.

On her way home, Ruby stopped in the middle of the sidewalk, overcome by worry. Was it too late to go back? Tell the shopkeeper she'd misunderstood? If she did, though, he'd take it back. The thought made her hold the notebook tighter. She stuffed it under her mattress when she got home and thought about it the rest of the afternoon.

That night, she closed the door, unwrapped the package, and sank onto the bed. Then she wrote her name in the inside cover with the new pen. The action was a sigh of relief. Descriptions of the city, the boardinghouse, and this mansion poured out of her. She noted it all in fierce detail, until her wrist hurt.

Shaking her hand out, she finally dropped the pen. Yes, she had made an extremely risky decision coming home with the pen and notebook, but it would be simple to feign ignorance if anyone asked questions. Say she didn't know how the accounts worked, that she thought the storekeeper had gifted it to her. It was worth it for this sense of relief.

To feel like herself once again.

The days passed without incident, but the guilt about the notebook burned bright in Ruby's heart. One afternoon, when her back ached so badly that she could barely take another step, she caught sight of herself in a mirror. Her reflection had hung throughout Wind Thorne, in dramatic family portraits that papered the walls. She'd often stared at those photographs, pleased to note that she was nearly as attractive as Elizabeth, with her long dark hair and deep-brown eyes. Now the girl from the portraits was nowhere to be seen.

Sunken cheeks stared back from the looking glass, and her eyes were dull, with deep circles of exhaustion beneath them. There was no question—she smelled like sweat now, too. Her hair was pulled back tight in a bun, and it was greasy, something her mother never would have allowed. Shame burned in her heart as she considered the many ways she'd disappointed her family.

That night, the servants were called to a meeting downstairs. Chester was already there, seated in the corner, his sleeves rolled up in a way that displayed his strong arms. He had been quiet, the past few days, since Elliot had officially left for training, but he seemed in good spirits.

Chester had been talking with one of the valets, but spotting her, he glanced over and smiled. She sat quietly and studied the chapped red color of her hands as if they belonged to someone else.

"Line up," Mr. Ward said, and the chairs scraped as the workers quickly got in line for the weekly inspection of their outfits. It would be extra floor scrubbing if one button was out of place, so Ruby stood up straight.

Chester hung back and fell in behind her. "You seem upset," he said, quietly.

The familiarity in his voice made her want to cry. Instead, she gave him a swift nod. "I'm fine." In truth, she regretted coming here with every ounce of her being.

Once the inspection was over, Chester pulled her aside. "I have news from home. Let's walk in the park on Sunday so I can share it."

Sunday was their day off. Each week, several of the servants talked of their plans, things like going to the cinema or seeing a play. Ruby had listened to their chatter, but whenever Millie asked her to join in, she had politely declined. Not because she didn't want to do those things, but because she didn't have any money.

"Tell me now," she whispered.

He glanced around the bustling room. Two of the servants were polishing their shoes, and a small group was gossiping by the door. "Not here."

Ruby was not about to wait until Sunday for news of back home. The idea weighed on her mind all throughout dinner. She made a point to finish her meal before anyone else and was quick to leave the table. Once she was on the stairs, she did not stop at her floor but went up to his.

Ruby tucked herself beneath a large table next to a small window at the end of the hallway, hiding under the cloth. It was the perfect hiding spot.

She'd sat beneath the table for so long that her back cramped and she'd started to doze off when the telltale footsteps came up the stairs.

Chester headed for his room, which was right next to the table. Ruby gave a slight cough, and he froze. Then he bid good night to the other servants before sitting down in the chair next to the table as if to fix something on his shoe.

Once the door to each room had closed, he whispered, "I'll leave the door unlatched."

She listened for the sound and then ducked out from under the table and into his room. He quickly shut the door and motioned for her to be silent before pushing open a window. It creaked, and her cheeks flushed as she wondered if this could get them in trouble.

Cold air rushed in, and Chester passed her his coat. He grabbed the blanket from his bed and climbed outside, onto one of the metal contraptions designed to help the family down in the event of a fire.

"Come on," he whispered, extending his hand.

Ruby followed him out the window, stepping onto a metal grate that overlooked the city. Her legs went weak. She was so high up, higher up than any tree. The buildings were right next to her. Ruby held tight to the edge of the windowsill as she marveled at their spires and frosted rooftops, the bright lights, and the river in the distance.

"This is beautiful," she whispered.

Chester took a seat by the closed window. "I've been out here every night, now that Elliot's off in training. Nothing else to do, and it's fun to be up so high."

Ruby considered her nights, where she'd fallen into bed with exhaustion. It frustrated her to think Chester was better equipped to handle all of this, but he'd worked as a farmhand for years. This type of work was nothing for him; he barely had to break a sweat. It probably would have been the same for her brother, since Brad had worked on the farm or in the distilleries his whole life.

"What's the news from back home?" she asked, bracing.

Maybe his father was ill and Chester had to leave to care for him. Could she endure that? Or would she try to go back, too?

Chester pulled an envelope out of his pocket and handed it to her. Quickly, she opened it.

> Dear Chester,
> This old man is grateful my oldest and youngest are okay. I had barely slept until you wrote, watching the fields to see if you'd come back home. There must have been something that spooked you here. I won't pry. I know you won't be back for some time, but when you do come, be careful. Ruby left when you did, to travel the world with a wealthy family member. They talk about it a lot.
>
> I love you, son. This is a difficult time, and I appreciate you watching out for Elliot. Your mother would have been proud.
>
> Sincerely,
> Jeremiah Mensley III

Ruby read the letter three times. Then she looked at Chester.

"It sounds like your father knows I'm with you," she said. "Does he?"

Chester hesitated, then nodded. "Yes."

Her stomach dropped. "How? *Why?*"

"I never said it in a way that anyone would know if they read my letters to him," Chester said, quickly. "Racine Thornhill might be your father, Ruby, but he's dangerous and he's never liked my family. I needed my father to be able to make his own choice about what to do in this situation, because what if someone does see us here in New York together? My father needed enough information to be able to protect himself."

Ruby put her hand in her pocket and squeezed the ring tight. Shame burned in her chest, not only to hear what others thought of her family but at what Chester's father must think of her. He'd always been so kind and humble. She'd never be able to look him in the face again.

"It's good you sent that letter about working as a governess," Chester said. "They believed it, even if they're telling a different story. You could go back with your head held high if you wanted to."

Ruby ached all the way down to her soul. It was even more humiliating to think that her family thought they were pulling something over on everyone, lying about her whereabouts, when Chester's dad was the only one who knew the truth.

"I don't know that I could go back with my head held high," Ruby mumbled. "However, I could go back without fear that they would blame you for my absence. If they believed you had anything to do with it, which was my main concern, I do agree that their interaction with your father would have been very different."

"My father's not vicious," Chester mused, picking at his shoe. "I don't think he could have survived an encounter with the mighty Racine Thornhill."

It was the first time since they'd been in New York that she felt irritated with Chester in the way she had back at home. "My father's not vicious, either. He's determined."

Chester gave her a half smile. "That's one way to put it."

When she went silent, he frowned. "Ruby, I'm just kidding. I'm glad your family's found a way to accept the situation. I'm also glad my father decided to stick around in spite of it all. I'm just saying things could have been different."

The apology helped, and finally, Ruby nodded. Chester seemed uncomfortable at her silence, but they didn't get to their feet until she started to shiver.

"You can come here whenever you want," he said, brushing snow off the blanket he was wrapped in. "It's peaceful."

Lips set in a straight line, she let his arm steady her as he led her inside. Ruby did not want to make a scene in front of Chester, but her heart ached to think of her family trying to explain away her absence, inventing some aunt to travel with as though she were a girl who'd gotten into trouble. Her parents would have been diligent to spin the narrative of her exploring the world and developing social graces, so much so that they might even impress themselves. Still, it offended her that Chester was so quick to judge her father.

It wasn't as though he'd intended to work outside the law. He'd been making whiskey long before it was made illegal. The fact that he didn't give up one of their major revenue streams just because some fellow in the government had told him to didn't make him vicious. In some ways, it made him brave.

Ruby was about to slip out of Chester's room and back into the hallway when she decided to set him straight.

"My father is someone I admire," Ruby said, in a low whisper. "You admired him, too—I could tell by the way you were always watching him, trying to figure out what made him tick. So, don't stand here and try to make him out for the fool or the villain, not to me. He's made choices that I don't agree with, but I've never walked a day in his shoes. I left that house for a lot of reasons, but he wasn't one of them, so I'd suggest you think twice before saying something like that to me about him again."

Chester listened to her tirade with a placid expression. Once she'd said her piece, he nodded. "I know it bothers you that you left, Ruby. It makes you feel unloyal. I'm going to tell you something, though. You're the most loyal girl I've ever seen, especially when your family hasn't done much to deserve that. But they loved you, and that's all that mattered."

Ruby gave a tight nod. "And don't you forget it."

The hallways were dark and quiet. It was simple to get back to her room. It was only once she was there that she could drop the bravado and stand frozen with anguish inside the bedroom door.

For so many years, Ruby had looked down on the Mensleys. She thought she was better than they were because she had so much and they had so little. Turned out, they had it all.

Chester Mensley was so close to his family that he'd dropped everything to stand by his brother. Chester could tell his father the truth, without fear of shame or retribution. Ruby, on the other hand, had been forced to flee her home because no one would protect her. Instead, she was here, in a dark, cold room with stains on the ceiling and only a stolen ring and a notebook for company.

Slowly, she sank onto the bed, laid her head face down in the pillow, and wept.

Chapter Eight

Upstate New York, present day

The house was blessedly quiet when Lindsey returned from dropping her aunt off at the airport. Sitting on the bed in the guest bedroom, the springs creaking with every movement, she sat in silence for a full ten minutes. It was nice to be alone.

Ever since learning about the licensing of her mother's jewelry, she had suffered through too many conversations with her aunt about feelings. Lindsey's biggest feeling was that she didn't want to talk about her feelings. She wanted to run back to her apartment in New York and hide from it all.

Now that Lindsey was alone and could have a moment to think, she was grateful she'd stuck it out. In the silence of the woods, she could take the emotion out of it and take action instead. Picking up the phone, she contacted an entertainment-lawyer friend in New York to discuss her options. The friend was sympathetic, but the law was not.

"The rights belong to your father," her friend said, tapping away at a keyboard in the background. "They'll one day pass down to you and your brother, but there's little you could do to stop him unless . . ." She clucked her tongue. "Maybe you could prove he's not honoring the request in your mother's will on how the work would be handled. Do you have that anywhere? In writing?"

Lindsey didn't have access to the will, but she had the number to her mother's sales agent. He had represented her work for years, and although Lindsey didn't know him well, they'd met at several of her mother's showings.

"Mikel?" she said when he picked up. "It's Lindsey, Stella's daughter."

"Lindsey! How wonderful to hear from you."

Mikel instantly launched into a whole song and dance about how great it was that her father wanted to share her mother's work with the world.

"This younger generation will fall in love with her," he exclaimed. "What a wonderful way to honor her legacy!"

Lindsey was stunned into momentary silence. "This can't be what she wanted. You knew her well, Mikel. You knew she was against this type of thing."

"Your father knew her best. This is the decision he's made." His tone softened. "It is hard when things change, Lindsey. This is very different, but it's a very different world. To be honest, I think it's beautiful that her work won't get lost in the sands of time."

Lindsey mumbled something and hung up the phone. For the first time since she'd heard the news, her eyes smarted with tears. She forced herself to get up and take a walk in the woods.

Sunlight filtered down through the trees, shining through the leaves in shades of cerulean. Lindsey walked quickly, trying to move faster than her feelings. In some ways, Mikel was right. Her mother's work had been showcased in Cooper Hewitt and several coffee-table design books, but with time, those accolades would cease to matter. Her legacy could be relegated to a byline in history.

Maybe her father did have good intentions about all of this, but she didn't understand why he wouldn't have talked to her and her brother first. In truth, he probably *had* talked to Jack. The idea pained her even more. The only way to know for sure was to call him, and she wasn't ready to do that.

He wouldn't bother to protect her feelings, to sugarcoat things. He'd demand that she handle it like a grown-up, which was fair. It was just that sometimes, Lindsey longed for the days when she didn't have to handle everything, the days when she actually had a parent looking out for her best interest, instead of pretending like she didn't exist.

Lindsey stopped at the edge of the river, staring down into the water. It was deeper than she remembered, murky with grays and greens. Quiet and still on the surface, but with endless activity beneath. It reminded her of a piece her mother had been working on when she died—a necklace with the fluidity of water and a stone in these exact shades.

The thought brought back her theory that her mother's last collection had been inspired by Wind Thorne. Lindsey's father had most likely forgotten about it, because he'd paid someone to pack it up and put it away.

The thing Lindsey could do, the thing that would give her some power over this situation, was to pull that work out of storage so he couldn't touch it. She could bring it here and compare it to her surroundings, to see if any of her theories were correct. Or, at the very least, to bring her mother close at a time when Lindsey needed her the most.

Back at the house, Lindsey spent the afternoon on the porch catching up with work and trying to figure out the best time to take a quick trip back to the city. Even though she'd requested PTO, she preferred to stay caught up instead of returning to fifty emails. It would also give her the opportunity to check out from everything happening here.

More often than not, people liked to comment that her work as a data analyst sounded mind numbing, but Lindsey enjoyed it. There was something soothing about the number patterns that passed through her head, like the notes on sheet music. Once she'd finally logged off late in the afternoon, she felt a bit steadier as she revisited the idea of retrieving her mother's last collection.

Lindsey poured a glass of sparkling water and took a seat back on the porch. It was screened in, quiet, and quickly becoming her favorite spot. The only sound was the occasional flutter of a passing bird or the drop of a pine cone on the forest floor, which was why she sat up straight at the unexpected crunch of a car coming up the drive.

Her aunt's house was isolated, and even though she felt perfectly safe here alone, she didn't feel comfortable with unexpected visitors. Quickly, she ducked inside and locked the front door, then stood behind the curtains, not quite sure what to do next. The black SUV parked, and much to her surprise, Otis stepped out.

Lindsey gripped the curtains a little tighter. He was tall, she realized, and looked well dressed instead of rumpled; he wore pale-green chino shorts, a white linen shirt, and a pair of sandals. Aunt Petra must have told him to just drop by, considering it hadn't even been a whole day since Lindsey had been at the house by herself.

Lindsey's hair was in a bun, she was sweaty from her walk, and she would have appreciated the solitude to sit and think more about the situation with her father. At the same time, Otis had already passed through her mind a few times today. The fact that he was here was enough to make her open the front door.

"Hey," she called. "In here."

Otis opened the porch door and stepped in, filling the frame. Their eyes met and he smiled. For a second, the air felt charged with electricity. She smoothed her hair with one hand, making sure the unruly strands weren't completely out of place, and was grateful she at least had on a linen sundress instead of a T-shirt and shorts.

"It's nice to see you," she said. "What are you doing here?"

"Oh, I was in the neighborhood." He held out a small box. "Wanted to bring you these. Your aunt told me she was headed to Europe today and you'd most likely need some sustenance."

The square box in royal blue felt familiar, and then, recognizing the name embossed on the top, her mouth dropped open. "You brought me caramels from Mountain Mint? Thank you."

Back when she was younger, the homemade caramels from Mountain Mint, the candy store in the center of town, were the highlight of her visits. She'd forgotten about them until this very moment.

Even though she was vaguely irritated with her aunt for sending Otis her way without warning, Lindsey had to give her credit. Sending him with chocolate was an impressive move.

"Well, I'm glad you stopped by." A quick glance at her watch showed it was nearly six o'clock. "I was just about to make dinner. Would you like to stay?"

"That sounds great." He smiled at her. "I'm happy to order us something, or we could cook?"

Lindsey considered the offer. Aunt Petra had stored the leftover sauce from the stir-fry the day before, and it probably just needed fresh rice and a new round of teriyaki, but cooking something new with Otis sounded much more appealing.

"Let's cook," Lindsey said, like it was the most natural thing in the world for them to be deciding together what to do for dinner. "I don't know what's in the fridge, but it's all up for grabs."

Lindsey led Otis to the kitchen, where they considered the contents of the fridge, followed by the freezer and the cupboards.

"What do you think?" she said.

"Two ideas," he said. "Shrimp scampi with seared tomatoes and spinach, or veggie burgers with sweet potatoes." He shrugged. "Definitely the home of an aunt."

"A health-conscious aunt," Lindsey agreed.

They settled on the shrimp scampi, and Otis got to work cutting and deveining, while she chopped garlic. It felt oddly normal to be standing with a person she didn't know, making dinner in a kitchen that wasn't hers, but maybe that was because she and her mother had cooked here so many times.

As if reading her mind, Otis said, "You know, I studied your mother's jewelry in college. I recognized your ring right away, but it took me a few to figure out why I'd never seen it before."

Lindsey paused. "I'm impressed that you know her work well enough to recognize this was something you hadn't seen."

"Well." Otis went in search of a pan and lit the gas stove. "I'm pretty meticulous about the industry. Your mother's pieces speak to me. The stones she chose aren't your typical choices. I read that she'd—" He stopped talking, looking embarrassed. "Sorry. I don't need to tell you anything about your mother. You already know, and besides that, you already said you don't want to talk about it."

"I was thinking about that today," Lindsey said, filling a pot with water for the pasta. "I'd like to hear your perspective. To hear what you noticed in her work. Makes sense you'd be drawn in by the gems."

"She had a gift for picking the perfect one for each piece. It's so subtle, but I can tell she spent ages making those choices."

Lindsey looked down at her ring. "You're right. She liked to say, 'The stone is the hero, but all heroes should be flawed.' She'd sometimes search for years to find the most perfect flaw."

Lindsey remembered the time her mother had nearly burst into tears when Lindsey's father gave her a raw opal he'd found on a business trip, to finish a piece she'd struggled with for months. Her father had looked on, pleased as punch. It was the first time he'd even attempted to find a gem to add to one of her pieces, but he said that when he saw the opal at a street fair in Italy, he'd gotten chills.

It was a story Lindsey hadn't thought of in years. Would her father put that design, that moment, up for public consumption? Maybe.

Her expression must have said too much because Otis, who had been about to pour olive oil into the pan, stopped. "You okay?"

"Fine." She added some capellini to the pot of water and stirred it. "Let's talk about your family. What brought them here? My aunt said they live right up the street."

"Retirement." The garlic started to sizzle, filling the kitchen with a delicious aroma. Otis gave her a rueful grin. "My parents are both people who would have been happy to spend their lives out in the middle of nowhere, raising chickens or alpacas or whatever suited their fancy. Instead, they spent most of their lives trapped in a suburb so that I could go to a good school, get a good education."

Otis sprinkled in some salt and pepper, and then, seemingly satisfied that the garlic was sufficiently browned, added the shrimp.

"I think they were incredibly annoyed, to be honest," he said as the steam rose, "when I fell into a fortune that I didn't quite earn. They wanted me to use the education that they had fought for, but at the same time, I wasn't allowed to major in petrology or mineralogy. I was stuck learning how to be an engineer, which wasn't the right fit. They knew it, and it all worked out in the end."

The fast-cooking capellini was soon ready, and Otis stepped aside as Lindsey poured it through the strainer. She pulled together a quick salad and, once it was dressed, added it and two glasses of pinot grigio to the table. Otis plated the shrimp scampi and set it in front of her with a flourish.

"Teamwork," he said.

They clinked glasses and dug in.

"What would you have engineered?" Lindsey asked. "If you would have deigned to do it?"

"How to excavate rocks."

Lindsey started laughing.

"That was always my passion," he said, waving a fork. "It's what made me happy, ever since I was young. Once my parents realized I could survive—that it wouldn't be a rocky road, if you will—they were fine with it." He considered one of the braised cherry tomatoes before taking a bite. "I was mad for a while, though. I thought they were only supportive because I'd started making money, but later, when my mom and I finally sat down and communicated, she told me that they loved it that I loved rocks; they just wanted to be sure I could survive."

"I get it," Lindsey said. "She was worried you couldn't squeeze money from a stone."

Otis laughed. "Exactly." He took a few bites and gave her a chagrined look. "Believe it or not, I usually don't talk so much about myself. You're a good listener. But I get the impression that's because you don't want to talk about you."

Lindsey took a sip of wine. "Sounds like a challenge. Well, I had a pretty normal childhood, considering. Back when my mother was still alive, my father spent less time at the office, less time focused on accomplishments, and more time with me and my brother. He tolerated all my phases."

The time that she wore black and put streaks in her hair. The six months where she only wore dresses that looked like something off the prairie, with her hair in two braids. The year she was in a band that played at nightclubs that catered to the under-eighteen crowd, singing songs completely inappropriate for her age.

"But I can relate to what you went through with your parents because my father did something similar after my mother died." The way Otis had been so open with her made her feel comfortable about opening up a little about her experience. "My father turned into this super-focused, career-minded man determined to put me and my brother on the right path for success. I was never really that close to either version of my father, but I liked the first one a whole lot more."

Outside the window, the sun started to set, giving the sky a pretty pink and orange hue.

"I feel bad saying that." Even though she was furious about the issues with the licensing, her mother would have wanted her to speak well of him. "The issue is that he's a total guy's guy now, and I just can't relate. My mother was so in love with him, but they were so different. That might have been what made it work."

They both finished eating, and Otis cleared off the plates. He sat back down and topped off their wineglasses.

"I bet he's proud of you, regardless."

Lindsey rolled her eyes. "He's proud," she muttered. "I'll give him that."

They sat in silence for a moment; then Otis asked, "What about Amrita? Are you still meeting with her tomorrow about the diary?"

Lindsey nodded. "I'm not sure how much I should pay for it."

"Do you want my advice?" Otis asked.

"I appreciate you asking," Lindsey said. "Sure."

"Don't buy photocopies. Buy the original."

"Of course. That reminds me." Lindsey got to her feet. "I have some things from Wind Thorne that I tucked away under the porch thousands of years ago. I want to show you."

He smiled. "Really?"

"Sure, if they're still there." Lindsey pictured the old diary and let out a breath. "I hope I'm remembering right about what I tucked away. Because if I am, I think you're going to be impressed."

Chapter Nine

New York City, 1926

Ruby had been working in the Wellsley home for over a month when Mr. Ward called a sudden and abrupt meeting for the servants.

Everyone gathered in the sparse, utilitarian servants' hall that smelled like sweat and onion. Some, like Ruby, had been in the midst of their duties. Chester gave her a questioning look, and she shrugged. It was curtain day in the main room, which meant a lot of heavy labor that her arms were already dreading, so she appreciated the moment to rest and hear the latest lecture from the butler of the house. His favorite topics, she'd quickly learned, were efficiency and discretion.

"Guess it's time for another talk on being unseen and unheard," Millie whispered, settling in next to Ruby. "I think I might have sloshed something at dinner last night, so I'm most likely in for it."

Ruby thought back to Wind Thorne, and the way her family would sit around the table and talk with abandon as the servants silently cleared the dishes from the table. Little did she know back then how it felt to clear those dishes without making a sound, when your arms were already tired and your feet were aching. Your spirit so tired it was hard to move.

Ruby regretted how she'd treated the servants back home. It was simple to pull up memories of moments she'd acted like a child, demanding the servants clean her chamber pot ahead of time, or drop everything to plait her hair. She'd never thought of the servants as people, other than Indira, whom Ruby had first loved for her beauty.

Perhaps the way she'd treated them was the very reason life had put her right here, seated where she was. Maybe she deserved chapped hands and aching muscles, instead of the grand life she'd failed to appreciate.

"Millie," she whispered as Mr. Ward moved toward the front of the room, "if I haven't said it, thank you for helping me. I couldn't do this without you."

Millie pursed her lips in that shy way she did when she was pleased. "You're a nice one, Ruby."

Mr. Ward took his spot at the front of the room, and everyone fell silent. He slowly scanned each face in the room, his silence weighing as heavy as a storm. Slowly, the energy in the room switched from boredom and grumbling to concern. The servants began to sit up a little straighter, and Ruby's heart pounded for a reason she didn't quite understand.

Behind her hand, she whispered to Millie, "What's happening?"

Millie didn't move a muscle, but she managed to whisper, "Trouble."

Mr. Ward cleared his throat. "It's been brought to my attention that Mr. Wellsley has questioned one of the purchases on our monthly account. He believes the store is in error but has asked me to speak with all of you first. I assume no one here has done such a thing?"

"What is the item, sir?" one of the men asked.

"A pen and a notebook."

Ruby's head went light. From the corner of her eye, she saw Chester's back stiffen, and she wondered if he'd guessed it was her.

No one answered, and Mr. Ward nodded. "I see. Each of your rooms is currently being searched by Mrs. Roberts. If nothing is found, I will present our findings to Mr. Ward and we shall be vindicated. However, if it turns out we have a thief in our midst, the proper authorities will be notified. You are to sit here in silence until she arrives."

Chester turned to look at Ruby the moment Mr. Ward turned his back to pull out a chair. She avoided his gaze and instead turned to Millie.

"This is not good," Millie said, in a low tone. "I once worked at a house where one of the lady's maids stole a hairpin with a diamond—she pinched it, simple as that. She was in jail the next day."

Typically, Ruby was amused by the expressions Millie pulled from the latest magazines, but now, Ruby was so panicked she couldn't even pretend to smile. "You really think they'd do that here?"

"Of course." Millie blew her bangs up, off her forehead. "We'll get a front-row seat."

Ruby's mouth was so dry she could hardly speak. Minutes passed that felt like hours until finally, Mrs. Roberts came into the room. She whispered something to Mr. Ward, and he clapped his hands.

Everyone fell silent and stared straight ahead. "The error belongs with the store. I will share the news with Mr. Wellsley, but I caution you, this has cast a shadow upon us all. Work silently, and diligently, to earn the favor of this home. Dismissed."

Millie got to her feet, grumbling. "He works us half to death and acts like we're up for a caper, when we didn't do a thing. No thanks around here. Let's do the curtains."

Ruby followed Millie, still careful to avoid Chester's gaze. She nodded at Mrs. Roberts on the way out, who nodded back.

It was a good thing the woman did not have the ingenuity to search for a loose floorboard beneath the bed, where someone might tuck a notebook.

Ruby was immensely grateful to her for that.

The moment Ruby was done with work, she rushed down the block to the corner store. When she approached the counter, red faced, the clerk glared at her with crossed arms.

"There is an issue." His voice was nasal and pinched with disapproval. "Your household refused to pay for that notebook you purchased."

Ruby's chest tightened. "Yes, that's why I'm here." She forced her tone to remain bright. "I did not understand how the accounts work. I thought I would be able to have them take it out of my wages, but apparently not." She shrugged as though she did not have a care in the world, and he adjusted his spectacles.

"I can pay you for it now." She gave him a hearty nod. "I have the money."

The servants had received payment the last Saturday of the month. Twenty-four dollars. It felt like a fortune, and she'd tucked it away in her sock.

The folded bills were warm, and her hands shook slightly as she unfolded them. The clerk rang it up and handed her the change. Ruby, who had witnessed her father sweet-talk the police more times than she cared to count, handed the clerk twenty dollars, nearly everything she had.

"Thank you for your discretion," she said.

He nodded. Then he cleared his throat and walked over to the file cabinet, where he pulled out a letter. He handed it to her. "It can be difficult to not understand the way things work in the beginning. Now you know. I do not expect to see such a mistake again."

Ruby pressed her lips together. "Yes. I apologize."

Outside, she forced herself to walk two blocks before falling against the edge of a rough brick building and bursting into shameful tears. Her entire body shook, her skin hot with embarrassment. The note in her hand—should she open it or throw it in the trash? The man at the counter must have wanted her to see it, so she tore the envelope open.

> Dear Mr. Wellsley,
>
> At your request, I can report that the one who purchased the notebook was your household helper

with dark hair, new to the position. If you would like me to speak to the authorities, let me know.

The words blurred in front of Ruby's eyes. She felt ill, knowing how close she had come to being hauled off to jail.

Ripping the note into tiny shreds, she started running. Her breath was freezing in her lungs. Ruby didn't mind. She ran faster, until she slipped and fell, almost hitting her head on the white snow.

That night, Ruby was so worried about how close she'd come to getting caught for stealing the notebook and pen that she decided to go and visit with Chester, to shake her nerves. She sat outside with him for the first time since that first night and confessed everything in a low tone. His face shuttered up, and she expected he would scold her. Instead, he stared out at the trees for a long while before speaking.

"I've stolen before," he said.

Ruby thought of his enterprise with Elliot and the card games. Stealing money from the workers' trucks. Her gold coin.

He looked over at her with a grin. "I'm sure you're shocked to hear it."

For the first time that day, Ruby smiled.

He scratched his ear and continued. "The first time I stole something, I was five. It was an army man, carved out of wood and painted. I remember this, because I stayed up late at night, giving the whole thing way more thought than it deserved."

"I'm sure you were worried about getting in trouble."

"It wasn't that." Chester stretched out his long legs and leaned back against the window. "I kept thinking about who the toy belonged to. Whether or not he would miss it or if he'd get in trouble for losing it, that sort of thing. See, I didn't care too much for army men. I just wanted to know what it would feel like to have one. We didn't have much, Elliot and me. My father finally came into money a few years back, when my grandfather died. He's doing real well now."

Ruby fiddled with the edge of her sleeve, thinking back to life at Wind Thorne. She'd had everything. Food, entertainment, time . . . Chester and his family, their life had been different. He was toiling on the farm from dawn till dusk, and on more than one season, his father had needed to sell off one of their cows to her family to make ends meet. But what her father really wanted was their land, a demand Chester's father always refused.

"It never felt fair, you know?" he said.

She looked up at the sky. "Is that the reason you took my gold coin?"

They'd never spoken of it. Now he paused and looked over at her.

"You looked so regal that night." His voice was low. "I couldn't take my eyes off you. I thought maybe it was the coin that had done all that, you know? I felt bad about it, though, a little worse about myself for taking it from someone like you."

Ruby looked at him in surprise. She never knew Chester saw her that way, not back then. They had a friendship here, but back home, she'd always assumed he didn't like her much, either.

"I forgive you."

"Well, that's good." He stretched. "I forgave myself a long time ago." Her mouth dropped open, and he held up his hands, laughing. "That's my point. This whole thing with the notebook—it happened. You made a mistake, and you learned from it, right?"

Ruby had learned that the relief from writing in the notebook had often been pushed aside by the persistent reminder that she had no right to have it. The fear that she'd get caught. She squeezed the back of her neck with her hand, remembering what a relief it had been to finally hand over the money.

"Yes." She nodded. "I'm still worried the family will find out."

"The shopkeeper isn't going to say anything." Chester was confident. "It's done."

Ruby had hoped as much. It took a weight off her shoulders to hear him confirm it.

They sat in silence, and she considered what he'd said, about her gold coin.

"Do you still have it?" she asked.

He knew what she meant. "No."

"Why?" she demanded. "You said it mattered."

"I gave it to Elliot." He fiddled with the laces on his shoes. "He was having a hard time that Christmas, missing our mother. I gave it to him because I wanted him to be the one to have those good, regal feelings. For me to be the one to keep the bad."

Ruby stared down at her hands. She'd done the opposite for her sister, taking her ring and running away. She'd been so selfish. Made too many mistakes to count.

"Life goes on, Ruby," he said. "You always get another chance to make it right."

"Until you don't."

His eyes met hers. "Until you don't."

Chapter Ten

Upstate New York, present day

Lindsey led Otis down the steps of the front porch to the yard. It was dark out, the bugs singing their summer song, as moths circled the light on the house.

"The ancient artifacts I collected should be under the porch," she said. "Carefully stored in the dirt, if memory serves. Let's go get them."

Otis began to look suspicious. "Under the porch? What does that mean, exactly?"

She pointed at the trellis that wrapped around the bottom of the screened-in porch. It had been fun going under there when she was younger, because it had been a good place to listen in on conversations, as well as find worms. Of course, she'd been a lot smaller then.

Otis groaned. "You know, I was trying to impress you tonight. I even put on the good clothes." He let out a hearty sigh. "It looks like I'm going to have to make that sacrifice."

"I feel guilty," Lindsey said, indicating the jeans and T-shirt she'd put on before they came out. "I changed."

She handed him a flashlight, and they walked the edge of the perimeter until he spotted the access point for utility workers. It was nice it was there because that meant they wouldn't have to wiggle their way through broken boards, but it also meant that people had been under the porch over the years. Someone could have easily found what she'd tucked away. Shining the flashlight first to check for snakes, Lindsey let out a breath and shimmied under the porch.

Otis was right behind her.

It smelled like a basement and was rough with rocks and dirt. Small slats of light shone through the boards from the porch light above. Lindsey kept her body close to the ground, mainly because she didn't have much choice, and tried not to think about all the creatures that could have made their homes in this dank, dark space. Something grabbed her foot, and she squealed.

Otis laughed. "Had to do it."

"I no longer feel guilty for ruining your good clothes," she said.

It had been years, but Lindsey remembered the exact spot where she'd kept her childhood treasures. She crawled to the far corner of the porch, to a small slab of cement with two levels. Mentally crossing her fingers, she shined the light into the crevice of the rocks and reveled in the reflection of the plastic bag.

Otis came up next to her. Their faces were close together, and for a split second, it felt almost possible to get caught up in a kiss.

She pointed with her flashlight. "It's back there."

"You want me to be the one to reach back there, don't you?" he asked.

"You know it," she teased.

He gave her a bemused look, cringing as he reached his hand into the tight space before pulling it out as quick as possible.

Even though she wanted to rip the bag open right then and there, she also wanted to do that in a place where she could sit up. They crawled back out, then brushed dirt and loose gravel off their clothes.

"You can officially add 'archaeologist' to your résumé," she said. "That counted as a dig."

"Unfortunately, I have to add 'entomologist' as well."

They headed into the house, Lindsey cradling the bag of artifacts.

"Let me get cleaned up really quick," Otis said. "You go ahead."

He went back to the bathroom. She suspected he was trying to give her a moment to revisit the find in private, which she appreciated.

The freezer bag had stayed in one piece for all these years, which was impressive. The plastic was not as smooth or malleable, but it was intact. Slightly yellowed and covered in dirt on the outside, but once she zipped it open, it was pristine.

Lindsey pulled out the full assortment of items and laid them out on the table, embracing the rush that came with the sudden flash through time. The pieces were everything she remembered. The diary, the chunk of turquoise—even brighter blue than what had colored her memory—several feathers that were the worse for wear, and oh!—she pulled a bracelet out of the collection. She squeezed it tightly in her palm before quickly hiding it behind the cookie jar in the kitchen, for fear Otis would see it and ask questions.

Lindsey picked up the diary. She had once kept a diary when she was young, and she could still remember the smell of the ink from the pen she used to write in it. Sharing her feelings on the page had saved her from a million embarrassing outbursts, but she'd finally stopped writing in it because she was afraid her brother would read it.

Lindsey wondered what had driven Ruby to keep these diaries, if writing had helped her in some way. Carefully, she opened the pages. It had been so long since Lindsey had read it.

Lindsey skimmed through the first few pages. It spoke about how weak Ruby felt, how strange it was to be back, and her apologies for not being able to be honest about everything that had happened. The words were much more interesting now that Lindsey was older, and she could hardly wait to read the whole thing. She flipped to the very back to search for the entry she'd read on repeat when she was younger. It was amazing how many phrases she remembered.

Otis stopped short when he walked back into the room. "Amrita gave that to you, after all?" he said, sounding puzzled. "I misjudged her."

Lindsey finished reading, then looked up at him, blinking. "What? No. This was with the collection from under the porch. I didn't tell you I had it when she showed me the diary because we'd just met."

Otis touched the front cover. "It's exactly the same. No wonder you knew it was authentic."

"Yes, I'm sorry I didn't tell you then."

He shrugged. "I get it." He turned his attention back to the objects. "This piece of turquoise is beautiful. Where did you find it?"

"In the woods at Wind Thorne." She admired it now, gently touching its rough surface. "I wasn't sure if it was from a collection of stones or fell out of a piece of jewelry or one of my mother's projects or what. It was one of the most beautiful colors I'd ever seen. I showed it to my mother, and she told me to . . ." She stopped, surprised that she'd even said that much.

"Put it in a piece?" Otis guessed.

Lindsey ducked her head. She didn't want Otis to know she'd once had aspirations to be a designer, because her work didn't begin to compare to her mother's.

"I remember being so happy to find the turquoise," she said, "but I did wish it was the diamond. Do you know much about the missing ring?"

"Only that I'd love to find it."

Lindsey nodded. "So, you're here because you're looking for the diamond?"

Otis gave her a half smile. "Not exactly."

Lindsey flushed and took a sip of wine. Noticing his glass was empty, she held out the bottle.

"Thanks." He thought for a minute. "I actually do know a little bit about the ring. My parents said it was the engagement ring of Elizabeth Thornhill, Ruby's older sister, and it went missing right before her wedding. No one knew who took it. The servants were questioned, but it was never found. It's supposedly still on the property, but I think that's wishful thinking."

"Ruby took it," Lindsey said, and he gave her a questioning look. "I found the part where it says it, right before you came back from the bathroom. She said she hid it away, and it would come back to her sister when the time was right. Unfortunately, Ruby wrote that only a few days before everybody got murdered."

Otis was about to take a drink, but he stopped. "So, it was still out there."

"Yes." Lindsey had reveled in that secret when she was younger and spent hours combing through every inch of the property outside Wind Thorne, trying to find it.

Now she opened the diary and searched for the passage. "There," she said, pointing at it. "I spent years trying to figure out what 'it will come back to her when the time is right' meant. For a while, I thought it was in the river. Either way, I never got lucky enough to figure it out. I should show this to my aunt."

"Yes, but you should have her cover that page up if she plans to put it on display, or you'll have everybody and their brother on the property searching for it."

"True." Lindsey hesitated. "It is possible a groundskeeper or one of the construction workers or someone found it ages ago and decided to not say anything."

"Always possible." Otis set his glass on the counter and gestured for the diary. He read the passage slowly, then tapped the page. "You think she would just leave it somewhere, though? It's too valuable."

The slow hum of the kitchen light above them, coupled with the easy lull of their conversation, felt so cozy that Lindsey felt grateful he was here to share this with her. She took a step closer and read over his shoulder. "I don't know. I searched the river and spent ages looking in the tunnels. I searched them endlessly, because they're endless."

"With a metal detector?" Otis asked.

"I'm sure my mother searched with a metal detector," Lindsey said. "I told her about what I read, and she'd asked to see the diary. I'd bet good money she swept the tunnels. She was fascinated by the story, too. It isn't fair that—"

Lindsey bit back the words. It wasn't fair that her mother never got to own Wind Thorne, especially considering how much she loved the property. It did no good to stew about the injustice of it all, because it wouldn't change a thing.

"What isn't fair?" he asked.

"I don't know." She paused. "Would you like to read the diary with me? I think it can be interesting to get a front-row seat to the past. We could bring the wine and have a reading session."

Otis stretched. "Only if you let me light a fire."

The idea of sitting together by the fire felt thrillingly intimate, much more so than some uncomfortable discussion about feelings. Lindsey kept her voice neutral, but she was already imagining what might happen if she reached forward to brush that unruly lock of hair behind his ears. "Researching ancient artifacts by the fireside, here we come."

Lindsey was struck by the quality of the diary itself. It was something that wouldn't have occurred to her back when she'd found it, but now, she marveled at the softness of the pale-blue leather and the heavy paper stock edged in gold. It had a tiny hook where the lock must have once been, but no actual lock or key.

When she'd first opened it, a loose page had fallen out. Holding it up, she said, "Let's start here. It's a letter. No envelope."

Otis had settled next to her on the floor with his legs stretched out and his back against the couch. He took a sip of wine, his eyes reflecting in the blaze of the firelight. "Who wrote it?"

"Ruby. She was the youngest sister in the Thornhill family, the one who supposedly took the ring from her older sister, Elizabeth."

She offered it to Otis, but he said, "No, you go ahead."

Otis listened as she read it out loud, his chin propped on his hand.

Dearest Family,
I realize that my sudden absence must be a shock to you, and I am sorry for any heartache this has caused, especially with Elizabeth's wedding on the horizon. However, I recently applied for a position as a governess, never dreaming I would be selected. Then I received a letter that indeed, I was.

I should have requested permission immediately, but I did not want to steal attention away from Elizabeth on her special day. I chose to leave in haste for several reasons that I will not discuss in this letter, but the main one is that I was frightened after what happened the night of the party. I do hope you'll forgive me for being a coward, but that is the truth.

I want you to know that I am safe, and my pursuits are honorable. I think I shall enjoy being a governess.

With love,
Ruby

"That's strange, isn't it?" Otis held out his hand, and Lindsey passed him the letter. "I don't understand why she'd go off to work somewhere. I'd assume her father would try to partner her off to someone with even more land. Isn't that what they did back then?"

"Maybe that's why she ran off." Lindsey thought for a moment. "Working as a governess for a high-end family would help her to see the world on their dime. Maybe she had bigger dreams." He handed the letter back and she reread a few sentences. "I do wonder what happened at the party. It seems odd that she'd just leave like that. There had to be a reason."

Otis leaned back on his elbow. "Didn't you say everybody died at some point? Maybe the family was always getting threats, and that scared her. She tried to change her fate."

"That's an interesting idea." Lindsey tried to remember if she'd heard anything about a rival farm or maybe a family that had threatened their illegal whiskey production, but couldn't come up with anything. "I haven't read anything, but considering the way they all died, I bet Racine Thornhill received threats all the time. I wonder if she was trying to run from all of that. Kind of a bummer to think it didn't make a difference."

It was one thing to know how a story was going to end and another to imagine how Ruby must have felt, thinking the choice to leave could change her fate. Especially if she never planned on returning but had eventually ended up right back where she'd started.

"What happened the night everyone got killed?" Otis asked.

Lindsey pulled a couch cushion down and nestled it behind her back. "It was actually on one of the smaller plaques at Wind Thorne; do you remember how there's educational vignettes all over the house? Well, sometime deep into the Depression, the family was murdered in cold blood. It's unclear whether it happened due to their whiskey trade or something else, but it was pretty brutal."

Lindsey flipped through the diary, considering the neat penmanship with loops in the letters. It had been written by a girl with hopes and dreams, without any idea that she wouldn't have enough time in life to make them come true. There were moments where Lindsey wondered if she'd run out of time, too, like her mother. Lindsey still hoped to fall in love, get married, and have children, but she also had moments where she knew fixing the relationship with her father and her brother should be on that list as well.

"It's sad that she died," Otis said.

"I know." Lindsey thumbed through the pages. "She would have died at some point, but this is different. She was murdered." The words hung there, somber and violent. She passed Otis the diary. "Your turn."

Otis flipped through the pages in silence before stopping at one. "This is interesting. She's being introspective about things."

He cleared his throat and started reading: "'I had thought I understood that there were many different ways to think and live because I had spent so many hours spying on the servants and other people, but now, I've lived another life. I understand not everyone has thick chocolate that pours from silver containers like lava. Not everyone has underclothes that are soft and cozy, instead of filled with bugs and scratchy. Not everyone has the freedom to spend all hours of the day creating secret worlds, learning about others, and moving through life with the slow and steady assurance of a cat waiting to be fed and brushed to a state of perfection. I'm surprised that the guilt I have for all I didn't know I had hasn't carried me down the river.'"

Lindsey frowned. "Goodness."

Otis handed the book to her, and she opened it to a random page and read: "'It's as if they don't care at all that I've returned. I don't know what I expected. It's possible that I've spent my entire life being pushed to the back of the hearth, and I only now started to notice. It's terrible. The way my father and uncle fight, the strain it's put upon us all. I don't like being here.'"

Lindsey wanted to keep reading, but it was his turn, so she reluctantly passed it back. He must have read her mind, because he stretched out and settled in deeper on his floor cushion.

"You go ahead. I like hearing you read it."

Eagerly, Lindsey continued: "'How long does it take to live in such a way that makes you begin to question if everything you knew before was false? Even this diary feels different now. Before, it brought me a sense of joy, but I'm afraid to see the truth behind my words. The girl I was no longer exists. That girl is an idea now, hazy and somewhere on the horizon.'"

"I felt that way sometimes, when I was close to her age," Lindsey mused. "It was after I went off to college. I came back home, and the things I'd started to accept, like how my father was fascinated with my brother and not me, I couldn't tolerate anymore."

Her first night back home from college was also the week of her twenty-first birthday. Her father's secretary had arranged a dinner for Lindsey, her father, and her brother at her favorite Italian restaurant, and she'd looked forward to finally having two or three hours of their full attention. Well, she'd sat at the restaurant alone for forty-five minutes before the two of them walked in, their cheeks flushed from a last-minute bike ride through Central Park.

"Why didn't you ask me?" Lindsey had said, marveling that they hadn't bothered to include her in such a fun moment.

Her father gave her a perfunctory kiss on the head. "Your brother's training for a race," he'd said, as if that explained everything. Looking at Jack, he said, "I'll race you again after this."

After this. Like her birthday dinner was another thing he had to knock off the list before getting back to what mattered.

The shame of that moment cut through her. The realization that, no matter how hard she tried, her father's focus would always steer toward her brother. She'd faked a stomachache ten minutes after the appetizers arrived and went home. She cried herself to sleep that night, instead of laughing and enjoying wine and dessert with her family, like she'd planned.

"Sorry," Lindsey said, now. "I probably shouldn't have said that."

"Why?" Otis asked. "No one's family is perfect. Was your father always like that?"

"No," she admitted. "He was busy but still involved. He checked out completely when my mother died."

"I've seen pictures of your mother, and you look like her," Otis said. "I wonder if that made it hard for him once she was gone."

Her shoulders tensed at the idea, and she braced herself against the hope that his theory was correct, and one day, she'd get her father back. That their relationship could still be fixed. It was still something she wanted, in spite of it all.

"Yes, I do look like her in some ways," Lindsey admitted. "You'd think that would make him care for me more, though, not less."

"Maybe it's not less," Otis said. "Maybe it's just harder."

Lindsey did not want to think about her father. It led her down this path of hope that her family could be whole again. In the end, her mother would still be gone.

Otis took the diary and turned to the next entry. His voice was deep and resonant in the quiet of the room: "'Elizabeth and I have talked in depth. Embraced and made progress. Yet, nothing much has changed. Elizabeth has moved on, and in some ways I have, too. I can no longer see her as the captivating creature I admired as a child. She can be selfish, and cruel. Leaving a conversation with a sudden turn of her shoulder if the mood suits. Such snootiness and entitlement. Perhaps I had the same airs? But once you know what it's like to be invisible—barely even human—you change. It's not right to treat others like they don't matter. I see her doing that a lot.

"'It's terrible of me to be so ungrateful. My father allowed me to return to a place that will keep me fed. How can I be so selfish, to keep looking for more? This is the dark thought that I've been brewing, the one I've been afraid to pull out into the light. There, I said it. I'm selfish. If I could change it all, I would, but I can't, so what can I do instead?'"

"My heart is breaking for her." Lindsey took another sip of wine, reading through some more of the entries. "Such regrets, but about what? I know I read this when I was younger, but it all went over my head. I never realized how much this girl was going through. I don't know why she's so upset. I'd like to read this from the beginning."

It was ten o'clock. Getting late. But the fire was crackling in the hearth, and the moths were hypnotic in the light outside the back window.

"Do you want to stay a bit longer?" she asked.

Somehow, they'd ended up close to each other on the floor. Her leg was resting against his. Now that she'd noticed it, she couldn't stop thinking about it.

Otis must have noticed, too, because the mood in the room shifted. He held up his wine and considered it in the firelight.

"The problem with longer," Otis said, slowly, "is that I can't guarantee I'd focus on the diary."

Turning, he met her gaze.

Lindsey's logical mind shouted at her to put on the brakes, but the other part of her, the part that relished the scent of sandalwood soap and ached to brush away that small smudge of dirt on his cheek, was more than happy to see what would happen next.

Otis lifted himself off his elbow and leaned in. Gently, he reached forward, and touched her cheek. Reaching out, she caught his hand in hers, and everything went still.

Slowly, excruciatingly, he traced his finger over her wrist. The warmth seared through her skin. He leaned forward and stopped. Then, his mouth was on hers. He kissed her with a ferocity that she hadn't felt in ages. He finally pulled back and took a long drink of wine, and she tried to catch her breath.

"All right. I'm staying so we can read more." He looked at her. "Right?"

Lindsey's gaze locked onto his. She picked up the diary, but her hands were shaking. If they crossed this line, moved away from the role of research buddies and into something else, there was risk. He was smart and attractive, and for the first time in ages, she was not only attracted to him but interested in getting to know him.

It wasn't the safe move to let him stay, but at the moment, she wasn't super invested in being cautious. Remembering the heat of his skin and that longing to keep that feeling going, she placed the diary on the ottoman.

"It's waited twenty years," she said. "What's another few minutes?"

Chapter Eleven

New York City, October 1929

Time passed in a blink as Ruby worked for the Wellsley family.

Once the trouble with the notebook had blown over, she started to appreciate her position and that it had put her right into the heart of New York City. Ruby lived in a stunning home in the center of the most interesting place she'd ever been in her life, and even if she wasn't the one wearing the dresses and being draped in jewels, she had plenty of opportunity to get out and explore. The winding paths of Central Park, the public library with the enormous stone lions, and the smell of the popcorn at the motion pictures captivated her, as did the time she enjoyed spending with Millie and Chester.

Ruby appreciated Chester in a way she hadn't before. It surprised her to think that they hadn't been close back at home, because now, she searched for the moments when she could talk to him about her day. There were times she even admired things about him that she hadn't noticed before. That his arms were strong, and his back. The charming way his hair fell across his forehead. Sometimes, she caught herself staring, but it was just because he was her one connection to home; she knew that. He'd become a good friend, and it made her free time more fun to have good friends to spend it with.

The work she had to do wasn't all that bad, either, as it provided her with money and freedom to do fun things. Plus, toward the end of her first year, the Wellsleys had discovered that Ruby was quite literate. They chose to increase the status of her position, having her work in the morning in correspondence and as a reader for their elderly father, which meant she only had to clean in the afternoons. This made the cleaning much more manageable, and the mornings, most enjoyable.

Not only did she get to sit in an ornate, well-lit room that overlooked the treetops in the park, but she was given the use of the most beautiful herringbone fountain pen. It soothed her to dip it into a well of ink and feel its nub bite into the delicious pulp of the stationery. She also had the opportunity to read the newspaper each morning and learn what was happening in the world, which informed her rare correspondence with her family.

Ruby still missed her sister but had slowly accepted that communication with her family had to be limited to the occasional letter filled with lies about her life. Four years passed in a breath, and Ruby's attachment to Wind Thorne faded along with the time as she adjusted to her new life as a servant.

Chester had returned home to visit his father several times over the years, but Ruby could not return, for fear her family would force her to stay. There were moments when she wondered if she should go back, but she had been away from home for such a long period that sometimes, she wasn't certain anything was quite as she remembered it. Besides, she had grown to enjoy her time in the city.

So much had changed, including her outlook and place in the world. She no longer felt like the lady of the manor, the petulant child who would make the servants change the chamber pots earlier than they should. She'd become a young woman, with grace, dignity, and a sense of how to work hard and serve for the greater good.

Ruby had also developed feelings for this life and the people in it. She loved Millie, as well as several of the other servants in the house, particularly the ones who boarded, as she did. Plus, her friendship with Chester had started to feel like something more, something bordering on romantic. Of course, that couldn't happen, since he was always writing love letters to Eleanor Cook back home, but what if they never returned home? What then?

These were the questions that consumed Ruby's thoughts as she debated how long she could remain a servant, and what strengths she could use to build a life on her own.

One morning in late October, when the leaves had started to turn color in the park, Ruby was sitting in the servants' hall, finishing up her tea. She was about to head up to do her correspondence work when a sudden scream made her jump and spill the last sips of Earl Grey down her dress. The scream transported her back to Indira's fall down the stairs, and that old sense of terror cut through her.

The cook rushed into the servants' hall. "People are diving out of buildings." Her expression was stricken. "The missus said so."

The men rushed to their feet, the chairs scraping against the floor.

"Are we back at war?" one of them asked.

Ruby and Chester locked eyes. He'd often worried there would be another war and that Elliot would be on the front lines, but the papers had given no warning of that. Ruby's heart began to pound even faster.

"I don't know." The cook rushed back out.

Ruby made haste to the main hall, determined to find out if there truly was trouble. It did not take long. Mrs. Wellsley was crying quietly on the fainting couch, while Millie, who had moved up to lady's maid, paced back and forth.

"Let me ring for your husband," Millie said. "We'll find out what the situation is."

Millie left the room and stopped to see Ruby. Millie gripped her arm and pulled her to the side, her face pale.

"Everyone's money," she whispered. "It's gone. That's what Mrs. Wellsley said. She said everyone's money is gone. Some of the men killed themselves, because they're ruined. Go look outside. I have to help Mrs. Wellsley."

Ruby ran upstairs to her room, which offered a better view of the city, and peered out her small window. Indeed, the streets were in chaos. They were full of people rushing down the streets in their business clothes, talking animatedly to one another.

She slipped out front and found Chester, who was speaking with a passing footman. His shoulders were tense, and he shook hands as the man continued on. Turning back toward the house, Chester seemed relieved to see her.

"The stock market has crashed," he told her. "The banks are failing, and several households have lost their fortunes."

"People were jumping from buildings?" Ruby asked.

"No, that's not true. People were panicked, that's all." They stood in silence, and he shoved his hands in his pockets. "Something terrible is about to happen to the city, though, Ruby. It's going to fall apart."

He couldn't be right. Ruby thought of the sundry shops, the bright lights outside the opera houses, the luscious smells from the restaurants. New York was full of amusement and opportunity. Ruby refused to believe it could crumble.

"It will work out." Her voice rang bright. "Hard times do. We are perfect examples of that, are we not?"

"Perhaps." Chester patted a pocket in his coat, as if checking on something. "Do you carry your money?"

"It's hidden in my room."

Chester kept watch up and down the street, as if guarding the house. "Sew it into your dress. From now on," he added, in a low voice, "I also want you to eat as much as possible, whenever you can. It's what we do for the livestock before winter, right? We need to do that for ourselves. I do think . . ."

A well-dressed woman walked by, wailing, her children held close to her.

Chester adjusted his cap. "I do think we're in for some trouble."

New York, March 1930

Ruby hovered in the doorway of the dining room, her heart pounding. The slightest creak of the wooden floorboards would alert her if someone had entered, but still, she didn't dare take another step forward. The loaf of bread on the wooden sideboard was so small it was practically a slice, and it would be noticed if even the slightest crumb was missing. Yet, her stomach ached, and she barely had the energy to put one foot in front of the other. Her hands shook with fear, along with the hunger.

"Don't." Chester appeared from the shadows, worry lining his gaunt face.

It was rare they spoke these days, as they were both so busy filling the roles of the staff, including Millie, who had escaped the city to help family back home. The Wellsleys could no longer pay for their services, but in exchange for their work, Ruby and Chester had a roof over their heads.

"What do you mean?" Ruby demanded, in a hushed whisper. "I am performing a final check of the table. Shall you ring for dinner?"

The look Chester gave her made her eyes sting. Turning, he strode out of the dining room.

Ruby squared her shoulders. It was frightening how close she'd come. If Chester hadn't been there, she probably would have done it. In the kitchen, she fetched a cup of water and drank it. It didn't make her feel full, but it helped her to go on.

The nights she still went up to Chester's "back porch," as they'd once called it, they could see starving people lining the front stoops of the streets. Ruby tried not to look too often, for fear her body was becoming the same. Folding into herself at night had become a negotiation of bones, with sharp angles and hollows that left no memory of the full figure she'd once had.

The need for correspondence had dwindled, but she still read to the senior Mr. Wellsley. He preferred novels, now, as the news made him think of everything their family had lost. Ruby liked the novels, too, as they helped her escape from all of this. Her head often ached from hunger, though, which made it less enjoyable to read the words. In addition to those duties, she was also required to assist with cleaning, serving, and the after-dinner cleanup. In exchange, she was fed, but not much.

Ruby often thought of how she'd turned her nose up to the food back home. What a fool she'd been, taking for granted the abundance of beef, eggs, and fresh milk. There were days when the physical yearning to drink frothy warm milk straight from the pail, the faded scent of grass blended with the sweet cream, made her knees go weak. It had never occurred to her that one day, the only thing she would have to put into her mouth would be stale water, bone broth, and, on a good day, a piece of hard, forgotten bread.

It brought to mind a time when she took a dislike to one of the smaller servants at Wind Thorne, because she gave mean looks to Ruby but fawned over Elizabeth. The servant stared with longing at whatever succulent dessert had been on the table, like freshly churned ice cream drenched in caramel sauce. Ruby never felt pity for those looks. If anything, they made her relish the taste of her dessert even more. Now she was paying for her past behavior. Wasn't that how it all worked?

Those rare times she and Chester still sat outside on the grate talking late into the night, those were the types of questions they discussed. Ideas of how the world worked. Ruby looked forward to hearing Chester's point of view because he saw things differently than she did. He didn't believe that things happened to people because they deserved it; he believed that each day was an opportunity to take on a new challenge and make something grow out of that. Lately, Ruby had found she had less and less strength to go talk with him at night, even though it had been one of the things she'd enjoyed the most.

Hunger made her brain soft. Some days, it was hard to focus on what she was supposed to be doing or remember the tasks that she had already completed. Distressing, yes, but she barely had the energy to feel anything.

Ruby wanted to return home, but she'd written to her family, asking if they'd like her to visit, and had not received a response. She'd had no choice but to stop paying the servant at the house down the road to watch for letters addressed to her, so it was possible a letter had arrived that had been tossed. Or perhaps, times were as difficult for her family as they were for her, and they didn't want another mouth to feed. It was also possible that they didn't want her to come back, that they had no desire to reopen the chapter on their daughter, which was an idea too painful to consider. Even if she had put herself in this position, it was frightening to think she might truly be alone in the world, especially when the world around her was falling apart.

Often, Ruby got herself through those hard moments by thinking about food. She closed her eyes and imagined what it would be like to eat a piece of toast. The crust feathery and light, layered with butter and jam. Or the memory of the summer days she and Elizabeth had picked blackberries fresh off the bushes. The thin skin of the berries, warm in the sunlight, burst in her mouth with juice and seeds as small as a splinter, leaving her something to work over with her teeth. Fluffy layers of lemon cake that her mother sometimes served with tea. Her fork would slide through the frosting like a knife, its lemon butter melting against her tongue, so tart and sweet.

These imaginings were often so deep and intense that her mouth would turn thick with saliva that she could swallow, imagining it to be something else.

On a Friday morning in March, Ruby awoke to the sound of hushed voices crying in the hallway. She tried to get out of bed. It was so hot, and the room spun beneath her feet. She steadied herself on the wall, dressed quickly, and opened her door, fighting back a searing pain in her head and a stiffness in her body.

"What is it?" Ruby asked, rubbing her eyes.

It barely registered that the cook and Mr. Ward should not be on her floor, but there they were, talking in low tones. Mrs. Roberts's face was streaked with tears.

"Florence. She's . . ." Mrs. Roberts put a handkerchief to her mouth and sobbed.

Ruby rushed to the older servant's room and pushed open the door. The doctor was examining the body as Mr. Ward stood in the hallway, wringing his hands.

A hand touched her arm. Chester.

"Ruby." He tried to lead her to the stairs, but she couldn't move.

The hallway seemed to spin. "I already saw." She sat right on the hallway floor, face hot with tears.

Florence was kind, one of the lifetime servants who had stayed without pay. She often insisted on giving Ruby her food, because she could not stand to see anyone suffer.

"Come." Chester led her down the staircase to the kitchen. No one was there, and he took two helpings of oatmeal and handed them to her. "You should eat." They sat at the table, and she devoured the food, tuned in to the sounds of steps on the stairs.

He put his head in his hands. "It might be time to consider if it would be safer for us to return. If we stay here, there's a very real chance we will starve."

"Where is your food?" she asked, suddenly.

"I gave it to you."

Ruby would have pushed her bowl back, but it was empty. Her whole body still shook from the sight of Florence. There had been something on her—vomit, maybe—and her gnarled hands had still clutched the bedsheets.

"Eat her share," she told Chester. "She would want that."

Chester tried to bring it to her, but the room was spinning, and Ruby pushed it away.

How was it possible that she had seen death already so many times in her life? Some people went their whole lives without ever seeing it, yet here she was once again, face-to-face with it. With another servant who had been her friend.

"Why didn't they help her?" The extra food in her stomach nearly made her sick. "They need to feed us."

"It's not their fault. They can barely feed themselves." Chester's hat was frayed to the point that threads were hanging off it, and he twisted it in his hands. "I saw Mr. Wellsley in the bread line when I was there."

Ruby shot to a sitting position, the rush to her head so intense that she fell back on her arms onto the table. "I had hoped they were buying the little they've had, or that one of their friends was providing for them. That they still had that." This family had always had so much money and an endless supply of friends who had the means to help if help was needed. "Surely, he was at the food line to volunteer, to offer service to those in need."

Chester shook his head. "He was there for food, Ruby. The picture of dignity in his fine clothes. Did not speak to a soul, but played with the latch on his watch over and over, perhaps thinking how much he would gain from pawning it. I was surprised no one snatched it from his hand. Maybe they did, by the end." He paused. "To be honest, I might, if I have a chance."

"I don't like to hear you talk like that." Mr. Wellsley had been good to them. "You need to be an honest man, Chester. You're a good person."

The same words she'd told herself repeatedly to keep from stealing a bite of that bread.

He put his hat back on. "You don't have to be a bad person to know how to survive."

Ruby ran her thumb over the ring in the inside of her pocket. A few months back, in complete desperation, she'd paid a visit to the pawnshop. The man had peered at the diamond in awe before pushing it away.

"I will not buy stolen items."

Ruby had taken a step back. "It's not . . ." But she *had* stolen the ring. From her family, from her sister. She had no right to sell it, even if she was going to starve. It was this realization that had kept her from trying to sell it again.

Chester frowned. "I couldn't get a thing at the bread line. I don't know that Wellsley did, either. They won't be able to keep us long, Ruby. They won't be able to feed us."

Tears burned her face, but crying took too much energy. She laid her head against the table and stared at the chipped wall.

I'll be next.

The fear clawed at the back of her brain like hunger pains. That somehow, she deserved this ending for being a part of a family that had allowed Indira to die. The thought was like a heavy blanket lying over her, shrouding her in darkness.

"Ruby?" His voice seemed far away. "Ruby!" He shook her, and moments later, water moistened her lips. Then, he was carrying her somewhere, jostling her like the train.

Ruby leaned to the side in time for her food to come up in a shudder, spilling down the edge of her mouth and onto the floor.

"She's ill," she heard a voice say as her mother wiped her face and laid her down in bed. The back of Indira's cool hand touched her head, lessening that feeling of being too close to the fire.

"Give her water," a man said. "Even if she can't eat."

Ruby stared at the patch of light on the wall, wondering at its sudden intensity.

Ruby did not know how much time had passed, but when her eyes fluttered open, Chester was sitting there. He moved forward quickly and held out a piece of jerky. "Here."

It smelled like salt and heaven, but she did not have the strength to chew it. The meat was too dry, and she choked. Quickly, he handed her a glass of water.

"What's wrong with me?" she managed to say, then had to close her eyes.

"Flu," he said. "A few of us have had it, but it hit you the worst. And—"

"Florence." The word came out a whisper.

"Yes." Chester's eyes were full of sorrow. "It's what took her. Ruby, if my father says it's safe, I will find a way to take you back home. We can't survive here much longer. I—" His voice broke slightly, and she squinted at him.

"What is it?" she whispered.

"I don't want to lose you." He swiped at his eyes. "Like I lost my brother."

"No, he's safe," she assured him, while trying to remember if her words were true.

"He could die at any moment." Chester's face was drawn, his voice as defeated as she'd ever heard. "One war, one training accident, and that could be it. I need to get you home."

She wanted to agree with him, to say something, but she'd drifted back to sleep. Waking for a brief moment, she saw Chester watching her, his eyes fierce.

"Save your strength," he said.

Her eyes closed once again.

The cobblestones clattered beneath the wooden wheels, and the blanket was heavy over her body. Her head jostled against the seat, but Ruby still drifted off to sleep. It wasn't comfortable, but she was so hot that the cool air felt delicious rushing through her hair, Chester keeping watch at her side. He had made an arrangement with a man to take them north of the city in his delivery cart, to a place where he had a friend who would let them on the train for the price of one ticket.

"Remember," Chester said. "Lie." He squeezed his hat in his hands and repeated the thing he'd been telling her since planning her return home. "You worked as a governess. Cared for children in a well-respected home. You ran away because you were scared of Indira's death, but a kind woman on the train took you straight to a nice family."

Ruby gave him a vague nod. He'd said it all before, but it seemed to help him, somehow, to know that she had a story to lean on.

"Never mention me. If your father thinks we ran off together, it will ruin your reputation, and he'd kill me on sight. Rosemary would, too. At least, your mother seems like she'd be a good shot."

Ruby did not have the strength to smile, or to think about what would happen when she returned home, but deep down, she was frightened. Her father would have to forgive her. She'd left in a moment of panic, too young to understand how lucky she was for her life on the farm. Surely, once she returned, her home could once again be a warm, welcoming place with a soft bed and plentiful food.

They eventually reached the train, and Chester moved to a seat on the opposite side of the car after boarding. He'd told her he'd watch her but could not be nearby, especially when they got close to Wind Thorne.

Ruby wasn't concerned about being seen. The train cars were sparsely populated due to the lack of jobs. She was more concerned that Chester had spent nearly all his money getting them on the passenger train since her body was too weak to steal a ride on the freight. He told her not to worry, that he would find food, shelter, and a job, but there were no guarantees of that these days. Through her half-asleep state, she held the ring that still lay hidden in the lining of her clothing.

Returning it to her family was the right thing to do, but in the few years they'd been away, Chester had become family, in a different sense of the word. It was devastating to think she wouldn't see him for some time, but the idea that he might not survive was unacceptable. It was possible he would be furious at her to learn that she'd held on to the ring all this time, but she would rather feel his anger than let him starve.

Using every ounce of energy and the back of the train seats for support, she drew herself to a standing position and made her way back to his seat. She did not stop; she instead pretended to drop her handkerchief, and set the ring on the seat next to it.

"You must use it." Her words were quick. "I could not."

He did not look at her, but from the set of his jaw, she could tell he was shocked.

Ruby returned to her seat, sweating and exhausted. Once they'd pulled into the station outside of town, a man boarded the train and gave a barely perceptible nod in Chester's direction.

"Ruby?" He had a kind smile. "I've been commissioned to take you home."

He helped her off the train, catching her elbow gently when she stumbled, and releasing her arm just as quickly. Ruby looked up at the train, wishing Chester would be at the window. She longed to see his face one last time, to know if her gift had hurt him, and if it had, that he'd forgive her. It was impossible to know.

The man he'd hired to drive her home had an old truck, and he helped her inside. They drove down the long main road shaded by trees toward Wind Thorne. In between the trees, the fields were covered with a light frost, and the reflection of the sunlight was so dazzling it hurt her eyes.

The stone entryway loomed into sight, and Ruby's body tensed. Chester had written to her family, pretending to be her employer. He claimed the family could no longer support her but was desperate to see her safe return, as she'd fallen ill. She hoped that, by now, they'd received the letter and would not turn her away.

The driver pulled up to the house. He opened the door and, as if picking up on her thoughts, said, "I've been paid to wait down the road for three hours. Place a white cloth in your window if you need help."

Chester had thought of everything, even down to a possible need to escape. She tried to step out of the car, but her legs buckled beneath her, and the driver shouted toward the open windows of the house.

"We need assistance!"

The front door opened. "Ruby?" a familiar voice called.

Ruby clung to the door, surprised to see her mother, quickly followed by her grandmother, her brother Brad, Elizabeth and Glenn, plus several of the servants. Her father and Uncle Peter were not there, and she half wondered if they were against her arrival or busy with the farm.

"Ruby!" Her mother rushed forward and held her up, pulling her in tight. Her mother squeezed her against her full figure, hugging her three times before moving back to see her face, and then hugging her twice more. By the fifth hug, Ruby sank into her mother and hugged her back.

The familiar scent of whiskey and perfume brought her straight back home, as did the sight of her family lined up outside the door. They looked exactly the same, and yet completely different; they'd aged, her grandmother stooped and her brother's hair now grayed. Their clothing was simple but not tattered, as so many of the fine garments were now in the city. No one made a move to come closer, and Ruby pulled in tight to her mother, using her remaining strength to sob into her shoulder.

Her mother also seemed overcome, and she patted her gently on the back. "We will get you straight to bed and get you a soup. You look half dead."

Ruby mumbled an apology.

"No." Her mother's voice was soothing. "I'll have none of that."

It was not the angry reception Ruby had expected. Her mother signaled Brad to help Ruby up the endless staircase and into her bedroom. She registered its finery from a distance—the wide, spacious room pretty and fit for a princess, as her brother helped her into bed.

"Welcome back, then," he said, as if she had indeed traveled the world. "I bet you have some stories to tell."

Her head sank into the soft pillow. When her mother patted down her blanket and smoothed her hair, it felt like Indira saying, "Rest now. You are home."

Chapter Twelve

Upstate New York, present day

Spending time with Otis had been an experience Lindsey wouldn't mind repeating. She'd intended to stay at her aunt's house to learn more about Wind Thorne and its history, but the summer might shape up to be something else entirely. The way he'd kissed her by the fire was the first thing that crossed her mind when she woke up before dawn the next morning. It would have been even nicer to wake up next to him, but it was too soon to think about all of that.

Lindsey kept most relationships at arm's length. She'd seen the devastation her father had felt when he lost her mother, and that had made it harder for Lindsey to push forward in her own relationships. Yes, she wanted marriage, kids, and all of that, but she couldn't imagine bringing a family into the world without the guarantee that she would always be there.

This attitude about romance was a coward's way out, according to one of her good friends, but it had served Lindsey just fine so far. She was perfectly happy to enjoy the occasional flirtation. Otis was here for the summer, and that was it, which was comforting, in a sense.

After pushing back the covers, Lindsey went off in search of a strong cup of coffee. Her plan for the morning was to read through this diary from cover to cover, before meeting with Amrita later in the day to buy the other diary. Lindsey was a little worried the asking price would be several thousand dollars, especially if Amrita knew who Lindsey's mother had been and made the false assumption that Lindsey was the one benefiting from her estate.

She found several white ceramic jars on her aunt's countertop. It took a little searching, but she finally found the one with ground coffee—Irish cream, by the smell of it. Lindsey poured a generous helping into the filter and drummed her fingers against the counter, waiting for it to brew.

While she stood there, the metal object she'd hidden behind the cookie jar caught her eye. Reluctantly, she pulled it out. The large squares of the metal bracelet were rudimentary in their cuts and unevenly pounded, but the thick link that held them together created a streamlined look of uniformity that, even all these years later, Lindsey knew she had been trying to achieve.

Her mother had loved the bracelet. She wanted Lindsey to wear it, to show it to the world, but Lindsey wasn't ready for that. She worried that people would comment, "Isn't that sweet, the way she's trying to be like her mother?"

Lindsey cradled the piece, trying to remember if it had been the last thing she'd worked on before her mother died. Metalwork had been a passion of her mother's back then because it was something they could do together. Her mother, always so cute in her rolled-up jeans and kerchiefs, would pull her aside and say, "Come on, Little. Let's go make some shine."

Her mother was entertained by the idea that most kids got to finger paint, while her daughter spent time smashing metal into shape with a hammer. Here, when they visited the grandparents, her mother had a studio in a barn in the back. Lindsey had loved the opportunity to make beautiful things alongside her, while storing a wealth of knowledge about settings, shapes, and cuts. When her mother died, Lindsey's desire to create jewelry in any form died right along with her.

Lindsey ran her thumb over the square of the bracelet, then put it on. Quickly, she took it off. The memories associated with it were too much, especially this early in the morning.

She moved to the living room with a cup of coffee and considered the space. The rumpled pillows on the floor still held the memory of Otis and her, and when she picked them up to put them back on the couch, the one she hugged the closest still smelled like him. A smile tugged at the corner of her mouth, and she settled into the couch to focus on the small blue book in her lap.

Two cups of coffee and one butterscotch scone later, Lindsey had finished reading the diary and was up pacing the room. The hardwood floors creaked beneath her steps as she read this one passage over and over again, certain she must be reading it wrong. Finally, she picked up her phone and called Otis.

Yes, it was probably much too early in the morning to call anyone, especially someone who might expect her to give it a few hours and even pretend they hadn't kissed. But after what she'd just read, she was not about to wait.

"Yes?" he drawled in a voice that was even huskier than the one from the night before. The fact that he'd picked up, no games, made her appreciate him even more.

"So, I spent the morning reading this diary," Lindsey said, getting right into it. "There are so many things. First of all, I think she was secretly in love with Chester, who was her neighbor and the older brother of my great-grandfather. I think she's lying about the fact that she worked as a governess. And unless I'm imagining things, I swear it gives the location of a hidden safe at Wind Thorne."

There was a pause.

"Is it really a hidden safe if she tells you where it is?" Otis finally said.

Lindsey laughed. "Okay, just listen to this," she said, and read: "'There are times when I think about what would happen if I went into my father's closet, found the key without being detected, and searched the safe in the library. What would still be in there? My family is losing everything. Is there anything left? I don't have a right to take anything, but they don't have a right to do what they've been doing. I don't dare, though. If anything is missing, it might tip them off that something's coming their way.'"

"Wait." Otis sounded surprised. "That last part—that sounds sinister. You don't think Ruby killed them, do you?"

"No, she died with the family." Lindsey hadn't even picked up on that part, because she had been focused on the safe. He was right, though. It did sound like she knew something bad might happen to them.

"The part about the safe sounds pretty clear cut," he said. "It doesn't sound like a secret."

"There's another passage, earlier," Lindsey said, trying to find it. "She's talking about her father, and it literally says something like 'in his hidden safe.' Now, my aunt gave me the full rundown on everything that was exciting about the property, but she never once mentioned a hidden safe."

"It is interesting," Otis said.

"Right? She mentions how her father kept everything valuable in there. I bet it's still there. We just have to find it."

"It could be in the walls or behind one of the shelves," Otis said. "Or under the floor?"

Lindsey laughed. "It could be anywhere."

"Should I bring a stick of dynamite?" Otis asked. "Because what are we supposed to do when we find the safe but don't have a key?"

"That is a problem I cannot solve," she said. "I guess we'd just have to get permission from my aunt to crack it open. She said I was more than welcome to explore Wind Thorne while she was gone. So, let's do it. If we find the safe, we'll search for the key."

She heard rustling, and Lindsey imagined him climbing out of bed and pulling on some clothes.

"See you in ten."

Lindsey had tried to call Aunt Petra to tell her the news, but the phone went straight to voicemail. The cruise had just left port, and she'd mentioned she might be out of touch for the first day or two. Lindsey wanted to talk to her, because it would be a little embarrassing to head to Wind Thorne with hopes of finding some mystery safe, only to learn that her aunt already knew all about it.

The door unlocked easily, and she tapped in the security code. She hoped she wouldn't do it wrong so that every security guard in the world showed up, but it went without a hitch. She was waiting on the front steps by the time Otis arrived, ready to greet him like the grand lady of the house. Stepping out of his SUV, he glanced up, nodding at the security cameras.

"It's probably good I don't have that stick of dynamite," he said, strolling toward her.

The masculinity in the way he moved reminded her of being on the floor with him the night before, and her cheeks colored.

"I promise we're not doing anything wrong." She squinted at him in the early-morning sun. "My aunt gave me complete permission to go in and explore."

"Great." He shoved his hands in his pockets. "Curious if she also said it was perfectly okay for us to break into a secret safe and loot the diamond ring that both of us are secretly hoping is in there?"

Lindsey laughed. "I'm sure that's what she meant."

They went in, and Lindsey noticed how quiet the house was with only the two of them. Their footsteps echoed across the main front hall, and lines from the diary floated through her mind.

Father Aaron is here too much. It's because he's the only one willing to listen to Uncle Peter ramble on about the war.

I wish Mother paid attention to the reasons behind Prohibition. She's a different person when she drinks. Was it always like this with her?

Elizabeth berated one of the servants so loudly in the main hall. I should be brave enough to tell her to stop. She has no idea what it's like to scrub floors until your hands are so chafed they bleed.

I do not have any right to say these things about my family. They allowed me to come back home. Why can't I find the same forgiveness in my heart?

That last one made Lindsey stop walking and put her hand to her chest.

"What is it?" Otis asked.

"I was thinking about the diary," Lindsey said. "I finished it this morning, and it's strange to see this place through her eyes."

Lindsey considered the expanse of the great room, the staircase that went straight up. She tried to imagine the parties and the energy, and then, the heartache of the time when Ruby had lived in this house.

"There's such sorrow here," she said. "I can actually feel it. It was such a long time ago, but it's like it's been sitting, waiting behind the curtains."

Otis was silent, and when she turned to look at him, his gaze was intense. "Your take on the world is beautiful. I want to tell you that now, in case this thing between us ends or whatever and I never get a chance to say it. You're beautiful, Lindsey."

Her cell phone chimed.

Saved. Maybe. Hard to decide.

Lindsey was drawn to Otis but hadn't expected him to say they might become a thing. She had to admit, she'd already caught herself thinking about him more than she should, and typically, her mind focused on more noble pursuits.

It whirred through columns of numbers, challenges from the math club she met with weekly, or the networking group where she set goals with other accomplished women. When Otis passed through her brain, too much of her time was spent analyzing the different shades of blue in his eyes.

Fumbling for her phone, she checked the text message.

"It's Amrita," she said, holding it up. "She wants to meet up today to show me the diary."

"Interesting." Otis seemed a little uncomfortable that she hadn't responded to what he'd said.

Lindsey slid the phone back into her purse, feeling guilty. Even though his compliment had hit a mark somewhere deep in her heart, the issues with her father made it impossible to be open. It was better to keep things light.

"The library is . . ." he said, turning his body in a half circle.

"This way." She pointed. "Let's go take a look."

The library itself was incredible. Two walls were filled floor to ceiling with leather-bound books in emerald, sapphire, and ruby covers. Some of the spines had titles and some did not, but for as old as all the books were, they looked perfectly preserved. The fireplace on the far side of the room was flanked by antique couches and a chair, while a large desk was over by the window.

Turkish rugs muffled their steps as they walked over to examine the books. The collection of *Farmers' Almanacs* intrigued her, and Otis pulled out one on cattle.

"These books are in surprisingly good shape," he said.

"It's pretty remarkable." Lindsey imagined her brother and Barrett smoking in this house, maybe two feet away from this very shelf, back when they used to sneak in. "My aunt did tell me that most of the things in the house had been covered and properly stored. There were no leaks, and few animals got in. Pretty lucky, considering."

Outside the window, the Hudson River sparkled through the trees of the forest. It was a lovely view, and she wondered what it would have been like to sit in this room, reading. Or spying on people, as Ruby had done.

One of the fascinating things about the young Thornhill girl was her complete disregard for other people's privacy. Ruby had mentioned in the diary that, when she was younger, she had thought nothing of hiding under a table and listening to other people's conversations. Lindsey couldn't imagine doing something like that around her father, mainly because she was pretty sure most of the things he said would be things she didn't want to hear.

"I'm going to take a look at the shelves," Otis said.

Using the flashlight from his phone, he checked the area where they connected with the walls. "These are flush, so the safe's not behind here. There could be a space hidden in the wall, though. But we'd have to pull out each of the books individually to check behind them to see."

Lindsey considered the massive expanse of shelves and books. The room was small in stature compared to the rest of the house, which lent it a sense of coziness, but it was still big. It seemed daunting to spend the next three hours of her life searching the bookshelves for something that might not be there.

There were no pictures, paintings, or even a tapestry that the safe could hide behind. Lindsey walked over to the desk, drumming her fingers against her lips. The paneling was solid oak and decorative, and she studied it for a long moment. She got down on her hands and knees, crawled beneath the desk, and tapped at the edge. The sound was dull next to the paneling.

"I wonder if it's hidden in plain sight," she mused. "I don't want to get my hopes up, but I think it's in here."

Lindsey studied the desk for a moment. The drawers flanked the desk on the left and the right, but in the middle, off to the left, the decorative wood panel seemed to cover nothing at all. She ran her hands along the edge of the panel. Her pulse quickened as she found a small latch. Pressing it, she guided the door open to reveal a solid oak block.

"Darn," she whispered, in disappointment. "I was hoping it would be in here."

Otis stood in the center of the room, staring up at all the books. "I'm willing to bet there's some sort of false back to one of those sections up there. But there has to be what, ten thousand books? At least?"

It was an impressive library. Unfortunately, the books looked about as dull as an old nickel, or Lindsey would have an entire summer of entertainment in front of her. She thought for a minute, trying to calculate how long it might take to look behind each one.

"I suppose I could spend ten minutes a day searching," she decided. "By the end of the summer, I might get lucky."

"It's also possible it's under the floor," Otis suggested.

They walked together across the library floor, each tapping the floor gently with dull pokers from the fireplace. Otis paused a few times, holding up his hand for her to listen with him, and tried again. Shaking their head, they moved on. Finally, she gave up.

"I think we're destined to search the books," she admitted. "It has to be up there."

Otis had taken off his overshirt, leaving him in a T-shirt that made him look more built than she'd initially noticed. He had to be fit, though, traveling the world to search for gems. The night before, when they'd been talking by the fire, he'd told her that he went on jewel expeditions to random mines at least three times a year, sometimes surviving on trail mix and dried fruit for days.

For her, the idea of jewel expeditions brought up images of a sled dog and panning for gold. When she told him that, he'd burst out laughing.

"Sounds exciting," he said. "But mine are more about hiking. I did use a pony, once, because she was better at climbing the terrain than me."

Now Otis studied the shelves for a long moment and shrugged. "If it's up there, a metal detector would find it," he said, running his hand through his hair. "It'll set off on the studs, but I do have one with a frequency reading that will help."

"Is it in your car?" Lindsey asked, not entirely sure what type of answer she expected.

He grinned. "It's actually back at my parents' house because I was hauling some mulch for them. I can go grab it."

"I love your commitment to this," Lindsey said.

Some people, like her father, would have been much too impatient to search for something without proof it was there.

Otis stretched. "Hey, once you discover a box of rocks that changes your life, you start to believe the unbelievable isn't that out of reach."

Lindsey smiled at him. "In that case, I think we should hunt for the key, too. She was pretty specific in the diary that it was in her father's closet, in some gap in the wall."

"Sounds easy enough." Otis hesitated. "Do you want me to run and get the metal detector and you start looking upstairs?"

Lindsey nodded and headed up. It felt strange to be in this gigantic house alone, and she stood in the first bedroom, feeling the size and scope of it all as she watched Otis pull out of the driveway. Her footsteps echoed as she walked back out to the main hall.

It must have been fascinating to stay at Wind Thorne back in the 1920s, with all the dazzle and the parties, the clothing. For a split second, Lindsey pictured the type of bracelet she would want to see on one of the flapper girls: several thin strands of pearls held together by thin wisps of gold that danced with movement.

It was a surprise to have that idea pop into her head. She studied it from a detached place, curious. Maybe it had come up because her brain had the time and space for it, but it might also have been due to being here, surrounded by this ornate, magical place.

It was hard to believe that her great-grandmother had actually worked as a servant here, then went on to own the home. It was nice to imagine her as the owner, but of course, it would have been owned by Lindsey's great-grandfather. New York was more progressive than some of the other states in terms of property ownership, but until the seventies, a woman still needed a man to cosign a loan. Besides, who did they buy it from, considering the entire Thornhill family was dead?

The bank, most likely. The purchase itself was probably for the land. Elliot would have bought it due to the proximity to his property, hoping to profit from the acreage or even the distilleries. No one was interested in the house, which was why it went to ruin.

Lindsey ran her hands along the gilded hallway table. She had so many questions, and she looked forward to spending the summer finding the answers. For now, she turned her focus to the task in front of her, which was to find the key to the safe.

Easier said than done.

Part of the problem was that Lindsey had no idea which room would have belonged to Mr. Thornhill. The primary bedroom, obviously, but every single room was practically its own hotel suite, complete with a fireplace, wide windows that overlooked the forest and the lawn, and a grand bed. Plus, there were so many cracks in the exposed brick walls of the closets that Lindsey only made it through three rooms before Otis was back with a sleek-looking metal contraption and two bottled waters.

"Did you find it?" he asked, cheerfully.

She wiped dust off her face onto her shirt. "Not even close."

Otis handed her a bottle of water. Grateful, she took a quick drink.

"This is a task," she admitted. "I've already been through three closets, but it takes a while to look in all the crannies."

"Let's divide and conquer," he suggested. "Where are we looking, exactly?"

Lindsey pulled up the photo she'd snapped of a page in the diary, where it gave the exact description of where in the closet Ruby had found her father's key.

Otis read through it, and their hands brushed as he handed back the phone.

"I'll take the end of the hallway," he said. "I don't know how the structure of 1920s houses works, but I have a feeling his room would be closer to the front. I'm happy to give you better odds on finding it."

The small act of kindness warmed her heart, and Lindsey got back to it. She was curious which room belonged to Ruby, but it was impossible to tell without more information. It was something she could hope to come back to later this summer, once she'd read the diary from Amrita.

Moving to the closet, Lindsey searched it from top to bottom to make sure that she didn't miss anything before moving on to the next room. Nothing.

In the next room, she paused. A door connected two of the rooms, and instantly, she felt foolish.

Poking her head out into the hallway, she called, "Otis!"

He ran out of one of the back rooms and came strolling toward her with a grin. "If you tell me you found that key, I'm taking you on a jewel expedition, like, tomorrow."

"I didn't find the key. But if it's going to be anywhere, I think it will be in here."

Otis joined her in the room and glanced around.

"Check out the door," she said. "There were lots of reasons a door would be between the rooms in old houses. Heating purposes, to make sure that both rooms could benefit from the fireplace. Easy access to a nursery, an older person, a thousand reasons. But the main one . . ."

"Husband and wife." He glanced out the window at the cattle field. "Great view. You can see everything from here. You think this is his room?"

"One way to find out," Lindsey said.

They headed for the closet and crouched down. Looking around the detailed space, with its carved shelves and ornate paneling mixed in with the brick, Lindsey felt a rush of affection.

"This matches up," she said. "Ruby described that wooden design over there. The way the shelf sloped and dipped over here." She ran her hands along the edge of the wall, searching for the small break in the wood. "Here." She stretched her fingers down into it, feeling around.

Lindsey sat back on her heels. "Nothing."

"No key?" Otis tried. "Maybe it's under the floorboards."

He ran down and got his metal detector. Even after sweeping it back and forth, he didn't get a signal. "Darn. I really thought we were going to find it."

"I guess it would have been too good to be true." Lindsey gave him a rueful smile. "Want to go 0–2 on the safe?"

Otis held it up like a sword. "Bet you I'll find it in ten minutes or less."

At three minutes and nineteen seconds, Otis found the safe.

Not in the bookshelf, where they'd expected it to be, but ensconced behind a secret door in the middle of the wooden oak block in the desk. She had been so close before, when she'd pressed the small latch and had found the block of oak, but the metal detector had pushed them to keep exploring. Otis discovered that the block was held together in the corner by four wooden pieces that, when removed, allowed the front panel to slide off. An old green safe rested inside.

"I can't believe it," Lindsey breathed.

Otis knelt down next to her. Reaching forward, he touched the lock, then gave her a wry look. "You knew this was here. You're messing with me."

She started to laugh at his reaction, and he got to his feet.

"I knew it," he said. "I knew you were up to something! You completely had me going. I bought into the whole idea that we were going to come here and find a safe that hasn't been opened in one hundred years."

"I'm not messing with you," Lindsey said. "I'm only laughing because it's pretty remarkable that this journal I've had hidden under the porch for the last twenty years of my life knew there was a safe here the whole time."

His face changed to cautious excitement. "You're serious? No one's been in it?"

It was impossible to tell without looking inside.

Lindsey's heart was pounding. The diamond ring, the one that she'd dreamed about seeing ever since she'd first read about it in the diary, could very well be inside.

"Time to call a locksmith," Otis said.

"Yes," Lindsey said. "I just have to get permission from Aunt Petra first. I couldn't get ahold of her earlier."

Pulling out her phone, she called her aunt using the app she'd sent for international calls. Her phone rang this time, but she didn't pick up. Lindsey imagined her having dinner on the luxury cruise ship, seven courses with delectable sauces and perfectly partnered glasses of wine lined up in front of her.

"Not picking up," she mouthed to Otis before leaving a message to call.

"Do you want me to pick the lock?" he asked.

She didn't know whether to be suspicious or impressed. "Can you do that?"

He shrugged. "There's always a first for everything."

"Then, no," she said. "We can wait."

They sat on the old-fashioned furniture in front of the fireplace, and after a moment, Otis looked over at her. "We should have read the diary here. It's the perfect setting."

She looked at her watch. "Speaking of, I'm supposed to meet Amrita in town for lunch in about an hour. Do you want to join us?"

"Yes, but before that . . ." He studied her with those intense blue eyes.

"What?" she asked, shifting under his gaze.

Otis grinned. Then, like he'd been doing it forever, he cupped her chin in his hand and kissed her.

Chapter Thirteen

Wind Thorne, March 1930

Ruby's eyes fluttered open in the darkness of the room. A man stood over her, gripping her wrist. She jerked away, drawing the blankets up close to her chest.

"Ruby, it's the doctor," her mother said. "He's here to check on you."

She rolled to her side, too exhausted to think.

"The flu coupled with extreme dehydration. Malnourishment." His voice sounded far away. "If you cannot get her to eat or drink, I cannot give you a favorable outcome."

There was the zip of his bag, the pinch of a shot. She dozed off during the examination, only half feeling it when he put a wooden stick in her mouth and lifted her eyelids to shine a light into her eyes.

It felt like morning and the room was bright. The smell of coffee drifted up from the rooms downstairs. Gone was the sound of carts and cars, replaced with the clink of silverware downstairs and the occasional low of cattle.

The next time her eyes fluttered open, shadows of the leaves stirred on the ceiling above. It took her a moment to take in the silence, breathe in the different smells, and realize the city was not outside her window.

A young girl stood next to the bed, holding a tray. "Miss?" she said.

The tray clattered slightly as she set it down on the bedside table. Ruby's mother swept over and cuffed the girl on the back of the head.

"Bring it to the *bed*." Her mother's voice was sour. "Can't you see she's ill?"

The slap cut through Ruby. It was an instant reminder of how it felt to be this girl, to be the one jostling the tray. Of Indira, and what had happened to her in this house.

The girl had dark eyes and strong arms. She helped Ruby to sit up against the pillows. Even though Ruby wanted to tell the girl to rest, that she could do it on her own, she was so weak she had no choice but to accept the help.

The girl brought a spoonful of soup to Ruby's mouth. The first bite was too intense, and she gagged at its sudden salty, creamy texture.

"It's chicken with rice." The girl's voice was quiet, soothing. "You must eat."

Ruby tried another small bite, this time swallowing the soup. She leaned forward and took another, her mother standing by wringing her hands. The servant dabbed at Ruby's chin with a napkin.

"Good," her mother said, returning to her needlepoint. "Keep eating. It's the one thing that will save you from this."

It took ages, but the servant fed Ruby every drop, followed by water. The girl wiped the dribble from Ruby's chin several times, which was embarrassing. Finally, Ruby took her hand and squeezed it tight.

"Thank you," she whispered.

The girl drew back, clearly surprised. Then she gave Ruby a small nod before darting out of the room with the tray.

Ruby pulled the pillows in close. She squeezed one tightly, amazed at the silken threads of its case and the softness of the feathers, before dropping back into a black hole of sleep.

Ruby opened her eyes. Outside the window, the wind blew through the trees. If she squinted hard enough, she was convinced she could see the smoke from the chimney at Chester's house. He hadn't said where he was going, but she knew he wasn't nearby.

Ruby had heard her sister downstairs, when she'd faded in and out of sleep, laughing or talking with their brother or Glenn. Her father and his boots stomping through the house, and the servants following behind to wipe up his tracks. Her grandmother, slowly making her way past the door. No one had come to visit, except her mother.

Even now, her mother sat by the window, working on a needlepoint. When Ruby yawned, she looked over and set it down. "How are you feeling?"

"I don't know." Her mouth was dry, and her head ached, but she could sip the cup of water next to the bed on her own. She waited to feel exhausted from the effort, but she didn't. "Better." She gazed at her mother, unsure what to say. "Thank you. For helping me." When she didn't answer, Ruby said, "Where is Father?"

"Cuts take time to heal." Her mother squinted at her. "You left quite a gash."

Ruby pulled the sheets closer. True enough. Perhaps being allowed to return was more than she deserved. She shouldn't expect grace on top of that.

Ruby considered the room. The heavy wooden dresser, the ornate fire mantel with the mirror over the top, and the heavy draperies pulled back to reveal the wide expanse of forest and fields. The sun was out, so the cows were out in the pasture, huddled together for warmth. She watched them, feeling dazed. The landscape of what she was seeing had changed so much.

"Elizabeth got married, then?" Ruby said, looking back at her mother.

"Mmm." Her mother pressed her lips tightly together, deepening the lines in her face. She focused on the needlepoint in her lap. "Glenn was not what he appeared to be. There have been some changes in this house while you were absent, most notably, that he required a place to stay." The needle whipped through her stitching as she talked. "Your father and I had no choice but to welcome them here. Glenn now works for us. Your sister is quite busy with the family business, since she can't be bothered to give her husband children."

Ruby winced. The servants had spoken of similar afflictions, where a wife could not give her husband a child. From what Ruby understood, it was not typically a choice. Her mother's words could become mean and sour, depending on whether she was drinking, a quality Ruby had tried to put out of her mind while she was away.

Still, Ruby had to think about self-preservation. Chester had told her to talk about her role as a governess as often as possible, to back up her story. Otherwise, her family would never believe her.

"She might still have children," Ruby said. "I'm sure it's not easy. I was exhausted caring for my charges. It's quite a task."

"Do not speak of that!" Her mother's whisper was full of fury. "You are *not* the help. You have been traveling the world with an aunt. You are never to speak of the other again." Her mother folded up her needlepoint with sharp, angry movements. Once she'd put it away, she got to her feet. "We will never tell anyone of that. We would be ruined."

Ruby studied her hands. The skin was still rough from the chemicals, the work she'd done. "The family was very kind. They didn't make it feel that way."

"Do not speak of it again." Her mother's teeth were clenched. "Never again. I will never understand why you did such a thing."

Ruby's head pounded, and her bones still ached with hunger. Still, she could not permit her mother to think of her as a disobedient child.

"I did it because Elizabeth was the only one willing to protect me from Uncle Peter," Ruby said. "She was leaving. I tried to tell you I was in danger, that he had cornered me more than once."

Her mother scoffed. "He's soft in the head."

Which made him more frightening. The moments he had appeared in her room with a placid look on his face and pulled her in for a tight hug. The time his lips had grazed her neck. Her cheeks burned with shame at the memory, and she wrapped the bedclothes tightly around her hand.

Her mother sat back down. She took a long drink from a glass sitting by the lamp. Whiskey. Even as the morning sun spilled in through the curtains.

"Ruby, hear me on this." Her mother cradled the glass, slowly rocking it back and forth. "It's important for you to know. You were a baby that cried all the time." Her mother's face scrunched up, mocking her. "The servants couldn't stand being around you. Did you know that?"

A dark pit formed in Ruby's stomach.

"I was the one who visited you in the nursery," her mother said. "Sang songs, held you. You scratched me like a cat, but I still held tight, and you'd cry and cry. It never ended. You'd cry when Elizabeth got a pretty dress." Her mother scrunched her face up again. "Cry when she could read and write. Elizabeth got engaged. You cried and cried." Her mother set down the glass. "I refuse to hear that horrible sound anymore."

Ruby lay back against the pillows, her body hot with shame. It had been so long since she'd been the victim of her mother's cuts, fueled by drink. Silence hung over the room like a shadow.

"He's gone to Europe," her mother finally said. "He'll be back. Ignore him."

Hot tears pricked at the corner of Ruby's eyes. The idea of being here in this house, so weak, without anyone willing to protect her was terrifying.

"I won't stay if he comes for me again."

"I see." Her mother's voice was calm. "Did you not come crawling back, begging for food and shelter?"

"I just want you to understand if I—" Ruby whispered, and her mother got to her feet.

"If you what?" Her voice was ice. "Do not presume to set foot in this house and tell me how it will be run. Tell your father to handle Peter. But I will handle you. If you speak so much of a word that reeks of a complaint, you will be dismissed from this home once and for all. I do not care if you crawl to the front door and ask for a loaf with your last breath, you will not get it. In fact, I will sit down at a fine table, eat it right in front of you, and lick the butter off my fingers. Do you understand me?"

The sour taste in the back of Ruby's throat sharpened. If only she could still place that flag in the window asking for help, but what good would it have done? Chester was gone. There was nowhere to go. Ruby couldn't survive on her own. Her mother knew that. They all did.

"Yes, ma'am," she whispered.

"Such a smart girl." Her mother gave her a tight smile. "I never gave up on you, Ruby. Now, get some rest and make yourself at home. This is your home, my darling. Assuming you show it the respect it deserves."

Ruby stared at the ceiling as her mother left the room. Finally, she sat up.

In the morning light, the room no longer looked so grand. It was aging. The curtains were worn, frayed in the sunlight, and the bedspread was stained from a spill. Even the walls by the fireplace seemed dirty almost, dusted with soot from the fire.

It wasn't what she remembered, but in so many ways, it was exactly the same.

The idea of getting out of bed was impossible those first few days, but with time, Ruby started to feel restless and curious about her family. She took small walks along the upper hallway, hoping to see her sister or her grandmother, but instead, she felt uncomfortable because the only people there were the servants, diligently cleaning. Would any of them believe that only moments ago, she'd been one of them?

Ruby knew she had to speak to her father, something she had not done since her arrival. He certainly hadn't come to see her. Once she finally had the strength to see it through, she knocked on the door of the library, where he was busy studying his account ledgers.

"May I speak with you, Father?" she said.

"Which one?" he said, barely looking up over his glasses.

The sound of a chuckle brought her attention to Father Aaron sitting by the fire, having a glass of whiskey and reading. She took a step back.

"Sorry." She wrung her hands. "I didn't mean to interrupt."

"You didn't." Her father pushed back his chair and stood, his expression dark. "The prodigal daughter returns. Have a seat."

Dread filled her at the thought of sitting with Father Aaron. The last time she'd seen him, he was carrying Indira's body out to a car, and she'd pictured that so many times since. How surreal to be here with him, in the blaze of the firelight, breathing the scent of woodsmoke.

Father Aaron gave her a wan smile as she settled into a plush green chair. His hair was cut closer than before, and he wore silver-framed glasses that made it hard to see his eyes. "Welcome home, child. I'm relieved you made it back. I hear the city is quite a bleak place to be right now. Lots of lack."

Images of the breadlines passed through her mind, as well as pictures of all those without jobs or homes. The sense of despair that she'd felt all around her. The fear that life might never be the same again.

Yet here she was, in this fine house, with well-fed people sharing drinks by the fire. It was hard to understand how they could have so much while some had so little, even as Chester was still out there, perhaps suffering the same fate that had brought her home.

"It was terrible," she said. "How have you avoided it?"

"Hard work." Ruby's father rang for a servant. The servant stoked the fire, added a log, and swiftly exited the room. "We expect to have a fine crop this year, the cattle are plentiful, and business is booming."

Father Aaron raised his glass. "Many blessings."

"Indeed." Her father squinted at her. "There is some struggle in town with a lack of jobs, some issues with food, but that doesn't affect us. It won't."

Ruby wasn't so sure. Considering that much of the town made up his customer base, it would affect him, once people were unable to spend their money on anything past survival. Surely, he realized that and was being glib due to the presence of someone outside the family here.

The three of them sat in silence. Her father was pleasing to the eye, with bright-blue eyes and high cheekbones too delicate for a farmer. But there was a steel to his spine as obvious as the marks on certain types of spiders, and she struggled to meet his gaze when he stared her down.

When he finally spoke, his words were cool. "Smart choice," he said. "To return. Not so smart to leave."

"I've come for forgiveness."

He laughed. "I think that's *his* specialty," he said, crooking his thumb at the priest.

In the past, that mocking tone would have silenced Ruby, but she couldn't continue on here without his permission.

"Father, I beg you. I was so foolish, leaving the safety of this home, the honor of our family's reputation. I was such a fool." Chester had scripted these words for her, but in truth, she hated having to say them at all. "I left because I was scared. Too weak to ask for . . ." Her voice trailed off.

His eyes flashed. "Too weak to ask for what?"

"Your protection."

The fire crackled. Her father frowned, staring at the flames. Finally, he spoke.

"Protection from what?"

"Uncle Peter. He—"

Her father held up his hand. "He drinks a lot."

If Father Aaron was shocked by this conversation, he didn't let on. He simply fiddled with the cross on his necklace. The three of them sat in silence for so long that Ruby wondered if she was expected to continue, but she had nothing more to say.

Palms sweating, she smoothed them over her dress. "I am sorry." She moved toward the door with the last energy she had. She looked over at the desk, remembering Chester sitting there on the day she'd left. His swollen face as he ate the breakfast she'd brought for him like he'd never see food again.

Her father's voice stopped her. "What would you do now?"

Ruby stood at the door, resting her hand against its frame. "Sir?"

"What would you do now?" He traced his finger over the rim of his glass. "If Peter gave you trouble?"

"He won't." She shrugged. "Now that I've told you."

Chester had pointed out that if she played upon her father's need to be perceived as powerful, he would make sure Uncle Peter stayed away.

He gave her a nod of approval. "You will be safe in this house, Ruby. I'm glad you've returned."

"Thank you, Father. Thank you so much."

She fought back the sting in her eyes and quickly left the room.

It took nearly a week to get her strength back. Ruby slept during the day, which sometimes kept her up at night. She spent the time waiting for sleep to return while gazing out the window at the sky.

The moon remained steady during these times. Its glow of white light, something Ruby could count on. The craters, the bumps, and the shifting clouds. At times it looked as if there were constellations of stars inside the gray that covered its surface, and she thought of Chester, wondering if somewhere, he was watching the same moon and thinking of her.

It took another week of rest, but she finally found the strength to go on a walk outdoors. She pulled on her coat and hat and, taking careful steps, went down the steps.

The house was still, and she walked out to the porch, wondering what she'd do if she bumped into Uncle Peter. She was certain he wasn't home yet but had no way of knowing. Finally, she crossed the yard and reached the edge of the woods, careful to not look for Chester's house between the trees.

The sudden crack of a twig made her stop and peer through the shadows. Part of her hoped it was Chester, unable to stay away, in spite of the danger. Instead, she spotted Elizabeth, hunched over on a stone bench in the arbor. Ruby was about to call out to her, but then she noticed her sister's shoulders heaving with sobs. The two still hadn't spoken, so Ruby hung back, unsure whether to offer comfort.

Elizabeth jumped as though startled by something and quickly wiped her eyes. She darted from her seat to the trees and, with sure steps, wove back to the house. Ruby moved on, wondering what it was that had made her sister sob in such a way. The guilt of knowing that Elizabeth might have cried like that when Ruby left made her walk a little faster.

Once she'd made it to the fields, she stopped next to a cluster of cattle to catch her breath. They were grouped together against the cold. Ruby was charmed at the way they lifted their heads to stare her down with inky-brown eyes, steadily chewing the cud from the hay they'd eaten for breakfast.

One of her favorite things to do with Elizabeth when they were younger was to feed the cows. They'd always laughed at the way a mouthful of hay hung down like a golden beard, the cow chewing as the beard grew smaller. Sometimes, when the cows finished eating, they'd low. One bull in particular would work up to it, flap his ears together, swing his tail like a rope, and tilt his head back to let out a loud moo, then look right at her and Elizabeth as if to say, *Your turn. What's on your mind?*

Ruby longed to share these memories with her sister, and hoped for the opportunity to soon approach her. Elizabeth had a set routine, according to their mother. She hosted weekly gatherings with friends, spent time strolling the fields, and worked as a bookkeeper on the farm. It wouldn't be hard to find her, now that Ruby was out of her room, but it might be difficult to find the right time to talk.

Ruby still didn't feel well, and the exertion of the walk, coupled with her heavy coat, made her dress stick to her sweating skin. She made it back to the house, wishing she hadn't pushed herself so hard. She took the porch steps slowly and spotted her sister once again. This time, Elizabeth was busy instructing one of the servants on how to properly prune the apple and cherry trees.

Ruby lifted her hand in an eager wave. Her sister stopped talking. Her eyes bored into her with such rage that Ruby dropped her hand, cheeks flushed.

Even though Ruby worried that Elizabeth had been upset that Ruby had run right before the wedding, Ruby had sent her a letter of apology from New York.

It had read:

> Dearest darling sister,
> I am so sorry to have left when I did, but I couldn't stay at Wind Thorne another day. The death of Indira affected me greatly, and caused me such fear. There are also other things that I will one day explain, but for now, I must beg for your forgiveness and wish you the happiest marriage to Glenn.
>
> With love,
> Your sister

It hadn't occurred to Ruby that her sister hadn't visited her room due to anger. Ruby assumed Elizabeth had wanted to give her time to rest or that it would have upset Elizabeth to see Ruby so incredibly ill. They had been so close that it didn't make sense that Elizabeth would carry such anger, especially after the letter Ruby had sent.

Unless she never got it.

Ruby would have to find a way to talk to her sister and explain everything. Her heart sank, because she would still have to uphold a lie to keep Chester safe and to protect the reputation of her family. She couldn't tell her sister that no, she hadn't traveled the world, but had cleaned a water closet and shivered through cold nights and, at the end of it all, thought she would die of sickness and hunger.

Heart aching, Ruby stared out at the woods and tried to catch a glimpse of Chester's house. Every part of her still felt so weak. Her legs trembled at the effort of standing too long, and a steady fog hung over her thoughts. It was a relief to have nourishment for her body, but what about her soul?

Facing this issue with her sister wasn't something she wanted to do alone. She had become used to having good people by her side, to support her through the difficult parts of life. Her friendship with Millie and Chester had been such a valuable part of the past few years. Millie was long gone, but Chester's home was right there. If only he were, too.

Their conversations had helped guide her through so many moments of confusion and loneliness. At this point, she knew him better than her own family. Yet she was stuck here, alone. The thought made her stomach hurt.

Chester planned to return sometime next year, and she suspected he'd timed it to marry Eleanor Cook, as she would be back from her university studies then. Ruby couldn't make the mistake of pining for him, when she'd been given a chance to start her life fresh, here at the farm. Standing next to the forest, staring at his house, was not going to do her an ounce of good.

She turned away from the railing and headed back inside. Her job was to take time to heal, then figure out what in the world her life was meant to be.

Chapter Fourteen

Upstate New York, present day

Finding the safe with Otis had made for a perfect morning.

"I'm tempted to push lunch with Amrita until tomorrow," Lindsey said. "It's been such a good day, I don't want to risk it."

Otis was still sitting on the couch, where they'd cuddled and talked for the past hour. Stretching, he said, "What do you mean?"

Lindsey waited to answer, instead focusing on the complicated task of closing the safe back up into the desk. It needed to look exactly the same as it had before they'd opened it, so the security guard or maintenance staff wouldn't stumble across it. Once it was in place, Lindsey stood up and brushed off her hands.

"I don't know," she said, going back to his question. "I think I'm just nervous she won't bring the diary, or she'll decide to not sell it or something."

"I'm sure if you give her enough money, she'd be more than happy to sell you the diary and anything else you want."

"You still don't like her," Lindsey said.

"Nope." He pulled on his baseball cap and got to his feet. "But I'm hungry, so let's go."

Otis offered to drive, so she climbed up into the brown leather seat of his truck, impressed at how good it smelled. It took a minute to place it all, but she decided it was a combination of mint gum, leather lotion, and his cologne. Rolling down the window, she enjoyed the breeze in her hair as they drove. She enjoyed their comfortable silence, and once or twice, she let herself think about their time on the couch.

When they pulled up, Amrita was already seated at an outside table in the small café. She wore a flowing purple sheath and a wide straw hat. Lindsey felt a flash of nerves and squeezed the door handle tight.

"What is it?" Otis asked, noticing her expression.

"I'm worried I won't leave here with the diary." Lindsey was so frustrated that Amrita was determined to profit from this. "She should just give it back to the estate."

"Then don't buy it," Otis said. "She can't sell it if there's not a buyer."

Logical, but no. The diary was an artifact, and it needed to return to Wind Thorne. It might hold a wealth of information on the history of the estate.

"I think it might be wise to give her that impression," Lindsey said. "It's a gamble, though. But if I play it right, maybe I won't get fleeced."

"How much is she asking for it?" Otis said.

Lindsey looked into the passenger-side mirror and swiped on some lipstick. "I don't know."

Otis paused. "You didn't ask for a ballpark? That's an interesting strategy."

Lindsey laughed. "If you mean a dumb strategy, it's not. I want to see her face, so I can get a better idea what to offer and when she's willing to cave."

He grinned and got out of the truck. "I like your style."

The town square had been deliberately developed into a rustic setup; the wooden buildings had wildflowers in their window boxes and small ponds and pathways out front. There was a small grocery store, an urgent-treatment center, a candy shop, and a local library, as well as several small restaurants. The area itself had become a haven for a well-heeled, academic crowd like Aunt Petra and Otis's parents, who preferred to spend their older years around trees, fields, and captivating views.

Aunt Petra knew everybody and had left Lindsey a list of names of restaurants to try and people to call if she wanted to be social. For now, Lindsey's focus was on expediting lunch as quickly as possible so she could get this exchange over with. Part of her worried that in the end, Amrita might retract her offer, and Lindsey would leave with nothing.

That would be a bummer, because Lindsey had developed an affection for Ruby. She admired the plucky spirit it must have taken to leave her home at such a young age, regardless of whether she actually worked as a governess or had just told that to her family to cover her tracks.

During that time period, most women from affluent families typically focused on societal pursuits. Ruby had never said it outright, but it was obvious she was pining for Chester. She hoped to marry him, but also, she wanted to run the farm with him. She had written about methods to better care for the topsoil and finding kinder ways to manage their servants. It was impressive, and Lindsey was sorry Ruby never had the chance to live that life.

Walking up to Amrita at an outdoor table with a yellow-and-white-striped umbrella, Lindsey gave her a perfunctory wave. "Thank you so much for meeting with us."

Amrita looked much more relaxed than she had at the antique show in her brightly colored dress and the several interesting pieces of jewelry she wore. Her hair was freshly set, and she sat up straight and proper.

"It's nice to see you," Amrita said once they'd settled in.

"You too," Lindsey lied. "Did you bring the diary?"

Amrita gave her a cheerful nod and patted her bag. "It's here. I spent some time this weekend reading through the pages myself." She put a hand to her heart, clinking her gold necklace. "I truly feel for the girl that wrote them, Lindsey. She was dealing with some heartbreak."

"From Chester?" Lindsey asked, wishing she could read it that very moment.

Amrita unfolded her napkin and placed it on her lap. "I can't remember his name. That's part of getting older. My memory isn't what it used to be."

Once they'd settled in, ordered, and chatted about the beautiful day, Lindsey brought up Amrita's mother, in hopes of learning more about her time at the estate. "It's such a strong piece of history to hear about one of the actual servants who worked there. Do you have any idea what she did?"

"I don't." Amrita fanned herself in the heat. "I really didn't learn much about my mother's time at Wind Thorne until she passed. I certainly wasn't interested when I was a child, and when I was a teenager, I was embarrassed she worked as a servant. She worked for several other families after Wind Thorne, and once we did speak about her work, those experiences were current." Amrita looked down at her hands. "I'm the one who is embarrassed now, for the way that I acted. I should have asked her more, learned more about that part of her life. I do realize all that her hard work gave to me."

For the first time, Otis seemed to warm to her. "There's a lot of hindsight for me, at least with my parents," he said. "It's funny how we don't realize any of that while they're raising us. It's a wonder they don't give up."

Amrita nodded. "I never had children. I imagine that would have helped me to see it all sooner."

Lindsey slid on her sunglasses. Her father had given up on her, or rather, on any hope that the two of them would have any sort of connection. She'd finally done the same.

"Now, tell me about you," Amrita said, smiling at Otis. "I noticed your bio said you work with gems?"

After the waiter came around and took their order, Otis talked a little about his work. He was so passionate and told them all about a recent trip to Nova Scotia, where he'd searched for garnets.

"It was such an astonishing place," he said, squeezing another lemon into his iced tea. "I didn't want to leave."

"I imagine that happens a lot," Lindsey said. "With all your travels?"

Even though she was not planning on getting in too deep with their romance, she couldn't help but wonder if he'd be around enough to even let that happen.

Otis wrinkled his brow. "You know, in some of the more beautiful parts of the world, I do wonder why I don't just give it all up and keep exploring, but home is home. I'm originally from just outside of the city, and it's impossible for me to imagine a life anywhere else."

Lindsey nodded. "I understand that. My grandparents had lived here ever since I was a child, and we spent summers and breaks visiting their house. That stayed with me and added to my sense of home."

"You didn't know your family owned the property at Wind Thorne until later in life, is that right?" Amrita said. "That's what it said on the website."

"Yes, that's true," Lindsey said, wondering how much Amrita had learned about her family online. "But we were still always walking around the field, sneaking into the house, and exploring the tunnels. It was like having a playground next door."

The food arrived with the inviting smell of sweet potato fries and freshly cooked burgers. Lindsey had ordered a salad, and right away, Otis dropped a few french fries on her plate.

"The musgravite is lovely," Otis said, once he'd added ketchup to his veggie burger.

Lindsey was confused, thinking he meant something about the food, and he pointed at Amrita's necklace.

Her hand went to her neck, and she fingered the stone, looking uncomfortable. "It's nothing special. It looks much grander than it actually is."

"It's pretty grand," Otis said. "You might want to get it appraised."

A ringtone paused the conversation, and hoping it was Aunt Petra giving permission to crack open the safe, Lindsey pulled out her phone. "Excuse me. I—"

Irritation cut through her at the name on the caller ID. It was her father, the last person she wanted to talk to. Quickly, Lindsey slid the phone back into her bag, and Otis gave her a questioning look.

"Everything good?" Amrita asked, and Lindsey nodded. "The food looks great. Lindsey, I should have ordered that salad."

The grilled chicken, jicama, watermelon, and mint was perfect for the hot day. The umbrella over the table offered some shade, but the sun warmed her shoulders, and she relished her cold drink of water.

"Were you still interested in touring the grounds at Wind Thorne?" Lindsey asked. "You'd mentioned you might be interested in doing that, instead of seeing the house."

Amrita brightened. "Yes, if that would be okay. I would like to see the tunnels. My mother spoke of them sometimes, but for her, the memories were not good."

"What do you mean?" Lindsey asked.

Amrita shrugged. "I think she was scared of them. Being underground, the fear they would collapse, maybe."

Lindsey nodded. "That's fair. My aunt had them checked for safety, but I don't know how she'd feel about letting in someone outside of the family. You'd probably have to sign a bunch of waivers, but I'd be happy to join you."

Amrita nodded. "I'd be willing."

"I have a question that might sound rude," Lindsey said, while savoring the sweetness of the watermelon. "I promise it's not meant to be—but did your mother tell you the reason she kept the items she had from the house?"

Amrita put her hand to her chest. "I think she loved the family and wanted to keep their privacy, even if they took advantage of her."

"What do you mean?" Otis asked.

"Well, she wasn't paid." Amrita wiped the corners of her mouth with a napkin. "I do know that. Room, board . . . that was about it. She told me she wished she'd never come to America."

"Where was she before that?" Otis asked.

Amrita set her burger down. “France.”

“Oh, she spoke French,” Lindsey said. “It would have been hard to communicate here.”

“She actually spoke Malagasy,” Amrita said.

Otis tilted his head. “She was from Madagascar?”

The waiter arrived just then to refill their iced tea and waters.

“My mother was born outside of Antananarivo,” Amrita said. “There was little opportunity and extreme poverty, so several of the people from that area moved to France to work. When she was there, my mother heard that others had gone to the United States and were doing very well, so she joined them, and ended up at Wind Thorne. The work was much harder than she expected, and there was not an opportunity to leave. She was quite young then.”

Now that Lindsey knew her great-grandmother had also been a servant at Wind Thorne, she was curious about her history. Annabelle could not have been from the same group as Amrita’s mother, because Lindsey’s ancestors were Eastern European and Irish. Her great-grandmother might have come to the United States to work, like them, but it was possible she’d already lived here. Something to research. Either way, Lindsey was curious if her great-grandmother had felt the same about working there.

“I am sorry to hear your mother didn’t have a good experience here,” Lindsey said. “It’s hard to consider the idea that in such a gilded age, in a gilded place, the working conditions didn’t shine.”

“Nicely put,” Otis said. He’d already finished his veggie burger and was fiddling with the clasp on his watch. “I’ve been to Madagascar several times. It’s a beautiful place, but still impoverished. It’s rich in gemstones, but a huge deposit of sapphires was discovered in Ilikaka in the late ’90s. The place went from under fifty residents to a boomtown almost overnight. The sapphires are some of the most striking in the world. They’re known for their diamonds, too, of course. Have you been?”

"No." Amrita pressed her lips together. "My mother did not have a desire to return. However, she was older when she had me, so her focus was on keeping food on the table. Not exotic travel."

They sat in silence. The lines around Amrita's eyes were pronounced in the afternoon light, and Lindsey wondered how old she was. Perhaps mid-sixties or early seventies.

"I found out something interesting this week," Lindsey said. "My great-grandmother worked at Wind Thorne. She would have been there when your mother was there. Her name was Annabelle. Did she mention her?"

It would be so interesting to have a real-time connection with her mother's grandmother.

"No . . . sorry." Amrita shook her head. "I don't remember that name."

"Darn," Lindsey said. "She was younger, too, from what I understand."

Amrita took a bite of her food. "Well, they might have known each other. I wish I could ask my mother. These are the things that come with loss, questions we cannot ask about the past. Once someone is gone, you never truly get to know the answers, do you?"

"No." Lindsey certainly had a running catalog of questions she would have liked to ask her mother. Right now, the main one was how she would want her work to be remembered. "My mother had a heart attack, so we were left without answers. It was hard on my whole family."

My father, too.

Lindsey pushed the thought from her mind. Her father, with his team-coach attitude about everything except the people on the actual team, did not deserve a pass.

"What other artifacts did she have?" Lindsey asked. Sitting up straighter, she added, "Wait. This is a long shot, but is there any chance she took a key that might belong to a safe? There's one on the property that hasn't been—"

Otis went into a coughing fit and nudged her leg under the table.

"Sorry," he sputtered, and grabbed his water. He held up his hand and took a long drink. Then, he said, "Sorry, guys. Lindsey, you were talking about the key collection you're building."

Lindsey frowned. Otis clearly didn't think it was a good idea to tell Amrita about the safe, but she wasn't worried. It wasn't as if Amrita, of all people, would break into Wind Thorne to find the safe. It had taken Lindsey a diary, a metal detector, and one hundred years to find it.

That said, Otis was used to dealing with high-value items. He probably practiced levels of protocol that she didn't need to consider.

"Why don't you tell her about it?" Lindsey told him.

"Sure." The sun reflected off Otis's sunglasses as he leaned back in his chair. "It's pretty cool. They're collecting all these old-fashioned keys for the doors and even found one that was used on the sugar jar, probably during the Depression. It would be interesting to showcase a few of them in a collection of older artifacts."

Amrita wrinkled her brow. "So, you need a key for a safe?"

"I don't know," he said. "Lindsey, is there a safe?"

"Yes, of course," she said. "My aunt has a modern-day one up in the office. But I was trying to think of old-fashioned things that might have keys."

"Oh. I see." Amrita took a drink of water. "Well, I can't help you there. I do have the diary, though. It doesn't have a key."

Lindsey regretted the entire exchange. Quickly, she said, "Yes. What did you hope to sell it for?"

Amrita finished chewing, then folded up her napkin. "I don't know. What do you think is fair?"

"I don't know." Lindsey toyed with her pinkie ring. "I think it can be difficult to give up something that's important to your family. I'd like to say this would be important to my family, but the more I've gotten to know you, I'm starting to see that your connection to the Wind Thorne household is significant. It clearly influenced your mother, to the point that she went back to protect her employers from thieves. It's special. I don't want you to sell it. I'm certainly not going to take it from you."

Otis didn't react, but Amrita certainly did. "You said you were going to buy it," she said, a hint of anger in her tone. "That's the entire purpose of this lunch."

"I thought we met so we could share stories and get to know each other," Lindsey said. "The diary belongs to Wind Thorne, yes, but it means more to your family than it does to ours."

"It doesn't mean a thing to me," Amrita said. "Thinking about my mother being stuck there, miserable . . . I'd as soon throw it in the trash."

Otis rested his hand on his chin, watching the exchange with interest.

"Oh." Lindsey had not expected her to become so openly irritated. Feeling uncomfortable, she wiped some precipitation from the ice off her glass. "I understand that, and it's good to hear. I mean, not good, but if that's how you truly feel—"

"It's how I feel." Amrita cracked her knuckles. "It means nothing to me. I'll give it to you for five thousand."

Lindsey's heart sank. She wanted the diary so badly that she could hardly keep her voice steady, but she was not about to pay that.

"This is awkward." Lindsey looked down at the table. "I've wasted your time, I think. I thought . . ." She hunched her shoulders, as if embarrassed. "I thought one thousand, at the most. I was totally off the mark."

Amrita's lips parted. "Yes, you were. This diary is an important piece of history. I'm much too old to just give it away."

"Oh." Lindsey ducked her head again. With a sigh, she reached for the check. "I understand. I'll get this. I'm so sorry for any misunderstanding."

Lindsey signaled the waiter to come get her card.

Amrita studied her in confusion. "I thought you wanted the diary."

"Of course I do, but it's too much," Lindsey explained. "Even a first-edition book rarely pulls in such a high price. I could do fifteen hundred, but that's as high as I could go."

Amrita scoffed. "Lindsey, we both know your family has the money."

So, she *had* done her research.

"Don't make that assumption." Lindsey kept her voice light. "If you're speaking of my mother's career, my father is the beneficiary."

Amrita's expression tightened. "Your aunt has resources. The estate is enormous."

"Exactly," Lindsey said. "The expenses to run it are immense, and as much as we'd like every piece of history that comes our way, we have to be prudent with what we can accept. I'm interested in the diary, of course. It's a diary. But it's also the fifteen-billionth expense we'd have this month."

Otis coughed, and Lindsey could have sworn there was a laugh behind it.

"Three thousand," Amrita said.

Lindsey held up her hands. "I wish I could."

Amrita sighed. She sat in silence for a long moment, running her fingers along the stitching on the strap of her bag. "I would still like to explore the property with you, so I don't want to leave here on a bad note. My mother had this for years. I remember her reading it."

"That's exactly why you should keep it," Lindsey insisted.

It was a risk to bluff, but if Amrita knew how badly she wanted it, the price would only go up.

"Lindsey, my mother would want me to profit," Amrita said. "She would. I want to do right by her. How about twenty-five hundred?"

Inside, Lindsey practically did a cartwheel. It was more than she'd wanted to pay, and her aunt would probably wonder at her for buying it, but the connection to Ruby was worth every cent.

Lindsey glanced at Otis. He shrugged. Then, she looked at Amrita and smiled. "Yes, I'll do that. Two thousand five hundred."

After getting Amrita's mobile payment details, Lindsey pulled out her phone and paid electronically. Once it went through, Amrita handed her the diary and got to her feet.

"Let's talk soon," Amrita said. "My mother would be so pleased." She gave Lindsey an air kiss and made her way carefully back to her car.

Once she'd pulled away, Otis stared at Lindsey with something bordering on amazement. "How did you do that?"

"What?" Lindsey asked, innocently. She held the diary tight.

"That woman came in here ready to fleece you, and you made her leave with half of what she thought she was getting. I mean . . . I'm sure she made copies, but that was some impressive negotiation."

Lindsey shrugged. "Like you said, supply and demand. If there's no demand . . ."

He burst out laughing. "I could barely keep a straight face when you said you didn't want it. Her face was priceless."

Lindsey's heart still pounded from the risk. "Can you imagine if she'd agreed with me?" She ran her hands over the smooth leather of the cover. "Like, 'Wow, you're right. This is meaningful. I'm keeping it.'"

Otis rolled his eyes. "Please. That woman planned to walk out of here with money today, no matter what. You're a tough negotiator. I'll keep that in mind."

Lindsey hid a smile and went to sign the check. She realized that the waiter had never taken her card because Otis had paid the bill already.

"Thank you," she said, looking up at him. "When did you do that?"

"When you were in the bathroom," he said. "Happy to do it, but I wasn't happy to do it for her. There's something disingenuous about her. That musgravite she was wearing, the stone she tried to play off as worthless? It's rare and it's expensive. I don't want to make judgments on what Amrita is capable of getting her hands on, but I will make judgments on her ability to be less than forthcoming about it."

Lindsey shrugged. "I don't know about that one. I sometimes get embarrassed when people dive too deep into my ring. If they recognize my mom's work, or that it's a unique piece, I can feel them calculating its value and wondering why someone as simple as me is wearing it. Besides, what kind of damage could she cause?"

"Probably nothing." They got to their feet and headed to the truck. "Still, I don't love the idea that she knows there's an untapped safe sitting in Wind Thorne."

"Well, who knows? It might be empty." Lindsey opened the diary and checked the date. It was from two years prior to the time Ruby had left Wind Thorne, and she felt a rush of excitement. "I can't wait to read this. I do have confidence in Amrita. The diary is legitimate. I knew the moment I laid eyes on it, since I had the match."

"Well, just because she has artifacts from the house doesn't mean she is who she says she is."

Lindsey paused. "What do you mean? Who could she be?"

"Don't know." Otis frowned. "That's the problem."

It wasn't like Amrita had tried to hang around all afternoon or asked strange questions. She seemed up front that she wanted to make a sale, and she was respectful of their time. Thanks to her, Lindsey now had another diary that would allow her to learn more about Ruby.

On the ride back to her aunt's house, Otis drove with the windows down and his sunglasses on, and he sang along to some blues song. He had a great voice, and she enjoyed watching the trees go by out the window, listening to him.

"Did you want to read this with me?" she asked when he pulled up out front.

"I do, but it's yours," he said. "You just paid a fortune for it, so you read it first."

"What about the safe?" Lindsey asked. "Do you want me to call when I hear from my aunt?"

"I'm definitely interested, but that's up to you," he said. "Either way, let's catch up later."

Lindsey hopped out of the truck and walked around to the driver's side. He looked so inviting in his sunglasses, his hair rumpled from the wind, that she fought back a smile. "When's later?"

"Friday?" he said, linking his fingers with hers. "I have some things with my parents tomorrow, but Friday's good. We could make dinner."

Lindsey laughed. "Or we could order pizza."

"Even better." He pulled her in for a kiss that made her grip the edge of the car door. "I'm all in."

Chapter Fifteen

Wind Thorne, 1930

The walk out to the forest and through the fields left Ruby exhausted.

Once she got back to the house, she settled into one of the larger chairs in the main room to catch her breath. The chair was out of the way, but it provided a view of the hall, as well as the library, office, and bottom of the staircase. She used to sit in this very spot, undetected, to write in her notebook.

It might be time to take up writing again. Not that she'd be able to be honest, not really. She had too many thoughts about her time in New York, her time with Chester, that she couldn't write about for fear of being found out. She had destroyed the notebook she'd used in New York City, throwing it in the fire as Chester helped her out to the buggy, her heart aching even then at the loss of those memories. She would have loved the chance to read it all now as the days stretched in front of her with nothing to do but recover.

The front door slammed, shaking the walls, and the heavy tread of boots stomped across the main floor. Ruby shrank back into the chair, certain it was her father, and wondering what had put him into such a rage.

"It's your stupidity that has caused this to happen," he roared.

Ruby hoped the men were not headed in her direction. They were not, as they went into the library and slammed the door. But through the wall, she could hear every word.

"You didn't plan ahead, so we won't have the equipment that we need to harvest the hay this summer." Her father spoke in a tone that was measured and matter of fact. "How are we supposed to feed the cattle?"

"The tractor might arrive on time, and if it doesn't, I'll find the part we need. Or borrow a tractor." Ruby recognized Glenn's voice. He sounded distressed instead of suave. "If we don't get the tedder, I'll have the field hands work around the clock to rake it."

"Sounds like you've got it all figured out."

"Yes. If everyone does what they're supposed to do, we should still be able to harvest half of it."

The silence that followed was louder than any shout. Ruby winced at a sudden bang, then realized it was a book that had been dropped onto the table.

"Half of it?" her father echoed. "What type of fool would allow us to lose more than half of our cattle feed because of a stupid mistake brought on by laziness and drink? You had one responsibility, the most important responsibility, and now it's too late to—"

"How was I to know the order would get delayed? You know what? I think you knew this would happen. I think you put me in this position so that you could step aside and avoid the fall, that's what I think."

"Oh, do you?" Her father's voice was low and measured.

"Yes, I do. You knew full well everything was about to implode. There's no access to anything anymore, no one has any money, and instead of failing in front of your entire family who worships you, you decided to set me up to take the fall for you. Well, I won't do it. I'm going to tell everyone the truth about—"

"Get out." Her father's voice was measured. "You and your wife are no longer welcome here."

Ruby sat up straight. Her sister? No, that couldn't be possible, not when the world was crumbling. Not when Ruby had just come back. Where was Elizabeth supposed to go?

Glenn, who had been so jeering moments before, was at a loss for words. "Sir, what?"

"Now it's 'sir'?" His voice was low and measured. "I think you heard me. You and your wife are no longer welcome to stay here. You will have to find another place to fail."

Ruby gripped the edge of her chair. Her father had to know how bad it was out there. He was just threatening to teach Glenn a lesson. Surely, he would not do this.

"You're right." Glenn's words felt heavy. "I failed you. I'm not up to the task, and I have cost you and your family deeply. I'm just not man enough to say it."

Even though Glenn's tone was pleading, she could hear the intense self-control it must have taken to say those words, instead of lashing out in a rage. Glenn spoke again, breaking the silence.

"Please, sir." His tone was full of contrition. "Give me another chance. We won't be able to survive out there. Your daughter won't be able to survive out there."

"That is no longer my concern. She married you, so you are responsible for keeping her alive. Yet, if you can't even run my farm, there is no chance that you can protect my daughter, is there?"

"No, sir." Glenn's voice broke, and she could imagine him fighting back tears.

Ruby's stomach ached. Last week, had she sounded just as weak and desperate? She wondered if the damage Glenn had done could still be repaired, like he'd said, or if their cattle would be affected.

The sound of her father's desk chair being pushed back was followed by the heavy tread of steps. She could imagine her father coming out from behind the desk, Glenn cowering in front of him.

"What did you promise me when you begged for her hand in marriage?" he asked.

"That I would keep her in the life that she is accustomed to."

"Then you'd better figure out how to do that."

"The only opportunity for that is here. At Wind Thorne. I disrespected you. I—"

"Beg."

"Please, sir. I never meant—"

Her father chuckled. "Kiss my boot."

There was silence. Then, a thud followed by a muffled cry. Ruby's hands flew to her ears, but it was too late; she knew exactly what had happened.

"Welcome back, son," her father said, chuckling.

The door to the library clattered open, and her father strode out the front door, toward the stables. Glenn rushed from the library with a rag pressed to his mouth. He looked around, eyes wild, and went upstairs.

Moments later, Ruby heard him shouting at someone, then her sister cried out. Ruby froze, then raced up the stairs. She got to Elizabeth's room in time to see that Glenn had her by the hair and was dragging her to the bed. Blood gushed from his mouth where her father had kicked him and was now smeared across her sister's face.

"Let her go!" Ruby cried, running up and punching him in the back.

Glenn's shock was quickly replaced by fury, and he lunged at her. Ruby ran toward the door, stepping aside just in time to shove Glenn out into the hallway. She slammed the door shut and locked it with the key. The doorknob rattled, and with a cry of rage, he gave up and stomped off down the hall.

Ruby stood at the door, frozen, as Elizabeth sobbed on the bed. In addition to wearing the blood from his face, she had a bruise puffing out on her upper arm.

Ruby still couldn't register the violence, the way he'd grabbed her. "I'll tell Father. He'll make him leave."

"Father knows." Elizabeth wiped at her arm as if trying to remove a spot. "Why do you think Glenn thinks it's okay?"

Ruby put her hand to her mouth. Their father had always doted on Elizabeth. The idea of him letting Glenn treat her like this was shocking. But at the same time, their father had always been clear that a husband was to be obeyed. Ruby had never considered the impact of that idea on her mother and, now, her sister. It was unjust, and instantly reduced Ruby's respect for her father.

Chester would never treat a woman like that. He had a gentle heart, full of kindness and compassion. In fact, if he witnessed such an injustice, he would put a stop to it.

"I'm so sorry, Elizabeth," Ruby said.

"Life goes on." Her sister looked at her. "You must apologize to my husband, for striking him."

Ruby nearly spat on the floor. "I will never apologize to him. I will never let him—"

"You don't know." Elizabeth's eyes were hollow. "The things he can do."

"I will not tolerate this. I will . . ." Ruby's words trailed off.

In truth, she was powerless to do anything at all.

"The best you can do is avoid him," Elizabeth told her. "Avoid all of this."

Ruby held her hands tightly together, trying to absorb the shock of all she'd seen and heard. "I'm so sorry I left," she said. "That I did that to you. Nothing can be undone, but I am here now, and Elizabeth, whatever I can do to help you . . ."

Her face shuttered up once again. "No help required. Shall we see if dinner is on the table? I didn't hear the bell."

"I know my apology isn't good enough," Ruby said. "I've wanted to talk to you for days, to see you and make sure you—"

"Make sure I what?" Elizabeth sounded more like their mother than she ever had in her life. "Do you have any idea how I felt when you left?"

Ruby stared out the window at the fields. It was so hard to not be able to tell her sister everything, to explain the choices she'd made. Where she'd really been.

Instead, she looked down at her hands. "I know."

"You don't know."

"Tell me, then," Ruby pleaded. "Please." Her sister didn't answer. "Elizabeth, I made a bad decision. You deserved to have the best day of your life, to enjoy every moment of your wedding with your family, and . . ." Tears pricked at her eyelids. "I was so scared that day. I ran away because I thought something bad would happen to me."

"Nothing bad was going to happen to you," Elizabeth said, her dark eyes wet with tears. "Give me a real reason. Please, tell me there was a reason."

"I thought Indira was murdered," Ruby said. "I still think she was murdered."

Elizabeth's mouth dropped open. "*That's* why you left?"

The blood on Elizabeth's face made Ruby feel sick. She got up and moistened a rag in the basin, carefully wiping it off. Her sister stood frozen while she did it, then touched her face when Ruby took the cloth over to the sink, where she squeezed out pink water.

"I saw her at the bottom of the stairs," Ruby said. "Someone killed her."

"Who cares?" Elizabeth demanded. "She was a servant."

Ruby drew back. "She was a human being."

"I'm sorry she's dead, but that's not why you left." Elizabeth considered the bruise on her arm, then glared at Ruby. "Did you steal my ring?"

Ruby flushed. "How could you ask me that?"

"Did you?" she demanded.

Slowly, Ruby shook her head. Elizabeth's dark eyes locked onto hers, and finally, they softened. "Uncle Peter told me you did. I told him you'd never do that to me."

"He attacked me that night," Ruby said, quietly. "If I would have stayed, he would have done it again."

Elizabeth put her hand to her mouth. "No."

The tears came so quickly that Ruby was embarrassed.

"I'm sorry I left," she said. "I love you so much."

"I love you, too." Elizabeth pressed her lips together. "But when you get older, you start to realize how little love really matters."

Ruby closed her eyes. Maybe if she'd been brave enough to stay, to face him, the light would have remained in her sister's eyes. If she'd been here, she could have fixed whatever had broken between Elizabeth and Glenn. If she'd been here . . . but then, Chester. She never would have had that time with him. Was that how it worked? A trade-off between the people she cared about the most?

"I missed you every moment. I . . ." Her voice broke as she thought how deeply she'd betrayed her sister. "I hope you'll forgive me one day."

Ruby reached out a hand. When the warmth of Elizabeth's skin touched hers, she pulled her sister in close, holding her tight. Was this forgiveness? Just as quickly, Elizabeth pulled back, and the two sat in silence.

"I'm so sorry," she said, again. "I'm so sorry I left."

"You were smart to run away." Elizabeth sank back onto the bed. "Why would you ever come back?"

Chapter Sixteen

Upstate New York, present day

Lindsey had no doubt the diary would captivate her from the first word to the last. It was the only thing that would even come close to keeping her mind off the safe at Wind Thorne. She still hadn't heard from Aunt Petra and was tempted to return to Wind Thorne on her own to look for that key.

The call of the diary was stronger. She poured an iced tea and settled into her chair on the porch, ready to learn more about Ruby. While the insects were lost in contemplations of their own, she opened it. To her surprise, several pages dropped out into her lap.

They were letters, with a Post-it note stuck to them that read, *These were folded up inside. They're letters from World War I, written by one of the Thornhill brothers. I thought you'd be interested.*

Eagerly, Lindsey started to flip through them:

> Dear Brother,
> It has been a journey with a surprise you won't see coming. We were in active duty, as I told you was coming, and it was not what I imagined. So much noise. You would not believe the sound of the explosions and shouts. Kept me on my toes with my head down, so I made out all right. It's risky business

making friends here, I guess. I've been telling you about Graham, but he was hit by a shell. Close enough to me to make my teeth rattle, but that was it. There's a soldier here who's taken on the job of being chaplain to us when we need it so that's a help because I might not have known him long, but the men here are some of the finest I've ever met. Graham was a swell guy.

Cattle cars moved us north so far that we'll be out of the action for months. We're near Paris, and you wouldn't believe it, but I fell in love with a girl. She's just about the prettiest thing you could imagine. Smells good when we all smell awful, but she's taken a shine to me.

Thank you for the cigarettes that you haven't sent. Smoking them yourself? I might not be on the front lines for some time, but a man has to live so don't forget your brother.

Dear Brother,
Thank you for finally sending a response. I am over the moon to think that you will finally meet her. I think you'll be a little surprised that your brother did so well for himself. You often thought I was the hopeless one of the two of us—don't deny it, you did!—but all that's changed. The thing I need to warn you about is that she is not educated. I know that our parents would have expected me to marry at my station, never below, yet you will see why I made the choice I did.

Dear Brother,
I was quite angry at your suggestion that I'd fallen for her out of loneliness. The thing you cannot understand is that I have not been alone since the start

of this thing. I always have someone by my side. I do not know what it is to be alone anymore. My battalion is a family to me and—I do not mean this to hurt you—any one of them would have stepped forward to help me if you did not. But I am grateful it's you because you are my brother, and you deserve to see your little brother making his way in the world. Our two families will raise our children side by side, and there will be days where you will wonder how I bested you in the end. (That was a joke—I hope you didn't let your wife read this.)

Dear Brother,
Oh, she is in a world of its own. Her beauty and grace are well beyond anything you will expect. She is skilled in so many things, but her English is not good. Her needlework will be a great loss to the milliner's shop where she works, I am told. She has a heart for children and their care, as well as skill in the kitchen and the home. You will find several places where she can be of service until I arrive. It would mean so much to me if you would take the time to introduce yourself and Rosemary, as we will all one day be sharing dinner together.

To whom it may concern,
I am sorry to contact you during such troubling times. Your brother fares well and continues to heal, yet what he wants the most is to know that there is still a place for him and the woman he plans to marry at the farm. He struggles with walking and may receive an early discharge. If not, he would like permission to send his betrothed to your home. She is highly capable and

> skilled in helping to maintain a home. On your word and wire transfer, I will make arrangements to send her with safe passage next month. Please contact me to confirm that this plan is pleasing to you.

That was it. Lindsey sat back in her chair, her heart aching from the sorrow that must have come from the young man who had fought in the war. The hope he'd had for the life back home.

Shaking her head, she set the letters aside and picked up the diary. She was already a live wire of feelings and wondered if maybe she should take a walk or something before delving into the life of Ruby. She was too curious, though, and started to read.

It took two hours to read the diary cover to cover. Lindsey had expected it would paint a picture of life at Wind Thorne, but when she was done, she sat in stunned silence. She'd never dreamed how detailed it would be.

This diary was written before Ruby left home. It painted a fascinating picture of what her life had been like before the Depression. She was obviously a lot younger, but the difference in her lack of awareness of the world was what struck Lindsey the most.

In this diary, Ruby had confidence that her interpretation of life was set and correct. She relished the household's small dramas and even seemed to have a small crush on her older sister's fiancé, along with absolute adoration for her sister. She was amused by her doddering grandmother and angry with her mother, and saw her father with equal parts of fear and respect. Interestingly, she also had a complete distaste for the boy she liked in the other diary, Chester. That was a surprise, given how much she pined for him later.

The things that Lindsey noted the most, though, were the references Ruby made to her uncle. It quickly became clear that he was the one who had written the letters tucked into the pages of the diary, because she often mentioned World War I and the changes it had brought about in her uncle. She didn't feel safe around him, and even though she never mentioned anything untoward, it was clear he made her uncomfortable.

One entry read:

I don't like being around Uncle Peter. He scares me. There are days he sits with that medical kit packed full of the little bottles and needles and stares for hours. My mother said he's like a walking corpse since he got back from the war. That he would have been better off killed than come back here, being as useless as he is with his injured leg, and that she would have rather had it that way. I feel guilty but I feel that way, too.

Lindsey was on Ruby's side in all things, but she still felt sorrow for this man and what he must have suffered, as well as returning to a family who didn't know how to help him. The needles—he was most likely hooked on morphine. Alcohol and drug abuse were huge problems when soldiers returned home because of the trauma they'd experienced. Morphine had been readily accessible in the medical kits, which only added to the problem.

It must have been confusing for Ruby to watch her uncle descend into that darkness. Ruby would have had no understanding of what had turned him into "a walking corpse," as her mother had put it. No one would understand, really, who hadn't experienced the horrors he'd been through.

Clouds hung low in the sky, and Lindsey felt stiff from sitting for so long. She decided to get a walk in while she still had the chance. A quick walk down the hill and across the footbridge would take her to the right path.

The one that led straight to Wind Thorne.

The difference between the hike from her grandparents' house to Wind Thorne back when she was younger was notable. The pathways were now trimmed and maintained, there were no weeds, and the wildflowers looked like they'd been set out as decorations at an incredibly rustic party. Aunt Petra had done a beautiful job linking the two properties, and once again, Lindsey had to wonder why her grandmother had waited so long to admit ownership of the estate next door.

Lawn crews had been hard at work earlier that day, leaving crisscross marks in the grass where the cattle fields had once been. Out of habit, Lindsey's eyes swept the ground as she walked, looking for the ring, as she'd done as a child. Finding it would have been about as likely as finding the gold coin Chester had taken from Ruby. At the thought, she came to a sudden halt as an echo from the diary passed through her mind like a whisper.

Elliot.

Lindsey's mouth dropped open. Ruby had written in detail about Chester and his family. She'd talked about him and his brother swinging on a tire swing when she was trying to read or throwing pine cones from the trees in a sneak attack as she and her sister walked through the forest. Her outrage was comical, given how much she adored the guy years later, but the detail that clicked was the realization that Chester wasn't just any neighbor boy. His brother was Elliot, Lindsey's great-grandfather. Chester had lived in the very house where she was staying.

It might have been a detail she'd known at some point in her life, that her great-grandfather had had a brother, but why would that interest her? Now, knowing the details about Ruby, Chester, and life at Wind Thorne, it felt like learning she was related to someone important from history. That tiny connection with Ruby warmed her heart and made the stories seem more real.

Lindsey stopped at the top of a hill and considered Wind Thorne. It really was stunning—the stretch of the cattle fields in gold against the blue of the sky. Inspired, she tried to imagine how she would capture its beauty in a piece. There were so many options, and in each one, she saw a stretch of thick gold with another layer of etching, as fragile as the wildflowers in the fields, with a sudden bite of a sapphire for the sky.

Lindsey brushed her hands over the top of a section of weeds, wondering at herself. It had been so long since she'd even considered designing something that she watched the idea from a place of detachment. The memories here were plentiful, but one in particular was pushing its way to the front: the first time her mother had taken her to see a silversmith work.

The man was melting silver in his workshop the day they stopped by. The shimmering pool of liquid metal was the most hypnotic thing Lindsey had ever seen. She stared at the hot, molten metal, breathing in the scent of minerals and fire, entranced by the way it changed shape and structure before easing into the mold.

That night, her mother found her trying to create the same thing with wet sand in a bucket of mud. It was then that her mother took her out to the workshop to teach her how to hammer a piece of metal into shape. They went back to see the same silversmith for weeks, until Lindsey had had her fill.

For all the time Lindsey had lost with her mother, it was those moments, those memories, that made it feel like her mother was still by her side.

Her phone chimed, snapping her back to the present.

Aunt Petra.

Good time to talk?

Lindsey called right away. She listened patiently as Aunt Petra talked about the cruise, describing how rough the water was as the ship pulled out, and how still it was once the journey began. The seven-course meals, and the endless entertainment, as well as the fun she was having with her group of friends. Finally, Aunt Petra asked how things were at home.

By now, Lindsey had made it to the back lawn of Wind Thorne. She sat on a stone bench with a trellis over the top. "What if I told you Otis and I—"

"Otis?" Her aunt sounded pleased as punch. "I told him he should come and see you."

"Well, he did." Lindsey paused. When her aunt didn't say anything more, she added, "He's helped me with some research, and you won't believe this, but we found a safe at Wind Thorne."

"A *safe*?"

The shock in her voice made Lindsey smile. "Yes. I wanted to get your permission to have it opened by a locksmith because I don't have the key. I'd love to do it now but can wait until you're here, if you'd rather."

For a second, Lindsey thought the complete silence on the other end of the phone meant the distance had affected their connection. Then, Aunt Petra came back on the line.

"I have the key, Lindsey," she said. "It's in my desk in the office at home."

Lindsey felt disappointed. "Bummer. So, we didn't really discover a safe," she said, laughing. "Otis did think it was a little too good to be true."

"No." Her aunt's voice was low and urgent, as if she'd stepped out into a hallway. "I didn't know there was a safe. Goodness, if this was an airplane, I would take the return flight back right now to open it with you."

Lindsey's heart started to pound. "Really?"

"Yes, that key was found when Wind Thorne was being remodeled. I took it to a locksmith, and they told me that it was for a safe built at the turn of the century. I'm pretty confident it will be a match. If not, yes, you can call a locksmith, but only if you have one of our security guards there with you when it's opened. I want you to be safe."

Lindsey got up and started pacing the grass. The idea of having access to all that history made it impossible to sit still. Anything could be in that safe, including the missing engagement ring or more information about Ruby.

"This is great news," she said.

"Yes, I think so." Aunt Petra sounded delighted. "Please make a detailed report of what you find in there. I bet there will be so many wonderful pieces of history."

"Do you want me to video-call you when I do it?" Lindsey asked. "Or wait until you come back?"

"No." Her aunt's tone was brisk. "Reception wouldn't be good enough for that. Besides, I think it's high time that you are given the right to move forward with abandon. Seek out joy, my child. Explore. Make the decisions that will affect your life in the best way possible."

Lindsey started laughing. "You're drinking!"

Aunt Petra's voice had a small smile. "No, but they do have several of those tasting courses that we've gone through. Take advantage of the moment, Lindsey. I give you my full permission to use my key and go into the safe. Love you."

"I love you, too."

Lindsey hung up and stared at the massive estate in front of her. This home held so many mysteries and had for more than one hundred years. Even though part of her was tempted to open the safe on her own, she wanted Otis to be there with her. Maybe because he'd been there when they found it, or maybe because she no longer wanted to feel so alone.

Picking up the phone, she called him.

Chapter Seventeen

Wind Thorne, April 1930

The same girl arrived at Ruby's side first thing each morning with a breakfast tray. Today, Ruby's plate was crammed with bacon, sausage, fruit, and a blueberry wheat muffin, alongside a fresh cup of coffee. The girl offered cream as well as a thick pat of butter, and at the kindness and the abundance of food, Ruby's eyes welled up.

"Miss?" the girl asked. "Is it okay?"

Ruby stared down at the tray, baffled at how she'd gone from near-starvation to this. Hot tears rolled down her cheeks. Gently, the girl with the dark eyes dabbed at her face with a cloth, like she'd dabbed at her chin after feeding her soup.

"You are still not well," the girl said, quietly. "I know."

Without her mother in the room, Ruby felt free to speak. "I had no food. But now, I have too much. And all that you've done for me . . ."

The girl studied her, confusion on her face.

"Thank you," Ruby said. "Please, what's your name?"

The servant could not have been more than fifteen, with a cautious smile.

"Annabelle, miss." The girl glanced up at her.

"Annabelle," Ruby said. "That's such a beautiful name. Please, call me Ruby."

"Your mother would not like that," Annabelle said.

"Then do it when she's not around," Ruby said. "I'm so grateful to you. Your care built back up my strength."

"You were quite ill," Annabelle said. "I was scared for you. I am glad you're better now."

Ruby smiled at her. "Thanks." She looked down at the enormous tray of food. "Would you like something? The wheat muffin?"

Annabelle's eyes widened, but she didn't speak.

"Please," Ruby insisted, handing it to her. "Shut and lock the door."

Quickly, Annabelle did what Ruby asked. Then, at Ruby's insistence, she sat in the chair next to the bed and ate quickly, but with a big smile on her face. Once she'd finished eating, she got to her feet.

"That was so good," she said. "Thank you."

"Thank *you*."

Annabelle curtsied and left the room.

Ruby wished she could have given her something more than a muffin. But she also knew full well the risk in doing anything that might single the girl out. It would get her into trouble.

The girl's sweetness reminded Ruby of her dear friend Millie, and Ruby wondered if she had fared well, out of the city and back home with her family. She'd often spoken of her many brothers and sisters, and Ruby worried that they would not have enough to eat. The circumstances she'd described were nothing like the comfort Ruby had come back to.

The farm supplied their family with so much, but Ruby wondered how they still fared so well, in spite of the struggles facing the rest of the country. Crops weren't bringing in money right now. She'd overheard her father note that the air smelled sickly sweet outside. The local farmers were burning their stockpiles of corn for fuel, since it was worth less than wood. Their family must have been doing so well because of the whiskey, but Ruby hoped her father had a plan in place, because at some point, people wouldn't even be able to afford that.

Once Ruby finished breakfast, she had enough energy to get up and dressed for another walk. She grabbed a hat, tied it under her chin, and set out on the same path she'd taken the other day. Past the forest, where she allowed herself one quick look through the trees to Chester's house, and out to the field with the cattle. Today, she planned to walk to the distilleries. They were out past the fields, hidden in small buildings designed to look like equipment sheds, even though her father had always ensured that law enforcement not only approved of his ventures but would also help protect them.

As she approached the fields, she hesitated. A large black army truck sat out by the warehouse that led to the tunnel system underground. It was a surprise to see it back there, as her family had stopped using that particular warehouse for barrel storage sometime ago, because it was too close to the road. Maybe that had changed while Ruby was gone.

Shielding her eyes, she studied the truck. It was the same type that had always been used to transport their barrels to the river, the kind of truck driven by the people Chester used to steal from. Well, that limited her options of where to walk, because it might not be safe to go back there alone.

Frustrated, she stood at the edge of the field, stuck watching the cows instead. Some of the bigger ones made her nervous. They seemed to stand at the ready, their heads tilted in her direction, eyes trained on her like soldiers. They were aggressive, sometimes pushing others out of the way to get food. Ruby took off her hat and turned her head toward the sun, unsure how to fill her day.

Boredom was a luxury she hadn't experienced in so long, but not necessarily one that she wanted. Her body was used to hard work. It wasn't that she wanted to go back to that, but she needed to do something with her life. Perhaps here on the farm, like whatever her sister was doing, because Ruby wouldn't be able to leave anytime soon. She had to admit, she didn't want to miss out on the opportunity to see Chester, whenever he returned.

It was hard to not get lost in the fantasy of what it would be like if she and Chester got married and could work together to run the farm. What would that be like, if her father welcomed him into the fold? It would never happen. The disrespect between her father and Chester's father was silent but blistering. Her father had always wanted the land that their house was on but had never found a way to acquire it. Besides, when Chester returned, they would have to go back to being strangers, as they'd been before.

Ruby started, realizing that a cow had walked right up to her. "I don't have anything to eat."

"Looks like you found a friend," a voice said, and Ruby's blood ran cold.

Uncle Peter stood a few feet away, leaning against the fence with a piece of straw in his mouth. His hat was pulled low, his eyes half shut. He was bigger than when she'd left, fuller in the face, like a plump pig primed for slaughter.

Ruby took several steps back, to put as much distance between them as possible.

It had been years since that day in her grandmother's room, when he had grabbed her hips and pushed his body up against her. Held her by the neck and made that lewd laugh when she dropped the coins. In that moment, she had felt numb, powerless, and trapped. She'd never jumped a train, searched for a job, or gone hungry. She lacked the grit back then to know those things were options, and in some ways, she probably owed this wretched man a debt of gratitude for opening her eyes to her simple naivete, because nothing like that was ever going to happen to her again.

With that in mind, Ruby picked up the nearest stick she could find and pointed it at him. "Beat it. Don't ever come near me again, you got that?"

Peter held up his hands, chuckling. "You feisty now, fresh back from the city?"

"I mean it." She pointed the stick at him. "If you come near me again, I'll . . ."

Would she kill him? No. That wasn't something she could carry on her conscience.

"I'll ruin your life in ways you can't even imagine," she said.

Millie had said that to one of the other housemaids once, as a joke. Chester had repeated it for weeks, over the smallest infraction, which never failed to send the three of them into peals of laughter.

Chester. Clouds drifted over the light-blue sky of the pasture, and she wished he were here with her now so she wouldn't have to face this man alone.

Peter adjusted his hat and made a clicking sound, and one of the cows from the pasture came toward him. He rested his head on the cow's forehead.

"This one's my favorite." Uncle Peter ran his rough hands over her shoulders. Then he picked up a stick from the ground and gave Ruby a pointed look.

Ruby tightened her grip, and her heart started pounding. But he just used it to scratch behind the cow's ears. The cow ducked her head, leaning into the rough wood. He patted her with his other hand before offering her food he'd tucked into his pocket.

"I call her Mary. She's smart, you know?" He kicked at a loose piece of the fence, knocking the board to the ground. "I admire that. It's not her fault the way that things turn out on a farm or that she's in line for slaughter, just like it's not our fault the way that our lives unfold. But there's a kindness in her, in this one. Those are the ones I try and keep around as long as possible."

Ruby stood, silent. She couldn't tell if he was threatening her or talking about the cow.

Uncle Peter looked her straight in the face then. His eyes had deep circles under them. "I already heard I'm to leave you alone." The words were stilted, with a touch of hurt. "Never meant to scare you, Ruby. Thought you were one of the good ones."

The words made her bristle. "I'm going back."

"Whatever suits." He dropped his stick and started pulling up dormant grass by the fistful. "I'm headed to the warehouses, got some work to do out there. Probably spend some time with Mary here first, though. Animals heal the heart, you know? People don't always do the same." He straightened up and opened his palm. The cow ate from his hand as if she'd done it a thousand times before. "I'll be seeing you."

The words echoed in her head as she walked back to the house. She moved as quickly as possible to get away from him, and nearly bumped into Elizabeth. She was leaving the barn, carrying a folder stuffed with papers, and fumbled to keep them steady.

Ruby helped and, once they were under control, gave her a tentative smile. "Hi. Sorry about that."

"It's fine," Elizabeth said. "I just can't mess anything up right now, since Glenn already did. We're on thin ice here." The skin around her sister's mouth was pinched. "I think Brad is kind of enjoying it. For once, he can do no wrong."

Ruby suddenly felt tired, and she rested her hand against the door of the barn.

"Are you okay?" Elizabeth studied her.

"Yes," Ruby said. "I'm still trying to get my energy back."

"Were you walking long?" Elizabeth asked, sounding concerned.

"No. The field got a little too crowded."

Ruby pointed at the field, where Uncle Peter was strolling along the edge, his walk steadier than she remembered. He led Mary by a rope and stopped every few feet, feeding her something from his hand and scratching behind her ears.

Elizabeth winced. "I understand that."

She made her way to the veranda, and Ruby followed with careful steps. They both took a seat on the chairs, Ruby grateful for the opportunity to rest.

Elizabeth watched their uncle in the field with disdain. "I think that cow is the only thing that truly loves him. Did you get to hear him singing to it?"

Ruby drew back. "That sounds revolting."

"He sings war songs." Her sister fanned herself with her hand. "The cow—"

"Mary," Ruby told her.

"It has a *name*?" Elizabeth laughed. "Mary just stands there and listens. Once . . ." She lowered her voice. "He actually bowed after he sang to her, like he was giving her a performance."

"No." Ruby couldn't imagine.

"Yes." Elizabeth gave her an eager nod. "He sang this slow song, like a love song. I don't . . ." The mirth died from her eyes. "There's something . . . I try to not be near him." She stared down at the folder. "It's good to laugh. I have to tell you, Ruby. I've been a little worried."

"About what?" she asked.

Elizabeth looked down at the folder. "We need to start stockpiling food. Next winter, it's going to get bad, I think. Like it was for you in New York."

Even though the Depression was in the village and the surrounding towns like a plague, it was nothing like it had been in the city. Here, they had plenty of food to eat. Ruby had settled into the idea that there would continue to be, with the crops and the animals.

"I'm sure it won't be like that." Ruby sat in silence. "Is that what Father said? What he's concerned about?"

"Everything is falling apart," Elizabeth said. "He blamed Glenn for making a mistake with the cattle feed, but the truth is, the tractor is broken, and we can't get the part because it's not available. It has nothing to do with our debts. That's its own problem, and it's a big one. We owe a lot, Ruby."

It felt a little harder to breathe. Ruby had thought she'd escaped this feeling, that she'd returned to someplace safe.

"Why are we so far behind?" she asked.

"Father took out some loans almost a decade ago, because Wind Thorne was so profitable, and he planned to expand. The Mensley property was a big part of his vision, though, and they refused to sell, so he used the money to build up the distilleries."

Ruby flushed at the mention of Chester's family.

"The rest of it was to keep up appearances." Elizabeth stared out at the trees. "Father's talking about taking out another a loan to avoid a foreclosure on the farm."

Ruby was confused. "What? No, we own the farm."

"It's the taxes." Elizabeth glanced at her. "Each year they've gone up, and we've been unable to pay. The foreclosure will pay for the taxes."

Ruby might not have understood what her sister meant if she hadn't spent the last two years of her life reading the newspaper from cover to cover. Now, though, she knew what her sister was saying. She also realized they were in serious trouble.

"Why haven't we paid?" she asked, chewing on her thumbnail. "We have plenty."

"We have debt," Elizabeth corrected. "Father and Uncle Peter have debt that you wouldn't believe. Father's doing everything he can, but it's too late. Brad's working harder than ever on the whiskey, but no one has any money to buy the things we're selling."

Ruby had a sudden sour taste in the back of her mouth. She had known the farm could not possibly be as safe from the Depression, as her father had claimed that first night.

"What are we going to do?" she asked.

"I don't know." Elizabeth drummed her fingers against the wood of her chair. "He's talking about taking out a loan from the Barbieris."

"*What*? No, that can't be." Her father had said countless times that the Barbieris were dangerous, not to be trusted. "What if we couldn't pay it back?"

"Exactly." Her sister pressed her lips together. "So, that's what you walked back into. Welcome home." She got to her feet. The folder in her lap slid to the ground, and a paper spilled out.

Ruby rushed to help pick it up. It seemed official. *The US Department of Labor* appeared at the top, and *United States of America* below that in a neat rainbow shape. It was followed by the title "Declaration of Intention," but Elizabeth grabbed it before she could read further.

"I apologize," her sister said, "but these cannot be lost."

"What's it for?" Ruby didn't realize the farm paperwork went beyond numbers and orders. It looked like each worker had to be documented, which was interesting. The idea of filling out all that information sounded important, and was definitely a part of the farm operations where Ruby would like to help.

"The servants. I think we have some new ones." Elizabeth avoided her gaze. "I have to file this. Reconcile it with our accounts."

"Why would we get new servants if we don't have any money?" Ruby asked.

"We have debt and complications." She gazed out over the fields. "I'm sure there are reasons."

The idea that they might not have enough food soon was a concern, without adding more mouths to feed.

"Where are they?" Ruby asked.

Her sister paused. "What?"

"The servants," she said. "I'd like to help work with them."

That was an area where Ruby's expertise would come in handy, not that she could share the information with her sister.

"Oh, I don't know." Elizabeth lowered her voice. "Uncle Peter brought them. Look, I shouldn't have said anything. They don't always stay. It depends."

If they were qualified or not, most likely. That was one issue Ruby had had to face in the beginning.

"Well, I'd be happy to help if you need me."

Ruby didn't want to just sit around the house. Everyone else had some sort of responsibility, and considering she was nearly twenty-one, it would be nice to have the same. Instead, everyone in her family still saw her as a child, because they knew nothing of her life away from home.

"Mmm." Elizabeth suddenly seemed distant. "I should get to it. Father wants to review everything after lunch."

Elizabeth headed inside, letting the screen door slam behind her. She seemed annoyed, and Ruby felt bad about pushing her. There was a hierarchy at Wind Thorne, and perhaps Elizabeth didn't want to share her work because it gave her a sense of importance at the farm. Fair enough, considering Ruby hadn't been here at all, but if they were anywhere near the point of collapse, she wanted to help.

Ruby sat a moment, watching Uncle Peter head out to the warehouse. The cow was back in the pasture, carving up the ground. Ruby considered the stretch of the farm before her. So much land, so much silence.

Picking up the flower she'd selected, Ruby followed her sister inside.

Chapter Eighteen

Wind Thorne, present day

"Didn't we start our day this way?" Lindsey asked, from her same grand-dame stance on the front porch. This time, she held up the key. "Well, maybe not with the key to the safe."

Part of her had worried that Otis would have other plans and she'd feel obligated to wait until morning. He did, as it turned out, have plans. He was at an art gallery two towns over, but the moment he heard she had the key, he said, "Give me thirty minutes. I'll be there." Lindsey filled the time making a cheese tray and packing a bottle of wine to drink by the fire, in case the safe proved to be empty.

Now that he was here, Lindsey leaned against the door as she watched him approach. He was all dressed up in a fitted navy suit with a black silk T-shirt that brought out his dark lashes and the blue of his eyes. His hair had been gelled into place, and as he swept in and gave her a kiss on the cheek, he smelled like a spicy cologne.

"You look . . . dashing," was all she could manage to say.

"Thanks." He held her gaze for a heart-pounding moment. "I don't know how I got so lucky to have someone like you call me, but to call me to explore a safe full of historical artifacts? That's incredible. I told you people who end up finding boxes of rocks are lucky, but I was just kind of saying that. I didn't realize how true it really was."

His charm was really growing on her.

"Well, I need your knowledge," she told him. "I'm hoping there's a diamond in there."

Finding the ring felt completely impossible, but to the other part of her, the part that had longed to see the diamond since she was a little girl, it made perfect sense. Of course she would find it; it was always meant to be that way.

"How was the art show?" she asked.

They walked into the house as if they lived there.

"Enjoyable." He adjusted his cuff links. "It's always interesting to see someone take their passion and turn it into something beautiful."

"I admired that about my mother," she said.

"Your work is stunning, too," he said, glancing at her. "I wonder if you ever intend to do something with it?"

Lindsey hesitated. "What work?"

"The bracelet." He stopped walking and shoved his hands into his pockets. "Look, I wasn't trying to be nosy. I saw you hide something that night, but I forgot about it until I went to get a glass of water. It was right there, in my sightline. I couldn't help but look because it was incredible. I'm sorry."

Lindsey thought of that moment on the walk this afternoon, when she'd conceptualized a piece—something she hadn't done in years. It had cost a lot to let go of that part of herself, back when her mother died. She wondered if Otis could see that about her.

"You're reading my mind, actually," she admitted. "I've considered getting back to metalwork ever since I found that bracelet. Since I've been here, really. Mainly because this is the place where my mother and I used to make things. I worked with her in her studio on the Lower East Side, too, on occasion. I haven't set foot in that in years, even though it's steps away from my apartment. It's all been on my mind."

Lindsey was surprised she'd shared so much, and she glanced at him. His gaze was trained on her, and he gave a slight nod.

"For whatever it's worth," he said, "I think we should put our time in the things that bring us joy. It might not be a practical way to live, but it's a lot more fun. You light up every time you see a beautiful piece. It's a part of you."

Lindsey wondered at the tug in her heart every time he was around.

"I'm surprised you'd notice that about me," she said.

"Oh, I notice more than you think." He shrugged. "It goes along with investing your time in the things that bring you joy." His grin was contagious. "Now, let's go open this safe."

Lindsey sat on the floor, cross-legged, next to Otis. He had taken off his suit jacket and draped it over the couch by the fireplace. They looked at each other, and she stuck the key in the lock. It fit.

"Step one, complete." She rested her hand on the cold metal. "I think we have to brace ourselves for the reality that the safe might be empty."

Otis grinned. "I'd rather brace myself for the possibility of what we're going to find when we open it."

Lindsey let out a breath. "Here goes. One, two, three."

With a sharp turn of the key, the lock clicked, and the door popped open. Her heart caught in her throat.

"Wow." She shined her flashlight inside, and her heart started to beat even faster. The safe was crammed with stacks of paperwork, jewelry, and what looked like bars of gold. "This is incredible."

Otis held up his hand before she reached in. "Can I make a suggestion? I think we should take a picture before we touch the safe, or maybe even film this so you can document it for your aunt. It's what we do sometimes when I'm looking at certain collections. It's a liability thing."

"Smart." Lindsey turned on the camera on her phone and handed it to Otis.

"You look," he said. "This is your big find."

It was a big find, indeed. The first thing she pulled out was a stack of paperwork. She flipped through it, describing each piece for the camera.

"This looks to be some sort of log about the workers," she said. "These are letters . . ." She stopped and skimmed over the first few words. "These are letters from World War One. They are similar to the ones Amrita gave me." Even though she wanted to stop right then to read them, to continue learning about Uncle Peter, there was so much more to look at. She reached for another paper, trying to avoid looking at the jewelry quite yet. "Here's another collection of paperwork." She sifted through it. "It has information about the cattle, the taxes, and . . ." Her heart skipped a beat.

Lindsey held the piece of paper in her hand, staring at it in disbelief. It was one of those moments when she wished her mother was by her side. In some ways, it felt like she already was.

"Otis, this is the design blueprint for the ring."

Lindsey set down the paperwork and reached into the safe, hands shaking. A black leather ring box was toward the very back. Slowly, she eased it open and her eyes smarted with tears. The diamond was a perfect circle of prisms, angles, and cuts so dazzling that it was impossible to tell where to look. The prongs were barely visible, cradling the diamond in such a way that the only thing visible was the cold vibrancy of the stone.

"This is it," she breathed, carefully taking it out of the case. "The one that's been missing for a century."

Otis lowered the camera for a quick moment to stare, then quickly put it back up.

Now that Lindsey had it in her hand, the legend that surrounded it made complete sense. This ring was spectacular, and she was unable to tear her gaze away.

"It is beautiful," Otis said. "But . . ." He held out his hand. "May I?"

Reluctantly, she watched as he shined the phone light on it.

"It's an incredible piece of history," he said. "It's just . . ."

The look on his face said everything.

"It's the fake." Lindsey's voice was flat. "Right?"

Otis cringed. "Thank you for not killing the messenger."

He handed it back to her, and she ran her finger over its smooth moonlike surface. It was stunning, regardless. Which meant the real ring had to be a true work of art.

"With something that valuable," Otis said, "it's logical they would have a piece of costume jewelry to protect it. I'd be interested in seeing the design blueprint, because that's what they would have given to the jeweler. They wouldn't have left him with the real ring unless they were standing right there with it. They didn't mark them with a serial number back then."

Lindsey pulled out the piece of paper with the design, and they studied it together, comparing it to the ring.

"It is fascinating." Each facet was represented and repeated in the copy. "My mother would have loved something like this. *I* love this."

She slid the ring onto her finger and stared at it, watching flashes of light dance in the deep patterns of the stone. "It's gorgeous. Like lightning on water." She met his gaze. "I can only imagine what you're thinking, watching me fawn over a piece of glass."

"You don't want to know what I'm thinking."

Lindsey's cheeks colored. "Hmm."

The day before, she hadn't known how to react to being called beautiful, before their lunch with Amrita. Even though they'd kissed by the fire, she'd still held him at arm's length, not sure quite how far she wanted to take this.

Lindsey fidgeted with the ring. "I'm having a hard time putting this back. My mother often said jewelry becomes interesting when it's a part of a person's life, a part of their story. This ring, it was a part of Ruby's story."

"Now it's a part of yours."

Lindsey ran her thumb over the smooth surface of the fake diamond. "I'm not sure what my story is, to be honest."

On one hand, she was an educated woman in her mid-thirties with a good job, great friends, and a lifetime of decent decisions. On the other hand, her choices lacked that spark of magic that would make her life well lived. Love was a big part of it, but until Otis had come along, that hadn't even been on her radar.

Still, they'd just met. It wasn't fair to put so much on him, especially considering all the issues in her family. But life could be cut short. She'd learned that much too young.

"What's on your mind?" Otis asked.

"I don't know," she said. "The weight of the history, I guess."

Lindsey set the ring back in its box and returned it to the safe. Carefully, she pulled out several emerald necklaces, one with rubies and sapphires, and two necklaces dripping in diamonds. She laid them out on the old Turkish rug and looked at Otis.

"What do you think?" she asked.

"Those look real," Otis said, handing her the camera. "May I?" He examined them closely. "These are really valuable."

They were lovely, too, in a style that would have been popular in the 1920s. Still, it didn't feel like much of a haul, considering the home's grandeur. If this was the entire collection, perhaps the family had not cared much for jewels or, more likely, had to sell them off during the Depression.

Otis took the camera back and aimed it at the safe. "Would you mind pulling out those gold bars? I'm so curious."

Lindsey grabbed one from the back. It was the size of a brick, and three times as heavy. She stared in awe at the soft, dull surface of the gold.

"Whoa," she said. "This is so beautiful. And illegal, right? They should have been turned in to the government. FDR's Executive Order 6102."

Otis laughed. "Numbers really are your thing."

"Well, I remember it from my economics class." Lindsey rested her hands on the cold bar. "By executive order, the gold was called back in 1933, I think, to try and stop the Depression. Since the government operated under the gold standard, they needed a certain amount of gold in the bank to back the dollar, but since people started to pull too much gold out of the banks, the government required everyone to sell it back. Looks like Wind Thorne forgot to follow that rule."

"They would definitely make an interesting historical display, unless you're still supposed to turn them in. We'll have to find out." Leaning down, he peered into the safe. "Did we get everything?"

"Yes. It's interesting that it's mostly paperwork." She tapped the stack sitting next to her. "This information alone is a jackpot."

The collection stood about eight inches high. There would be a wealth of information and history, and she could hardly wait to go through it all, page by page.

Lindsey gestured for him to point the camera at her. "I'm taking some of this out to read tonight," she said, holding up a handful of pages. "I'll put it back after I've made copies."

"Your aunt will be excited," Otis said. "Those necklaces and the paperwork are the biggest take, in my opinion."

"I wish the ring had been there." Lindsey peered into the safe, still hoping to find the actual diamond ring. Quickly, she ran her hand over the interior to be sure there weren't any hidden compartments. Finally, she went through all the jewelry boxes, searching for it. "Nope." She gestured at the remaining mountain of papers, the jewelry, and the gold bars. "Not a bad haul, though, considering."

"We should catalog it," Otis said. "Get an insurer in here. I'm sorry you didn't find your diamond. I could have lied to you . . ."

"Yes, you should have!" Lindsey laughed. "Given me a few minutes of glory. I wouldn't have known the difference, sadly."

"That's the point of costume jewelry," he said. "That one is a strong piece all on its own."

Lindsey took one last look and shut the door of the safe, then used the key to lock it. Otis turned off the camera. Together, they slid the safe back into the compartment in the desk and carefully put on the lid, followed by the wooden corners to conceal it.

Tomorrow, Lindsey planned to get everything copied and appraised, but for now, she was eager to get home and go through the paperwork she'd removed.

Otis stood up, then helped her to her feet. Heat rushed through her as he pulled her in close. The fabric on the lapel of his suit was soft as she rested her cheek against it.

Looking up at him, she said, "We still on for dinner Friday?"

"If you're interested," he said.

She smiled. "Well, what do you think?"

Chapter Nineteen

Wind Thorne, January 1931

Winter hit. The nights were long and dark at Wind Thorne. Ruby often lay awake, wondering if Chester was well and if he ever thought of her. The time in New York City felt like a vague memory at this point, something she might have imagined.

The Depression had shown up in town with the sudden intensity of a blizzard. It started with the abrupt closing of the general store, the one every farm within thirty miles relied on for basics like soap, sugar, and candles.

"We have to go." Her brother had burst in through the front door during dinner, shotgun in hand. "I've gotten word Don's General has shuttered up. They're going to be looting the store and taking the last of the supplies. We need the cattle feed."

Her father, who had been halfway through his beef stew and mashed potatoes, let out a burst of profanity. He ran to the front door, immediately followed by Brad and Glenn. The truck roared to life outside and sped down the front lane toward town.

Elizabeth stood, her hand resting on the back of the chair.

"The store." Her mother sounded a bit stunned. "What will we do without the store?"

Their grandmother folded her napkin and got to her feet. "Like rats on a sinking ship." Picking up her drink, she said, "I'd like to see the show."

Ruby's mother snapped to life and instructed the footman, Herisoa, to get the car ready. "Come along." Ruby bundled up against the cold and then headed for the front door, holding her mother's arm tight.

The women piled into the motorcar, with Ruby's grandmother up front with the driver. She was holding a glass of whiskey.

Ruby's mother stared out the window of the car as they drove. "Such fools. Trying to loot something where nothing will be left."

The five-minute drive to town brought them to Main Street, where word had spread fast. Farmers and families from miles around had converged. The boards had been ripped off the windows, and the front door hung open, flapping in the wind on one hinge. Men heaved out bags of feed, loading it into their wagons and the flatbeds of their trucks, shouting orders at one another.

A young boy rushed out cradling several jars of preserves, and as Ruby watched, one of the farmers ripped two of them from his hands, making him stumble and drop the rest. One shattered like blood across the dirt road. A man rushed up, fists raised, and the farmer left the jars before running back into the store.

Ruby's grandmother cackled, holding up her drink. Her faded eyes were sharp, her pupils so small they were frightening. "Go get something, girls. I want to see what you're made of."

"Let's leave." Elizabeth's voice shook. "I don't like this."

Ruby squeezed her hands tight. Her heart pounded as she remembered the fights for bread she'd seen in New York.

Their father walked out then, brandishing a shotgun. He fired once at the sky, and everyone fell silent. They took a step back as Glenn and her brother came through, carrying large bags of pasta, rice, and what looked like sugar.

"Thank goodness," her mother murmured as they put it in the truck. Their father stood guard as they went back for more.

Ruby's cheeks burned with shame. Outside the store stood mothers with small children clinging to their skirts, men with bent backs who no longer had the ability to work the land—the same people her family nodded at each week in church. Everyone was desperate, yet her father had muscled his way in and taken the most. It wasn't right, but Ruby could not say or do a thing without being cast out of the house altogether.

The drive back was bumpy, and she leaned her head against the icy pane of the window.

"That food, it isn't enough to last," Elizabeth said. "We should have taken more."

Ruby looked at her in disbelief. "It's more than the others got."

"I'm not worried about them; I'm worried about us." Her sister stared out the window. "I saw you when you came back. You were just bones."

"We have a farm." Her mother's words were short. "It gives us what we need."

"Right, but . . ." Elizabeth's voice went so quiet that Ruby had to lean in to hear it. "What about when we don't have that anymore?"

Her family was no closer to eliminating the tax debt on the farm than they had been before the winter, and her father had received a notice that Wind Thorne would be seized in a matter of months if the matter was not resolved. The men began meeting without Elizabeth. She still managed the paperwork and informed Ruby that, if anything, the situation had gotten worse.

The remaining general store was two towns over and half a day's ride away. It was still open but had started to refuse their family credit. That made it impossible to acquire basic needs to run the house, such as flour, soap, and sugar. Her brother continued to trade barrels to keep them fed, but as time went on, the remaining whiskey in the warehouse was getting so low that Ruby worried they'd be unable to trade anything at all.

Not to mention that the remainder was constantly consumed by the rest of her family. Then, they'd thrash about with theories and ideas of what to do, while her father took action. He hunted, bringing home geese and rabbit so they could have meat on the table. He didn't want to touch the cattle, as he saw the herds as their last resort for survival. Yet keeping the animals fed was a burden in itself.

No matter how many deals Brad made, he couldn't acquire enough feed to make up for the mistake Glenn made in ordering the equipment needed to harvest the hay. The cattle suffered, and when Ruby took walks up to the pasture, she noticed that they'd started to show signs of starvation. Their fur, normally so smooth, stood up in matted clumps. The ground was completely shorn beneath the muddied snow, and they stood cold and tense, heads hung low and their backs arched, as if trying to escape the rumbling pains in their stomachs.

Uncle Peter was often out there as Ruby walked. One time, he stood at the side of the pasture with Mary, feeding her from a bagful of snow-crusted grass he'd plucked from the front lawn. "It's not enough," he called when she paused on the frozen tundra, cheeks flushed with cold. "It's something, though. To keep her fed."

Ruby raised her hand and kept walking. In those moments, she wondered if her anger for Peter was misguided. Things had not been easy for him. One night, she'd heard him ranting to Brad while they warmed their hands over a bonfire in the front yard. Peter described the sound of the shell landing next to him in the trenches and how the body of his friend had protected everything but Peter's leg during the violent explosion. He moved too close to the fire as he told the story, and Brad nearly had to wrestle him away from the flames.

It wasn't that Ruby believed him to be a good person, not really. But the fear that she'd had for him was less, because she understood that somewhere inside him, his sorrow ran deeper than rage.

The need to ration their food heightened with the deadline for the taxes. It slowly became common knowledge that her father planned to meet with the Barbieri family. Her mother's expression became sour and accusatory, and her father often sat outside under a tree, looking defeated.

Too many nights passed with Ruby staring out at the sky, feeling completely alone. Her sister no longer had time for her, on top of her responsibilities and her troubles with Glenn. It made Ruby miss her friendship with Chester and Millie, because she'd always had someone to talk to. Here, she didn't, and the nights were more frightening than ever with her worry about what might happen if her father went through with the loan.

It would only be a temporary fix, leading to bigger problems down the road. Even though her family had always skirted the edges of crime, no one considered their family dangerous. People knew not to cross her father, to stay out of his way, but it wasn't as if he was out there committing crimes. That could change if her family became indebted to the Barbieris.

Back in New York City, Millie had been besotted with the idea of bootleggers and gangsters. The Barbieris were constantly in the paper for terrible illegalities, and Ruby's cheeks would color as Millie waxed on about how romantic it must be to know someone in the bootlegging trade.

Chester had waggled his eyebrows at Ruby more than once, as if to say, *Go on, tell her*, but Ruby refused. Her family wasn't like the gangsters in the paper. Now they might have to be, if her father was foolish enough to make this deal.

Ruby rested her forehead against the glass of the window. The outlines of the trees were etched in shadows against a moonless sky. It was so dark, which made her thoughts feel even darker, until a sudden idea brought a glimmer of light. Quietly, she moved to the writing table and quickly penned a letter.

Everyone was asleep as she crept down the stairs and made her way to the forest. With careful steps, she picked her way through the darkness, avoiding the sticks that snapped and echoed in the silence. She made her way across the small bridge that led to the Mensley house, nearly slipping on the light frost that covered the wood.

Ruby hadn't been back this way in nearly a year, because Chester was still not home. She had not spoken to his father, even though she'd spotted him a couple of times working in the forest. Now, though, she stopped in the clearing at the edge of the woods, clutching the letter.

It had to be near one in the morning, and the Mensley house was dark. For a brief moment, she imagined it was one of those late nights where she and Chester had sat outside in Manhattan, looking at the city and talking, but at a sudden sound in the forest, she walked swiftly across the yard and to the front porch.

Ruby had no idea what Chester's father thought of her. She had no idea what he'd do with the information in the letter. She had to write to him, though, because it was the one thing that might help her family survive. Quickly, she slid the letter under the door.

Heart pounding, she'd just made her way back into the forest when the front door creaked open. The silhouette of a man stepped outside, and she ducked down behind a tree.

"Ruby?" a voice whispered. "Is that you?"

She froze. *"Chester?"*

Ruby flew from behind the tree and across the yard. She was half worried she was wrong, that the voice had indeed been his father. But no, Chester was running down the steps toward her.

They stopped inches away and stared at each other. For some foolish reason, Ruby's eyes sparked with tears.

He let out a chuckle that was so familiar, so Chester, that she put her hand to her heart.

"I wasn't sure I'd ever see you again," she said.

"Oh, Ruby," he said, quietly. "Knowing I would see you again is the only thing that's kept me going at all."

Chapter Twenty

New York, present day

Lindsey eased open her eyes.

Otis.

The thought hit her, and she pulled the sheets close.

The two had left Wind Thorne once they'd closed up the safe. They'd kissed furiously against the side of the car, beneath the tree in the yard, and then at the front door of her aunt's house. There, Lindsey had hesitated, not sure whether she was ready to let him in.

"I can't do this if it's only for tonight," he said.

It was the push she needed to put on the brakes.

"It's getting late."

Hurt crossed his face, but he'd nodded. They'd stood in silence for a brief moment. His eyes were so blue, and everything about him pulled her in, but slowly, she dropped his hand. The tears fell only once his car had headed back down the driveway and she was back to being alone.

Now Lindsey stared out at the morning through the curtains, watching the dawn unfold. The birds were chirping, and the mist danced in unfurling wisps. It was strange to think she could have been sharing this view, maybe nestled in the crook of his arm, but it had been the right choice to end the night when they did. Lindsey was already too invested in their developing relationship, and that was dangerous.

It was one thing to date. The guys she'd gone out with over the years were good people, but none of them had ever left her with a sense of loss when the relationship had run its course. But Otis had captivated her since the moment they'd met, and she didn't quite know what to do with that.

The more she learned about him, the more she looked forward to spending time with him. That was an uncomfortable place to be, because she didn't need additional heartache. If her relationship with her father and brother could fall apart so easily, then how could she believe in a lasting connection with someone she barely knew?

Besides, Lindsey had more than enough to focus on, given the discovery of the safe. She'd wanted to discuss it with Aunt Petra the night before, but the time difference had made it impossible. Now, relieved to put her mind to something other than relationships, she grabbed her cell from the bedside table and placed the call.

Once Lindsey had explained what they'd found, Aunt Petra gave a very uncharacteristic shout. "This is wonderful!" she cried. "Are you sure?"

Lindsey laughed. "Am I sure the safe was full? Yes! We took a video, so you can see everything."

"How incredible," Aunt Petra said. "Please send it. I can't wait to see the jewels or learn what's in the paperwork. Will you make copies? There could be so much in there with historical significance. Plenty to keep you occupied until I get back."

Aunt Petra wasn't due back for more than a month, but Lindsey was inclined to agree. The stack of paperwork was incredibly dense. There were pages of information on the general workings of the farm, along with details about the family, several official-looking forms, and even a few local bills. It was all interesting, and would certainly create an in-depth chapter into the history of Wind Thorne.

"I agree," Lindsey said. "Let me send you some photo files. I can—"

The email alert chimed, and she glanced at it. "Oh. Hold on."

It was an all-hands call from her boss. Quickly, she skimmed the email.

"I actually . . ." Lindsey hopped out of bed and started to get dressed. "I have to go to the city. Turns out a presentation we planned to give in July is happening today."

"Oh, dear." Aunt Petra sounded worried. "You can't possibly be prepared for that."

"I am, actually," she said, quickly brushing her hair. "The client is in China, and they asked us to hold the presentation until their visit in July. They need to do it virtually, now, because someone's trying to buy them out. The meeting isn't until seven tonight because of the time difference, so there's still plenty of time to get there and to prep. My boss wants us all to meet at the office."

"Well, be safe on the drive." Aunt Petra's voice was hesitant. "There won't be time to get everything appraised and insured before you go?"

When Lindsey had asked for permission to be here for the summer, she'd promised her boss she could be in the city within a few hours' time. If she couldn't uphold that, she'd lose the option to work remotely. She'd probably lose her job, too, considering the importance of the client. The items in the safe were exciting, but they would still be there tomorrow.

"I wish I could." She glanced at the clock. "I really have to get there."

"I understand," Aunt Petra said. "I'll have security keep an extra-close watch on the house, but considering everything's been hidden for a hundred years, it should be fine one more day."

"My thoughts exactly," Lindsey said. "To be honest, I'm willing to bet Barrett and Jack were alone in the room with this safe at least a hundred times and had no idea."

Her aunt laughed. "I bet you're right."

Once they'd hung up, Lindsey threw together an overnight bag with her toothbrush, laptop, and the paperwork from the safe before getting on the road. It didn't bother her to make the trip, because she'd planned on heading into the city at some point soon, anyway, to stake a claim on her mother's final pieces.

That is, if her father hadn't gotten there first.

Her mother's sales agent must have told him about her phone call, because her father had never tried so insistently to connect. She'd sent him to voicemail on three different occasions, and after that, her brother had tried to get in touch, too. Neither had reached out to Aunt Petra, so it wasn't as if there was some emergency.

Finally, Lindsey fired off a text to both of them:

> I'm on vacation for the next couple weeks and can't get on the phone. Is it something urgent?

Her father replied back:

> Not urgent. However, I would like to speak to you at your earliest convenience.

The formality was annoying, so she didn't respond with anything other than a thumbs-up emoji. It might be rude, but she still couldn't believe her father hadn't bothered to discuss any of this with her. She did not plan to talk to him until she had the final pieces of her mother's collection in hand.

Lindsey slid on her sunglasses as the first rays peeked over the trees lining the roads back to the city. It was a strange feeling to leave Wind Thorne to return home for such a brief period, like being suspended somewhere in time.

She headed out onto the main road, the paperwork from the safe in a file next to her on the front seat, alongside Ruby's diaries. Lindsey had grabbed them at the last minute. A few letters from Ruby were also in the stack of paperwork.

She'd written the letters while she was in New York, claiming to work as a governess. Her tone was light and breezy, but something about it rang false, and Lindsey looked forward to reading them in her cozy apartment, with the view of the city in the background.

With some luck, maybe she could figure out what Ruby was really doing during the time she was away.

Lindsey's apartment was the fifth floor of a walk-up in an old brownstone. It was in a part of the Lower East Side that had been affordable back when her mother bought it. Lindsey returned with enough time to shower, change, and meet a friend for a bowl of soup at her favorite Thai restaurant before heading into work.

Her office building was a sleek space in the Financial District. It was on the forty-fifth floor and had a view of the Hudson, and the break room never ran out of snacks, since everyone worked remotely. It felt like a reunion when the team actually showed up at the office, and true to form, they spent the first fifteen minutes catching up before they buckled down to prep for the online meeting.

Once it started, Lindsey's boss spoke first, then Lindsey talked in depth about her analysis. Specifically that, based on the metrics, it wasn't necessary or advisable to sell the company unless they wanted to, and now they had the data to prove it. She was delighted to see the relief on their faces at the news. Moments after the meeting was over, the company put out a press release stating they had no plans to sell.

Lindsey celebrated with her team at the sushi restaurant down the block. On the walk home, staring up at the buildings, she wondered what her father would say if he ever learned she had influenced the decision of such a large business. He would be surprised, most likely, and maybe even proud.

It bothered her to realize how much that would mean to her.

The next morning, in that moment between being asleep and awake, it took her a moment to remember why she was at her apartment instead of at Wind Thorne. She planned to head back as soon as she'd acquired her mother's artwork from the storage unit, but she couldn't do that until the building opened.

In the meantime, she settled into her favorite spot on the white overstuffed couch, tucked her feet beneath her, and read the papers she'd brought with her from the safe.

The operations of the farm piqued her interest. She decided it would be best to compile the data into a spreadsheet to better analyze it for the grant, and she added that to her mental checklist of things to do when she got back to Wind Thorne. Taking a sip of coffee, she moved on to the letters Ruby had sent back home.

There were only six total:

> Dear Family,
> Merry Christmas to you! I send tidings of Thanksgiving, as well as a deep longing to be back at Wind Thorne during the coziest season of the year. I can practically smell the pine boughs that decorate downstairs. Elizabeth, I would love to sneak a mulled wine with you. It has been quite an interesting experience celebrating Christmas with this family in New York. The parties are so elaborate and the gowns like nothing I've ever seen. Elizabeth, you would be mesmerized. I do hope that you have a merry Christmas and that one day we will be able to celebrate together. Until then, I am thinking fondly of you. Ruby

Lindsey was interested to hear Ruby's cheerful tone. It was hard to tell if she missed being home.

> Dear Family,
> I apologize it has taken me so long to write. We have been busy on holiday in Europe. The children were sick nearly the entire time, and then I fell ill, as well, and spent most of the time laid up in bed. Not exactly the holiday I'd been hoping for, so I didn't see hardly any of the sights. The good news is that the family often travels, so I'll have another experience to see it all.

That one gave Lindsey pause. She was surprised to learn that the family was kind enough to allow Ruby to stay in bed instead of doing her job. Lindsey would have thought that the governess would have been expected to get out of bed and get to it, no matter what.

Feeling suspicious, she read on:

> Dear Family,
> Happy spring to you! You are often on my mind. Why do you never write? I've sent several letters to you and have not received a reply back. Perhaps there is some issue with the mail? I do not want to trouble my employers, so I have asked a neighbor to collect my mail. I will only ask for her help briefly, so I just want to know that all is well and that you have heard from me.

> Dear Family,
> I was so happy to receive your letter. It seems that there has indeed been some issue with receiving mail at the address that I have given you because I did not receive the ones you had mentioned. I have sent you the corrected address and am so delighted that we have worked this out. It is not costly to pay my neighbor

for her help, and I am proud to say that I earn a good wage. I do hope that one day you will come visit me in the city.

Dear Family,
Watching the children play reminds me of the many times that Elizabeth and I would play together outside. Making daisy chains, milking the cows, and catching butterflies are all things my charges do not get to experience. Elizabeth, I hope you are doing well and enjoying your marriage. I wish I could have been there, and I think often of you.

Dear Family,
Forgive the short notice. I was looking forward to seeing Mother when you come to town for business, but I've just been informed by my employer that we will be headed to Europe again during that time. I am so sorry and hope that we can try again one day.

The letters told a story, but Lindsey was certain they only told the story Ruby wanted her family to hear. It didn't make sense that she would have a friend collect her mail. If she was indeed working as a governess, perhaps the family she'd worked for was not nearly as nice as she'd tried to make them seem.

The letters had still been in the envelope, and Lindsey considered the address that Ruby had given. It was over by the park, but it didn't sound quite right. She pulled it up on Google Maps and, when it didn't appear there, tried to find it on a map from the 1920s. Well, that explained it. The family couldn't write her back because the first address didn't exist. However, the corrected address wasn't on any of the envelopes, so she had no idea where it was located.

Getting to her feet, Lindsey looked at her watch. It was close enough to the time the storage building would open that she could get dressed and head over, but she couldn't help but worry at what she'd find. It was one thing to imagine acquiring her mother's final pieces, but quite another to do so.

Much like Ruby's letters, Lindsey had painted a rosy picture of what it all would look like. The artwork would be there, she would sit in reverence, and she'd feel a connection to her mother all over again. In reality, that might not be the story at all.

It was very possible the work wouldn't even be there, that her father would have taken it. Or that the collection, since it was unfinished, wouldn't spark any feeling in Lindsey beyond a sense of injustice that her mother had never had the opportunity to finish it. That she'd walk out of there feeling worse than before, because the opportunity to connect with her mother would be long gone.

Lindsey pressed her fingers against her temples and stared out at the treetops. She had no idea how any of this would go or how it would make her feel, but the truth of the matter was that there was only one way to find out.

She headed out the door to take a look.

Chapter Twenty-One

Upstate New York, 1931

It was the middle of the night. Standing there, talking to Chester, was dangerous. Still, Ruby could not bring herself to leave his side.

"Let's go somewhere safe," she said. "If we're found out . . ."

It would be nothing for her father to pull out his shotgun in the name of her honor.

Chester's expression was grim. "My father told me not to see you. Not for some time."

Tears spilled down her cheeks. The loneliness of the farm was something she'd absorbed, something she'd accepted. Being away from Chester was possible when he was far away, but she couldn't just walk back home, climb into bed, and pretend he wasn't nearby.

"Please," she whispered. "We can go to one of the abandoned distilleries."

Chester tugged on a tree branch, watching her. Finally, he nodded. "Give me a moment." He ran inside, and she waited, arms wrapped tight around her body, worried he would not come back.

The door opened and he was back, a bag over his shoulder.

"Come on," he said. "We have to be quick."

The distillery Ruby had in mind was as far back on their property line as they could get. It was buried deep in the woods but close to the road, with a mile-long path leading in and out. They walked to it at a quick pace, careful to keep as silent as a pair of foxes. She could tell he was on high alert, his body tense, ready to explain away the reason they were together.

It had been years since Ruby had been back to this warehouse, long before she had left, and she worried it wasn't as remote as she remembered. Her family might have put it to use again, trying to increase production as much as possible to pay off their debts.

She suddenly stumbled over a dip in the pathway, and Chester caught her arm. Warmth spread through her. He lit a match and shone it for a split second on the road, like the flash of a firefly. Deep ruts roughed up the mud, as if a large truck had passed through. She hesitated, unsure whether or not to continue.

"Come on." He hadn't let go of her arm.

They made their way to the small warehouse, and Ruby was relieved to see only a broken door keeping it closed. Once it shut behind them, Chester took a board and rigged it underneath, probably so it couldn't be opened from the outside without a loud warning.

It was much warmer inside, and the smell of damp stone and old wood was all around. Chester flicked on the flashlight. Ruby winced at the cobwebs and the fluttering noise somewhere down the stairs.

"You don't use this one anymore, right?" he asked.

"No. I saw a truck out here a while back, but I mentioned it to my sister, and she said they don't use it, that the driver was probably just looking for a shaded spot to take a break."

Chester nodded. "Then let me go first to make sure the stairs will hold."

In some of the warehouses closer to the farm, the stairs were made of stone, but these were wood and had seen better days. They shifted slightly beneath Chester's weight but didn't crack.

"It's safe," he called. "I'll shine the light."

Ruby went down the stairs as quickly as possible.

Chester set up the flashlight to illuminate the cavernous space. The floors were planked with wood, and the walls reinforced with wooden beams structured to avoid a cave-in overhead. The room was half the size of her bedroom back home but still capable of storing several barrels. It was one of the first spaces her family had ever used to produce whiskey.

"I have a confession." Chester ran his hand over one of the wooden storage shelves, then wiped away the dirt on his trousers. "I used to come here all the time. Sneak in."

"What?" Ruby was shocked he'd take the risk. "Why?"

Chester shrugged. "Adventure. I needed a clubhouse." He sat cross-legged on the floor. "Why did they leave it?"

"Too close to the road," she said. "If the police decided to do a raid—which they wouldn't, considering how much my father has paid them over the years—it would be first on the list. The most interesting thing about it is . . ." She walked over to the wall, constructed floor to ceiling with several worn boards. It only took a small tug to pull aside one of the boards and reveal a long, dark hallway.

"The tunnels." Chester smiled. "My favorite part."

Her mouth dropped open. "You've been back there, too?" She resecured the board and took a seat on the ground.

"Of course. I had to see what they were."

The tunnels had been built when her grandfather was still alive. He had made his living from farming but also mined for sand to supply to the cement makers. Her father continued building on them to make an underground world for the whiskey production, and Ruby had spent hours exploring every inch of them.

"What would you have done if my father caught you?" she asked, studying him. He looked older, with deeper lines in his face.

"I would have been stuck working for him, I guess." Chester leaned back against the wall. "If he didn't kill me first."

The two looked at each other. Ruby was tired, but her body buzzed like the lamps in the city. So much had happened since she'd been back, but the current of missing this connection, this type of conversation, had run through it all.

"How has it been?" he asked. "Being back home?"

Ruby let out a slow breath. "Complicated."

Everything that had happened since he'd left her at the train station came tumbling out, including Uncle Peter, Elizabeth, and the debt on the farm. She left out the loneliness, the ache that she'd felt at his absence, but didn't hold back on her fears. Finally, she dropped her eyes in shame.

"That letter under the door," she admitted, "was to tell your father what was happening. You once said he had money saved from when your grandfather died, so I asked him for help."

It had seemed like a good idea when she wrote the letter, but now, she wasn't so sure. What if Chester thought she was trying to take advantage of his family?

To her relief, he gave her a vehement nod. "Good. You can't get mixed up with the Barbieris. There's no going back. Besides, you'd lose the farm for sure. I've heard too many stories where they give people help, but then in the end, they take everything."

"I know." She lifted her chin. "My father wouldn't even see it coming. He stands too much by honor. He'd expect that if he borrowed the money and returned it, that would be that."

"Honor?" Chester echoed.

They looked at each other, and Ruby couldn't help but laugh.

"Well, his version of it, anyway," she said.

Her father had no qualms about hurting other people. Lying, cheating, and stealing all chalked up fine in his book. Yet he stood hard and fast on one principle: "Do what you say you're going to do." To him, the man who would break a business deal was a man with no honor.

"Your father certainly has his own view of the world," Chester said, fiddling with a tie on his boot. "It's served him well, in many ways. And I'm sure it's caused you pain, in many others."

Ruby looked down at her hands. This was one of the many things she'd missed about talking with Chester. The honesty. The ability for both of them to say what they truly thought, without fear of repercussions.

"What about you?" she asked. "I've thought of you so many times."

His eyes met hers. "You did?"

"Every minute."

Silence fell between them, and he held her gaze. Her body flushed with embarrassment at the confession, but more, that he didn't react. In fact, it didn't seem to matter much to him at all.

Then he said, "It was hard to know you were back and that I couldn't be. I thought of my father, a lot, managing all this on his own. It was hard to think how lonely he must be, and now that I've come back, it feels like Elliot should be here."

Ruby's breath caught. "You're back for good?"

"Yes." His eyes met hers again, and he looked away. "Elliot's doing well. My father has gotten many letters from him."

She thought back to the stricken look on his brother's face, that day in the boarding hall. "What does he say about being in the navy?"

Chester gave her a half smile. "He likes it. Hard work, and the guys respect him. The food is excellent, he said."

"What about you?" Ruby asked. Chester's face looked thinner than it had in the city, but his shoulders seemed strong. "Have you been able to eat?"

She wanted to ask him if he'd sold the ring or if he still had it, but she didn't want him to think that she cared more for it than him. If he'd had to use it, she would be grateful that it had kept him alive.

"Yes, I've managed. I took the train north until I could find some logging work. They had food at the camps, decent wages. I settled into a place that had beds for all of us and sent some letters to my father and Elliot. I didn't mind the hard work, but the pests and the danger on the job started to get to me."

Ruby remembered some of the articles she'd read out loud from the newspaper, about the logging industry. Some of the stories were horrible. She shuddered to think that all this time, Chester had been at such risk. It explained the weight that seemed to hover over him, the fact that he seemed older, somehow.

"There were some accidents." His voice was quiet. "My father kept telling me to come home. One of my chaps got hurt real bad. Didn't make it. I decided it was a good time to go."

Ruby's heart ached to see him in pain. It reminded her of that day in the forest after Indira's death, when his face was bloodied and bruised, but the only thing he could think about was his brother.

"I'm so sorry," she said. "You must miss him something awful."

"He was a good one." He avoided her gaze. "Don't meet too many of those, you know?"

She nodded. Then, the emotion of it all caught up to her, and she buried her head in her hands.

It had been so painful to part from him in Manhattan, to leave him with only the ring and the hope that somehow, he'd manage to survive. She'd come here, like a coward, and he'd had no choice but to stay away, for fear everyone would know that they'd left together. That whole time, he'd been risking his life, working in terrible conditions. He—instead of his friend—could have been the one who didn't make it.

"Ruby, what is it?" he asked.

She squeezed her eyes tight against the tears, fighting to control her feelings. It wouldn't be fair to say the very thought of him facing any amount of pain was enough to break her in two, that she loved him with every breath in her body, because there was nothing he could do about it. Even if he felt the same, he had made a commitment to Eleanor Cook years ago, and she knew full well he would uphold that.

"Ruby," he said, quietly, "have I upset you?"

"No. I'm just so glad to have you back with me." The agony of saying the words nearly broke her, because it would never be the same. Not like it was in the city. "It was one thing to not know what was happening, but now, to think that you could have been the one . . ." She lifted her head and found him staring at her with an unreadable expression. In spite of her resolution, she said, "I couldn't bear it."

Chester got to his feet. "We should get back."

They walked in silence through the forest, and Ruby was angry at herself for telling him that, for making their situation harder than it needed to be. Once they were in the clearing by his house, he stopped and studied her for a long moment.

"I'm sorry I said that," she told him. "You were a good friend to me, that's all. I missed you."

"I feel the same." He shoved his hands in his pockets and gave her a hesitant smile. "Do you want to meet tomorrow afternoon? We can sit and talk in the forest across the road. No one will see us there."

His smile filled her heart. "I would love that."

For the next week, Chester waited for her every day in the clearing in the forest in the late afternoon. Each moment with him was a revelation as they talked about their time in Manhattan, their lives, dreams, and disappointments.

Chester knew so much about so many things. She loved the moments he would point out a piece of nature, like a small hawk resting on a treetop, waiting to fly across the field. When he would discuss different variations of rotating the crops to rest the soil, a technique he'd learned from his father that had served them well on their farm.

Everything she saw after their talks seemed to flow through the filter of Chester, as if he were always sitting right next to her.

Chester was a brilliant farmer. He had learned so much from his father and from the books he'd devoured from that massive library at the house where they'd worked in the city. Because of his reading, Chester knew of maps, weather patterns, and changes in farming that few people in this area of the country had the time and freedom to learn about. It was hard to not get lost in the fantasy of what it would be like if the two of them could work together to run the farm. Of course, those thoughts could not be brought out in the light.

One day, they sat on a thick wool blanket on the ground reading poetry. The Robert Frost book she'd brought from the library in her home was passed back and forth like a drink, each reading a poem out loud. Chester was near the end of "Stopping by Woods on a Snowy Evening" when his words faltered.

"What?" she asked.

"This line." He closed the book and ran his hand over his face. "It reminds me of you."

"It does?" Her heart started to pound. "Read it."

"No."

Ruby tried to swipe the book from him, and laughing, he held it up high in the air. She reached for it and lost her balance, crashing into him. He steadied her, their faces close together, and time seemed to stand still. He was the one to pull away, fumbling to find the page once again.

"Here," he said. "It's this part."

> The woods are lovely, dark and deep,
> But I have promises to keep . . .

"What does that have to do with me?" she asked.

"I don't know." He picked at the edge of the blanket. "I can't explain it."

The words echoed inside her mind, and she sat in silence, her face still warm from being so close to his. It meant everything to spend time with him; it had put purpose back into her life. She heard the message, though: Being with her felt dishonest.

Besides, what was the point of spending this time together, only to lose him to someone else? Loneliness had haunted her before his return, and now, she couldn't stand the thought of feeling that way again. She wouldn't have a choice, though, once he married Eleanor Cook.

It was inappropriate to think these thoughts. Yet, it was more inappropriate for her to imagine he belonged to her, when he didn't. Would he understand if she told him that? Could he feel the same?

Like always, Chester seemed to know in an instant that she was troubled.

"What is it?" he asked, closing the book.

Ruby squeezed her cold hands together. It wasn't smart to talk to him about this. It could ruin everything. Still, she couldn't continue pretending he wasn't in her thoughts every second of every day, and had been ever since they'd left New York City.

"Ruby, please." His voice was low. "Tell me what's wrong."

"I'm so glad you're back," she admitted, quietly. "I often think about the time we spent together in the city. It was like we were family."

He got to his feet. "Ruby, I—we—" He turned away and stood in silence.

"'We' what?" She got to her feet and stood in front of him, her arms crossed. "Tell me."

Reaching for her hands, he said, "You can't think of me in that way. I understand there have been moments where we both . . . but those were moments. They're not something that would be smart or safe to—"

"It wasn't a moment to me."

He dropped her hands. "It's not the same between us here. It can't be. I don't think we should keep meeting like this."

Her body burned with heartache and shame.

The past few years, Ruby had spent so much time thinking of him and hoped he might feel the same, but as it turned out, she was alone in all of it. They'd been friends, and he'd watched out for her, but it had meant something different to him.

Silently, they made their way to the road and went their separate ways. She slipped back home and up the stairs alone, as if Chester had never been a part of her life at all.

The next morning, Ruby woke feeling restless, groggy, and unsure why she was upset. The sun streamed through the curtains, and it came back to her in a rush.

What had she done?

Getting into her feelings about him had been a mistake. Selfish, really. Chester was engaged. She knew full well that talking about all of that would complicate their relationship and make it hard to spend time together. On some level, maybe that's what she wanted, because it was too painful to be around him and maintain a level of polite formality.

On the other hand, it would be an absolute crime to give up the one person who meant more to her than anybody because she couldn't maintain a certain level of decency. She did not want to lose his friendship, and she was determined to tell him that.

Ruby grabbed a hat and a fishing pole and headed up to the river. She picked a spot farther up than she'd usually go but that could be seen through the trees from Chester's house. She hoped that if he saw her outside, he would come see her. No one would find it suspicious for her to have two words with the neighbor boy if he happened to walk by, especially when he'd been away for so long.

Her hands trembled as she cast the line. The metal of the rod was cold in her hand and made a squeaking sound as she reeled it back in as slow as possible, hoping she wouldn't actually catch something. She fished until her face was chapped with cold and her arm ached, but his house remained dark. Frustrated, she finally reeled in the line and walked back home.

Later that day, Ruby went for a walk through the fields, taking her time, hoping to bump into him so she could apologize. She headed to the abandoned distillery in hopes that perhaps he might be there. Foolish, since he'd clearly stated they needed to stop meeting altogether.

At the same time, she couldn't help but wonder if he had feelings for her, too. That night outside his father's house, he'd said, *Knowing I would see you again is the only thing that's kept me going at all.* He cared for her, no question, but he was also an honorable man. It wouldn't be right to keep spending time with Ruby, now that she'd spoken her feelings. Especially since he'd promised to marry someone else.

The distillery door was heavy as Ruby pushed it open, and she blinked in the sudden darkness. It looked different in the daylight, with the cracks in the wooden walls letting the sunshine spill in once the door was shut. The cobwebs were still there, though, and the dust. She made her way down the steps, clinging to the railing, and settled into the spot on the ground next to the wall where she'd sat with Chester that first night.

Ruby buried her head in her hands, trying to fight back the sorrow coursing through her.

Every time she thought of the way their eyes had met after that one poem, Ruby couldn't help but think that he felt something for her, too. It would be impossible to have the connection they did, the friendship and history they'd shared, without feeling something.

Ruby rested her head back against the wall. She had stayed up half the night crying and was tired from the disappointment of it all. Closing her eyes, she decided to take a short rest, in hopes that when she opened her eyes, he would be there.

But when Ruby opened her eyes a short time later, blurry with sleep, the man standing over her wasn't Chester.

Chapter Twenty-Two

New York City, present day

Lindsey slid open the door to the storage unit, the hinges screaming in protest. Or maybe that was her heart, because she was still not convinced it was right to do this. The pieces might not be there at all, and if they were, she still wasn't certain she was ready to see them.

Knowing there was still one final thing out there that Lindsey had not yet discovered was a way to keep her mom alive. But once Lindsey saw these pieces, that would be it. Her mother would truly be gone.

Lindsey rested her hand on the cool metal of the doorframe. It wasn't too late to walk away, but the longer she waited, the more likely it became that her father would remember these pieces and take them. He might have done so already. With that in mind, she squared her shoulders and walked in.

The room was small and clean. The floor had hardly any dust, and the only objects in the room were three black heavy-duty storage containers with yellow handles. If her father had already been here, the containers would only be filled with scraps.

Lindsey's hands shook as she lifted the yellow latches. The smell of plastic wrap hit her, along with relief, as she recognized the dull gleam of the metal. Carefully, she pulled out the closest piece.

It was packed in bubble roll and cellophane, with tape wrapped around it. Her intent had been to take a trip down memory lane right here and now, but the pieces were so well wrapped that she would be better served to keep them that way for the drive back out of the city. Still, she had to look at just one.

She lifted out the nearest package and carefully sliced it open with the scissors she'd brought. The object was lightweight. Earrings, maybe?

The gold necklace rolled out into her hand, and she let out a small yelp of excitement. The shape and pattern of the necklace was an exact replica of the stonework that lined the bottom of each window at Wind Thorne.

Lindsey let out a breath as she shut the door to her apartment, all three cases brought up and safely stowed away. She'd struggled to carry each one up the stairs one landing at a time, careful to keep eyes on the others. The bins were heavy, and she was sweating through her shirt, but it was well worth it. Her assumption had been correct—her mother's last collection was based on Wind Thorne.

Up in her apartment, Lindsey lined the black storage containers neatly against the wall and collapsed on the couch. Her emotions were on overdrive, and before she hit the road, she wanted to call her father. Being here, seeing her mother's work, had made her feel brave enough to do it.

He picked up the phone on the fourth ring. She had just told him that she would not be available for some time. It wasn't a surprise that he sounded cautious and, in spite of the niceties, annoyed.

"Lindsey." Like always, his voice was loud across the line. "Good to hear from you."

Lindsey got right to it. "I assume Mikel let you know we spoke. I know about your plan for Mom's work."

"He told me you called." There was a commotion on the other end of the line, and her father seemed to cover the receiver. Back on the line, he said, "It's incredibly busy here today. There will be interruptions."

"That's fine." Lindsey cleared her throat. "I've had an extremely difficult time in the past few months trying to understand some of the choices you've made regarding my mother."

The phone went silent, and it took her a moment to realize she was on mute. Lindsey pressed her palm against the window in frustration, wondering if he was having an entire side conversation. The background noise started up again, and she couldn't keep the anger out of her voice.

"I can call back," she said. "It doesn't sound like it's a good time to talk."

Lindsey was prepared to hang up, but he said, "Hold on. I was just telling my secretary to give me ten minutes to talk to my daughter." In the background, a door shut and it was silent. "I'm here."

"Now I'm your 'daughter'?" Lindsey said. "I don't remember that same courtesy when you took the family trip to Snowmass without me."

She had so many grievances against him that she was surprised this was the one that had come flying out. But it was the most recent—other than selling off her mother's lifework piece by piece, of course.

"The ski trip?" her father said. "Lindsey, we did not intentionally exclude you. It was a guys' trip, and there was some sort of last-minute issue with the place I had booked in Aspen. A pipe burst or something. I called over to Snowmass because I knew the owner would remember me and get us in. I was trying to save the trip."

The apology was disarming. Granted, he hadn't actually apologized, but it's what he meant, in his own way.

"Now, as for the licensing of your mother's work, that's a decision I've made." His tone was abrupt. "It's a monetary choice."

Lindsey's stomach dropped. It might have been tolerable if he'd said he was doing this to keep her mother's legacy alive or to share her art with the world. Instead, it was in fact about money.

"Is there some sort of monetary need that I should know about?" she demanded, her voice tight.

"I don't understand what you mean."

Her father had a knack for avoiding direct questions. She tried again.

"What do you think is more important, honoring my mother's legacy or making money off of her?"

Lindsey's stomach clenched at the words. It wasn't right. The idea had been bearable when she'd gone with Mikel's take, that her mother's legacy would live on, but not this.

"This isn't the right choice," she pleaded. "Mom wouldn't have wanted this."

"I do feel your mother would have stood by me on this one."

"No, it's—"

"Lindsey, I have to get back to work." He sounded frustrated. "I'm glad we've had the opportunity to speak. Please do not contact Mikel about this without patching me in on the call as well. His time is valuable, and we need to treat it as such. I'll keep you posted on any developments. Let's talk again soon."

His tone was final, and she could imagine him turning away from whatever million-dollar view he was looking at out the window before getting back to work.

Lindsey hung up the phone, her cheeks still flaming with frustration. Her father was doing this for completely selfish reasons. It was shocking, in some ways, and par for the course in others.

She almost called her brother. There had been phases through the years where they had actually been good friends, sometimes even close. Given the immediate pain of speaking to her father, she wasn't ready to feel that pain with him, too. Besides, he couldn't tell her anything new about the situation, other than if there was a reason their father needed money.

Lindsey thought she knew the answer to that one. Her father liked nice things. He never saw money as a hindrance to getting them. He was probably determined to enjoy the last few years of his life and dating several women who preferred to be wined and dined. Or maybe one woman.

Lindsey paced the room. It was an angle she hadn't considered. If her father remarried, his new wife would have more authority over her mother's work than she and her brother would. The thought was so unsettling she wanted to scream.

Lindsey considered the crates lined up by the door. She'd felt guilty for taking them from the storage unit, like she was stealing from her own family. Now she was glad she'd taken the initiative.

Lindsey would protect these pieces. The rest of her mother's work could be turned into some mass-market carnival, a way for her father to capitalize on the best of everything and use her mother's work as some sort of cash grab. These pieces, though, the ones that echoed the time with her mother at Wind Thorne . . . those pieces belonged to her.

Chapter Twenty-Three

Wind Thorne, 1931

Ruby stared into the dirty face of a man with wild eyes. She let out a shout and tried to scramble backward, but the wall was right behind her. He grabbed her arm as she tried to get to her feet.

"Help." The word dropped from his lips, and she froze. "Help." He hit his chest, shirtless and emaciated.

His grip was almost gentle. She nodded, and he released her arm. The stench of the man was overpowering, and she took a couple of steps to the side, debating whether to run. He moved away and pointed at the tunnel.

"Help," he repeated.

He looked like one of the servants, she realized. Dark hair, distinctive dark eyes, and the same skin tone as Annabelle.

Had he gotten lost? Trapped in the tunnels and turned around? She didn't recognize him, but her uncle had brought on several new field hands. It was hard to know because she rarely saw them close up, unlike the servants in the house.

This man needed food, water, and to get cleaned up. Uncle Peter managed the farmhands, but she hesitated to bring this man to him, for fear he'd be punished for wandering off. Instead, she could find out his identity from her sister, who helped manage the household staff, and get him fed.

Ruby moved to the staircase. "This way."

The man let out a sound, and she looked at him in confusion. He pointed toward the tunnel, and she shook her head.

"No, up there." She pointed and started to go up the stairs, to show him.

He let out another cry. If he wouldn't come, she'd have to bring her sister here. Beckoning at him, she tried one last time, but he refused to go.

"I'll be right back." Ruby held up one finger and pointed at herself, hoping he'd understand. Then, she started to climb the stairs.

The man let out such a cry of agony that Ruby stopped and stared at him. He didn't seem to understand she was coming back, and he must have been scared to think that she'd leave him. She couldn't stand here looking at him, though, because that wouldn't be any help at all. Then, it hit her.

"Are you hurt?" She came back down. If his leg was injured, that would explain why he couldn't walk up the stairs. "What is . . ."

Ruby stopped. His ankle was caked over with blood, bright with infection. It had a chain wrapped around it, which had been broken.

He was a prisoner. Escaped, hiding out here.

She ran up the stairs to get help.

"Elizabeth!" Ruby banged on her sister's bedroom door. She was out of breath and sweating from running all the way back from the warehouse.

Elizabeth opened the door, her eyes rimmed red, but she was smiling.

"What is it?" Ruby asked.

Elizabeth pulled her into a tight hug. "We've been saved! Mr. Mensley heard about our troubles from one of his field hands. He met with Father this morning and offered a loan to us, no interest."

"Really?" Ruby held her sister tight. "That's wonderful news!"

Even though Ruby had asked for his help, she didn't think he'd agree. Certainly not so quickly.

Chester's face ran through her head. He'd helped her in the city, helped her get safely home, and now this. Surely, he'd had something to do with his father's decision, and her eyes smarted with tears.

"I know." Elizabeth started laughing and brushed her tears away. "He said if we didn't own Wind Thorne, it could put his farm in jeopardy, too. So, he's talking to the bank this afternoon." She ducked her head. "Uncle Peter is angry about it, of course. He's ranting that Mensley is rejoicing to see us cooking on the spit, or something like that. I think Father's just happy the ordeal is over."

Ruby wanted to talk to Chester so badly, to thank him. Her family had been angry at the Mensleys for years, ever since Mr. Mensley had refused to sell his farm when Wind Thorne needed the land to expand. This would make all the difference.

It might be possible to begin speaking to his family without suspicion. To be friends with Chester out in the open, instead of hiding in the warehouse. The thought brought her back to the reason she'd sought out her sister.

"I need help." Ruby settled onto the softness of her bed. "I was in the warehouse, the one by the forest, and—"

Elizabeth's face changed. "Wait, what?" She pulled Ruby into her bedroom and shut the door. The curtains were down for cleaning, flooding the room with light and making the worry lines on her sister's face more pronounced. "Ruby, why? What were you doing back there?"

It still wasn't safe to tell her the truth about Chester, that she was back there looking for him.

"It was on a walk," Ruby said. "I needed to rest, and the next thing I knew, a man was looking at me. He was starving and dirty and had a chain on his ankle." The words came out in a rush. "He needs help."

Elizabeth paced the room. Her face was pale, and her hand was at the neck of her dress. "You can't help him."

"He's not going to hurt me," she insisted. "He would have already if—"

"I mean it." Elizabeth's eyes were panicked. "If Father finds out you were back there—"

"Don't worry about me." Ruby was baffled that her sister couldn't see the bigger picture, that the man might die without assistance. "I'm fine. That man is not."

"You said this man was a prisoner, yes?" Elizabeth's voice was brisk. "That means he's dangerous. I'll inform Glenn, and he will get him the assistance he needs to get off our property. But I'm telling you, do not go there again. If anything happened to you—" Elizabeth turned toward the window and put her head in her hand. "Do you know what it was like for me, when you left?"

"No." The word came out a whisper.

"I cried every day. The first three months of my marriage, I sobbed into a pillow, thinking you were dead. It was only when we got your letter that I knew you were safe, and then, I was furious. Furious you weren't there for me, furious that you'd put us through all of that." Elizabeth turned, her eyes pleading. "Don't put me through that again. Be careful, Ruby."

Shame filled her heart. "I'm so sorry."

"I know. You—" She pressed her lips together. "Glenn can handle it."

Ruby gazed out the window. She couldn't see the warehouse, but she half wondered if the man had climbed up the steps in spite of the pain in his ankle.

"I hear you." Ruby kept her voice light. "I'll be careful. I promise."

Restless and worried, Ruby returned to the river with her fishing pole. She needed Chester to understand she was desperate to talk. Even if he did want to keep his distance, he had a kind heart. Ruby was certain he would help her if she needed it.

Ruby settled into a patch of dormant grass alongside the shore. The sky had turned gray and the wind had picked up, chilling her to the bone. Still, she cast the line and listened for the sound of twigs cracking or any indication that the man from the tunnel had come out to the forest.

Elizabeth had said she'd have Glenn handle it, but that was doubtful. These days, Glenn spent too much time away from the farm, gambling with Uncle Peter in a club that distributed their whiskey. So many of the men had been going there, to find amusement at a time when there was none, and she feared he wouldn't be back in time to help.

Ruby hated the idea that the man was suffering, regardless of what he'd done. It was a desperate time, and she remembered back in New York, hearing of dignified people doing terrible things just to survive. She had to help him, but Chester was nowhere in sight.

Ruby got to her feet, frustrated. She gathered up her fishing pole and stopped at a surprising series of stones in the grass. They were laid out in the shape of an eleven, and her pulse quickened.

To anyone passing by, it wouldn't look like anything other than some rocks scattered on the shore. Yet they hadn't been there before, so she knew Chester must have left them for her to find. He wanted to talk with her tonight at eleven.

Ruby rushed back to the house, heart pounding with relief. She planned to get there first to warn him about the man. Together, they could figure out what to do to help.

Chapter Twenty-Four

New York City, present day

The proximity of her mother's artwork made Lindsey long for her. It had been years since she'd died, nearly a lifetime, but it was a pain that never quite went away. For once, Lindsey felt ready to face those feelings, so she decided to pay a visit to her mother's art studio.

The steep stairs that led to the basement of Lindsey's apartment smelled of cold, wet brick and something sour and sulfuric. The space had a low ceiling and a flickering bulb that very well could have been there since the last century, giving off a low yellow cast of light that shaped a vague path down the hallway. So many years had passed since Lindsey had been down here, and she took slow breaths, proud of herself for coming this far.

Back when her mother had purchased her apartment in this building, she had also purchased the rights to one of the storage rooms. Such valuable real estate could probably be turned into some sort of living situation of its own, now, but her mother had had other ideas for it. She'd turned it into an art studio.

Her father had closed off and cleaned up the space following her death. Lindsey had tried to find refuge in the space but couldn't face the memories. The idea of being that close to her mother and yet so far away was too much, so she'd stopped visiting it altogether.

Now she turned the key in the lock. The sound of metal grating on metal was familiar even after not hearing it for so long, and she pushed open the door. The faded scent of the lavender candles her mother had always burned still hung in the air like a ghost.

Lindsey flipped on the light. Joy was the first emotion to hit, followed by a certain level of disbelief. Being there felt like falling through time. Her mother had painted the brick walls white and had several work stations set up over by the windows. They were covered with blurring papers that her mother would peel off to let in the sunshine and do her work. Now Lindsey slowly removed one of the papers, watching as the edges disintegrated like ash in her hands.

She went over to several small lidded bins filled with neatly organized metalworking equipment and pulled open one of the drawers, where she remembered keeping her pieces. Sure enough, she found a metal bracelet that she'd started and left unfinished. Several more just like it would be in the drawers.

Now she studied the bracelet in the light and saw what she could do right there, in the moment. The tension immediately drained from her shoulders, and for the first time in ages, the tightness around her mouth relaxed. Pushing back her sleeves, she got to work.

Lindsey had left her phone up in her apartment, and when she returned, hours later, the sky was dark and the buildings around her were lit up. She checked her texts and messages, embarrassed to see that two of them were from Otis. She'd completely forgotten their pizza date.

Lindsey squeezed the phone tight and called him. "I am so sorry," she said when he picked up. "I had to go to the city yesterday for work and didn't plan to stay, but some things came up. I meant to text you to reschedule."

"No problem." He sounded a little cautious. "You didn't have to call."

Lindsey could tell he was confused that she'd stood him up. It was rude, and it wasn't like her to disregard other people's feelings. Especially people she cared about.

"Of course I did." She squeezed the phone tight. "I shouldn't have let the time go by like that. I'm typically precise. It's just that . . ." She sat on the couch and stared out the window. "Look, my family's been complicated lately. Staying with my aunt was not something I planned. So, I'm just trying to get everything organized with work and—"

The words felt completely surface. Lindsey wanted to tell Otis about her father and the heartache he had caused her over the years. How it had been a big step for Lindsey to revisit her mother's studio. Talk to him about opening that bin, seeing the first piece of art, and knowing down to her soul that those pieces were connected to Wind Thorne. She was still so confused about all of it. It felt easier to avoid the issues and just keep this thing with Otis simple and light.

"I'm sorry," Lindsey said. "I can't believe I did that."

"I get it," he said. "It's a little hot today for pizza anyway."

She forced a laugh. "Hey, since I'm here, I might stay a little longer and visit that jewelry shop. The one that was listed on the blueprint we found for the ring? It's old and still in business. I was also thinking I might try to figure out where exactly Ruby worked as a governess because her information is not adding up. I'm starting to suspect she didn't actually do that."

"Sounds like you might be there for a few days," Otis said. "Enjoy New York. It's a fun city. I'll try you sometime next week."

Lindsey was on the edge of asking if he'd like to join her, to continue their research, but she held back. If she let him in at that level, there would be heartache and complications down the road. She needed to face the problems with her family first before setting herself up for a new round of issues.

"I've got to run," Otis said.

My thoughts exactly.

"Keep me posted on what you find," he said. "I won't be around next week when you get back because I've got some work things, too, but I do want to hear what you find. This whole journey with Wind Thorne speaks to my history-loving heart."

They hung up, and Lindsey sat on the couch, staring straight ahead. It was disappointing that he wouldn't be there when she got back, because as much as she was scared to let him in, she didn't want to lose him altogether. She wanted summer to continue as it had started, keeping it light over dinner and research, and maybe a few moments by the fire.

The disappointment validated her hesitation. She was too attached to him and his friendship. It wasn't fair to either of them if she couldn't let him in. Shaking it off, she got to her feet.

It was time for a quick dinner; then she wanted to get back. She had some ideas to improve the bracelet. For the first time in as long as she could remember, she looked forward to going down to the studio to work.

Chapter Twenty-Five

Wind Thorne, 1931

The crunch of feet through the woods made Ruby's heart pound. She listened closely, half worried it would be her sister's husband, drunk and showing up late to help. Squeezing her hands together tight, she stayed silent until she recognized Chester's silhouette.

"I'm here," she whispered.

He stopped. She picked her way to where he stood in the darkness. Leaning in, she could feel the softness of his hair as she quietly filled him in on the man hiding in the distillery. His body stiffened and he drew back, giving her a questioning look.

"I have supplies in here." She patted her cotton sack. It had a cowhide flask full of water, several apples from the cellar, dried venison, and a flat loaf of bread. She'd also brought antiseptic and bandages, although they would do little to help with the infection.

"Let me go in first," he said. "I'll be right back if it's safe for you. Run, if you need to. The front door of my house is unlatched, and my father would protect you."

Ruby gave him a grave nod. "Be careful."

Chester's shoulders were broad as he crept through the forest, toward their property. The silence was dreadful once he was gone. She sat on a downed tree, still as a hawk in the darkness. She imagined dreadful things, like him stumbling into an ambush.

Twigs cracked in the forest, and Ruby froze. The sudden rush of a rabbit made her jump, and her heart ached for Chester to return. She couldn't bear it if anything happened to him.

The time she'd been without him, not knowing where he was or what he was doing, had been so painful. Now that she had him back, she couldn't imagine losing him. It was inevitable, though. She would lose him when he married Eleanor, and life would have no choice but to go on.

Ruby blew on her hands to warm them. The sky was so beautiful that it was hard to believe there could be such a thing as heartache, but it was always there, waiting its turn. Predictable as the moon.

"Ruby." Chester's whisper cut through the woods. "It's safe."

The soft glow of the flashlight darted across the wall as they walked in. Using a low whisper, he called, "Hello? We're here to help."

No sound. The wooden stairs creaked beneath their weight. Ruby worried the man would be down there, dead on the ground. He was nowhere to be found, but they did see a smear of blood on the dirt near the entrance to the tunnel.

"He wanted me to go back there with him," Ruby said.

"I'm glad you didn't." Chester pulled back the board. "I'll see if I can find him. Stay here, and if anything happens, scream."

"No, I'll come."

"Fine." Chester nodded. "Then stay behind me, and if anything happens, don't waste time screaming. Run."

It was cold underground, and Ruby's teeth began to chatter. Her eyes adjusted to the dim lighting that bounced along the wooden walls with each step. After losing her footing against a rut in the ground, she pitched forward and grabbed Chester. His body tensed, then he relaxed.

"Hold my shirt," he instructed. "It'll be easier to navigate if we stick together."

The warmth of the fabric was a comfort, and she plodded on with careful steps. Every few feet, Chester called out "Hello?" without an answer.

Then, the smell in the air seemed to change.

Chester seemed to notice at the same time.

"What is that?" she asked.

Instead of the cold, rich smell of stone and earth, it was the faint odor of ammonia. They walked forward, and the smell got worse, getting stronger with each step until he drew back.

Ruby let go of his shirt, recoiling at the sudden scent of urine and feces. Chester shone his flashlight, and they found an entire area used for defecation, with rodents slinking through.

"What is that?" she whispered.

Chester moved forward with purpose, his strides quicker.

Ruby followed behind, unable to think of anything but the smell and the rats. She shuddered, turning her mind to even worse thoughts like the tightness of the space, and what would happen if it all came crashing down. Chester rounded a corner and came to another abrupt stop.

"No." The word came out as a breath.

In a small, dank enclosure of the tunnel, five people were sleeping on the ground, three men and two women. They lifted their heads at the flashlight, and the two women scrambled back, their dark eyes filled with fear. One of them, the largest man, muscular and furious, had his foot chained to the wall.

Chester turned to Ruby. "What is this?"

It was her property, her family. But she had no idea why there were people here, filthy, hungry, and trapped in the tunnel. It was impossible that her family could be responsible for this. Yet, she couldn't stop thinking about Uncle Peter's trips to Europe, the large truck parked outside the distillery after he returned, and how they suddenly had new servants each time. Was this how he did it?

Chester took a step forward. "We're here to help. Who can tell me how you got here?"

No one answered.

"Do you speak English?" he persisted.

One of the women shook her head. Her eyes were dark, and the resignation in her face was heartbreaking. It was as if she knew things weren't right, but she understood she was powerless to do anything but try to survive.

Chester turned back to Ruby. "Quick, give them the food."

Ruby rushed forward, distributing food that was no longer plentiful, with so many mouths to feed. She wanted to run back to the house and get them so much more, but Glenn could be home at any time. If Elizabeth really did tell him that Ruby had found a man in the . . . Ruby stopped, realizing that her sister had never intended to tell him. Glenn would have told her father, and who knows what would have happened. Elizabeth had just said it to keep Ruby away, because she knew full well that her family was keeping these people in deplorable conditions.

The idea that her sister knew about this—and hadn't done anything to stop it—made Ruby's head feel light. She rested her hand against the wall, scared that her legs might go out.

"Do you have any idea why they're here?" Chester asked.

Ruby stared as the people devoured the food put in front of them, barely pausing to chew. The stench made her dizzy, along with the disbelief that her family could do something so terrible.

"Ruby." Chester touched her arm. "Are you all right?"

"No." She remembered the immigration papers she'd once seen in Elizabeth's folder. "I bet they came here to work. I don't understand why they're in here, though."

Chester frowned. "I have some ideas." He drew back as the man whom Ruby had met earlier walked into the room. Chester indicated the food they'd brought, and the man rushed over to eat with his family. Then, he held up the chain, showing it to Chester.

"He wants me to put it back," Chester guessed, looking to where it once connected to the wall. "So he doesn't get found out."

Even though it tugged against every instinct Ruby had to help these people and release them, she nodded. If they didn't fix the chain, this man would get in trouble for trying to escape. He did not want to leave his family (or whoever they were to him), because if he did, they'd be punished for his absence. Quickly, Chester helped reattach it to the wall, and the man bowed at him, grateful.

"We'll figure out how to help them," Ruby said.

"It'll take time," Chester said. "We need to understand what's happening here first."

"We'll figure it out." She stepped forward and put her hand to her heart. "We will be back; we will help."

The people didn't seem to understand. Slowly, she mimed out the words, repeating them. The man with the chain gave a slow nod and said something to another man, who nodded. The rest of them stared blankly at her, some already collapsed against each other in exhausted sleep now that they'd been fed.

Tears ran down her face the entire way back to the main room. There, she leaned over and retched. It was the panic. The feeling of sweat and horror and being absolutely powerless to help. Because as much as she wanted to step in and make things right, she couldn't. It was impossible.

"Let's go." Chester's voice was grim. "It's not safe. Whoever's behind this could come in at any moment."

Ruby and Chester walked through the trees in silence until they found a clearing, and Ruby sank down onto a fallen log. Chester sat next to her. His entire body was tense, and he stared down at his boots.

"Your family has been involved in a lot of things, but I never would have thought they would do this."

"Chester, I'm so sorry."

That made her sound complicit, like she had something to do with it. *What must he think of me?*

Cheeks flaming, she said, "I had no idea they were being treated like that. My family doesn't always treat our servants well, but I never imagined something like this. It's horrible."

The words were insufficient. The image of that man's wound, the blood and infection on his ankle . . . It made her feel sick. She'd heard rumors that her father harmed anyone who crossed him, but what could these people have done? That man, the one bleeding and chained to the wall, did not deserve whatever had happened to him.

Ruby ran her fingers over the rough bark of the log, thinking about the moment the man had banged on his chest, begging for help. The way she'd run to her sister. Ruby stared out at the woods, its darkness like claws squeezing tight at her heart.

Her sister panicked the moment she heard Ruby had been back here at all. Instead of helping, she'd tried to keep Ruby away. To protect her? Maybe. But these people needed protection, not her.

There had to be a reason behind it all.

"Do you think it's a quarantine thing?" Ruby asked, keeping her voice low. "Make sure they aren't bringing in lice or the flu or . . . I just don't understand why they wouldn't have put them in one of the barns. We have the room."

"Ruby . . ." Chester's voice trailed off. "Do you not understand what's happening?"

The moon was still out, and a silver mist blanketed the clearing. It was odd to think that at one point, she and Chester had looked at the same moon in New York City. That moment was so far from their current reality, but that memory made that time seem real again.

"Ruby?" he pressed.

"I don't know," she said. "I wish I did."

"Those people—and maybe all of your servants . . ." Chester frowned. "I think they're being brought here under false pretenses."

"I agree. They come here to work, for a better life. Not to live like that."

"No, I mean . . ." Chester paused, squeezing his hands. "Those people in there, they don't look like they're here for a better life. They look like they're trapped."

Ruby shivered. She looked up at the moon, trying to let its beauty dull the pain of what he was saying. "There has to be an explanation."

Chester got to his feet. "We need to get them out of there. I could bring them over to my father's house, get them cleaned up, and keep them hidden until we know where they're from and what they're doing here."

"You wouldn't be able to keep them hidden." Chester's house was much too close to Wind Thorne for that. "Not there, not out in your barns. You'd get caught."

He kicked at a rock on the ground, sending it across the forest floor. "We'll have to get organized, put a plan into place. Can you talk to one of your servants? Find out what's going on?"

"I'm close with Annabelle."

The young girl was one of the few who seemed happy to interact with her.

"I need you to find out if this is how all servants are introduced to Wind Thorne. If it is . . ." He shook his head. "Maybe there's another explanation, but I doubt it."

"What do you mean?" she asked.

"I don't think your family just sells whiskey, Ruby," Chester said. "I think they might sell people."

Chapter Twenty-Six

New York City, present day

Lindsey had only intended to extend her stay in the city for the weekend, but she didn't step back out of her apartment for several days. When she was working on the projects alongside her mother, a certain peace had always come with being in the studio. Now that peace had been replaced with regret that she'd let grief keep her from doing something that she loved for so long.

Now, each day, Lindsey got up and logged on to her computer, the three screens shining with rows of data. Once she'd completed her daily tasks for work and followed the staircase to the basement, her hands started tingling with anticipation. She'd added several tabletop lamps to the studio, as well as a string of fairy lights, outfitting the dark space into something that lit up like the inside of a diamond every time she walked in.

While she worked, her mind clicked through a slideshow of memories. Endless images of her mother's smile, the clothes she wore, the way she smelled, and the conversations they shared. Some of these memories made her laugh, and others left her sobbing at the edge of the table, but she moved forward through them all, revisiting a lifetime that she had practically removed from her brain.

Her hands became sore and blistered from cutting out small pieces of tile to place on the bracelet that she'd designed to mirror a mosaic. Her skin was raw from washing the places where the resin touched it, where she ground up stones and sand to texture the intricate designs. Then, she turned to wire weaving, which pinched her like the sharp strings of a guitar, the shape of the metal never quite right no matter how much she twisted and bent and turned it. But she tried, and she kept trying.

Finally, on the day she'd finally managed to make the piece look how she'd imagined it, the regret inside her, the anger that she'd wasted so much time on, had passed. She stopped and looked around the studio, surprised at all she'd accomplished.

Lindsey had stayed away from her art for so long because she'd been afraid of the pain that might greet her in the middle of it. Now, as her eyes scanned these striking pieces of jewelry, she understood that exultation waited there for her, too.

That afternoon, she cleaned up the studio and packed away the pieces she'd made. She was ready to move forward, to go back to Wind Thorne for the summer. She'd bring her mother's pieces with her, knowing that when the time was right, she would be able to look at them through the eyes of joy, in the spirit in which they'd been created.

In the late afternoon, Lindsey sat out on the "balcony," the small outdoor space of her apartment. It was really just a sliver of about fourteen inches that opened into the gap of the stone buttresses that made up the bottom of the window frame. The space could be accessed by opening the entire window into her apartment, like a French door. Lindsey liked to bring her small dining room chair out, half of it on the balcony and the remainder inside, her knees resting against the stone partition like a seat on a Ferris wheel.

The air outside was thick from the heat of the day, and the dusty, sweaty scent of the city rose up from the street down below. Lindsey considered the buildings across the way, noticing which windows were lit and which were dark. She had sat here so often during the pandemic, waiting for the world to get back to normal. Now that it was, she wondered how it was possible she was still sitting here alone.

Spending the week twisting metal and pounding it into shapes had been cathartic, but she was still lonely. Her typical group of friends had scattered for the summer: some up north, others to the Hamptons, and others back home to see family. If she sent out a mass text, she could probably still find someone to grab a bite with, but that didn't sound appealing.

Halfheartedly, she scrolled through her phone and stopped on a social media post. It showed Otis at a Mets game. Her cheeks flushed to learn he, too, was in the city.

She would love to grab dinner with him. In a relatively short period of time, he'd become a good friend. He was kind and respectful, and the moment she'd indicated she needed space, he'd backed off.

Lindsey regretted pumping the brakes with him, but at the same time, she needed that time to figure things out. Now, after a week where she'd faced her feelings about the loss of her mother and reconnected with her passion for metalwork, she felt more capable of facing the complications that might come with letting someone new into her heart.

The idea of spending time with Otis was incredibly appealing. She wanted to continue to do research at Wind Thorne, get to know him, and learn more about his work. Plus, when the summer ended, their relationship could continue on, as they both lived in the city. Heartache was not inevitable. Instead, there might actually be the possibility of something more.

With that in mind, Lindsey picked up the phone and called him.

Otis answered after three rings. "Lindsey?"

Based on the noise in the background, he was out somewhere. Suddenly, she felt embarrassed for calling instead of just texting.

"Yes, hi," she said. "Sorry. It sounds like you're busy. I just—"

"I'm glad you called." His voice was gruff. "Hold on."

After a muffled sound, everything went quiet.

"Hey, sorry for the noise," he said. "What's up?"

The evening sun warmed her upper thighs, and she took a drink from her water bottle. "Nothing." She hesitated, then decided to tell the truth. "I saw you were in New York, so I wanted to see if you'd like to grab a bite to eat?"

He paused long enough to make her heart sink.

He matters to me, she realized. *I'll be disappointed if he says no.*

"I just had a plate of fried pickles," he said.

"Oh." She gave an awkward laugh. "Then, no worries. Never mind, I just thought I'd—"

"Wait, don't hang up!" He laughed. "I just mean I need some vegetables or something to save me from all that."

"Pickles are vegetables."

"Like wine is fruit." His voice was warm. "Let's sit outside somewhere. It's a nice night."

"Great." Lindsey shielded her eyes and scanned her street. "There's a great place next to my apartment. I can drop you a pin." The Ethiopian restaurant had small tables on the sidewalk that were never completely full but never completely empty. At the moment, they were somewhere in the middle. "What do you think?"

"I think I'm glad you called."

Otis strolled down the sidewalk dressed in sporty gray shorts and a white short-sleeved button-up shirt that looked crisp and cool in spite of the heat. Expensive sunglasses pushed back his wavy hair, and he seemed more like a city guy here than he did back in the woods. Lindsey smoothed her hair, surprised at how happy she was to see him.

It was one thing to see Otis at Wind Thorne and another to see him here, with her actual home less than a block away. So much of her adult life had been lived on this block: getting last-minute groceries or a bottle of water from the convenience store, buying flowers for herself at the florist's shop, or picking up an egg and cheese sandwich on the way to work.

"Hi," she said, half rising from the metal sidewalk chair. "You made good time."

"I was only a few streets over." He leaned in and kissed her cheek, which instantly gave her heart flutters. "One of my good buddies lives in this part of town. I come here all the time."

"Isn't it wild how we can pass the same person a hundred times on the street and never pay attention unless we have a reason?" she asked, pouring him some water from the glass bottle on the table.

He gave her a flirty grin. "I would have paid attention if I saw you. Even if I didn't know you at the time."

Lindsey's cheeks burned. He was already turning on the charm, and instead of running from it, she was relishing it.

The waitress stopped by, and soon they had drinks and plates in front of them before they could fully catch up on the week. Diving into the shiro wat, Lindsey closed her eyes, enjoying the spicy flavor of the curry.

"When are you headed back?" she asked.

He'd mentioned he had some work commitments that would keep him in the city for a few more days.

"The weekend, I think," he said. "What about you?"

"I was planning on sticking around a few more days, too," Lindsey said.

"What do you have?" He dipped some bread into the sauce. "Work things?"

"No, it's still that research on the Thornhill family I was telling you about on the phone. I'd like to show the blueprint of the ring to the jeweler, try and find the family Ruby worked for, and that sort of thing.

One of my main goals is to find the servants from Wind Thorne in the immigration logs at Ellis Island. I'm especially interested in tracking down my great-grandmother. I think all of those details would be nice pieces for Aunt Petra to add to the museum and the grant application, don't you?"

"For sure." The sun dipped between the buildings, and Otis slid on his sunglasses. "I'm curious who Ruby worked for, because I agree that she's hiding something. That girl never traveled the world."

"You sound so certain." Lindsey wiped her mouth. "Why?"

He gestured with his fork. "Because she writes in such great detail about things that I think she would have written all about it. Riding on a ship across the sea has to be one of the most romantic things ever, and there's not a word about it. She also doesn't say a thing about the kids she supposedly watched. Those kids could have been a menace, but she would still mention them, I'd think. There's nothing there."

Ruby nodded. "I think she was tricking her family."

"To what end, though?" he asked. "Do you think she and Chester eloped?"

"No." Lindsey had considered that, but in the diary from under the porch, Ruby was pining for Chester. That was after Ruby had returned home from her adventure, so unless they'd had to break up . . . "Well, maybe. Maybe they did elope."

"And they had to break it off when they went home," Otis pointed out. "For fear of getting caught. Or if he was supposed to marry someone else."

Lindsey raised her eyebrows. "That would be scandalous. Especially if Ruby took her sister's engagement ring to marry him."

"I don't know." Otis took a long drink of water. "Your girl Ruby seemed like an upstanding, honorable person. Stealing from her sister to fund a romance doesn't match up."

"Love makes people do wild things," Lindsey said.

"It does?" Otis raised his eyebrows. "What wild things have you done?"

Lindsey wished she hadn't said anything. There were couples seated all around them, with so many of them holding hands or sharing a bottle of wine that the environment was already full of romantic energy. It would be a little embarrassing to tell him that she'd never really been in love, but the wine made her bold.

"I wouldn't know," she admitted. "I've never felt that way."

Otis studied her. "Never met the right person?"

"Guess not." She shrugged. "To be fair, I always dated the guys that were all wrong for me, but they were the ones I recognized, you know? My brother and dad are these sporty alpha males, and as much as that doesn't fit with me, I was used to being around that. So, I'd feel annoyed to be with a guy who'd only want to go jog, or find a place to rock climb indoors, or go to a sporting event for a big date night. But it wasn't fair, because I knew full well what I was walking into every time."

"Hmm. I went to a Mets game." Otis adjusted his baseball cap. "Does that put me on the eligible list or take me off of it?"

Even though he was smiling, the question was somewhat serious.

"Don't get me wrong." Lindsey took a drink of water, thinking. "I like sports. I like cheesecake, too. I just don't eat it every day."

"So, if I take you to a baseball game once a year and order you cheesecake on the way home, I still have a shot?"

Lindsey laughed. "You had a shot the minute you told me you're not the guy to ask to hold a Fabergé egg."

Their eyes met, and for a split second, she truly thought he was going to slide their food aside and kiss her. Instead, he took her hand and slowly traced the lines on her palm.

"Do you want to help me research the Thornhills?" she asked, once she'd caught her breath. "Find out if Ruby and Chester secretly married?"

"We can look it up right now." Otis gently let go of her hand and pulled out his phone. "The Municipal Archives would have a record of it if they were married in New York. Give me their full names, if you know them."

Together, they wrote out the possible variations on the paper place mats. Otis had surprisingly neat handwriting. She peered over his shoulder as he punched them in. Nothing came up.

"Doesn't mean they didn't get married," he mused. "Just means they didn't do it in New York."

Lindsey pulled up the ancestry site and searched there. "It's not listed on here. I don't think they ever did. I think she was still pining."

"You're probably right." He folded up his napkin and set it on his plate. "Do you see either one of them on the site?"

Lindsey squinted at the screen. "Nothing's coming up."

"Darn. Then what did Ruby want with the ring?"

"I'm not sure." Lindsey thought for a moment. "Maybe to pay for the trip, so she could run away with Chester. It's just that, in the diary Amrita gave me—"

"Gave?" Otis said, laughing.

"The journal where she tried to fleece me," Lindsey corrected. "It didn't seem like Ruby was interested in Chester at all. They were friends, but he annoyed her, so I'm not entirely sure when that changed, because it's a completely different story in the diary from under the porch." She took a final bite of food. "The first thing I want to find out is if she actually had a job. That would answer a lot of these questions. There's an address listed in one of her letters where she asked her family to send letters." She pictured the tight, careful handwriting. "I'm going to go take a look tomorrow to try and find where it is. Her actual address would have to be nearby, if she left her mail with a neighbor."

"Unless she was lying about that," Otis pointed out.

Lindsey pushed her plate aside. "Why would she lie?"

"Well, she probably didn't want her father to show up and drag her back home," he said. "So, saying the mail was with a neighbor would be a safeguard against that."

Lindsey sat back and considered that. The city, even now, was bustling and alive. The tables were now full of customers, people were walking along the street, and the easy feel of summer was in the air. It felt like freedom.

Back in Ruby's time, such a thing would not be allowed. Ruby was from an influential family, and it would not have been good for their reputation to have her in the city, alone. Of course, that wasn't how Ruby had painted the situation for them.

"Based on what she writes about her father," Lindsey said, "he would have no qualms about showing up and demanding her whereabouts from whoever."

"Fair point."

The waitress returned and cleared their plates, then dropped a dessert menu.

Lindsey thought for a second. "But the servants most likely collected the mail back then, right? So, she could have made a deal with one of them to give her any letters, and if her father did come to the house, the owners really would be clueless."

Otis gave her a slow nod. "That makes more sense. So, the servant would collect the mail and pass it off to her."

"Maybe." It sounded simple, but at the same time, Ruby didn't seem particularly worldly. Giving her family a different address was most likely the height of her intrigue.

Otis looked at his watch. "I should probably get to bed."

Lindsey's shoulders tensed. "Oh." She'd hoped they could hang out after this, maybe take a walk.

He signaled for the check and waved her off when she pulled out a card. "No, let me." He handed the waitress his card. "Sorry to eat and run, but I have a meeting at four in the morning with a buyer on the other side of the world. I'll be free around ten, though, if you want me to come with you."

"I have to work, too, but not that early," Lindsey said, laughing. "Want to meet up at one?"

Their eyes met, and warmth spread through her.

"I'm really glad you called," he said.

"I'm really glad you answered."

Lindsey spent the evening flipping through some of the paperwork from the safe. Most of it was pretty mundane, but she kept coming back to the records on the income at Wind Thorne. It was a little shady, probably because their main business was bootlegging, and they had to find a way to hide that money. It was interesting, though, because the family seemed to have a few additional revenue sources that were unclear, and whatever source that income was from, it was lucrative.

Lindsey flipped on the small lamp on her desk, studying one section in particular. The alcohol sales were easy to spot. They were coded as "the oaks" and specified with a "b," probably for barrels, or "btls," for bottles. The records made it possible to figure out which sources had supplied the barrels, along with how much or how little Wind Thorne had paid for them. The bottles all came from the same glass supplier in the city.

Still, those items didn't have anything to do with this other source of income, the one she couldn't quite place. Tobacco, maybe? It couldn't have been cattle meat, or anything to do with livestock, because the numbers didn't show the level of reduction or influx that would match the output. Lindsey racked her brain, trying to think of what a farm could supply that would bring in the amount of profit she was seeing.

Maybe it was a payout from the Agricultural Adjustment Act. The federal government had put it into place during the Depression to limit certain crops in an effort to stabilize pricing. Perhaps Wind Thorne had been a part of that, and the government was subsidizing them to not grow corn, wheat, or one of the other crops that needed to be pulled back from the market.

The payouts were so large, though, that it was hard to imagine the government handing that money out for nothing. Besides, why wouldn't the bookkeeper just call it a subsidy? It was strange to leave it unmarked.

Tapping her fingers against the pages, Lindsey gave up on trying to figure it out and instead moved on to some of the other paperwork.

The moon was up by the time she got drowsy and headed off to bed. Her mind kept sifting through the different possibilities of what the numbers meant. Finally, she drifted off, thinking of the way Otis had held her hand at dinner.

Early afternoon, Lindsey and Otis stood outside a brownstone in the Upper East Side of Manhattan. It was an upscale area, with Central Park across the road, and a sense that everything was cleaner and quieter.

"This is the address," Lindsey said, adjusting her ponytail. The air was stifling, and she shielded her eyes against the sun. "Should we ring the bell?"

"Sure, if you want to get arrested." Otis wore his Mets hat and a sun shirt, and he studied the building intently. "I'm wondering . . ." He spun in a slow circle, taking in their surroundings. "Did you bring the diary?"

Lindsey lifted an eyebrow. "Why?"

"Well, hear me out," he said. "There was such a good description, you know?"

Lindsey knew exactly what he meant. Ruby had a knack for explaining exactly what something looked like, down to the most mundane details.

"I'm thinking that if we take some pictures and compare this area to the diary, we might be able to figure out where she stayed."

Lindsey gave him an eager nod. "It's possible." Quickly, she snapped a picture of all the houses in the row. Some were enormous, like small mansions carved from brick and stone. "We should also find pics from the '30s, because I'm sure a lot has changed since then."

Across the road, a white Clydesdale plodded along the edge of the park, pulling a carriage. "Well, maybe not that much," Lindsey said, laughing. "Okay, next stop. The shop where the ring was made. I did bring the paperwork for that."

It was too hot to walk, so they took the subway to the small hole-in-the-wall shop in upper Manhattan. The sign above the door looked like something from the '50s.

"Schroeder's," Otis said, patting the brick wall with affection. "I've been here. It's been a while, but this place has been here forever."

History practically breathed out the front door. It was the type of place where the pictures on the walls of celebrities and society people didn't just demonstrate how many well-heeled people they served; the photos also honored the friendships of the people who had come here for years. Lindsey marveled at the black-and-white images of presidents, movie stars, and, as Otis pointed out, a few members of the Rockefeller family.

The shop displayed a remarkable collection of jewels, everything from diamond necklaces made up of several shapes that looked like eagles, accented with emerald and citrine, to sapphires that dripped down in a waterfall cascade like tears. The jewels were dazzling, the lighting done in such a way that the diamonds seemed to dance. Lindsey studied them like a collection in a museum, mesmerized.

"Stunning, right?" he said in a whisper. "I used to come in here just to see what they had. Tried to get them to hire me, but they don't go outside their family."

"My family does the same," Lindsey said. "Except it's more like, 'My father doesn't go outside the men in our family.'"

One year in college, Lindsey had needed to get an internship to fulfill her credits. She wasn't interested in law, but her father's firm had several opportunities in corporate finance. He refused to even interview her, claiming he didn't believe in nepotism.

Two years later, her brother was working in the accounting department at her father's practice, and Barrett was offered a sales job that, ultimately, he'd turned down. When Lindsey mentioned the hypocrisy, her brother claimed their father had had a change of heart with their cousin after the internship issue. True or not, he'd never once uttered a word of apology to her.

"Can I help you?" A woman stepped out from the back and took a place behind the counter. She was older, with sharp eyes, and Lindsey saw her glance at Lindsey's pinkie ring.

"Yes." Lindsey smiled at her. "I found a rather remarkable reference to your shop at an estate that's now a museum called Wind Thorne. I was curious if you'd have any additional information related to this ring blueprint." She pulled out the paperwork. "The diamond ring itself came up missing nearly a century ago, but when we found this, I wanted to delve into it a little bit further."

The woman put on a pair of reading glasses. Her eyebrows lifted slightly as she studied it, and she finally said, "This ring looks like an impressive piece. My father didn't keep the best records, but he did keep some. I'd be happy to look into it. Did you happen to bring the ring with you?"

"No."

"Hmm." The woman studied the paperwork again.

Lindsey remembered the video. "Actually, I have a video of when we found this, and the ring. You're welcome to see it if you'd like."

When the woman nodded, Lindsey queued up the portion of the video where Otis had zoomed in close on the design. The woman studied it for a long moment and paused the frame. She zoomed in and lifted her eyebrows before handing the phone back.

"You said that the real ring has been missing for quite some time," she said, peering at Lindsey over her glasses. "Where did you find that one?"

"In a safe that hadn't been opened in nearly a hundred years." Lindsey gave a little laugh. "I know this sounds a little far fetched."

"I've heard stranger things." The woman gestured for Lindsey to hand her the phone, and she took another look. "It's hard to tell from this, but I'd be doing you a disservice if I didn't ask—you're sure the ring you found was a fake?"

Otis gave her a slight nod.

"It was," Lindsey said. "I was with a gem dealer when I found it, and . . ."

The woman laughed. "Never trust a gem dealer. I bet he's cute, too."

Otis raised his hand. "I'm the gem dealer. I don't know about the 'cute' part, but the ring we found was definitely the replica."

"Hmm." The woman eyed him. Then she looked at Lindsey. "Get a second opinion."

Lindsey could see how this woman in the jewelry shop—a corner store that had to be guarded with a metal door, bulletproof glass, a buzzer for entry, and at least five cameras—could fall into suspicion so easily. From her point of view, Lindsey's immediate acceptance of the appraisal was shortsighted; maybe she should have put the ring under lock and key until she'd had it formally evaluated. But she trusted Otis, and there was something to be said for that.

"Thank you for your vote of confidence," Otis said.

"You can't be too careful," the woman said. "Costume jewelry can still be worth a fortune, especially a piece that's historically significant."

"He said all that," Lindsey confirmed, and the woman grunted.

"I'll give you a call if I find anything." She raised her eyebrows. "But do get it double-checked."

Lindsey was mortified when they left the shop. "She was so mean! She basically called you a criminal, and you were standing right next to me."

Otis was laughing. "I bet she deals with a lot of criminals. Look, she's right. Not about the 'criminal' part, but it's an important piece. You need to get it insured and appraised."

"I know." Lindsey felt slightly guilty that she hadn't done it before she'd left town, but there hadn't been time. Plus, she'd lost herself in metalwork and stayed much longer than she'd planned. "I had to get here, but I also kind of figured that if it's been there that long, what's going to change?"

"True." Otis looked at his watch. "What's next? The servants?"

Lindsey nodded. "Yes, I thought that would be interesting."

"Are we jumping the ferry or doing this online?" he asked.

It had been years since Lindsey had taken the ferry to the Family History Center at Ellis Island. It was a fun ride that stopped at the Statue of Liberty before moving on to Ellis Island. The one time she'd taken the boat with her mother, they'd stopped at both places.

"I'd love to do the boat," she said. "But it's getting late, and by the time we get there, we wouldn't have much time."

"Agreed," Otis said. "Am I coming to your apartment?" She nodded, and they started to walk. It was hot, and he said "Hold on" before ducking into a shop and returning with two ice cream cones.

"Thank you," Lindsey said, brightening. He'd gotten her lemon custard, one of her favorites. "How did you know I like this?"

It was a somewhat random flavor, right up there with peach.

"You mentioned it," he said, and her heart beat a little faster to know he'd paid attention. "I think it was during our appraisal days."

How sweet, and how unexpected.

"Thank you," she said, and smiled at him. "You know, I studied some paperwork last night, and this is interesting—Wind Thorne has all this money coming in, but I can't figure out what it's from."

"Bootlegging," Otis said.

Lindsey took a bite of her cone. "You'd think. But I could see where the whiskey trade was and how it was hidden. This is something else."

They arrived at the brownstone, and Lindsey led him up. He walked through, taking it all in. She rested her keys on the counter before finishing her cone and watching him. She typically felt possessive when new people came into her apartment, but with him, it felt fine. Peaceful.

"This is a great place." His eyes were so blue when they caught hers across the room.

Lindsey took a seat on the couch, and he did the same. They both sat in silence for a minute, and when he looked at her, Lindsey's heart started to pound.

"Should we look all this up?" she said.

Otis took her hand. "Not quite yet," he said, then leaned in to kiss her.

Chapter Twenty-Seven

Wind Thorne, 1931

Ruby tossed and turned, the images of what she'd seen in the tunnel and the questions from Chester replaying in her mind. The moment she heard the servants moving about the next morning, she rushed out of bed to search for Annabelle. Ruby found her scrubbing a back hallway alongside Haja.

"Annabelle," she called, "can I see you for a moment? I need your help with something."

Annabelle bustled over as Haja squared her shoulders and scrubbed a little harder. Ruby remembered that feeling, when another servant would be singled out to do something special while she was left mopping floors. In some ways it felt like moments ago and, in others, as if years had passed.

"Thank you." Ruby smiled at Haja. "I appreciate your hard work."

Haja didn't look her way.

Ruby led Annabelle downstairs, into the library. The walls were thick enough that no one would hear, and the lock gave fair warning before anyone could walk in. If they were discovered, it would be simple to pretend that Ruby needed assistance drawing the draperies or some other such nonsense.

Ruby gestured to the couch, and they took a seat. Annabelle gave her a questioning look.

"What is it, miss?" She looked curious.

"Well, I wanted to ask—"

Ruby stopped. It was cruel to even speak the words, let alone ask another human being if they were true. Her eyes smarted with tears, and she reached out her hands. Annabelle took them and waited.

"I understand if you do not want to tell me." Ruby kept her voice low. "I also want to give you my word that nothing you say will put you in danger and that your name will never be used."

Annabelle, who had been looking up at her with a curious smile, dropped Ruby's hands. Her face became cautious, and the exhausted circles under her eyes seemed more pronounced.

"What was the circumstance of you coming here to work?" Ruby asked. "Did you apply for the job?"

Ruby remembered the indignity of going from house to house, being looked over like livestock, back when she and Chester were trying to get a position. One of the butlers had actually squeezed her upper arm, shook it like a piece of spaghetti, and laughed. But if Ruby had wanted to leave that interview, walk right out the front door, she'd had the power to do so. The men in the tunnel, their ankles chained to the wall, did not have the same choice.

"Annabelle," she said, "did you apply for this job?"

"I do not know what you are asking."

It was still possible Chester was wrong, and this whole thing was a misunderstanding. Ruby wanted that to be the outcome, because she couldn't bear to believe her family could be so cruel.

"I'm asking how you started working here." Ruby tried to make her tone sound curious. "Did you have to come and speak with my father to get hired on? How often do they pay you?"

Annabelle's cheeks colored, and she looked down at her feet.

The sudden, horrible realization made Ruby feel lightheaded. "Please tell me they pay you."

In New York City, the decision to switch to working for room and board was a choice Ruby and Chester had made together. It was the only way the family could keep them on, and it was better than being without both food and shelter. But the Thornhill family was struggling now, too, so perhaps they had a similar setup with the servants.

"Things are complicated right now," Ruby said. "But they paid you in the beginning, didn't they?"

Annabelle fidgeted with the cuff of her sleeve. "No. Never."

Ruby drew back. How was this possible?

"You've never been—" she started to say, but Annabelle spoke up.

"We will be paid," she said.

"Thank goodness," Ruby breathed. "I couldn't imagine—"

"It's only that, right now, we still owe for our passage."

The clock ticked loudly in the silence.

"What do you mean?" Ruby whispered. "Your passage?"

Annabelle glanced toward the door, and she lowered her voice. "Peter got us to America, in exchange to work for him. We were allowed to skip any immigration problems, since we came with him. He promised weekly pay, but did not say how much then. Now we know it is two dollars a week, and it goes to our debt."

Before Ruby could gasp out a protest, Annabelle continued. "My mother once complained, and I didn't see her for three days. When she came back, she worked harder than ever. She did not speak of it again."

Ruby paced the room, trying to breathe. She knew what it was like to fall into bed tired to the marrow of her bones. Feet swollen and aching, hands hurt and blistered from the hard work on someone else's home. She could not imagine having to do all of that without having a choice in the matter, and to be punished for any word of complaint.

Ruby swallowed hard. "You don't know where your mother went? During that time?"

"No. She has told me never to argue with them." Her eyes filled with tears. Taking Annabelle's hands again, Ruby sat with her on the couch. "Miss Ruby, I am tired," she said. "I do not think this is right.

I never wanted to leave my village, and my mother brought us here because she thought our lives would be better. Our lives are so much worse. My family back home thought we were going to send money, but we can't. Instead, Peter makes us write letters saying how happy we are. We are trapped here."

"Is it the same for everyone?" Ruby asked. Thinking of Chester's words, she said, "Does everyone stay?"

"No." Annabelle stared down at her feet. "Some of the men have left. A few of the farmhands told us they'd seen them at other farms."

"What about Indira?" Ruby asked, quietly.

Annabelle bowed her head. "She was the first to leave from my village. The one who we all wanted to be, coming here for a better life."

The front door slammed, and footsteps moved down the hallway. Quickly, they got to their feet.

"There is much more to be said, but we must be careful." Ruby glanced at the door. "Please, do not tell your mother we spoke. Do not tell anyone. But this will not continue, I promise you that."

Hope flashed in Annabelle's eyes, but it was short lived, probably as she weighed how unlikely it was that Ruby would be able to force a change. "Yes, miss."

Once Annabelle had left, Ruby sat in silence on the settee. The heat from the fire was on her skin, the burn of anger growing hotter on her cheeks. Her hatred for her uncle ran so deep that she could barely think. The man had no conscience, no honor. The things he had done to these people were awful. Yet, they still went about their business each day, serving the meals, cleaning the floors.

The rage they must feel. The betrayal.

Not to mention the fear.

Most barely spoke English. Annabelle did, because she'd arrived at Wind Thorne at a young age, but many of them struggled to communicate. Without that ability, they had no way to get back home. Her uncle knew this and took advantage of it, ripping away any opportunity for dignity. If screaming in his face would have solved anything, she would have welcomed the chance.

The only way to change this situation, though, was to take action. To find a way to help them. But she had to be careful around him, so he had no idea she knew.

Did everyone in the family know about this, everyone but her?

Ruby's heart sank at the thought. Yes, her sister knew about the man in the tunnel, but it was possible she had been sold a different story, that she knew nothing of what was really happening. That their mother, their grandmother, knew nothing. Because if they did . . .

Ruby squeezed her eyes tightly shut. Family could be forgiven all sorts of faults, but not this.

This was unforgivable.

The door slammed behind Ruby as she rushed out of the house, and she stopped suddenly to see her father in his thick winter coat, slumped over in a chair, a glass of whiskey resting alongside him.

It was barely nine o'clock in the morning. Her father was always up with the sun, but he looked like he might have been up longer than that: dirty shirt, unshaven, the stench of whiskey radiating off him. Feeling cautious, she moved toward the steps. The creak of a board gave her away, and he opened his eyes.

"Daughter." He stretched one hand out and beckoned. "I was raised on this farm. Did you know that?"

"Yes, sir." Her voice was low, cautious.

Her father had always seemed to have a way of knowing everything that happened on his farm: secrets behind closed doors, deals Peter tried to make behind his back, even the very moment someone thought of betraying him. Ruby wondered if he had seen it in her, sensed that she had figured out more than he wanted her to know.

"Peter and me, we were raised here." He reached for his glass but seemed to change his mind and put his head in his hands instead. "My father, he was a big man. Strong, smart. He built this place with his bare hands. Cut down the trees. Tunneled for sand."

Ruby's shoulders tensed at the mention of the tunnels.

"He taught me many things, but he said, 'Son, if you want to be successful in this world, you have to change with the times.'"

The air felt still as her father watched her, like before a lightning strike.

"I changed," he said. "There was a time I didn't even like whiskey." He held up the glass and tossed the rest of his drink over the edge of the railing. Some splattered on the boards. "Without it, though, we would have had to give up this place long ago. It saved us. Then, we needed to be saved once again." He surveyed the expanse of the fields and leaned back in the chair. "The Mensleys." He laughed again, a joyless sound. "Chester's back, did you know?"

If this was a trap, she couldn't walk into it.

"His father must be delighted." She folded her hands. "Elliot, too?"

"No, not Elliot." Her father kicked his boots against the floorboards, rocking in the chair. "I had to listen to Mensley blather on, you know, while he smoked my cigars and drank my whiskey, because I need his money. I learned Elliot's in the navy, Chester dislikes hunting, and Mensley likes to eat oatmeal every morning but has a hard time getting it. I sent him home with some, of course." He stopped rocking. "Ruby, I've tried to do right by people."

The sky was so bright. It hurt her eyes.

"Father, I—"

"This is *my* farm. No matter what I have to do to keep it." His glare was as sharp as an axe cutting through a tree. "We change with the times. We do what's necessary. It's what needs to be done." Nodding, he got to his feet and took plodding steps toward the front door.

Ruby's heart ached. Her father had seemed so strong to her once, so handsome and sure. It was impossible to feel pity for him, even in his broken state, knowing the harm he'd caused to so many others.

"What about doing what's right?" she asked.

Her father stopped to steady himself on the doorframe.

"Talk to Father Aaron about that one."

Ruby walked out to the fields, trying to outrun her thoughts. The herd of cattle was just ahead of her, and she slowed, watching them.

Each week that passed, they had become more emaciated. Now she could count the ribs on the one closest to the fence. There was a time when it would have walked over to her, curious. Now it stood there, its face blank and its back arched.

"What can we do?" she whispered.

Slowly, she walked the edge of the field. She started when she found Peter standing in the shadow of a tree. Like her father, his eyes were wild, and he reeked of whiskey. He gestured for her to move closer. She planted her feet firmly in the dirt, staring at him.

This was the man who had taken people from their homes. Lied to them. Left them dirty, starving, and trapped in a place that wasn't their own. Rage filled her, but also a despair so deep that her hands started to shake. She would never be able to look at him again without the image of those chains in her mind, the stench of those tunnels. She wanted to scream at him, to insist he admit to it all and fix it, but it would do no good.

"Why are you looking at me like that?" Peter demanded.

"I'm not afraid of you," she told him.

"Glad to hear it." His voice echoed across the fields. "You can't survive when you're afraid, Ruby, and this world is all about survival. You have to help others see that. Help those who can't help themselves. That's mercy. That's goodness."

"You're trying to talk to me about goodness?"

"I'm trying to get you to understand," he said.

He was drunk. But if he was going to tell her what he had done and try to justify it, maybe that was another way to solve this mess. She could help him to see that it wasn't right, convince him to return the servants to their homes.

"Look at them." Peter gestured out at the field. "They're not going to survive, and they're going to suffer along the way."

Ruby looked out at the cows. This was the only thing she shared with Peter. If she hadn't been so angry, she might have said she understood, that seeing the cows without enough food hurt her, too.

His voice broke. "I did what I could for her, Ruby. I tried." He took a step to the side, and Ruby gasped.

Mary, the cow he favored, lay in a crumpled heap behind him. The cold, coupled with the lack of food, must have taken her, and it wouldn't be long until the others followed. Ruby took a step forward, her heart filled with regret.

"I'm so sorry," Ruby said, quietly.

He nodded. "I couldn't let her suffer."

Peter mopped his brow with a handkerchief stained with something. It was then that Ruby noticed Peter's shotgun propped up against the tree. The smell of iron hung heavy in the air.

Out in the field, the herd remained, huddled together. They might not make it, but they still had the chance.

"I saved her." He knelt down next to the cow's dead body. "From all of this."

"No," Ruby whispered. "You killed her."

Peter put his head in his hand. His shoulders shook, and moments later, he was sobbing.

Ruby turned and ran, through the fields and deep into the forest, until the only thing she could smell was pine.

Chapter Twenty-Eight

New York City, present day

Lindsey woke up in Otis's arms, the early-morning streetlights shining around them like stars. He stirred and reached over, running his hand down her arm.

"Hey," he said.

"Hi." She pulled the sheet up close, feeling shy now that they'd crossed that line of intimacy.

"Your apartment has a great view," he said. "It's so wild to think we're surrounded by buildings at the moment and, in our other life, we're surrounded by trees."

Lindsey smiled. "It makes me think of Ruby, how she must have felt coming here."

"You think of Ruby a lot these days," he said. "What draws you to her?"

"I don't know." Lindsey stretched, thinking. "It's the connection, I think, to my family, my great-grandmother. We don't know much about Annabelle or Elliot, other than what we've learned from Ruby's diaries. It's nice to know that Ruby watched out for my great-grandmother and made a point to be kind to her when she worked as a servant. I also like Ruby's spirit. That she tried to figure things out and do better. It's a reminder to me to not give up just because things are difficult."

"What's difficult for you?" Otis asked.

Lindsey gazed out the window. The sun still wasn't up, and their conversation felt cozy. She took a drink of water from the glass on the bedside table, then snuggled in closer to him.

"Well, I've been having a hard time lately," she admitted. "I hadn't been to my aunt's house—which used to be my grandparents' house—in years. I was . . ." She squared her shoulders. "I was the one who found my mother when she died, which was in the woods there, so I've avoided it."

"I'm so sorry," Otis said, squeezing her hand.

"It's been years," she said. "But it's still hard. Then, right after I got there, some things happened with my mother's work that kind of knocked me down."

Otis traced his thumb along the inside of her arm, listening.

"With all that going on, I wasn't in a place to jump into anything with you." She met his gaze. "I'm probably still not in a place to jump into anything with you, but I couldn't stand to miss the chance. So, here we are, and I might be less than what I want to be for you for a while, but I really want to try."

Lindsey fidgeted with the sheets. She was afraid he'd look uncomfortable or change the subject, but instead, he gently tucked a strand of hair behind her ears.

"I'm glad you said all that. You never have to be anything more than what you are," he said. "Not with me."

Lindsey rested her head on his shoulder. "I'm not used to talking like this," she admitted. "My father and my brother have no interest in talking about feelings or issues, and as a result, we don't have a great relationship. They do well together, because they communicate in their own way."

"Was it always like that?" he asked.

Lindsey thought back. "In some ways. They were interested in sports and had their relationship, but it was fine, because I was close with my mother. Once she was gone, not knowing how to relate to them bothered me. I've leaned on my aunt quite a bit."

"She seems like a good person to lean on," Otis said. "You can also lean on me, you know. I'm not going anywhere."

The words made her squeeze his hand a little tighter. For years, she'd felt the need to handle everything on her own. It was nice to know that she didn't have to be alone and that, for the first time in ages, she didn't want to be.

That morning, they started researching Ruby over breakfast. While he studied the pictures of the houses on the block where Ruby received mail, Lindsey began to check into the servants.

The immigration paperwork was primarily a form signed and stamped with approval to enter the United States. It contained basic information such as name, age, and eye color, but also details like the country of origin.

"This is great information," she mused, taking a bite of the avocado toast that Otis had gotten for the two of them. "If I compile it all into a spreadsheet, it'll be simple to compare and contrast the details about the servants who worked at Wind Thorne. I could even do random stuff, like figure out if the majority of the workers were tall or small."

Otis grinned. "Sounds like you're making progress."

"Not entirely," she admitted. "That said, I'm hoping the immigration records in the national archives can help me to make connections with the modern-day families. The individuals won't be around anymore, but it might still be possible to speak to their children about their parents' time working at the estate."

It could help her compile an oral history to paint an even more detailed portrait of what living at Wind Thorne had been like.

Lindsey went back to the paperwork, and she and Otis worked in silence for an hour. He sat at her tiny kitchen table, and Lindsey was on the couch with her feet tucked underneath her. It was cozy, but as time went on, she started to get frustrated. In spite of all the information she had, it seemed like each time she searched for one of the servants in the immigration database, nothing came up. It was like the person didn't exist.

"Am I doing this wrong?" she finally demanded. "There have to be at least 120 pieces of paper here, and I've only found five of the servants on record. Can you come look?"

Otis stayed focused on his phone. "In a sec. I'm wrapping up something that I think you're going to like."

While she waited, she pulled up some examples of 1930s immigration forms from the internet to see if she was working with the right forms.

"These actually look different from what I have," she mused. "Not by much, but . . ."

Otis got up and peered over her shoulder. "There's no number at the top," he said, pointing.

"Exactly," Lindsey said. "There's a signature, but . . ."

"Can I see one of those?" he asked.

Lindsey handed him one of the sheets of paper. He typed the appropriate information in, just like she'd done, and nothing came up.

"Huh," she said, puzzled. "I hate to say it, but I'm guessing the forms I have were designed to gather information from potential workers. Only five are documented, so the rest probably never made it into the country."

"Why keep the paperwork, then?" Otis said.

"True." Lindsey tapped at the page. "What if these are forgeries? Do you think it's possible the workers at Wind Thorne weren't documented?"

"Maybe," Otis said.

"Hmm." Lindsey drummed the pen against her lips. "I'm going to email immigration with some pictures of these forms and see what they say. I mean, my great-grandmother definitely came into the country. I need to find her form."

Lindsey took another look at the paperwork. It seemed like a lot of effort to gather so much clerical information and not use it. There had to be some sort of an explanation, even if it did turn out that the workers weren't registered.

Quickly, she sifted through the papers before finally finding Annabelle Rakoto. The paper looked exactly the same as the others, with the same missing information. When she typed her great-grandmother's name into the database, she wasn't there.

"I have to be doing this wrong," Lindsey said. "I'll send them hers, specifically, to see what they can make of it."

"That's a good plan." Otis stretched. "No reason to jump to conclusions when we don't really know what we're looking for, right? Speaking of, I'm ready to share my presentation with you."

"Presentation?" Lindsey said, laughing. She grabbed her coffee and joined Otis at the table. "What do you mean?"

"I found out where Ruby lived."

Lindsey's heart soared. "You did? Why didn't you say anything?"

"Because accusing Wind Thorne of using undocumented workers was much more exciting and illicit," he said. "Come here, though. Check it out." She peered over Otis's shoulder, and he zoomed in on an elaborate home four doors down from the building where they had been standing.

"Okay, look at this while I do a dramatic reading." He picked up the diary and cleared his throat before reciting, "'The house is five stories and it goes straight up. I love how on the outside, the ground floor is backed by stone. The next two floors are brick, and the top floors are once again stone, with carvings over arched windows. It's a work of art. I wonder if people feel intimidated looking at Wind Thorne the way I feel looking at this place.'" Otis tapped the picture for emphasis. "Stone, brick, brick, stone, and stone with arched windows." He looked at Lindsey. "It's a unique combination. No other place on the block has it. This is it."

Lindsey held her breath. "Did you look up who lived there?"

"Of course." He gave her a playful smile. "Ruby worked for the Wellsley family. Very wealthy, and always in the society pages. They seem like good-enough people, based on what I read. Definitely rich."

Otis pulled up several screenshots, and Lindsey leaned in. She stared in awe at the well-dressed family. They were photographed at all sorts of society events, including a charity ball, the opening of a theater, and a party that appeared to be at a bank. The woman was stunning, the man a typical, portly picture of success from the early twentieth century.

"Did they have children?" Lindsey studied them with interest. "Maybe Ruby really was a governess."

"They had kids, but get this—the kids were primarily at boarding school the years Ruby was in New York."

Lindsey set down her coffee mug. "We were right."

"Ready for the grand finale?" he asked.

Feeling numb, Lindsey nodded. She wondered if he was about to pull up a copy of a marriage license or something.

Otis clicked open a photo full of servants. Many had dour faces, but a select few had bright smiles.

"This was taken Christmas, 1928, for a local magazine to showcase Wellsley Manor and its staff." Quickly, he clicked over to the Wind Thorne website put together by Aunt Petra. He pointed at a photograph of the Thornhill family. "This is Ruby," he said before clicking back to the group photo of the servants. "And . . . voilà! There she is again."

Lindsey stared at the picture in disbelief. "She worked as a servant," she breathed, taking it in.

A large group of servants dressed in smart black uniforms lined up in formation next to a sweeping staircase. Many of them looked thin and tired, but Ruby was noticeable with her regal air and dark eyes. She stood next to a smiling, pretty girl. The way their elbows touched gave Lindsey the impression that the two were good friends.

Quickly, she scanned the group of men. Most of them were older, and she considered the younger ones carefully. Finally, she tapped the phone, pointing to a handsome young boy with broad shoulders and an open, charming smile.

"That's Chester," she said, feeling a rush of affection. "I'd bet you a million dollars. He looks exactly like the pictures I have of my grandmother when she's young. The same eyes. He and her father were brothers." Lindsey smiled, amazed to see all this history come together. "This is so interesting. Thank you. I can't wait to show it to Aunt Petra."

"It's fascinating. Why do you think the two of them worked as servants?" Otis asked.

He got up and rummaged through her cupboards, returning with the only snack option—chocolate-chip protein bars.

"Who knows?" Lindsey sat back on the couch and opened one. "Maybe it was to be together, and this was an opportunity to live in the same place. Then, they had to come back home when the Depression hit and New York fell apart."

It was hard to imagine, gazing out her window at the vibrant city.

"Everything about this keeps me guessing," she said.

Knowing that Ruby had lived in the city on her own, with the boy next door, left her with so many questions. She didn't know how much paperwork she'd have to sift through to get there, but Lindsey was determined to find out the answers.

"When are you headed back to your parents' house?" Lindsey asked.

"I was thinking tomorrow, but it depends on you." Otis sat next to her. "What are you thinking?"

"Tomorrow." She looked at the folder full of paperwork and thought of all the additional information back home. "I want to get back and start looking through everything. See what I can figure out."

Otis nodded. "I'm right there with you."

The next morning, Otis had some things to wrap up, and Lindsey wanted to get in one last work session down in the studio. It was light, fun, and relaxing to work on one of her new ideas, and by the time she emerged, it was early evening. She packed everything up, retrieved her aunt's Land Rover from the nearby garage where she'd parked it, and loaded up her mother's art.

Before getting on the road, she texted Otis:

Headed back.

The skies were dark, and it had started to rain. It was really coming down by the time Lindsey pulled out. She was tempted to wait one more night so she wouldn't have to drive in the rain, but then she'd have to unpack her mother's pieces and park the car again, which sounded like way more effort than driving slow.

Her cell rang thirty minutes in. The number was unfamiliar, and from New York. Possibly a work call, so she picked it up.

"Lindsey." It took a minute, but then she recognized the dry, nasal voice of the woman from the jewelry shop. "I was so interested in the ring that I researched it the moment you left. We indeed have a record of it. I was curious if you'd like me to send you the information that we have or if you'd like to swing by. It turns out, some additional work was completed on the original ring after the costume piece was made. Several years later."

Lindsey hesitated. Otis might still be in the city, and she could ask him to go. But the shop was across town from his apartment, and it would be a hassle.

"Send it to me, if you don't mind," Lindsey said. "Was it a repair?"

"No, it was an inscription," she said. "Commissioned by Elliot Mensley the summer of 1935. I'll text it to you."

"Oh." Lindsey bit back the words *Elliot was my great-grandfather*. "Yes, please. Thank you for all your help."

Lindsey pulled into a rest stop and waited for the photo text, baffled. She clicked it open and stared at the words in confusion.

"No, this can't be right," she said.

The work commissioned in 1935 was a message to be engraved on the interior. The inscription read: *2.27.32 R E Forever.*

Lindsey picked up the phone and called Otis.

He picked up on the first ring. "Hey, I'm going to leave in the morning. The rain's made it a mess here. Are you already back?"

"No, but I'm on the road, and I am losing my mind." Quickly, she explained about the ring. "How did my great-grandfather end up with the ring? I'm having a hard time processing this. Take a look at this inscription."

Lindsey sent the picture and put him on speaker. She knew the second he read it, because he blurted out, "The family was killed in 1931."

"Exactly," Lindsey said.

Otis went silent. "You don't think he killed them, do you?"

Lindsey's heart dropped. "No. He wouldn't do that."

The words sounded foolish, even to her own ears. She knew nothing about her great-grandfather, not really. Only what they had read in Ruby's diary about him. The police had never caught the killer; they had just chalked the murder up to organized crime.

"Well, he had the ring," Otis said. "Your family also ended up with the property. Do you know how that came about?"

"No. I . . ." Lindsey paused, staring out at the rain. "I don't know."

Even though she did not want to consider this angle, it made sense. What if her great-grandmother, Annabelle, had been poorly treated while she worked for the Thornhills? Perhaps Elliot sought revenge on her behalf. The thought was unsettling, but it would explain why the property was left vacant and her grandmother refused to have a thing to do with it.

"I don't know," Lindsey said. "I have to think on this one."

They sat in silence.

"Well, I don't know what to tell you," Otis said. "Except that you're going to have quite a bit to report back to your aunt."

The rain started to come down hard, and Lindsey pulled into the parking lot of a small bakery in Poughkeepsie to wait out the storm. While she waited, she considered the collection in her back seat. She felt almost guilty, like she'd pulled off a jewelry heist in the highest degree, but she was beyond grateful to have these pieces of her mother's work.

Lindsey could hardly wait to see them, to take the time to sit and study her unseen work. It would be like having a conversation with her mother all over again, something she'd been waiting for since the moment she'd passed. Lindsey planned to speak to her father about the pieces only once she'd spent the time that she needed with them, and determined what role she wanted them to play in her life. This opportunity felt freeing, as if it had opened something in her heart that had been closed off for too long.

The rain eased up, and she pulled back onto the road. She turned up her music and started singing, just like Otis had done that one day. For fun, she rolled down the window and relished the feeling of the light mist on her arm and the sound of her voice in the dark night.

When she finally made it to Aunt Petra's, a few branches from the storm were down on the drive up, and it had started to rain harder again. Lindsey parked closer to the house, since she didn't have an umbrella. The headlights reflected off the front porch, where the screen door had blown open.

"Oh, look at that," she said, surprised.

The wind had been strong enough to not only blow open the door, but to break the glass pane next to the front door. She started to get out of the car to take a look, but suddenly, it hit her.

The wind hadn't done that.

Someone had broken into the house.

Chapter Twenty-Nine

Wind Thorne, February 1931

Soon after Ruby found people in the tunnels, they disappeared. No trace except the stench and the refuse. It took some cautious snooping, but she finally found a paper trail that led to a farm two counties over.

Ruby met with Chester in the secluded spot in the forest to discuss it. The light dusting of snow on the ground and a chill in the air encouraged her to pull her coat close.

"I know where they went," she said. "The records are buried in my sister's files. They're at a dairy farm twenty miles away."

The sale had been to one of the wealthier farms in the region. They'd paid an exorbitant amount of money for an exchange that trapped the workers into servitude. Based on her sister's paperwork, this had happened many times before, involving several farms in the area.

"They make contracts with each of the servants." Ruby felt her cheeks flaming with fury, thinking about it. "My family has paperwork that they probably forced them to sign, and the new owners hold their immigration papers until their debt is paid off."

"What debt?" Chester demanded.

Ruby sat on the cold ground, leaning against a tree. Her coat was long enough that the snow didn't seep through, but it still left her chilled.

"The passage overseas," she said. "They have to work to pay it off. Annabelle said my family doesn't tell them until they're here and it's too late. Of course, the money earned is so low it would take years for them to make good on it."

The injustice was blistering. Slavery had been abolished in 1865. Yet a different form of slavery was thriving thanks to people like her father, who thought he was above the law.

"Do you have the exact address of the farm that bought them?" he asked.

"I do." Ruby lifted up a patch of decayed leaves and watched them flutter back to the ground. "Do we turn them in to the authorities? My family is protected around here, but surely their reach only stretches so far. Do you think we could inform the police in that county?"

Chester settled in next to her, deep in thought. Finally, he spoke. "Elliot's about to be on a six-month furlough. He comes back home next month. I've been talking to him about this situation."

Ruby sat up straight. "I don't think that's wise."

It felt dangerous to bring other people into this terrible secret. Like it could quickly spin out of control. On top of that, Ruby didn't know if she could trust Elliot. He had been annoyed when she'd stayed in Manhattan with him and his brother, instead of returning home like a dutiful girl.

"Elliot could help. He . . ." Chester went quiet. "You're upset?"

Her throat was so tight, it was hard to speak. "I'm scared."

"It's a difficult thing, but—"

"It's not about that." Ruby looked down at her hands. She'd forgotten gloves in her eagerness to see Chester, and her skin was red and chapped from the cold. "Elliot knows the truth about New York. It makes me nervous."

What if he decided to tell everyone that Ruby had stayed in a room with the two boys? Her family would send her away in a heartbeat.

"Ruby, you can trust him." Chester seemed puzzled. "He's family."

The statement was so absurd that she nearly laughed out loud. Her family didn't have one person she could trust, not really. Elizabeth, maybe, but when it came down to it, her sister would give her the gate for Glenn. Even if it was just self-preservation.

"Family?" she scoffed. "Since when does that mean anything?"

Chester took her hands. The touch of his skin, the warmth and the calluses of his fingers, made her entire body flush.

"Ruby, I am so sorry your family is the way it is. Mine's different. We're loyal to one another. Hurting you would be hurting me. Elliot knows that. He knows that I . . ." He squeezed her hands tightly, then let them go. "You can trust him. To the end."

Chester was so honorable. So good. Such a different person from what she'd expected him to be, so long ago. If he trusted Elliot, she would do her best to do the same, in spite of her nerves.

"So, he wants to help?" she asked.

"Yes." Chester nodded. "He knows a lot of people from his work with the navy. Ones with boats that can help the people get back home."

Ruby had never dared hope to accomplish something like that. The thought nearly brought her to tears. If they could help these people escape, if there was still room for this to be fixed, it might still be possible to make it right.

"Elliot and I have talked about it in detail, and we think the best thing to do is travel back with them. That would ensure they're returned safely, and not put into another bad situation."

"Is that safe for the two of you?" she wondered.

"It might not be safe, but it's right."

The sun dipped behind the trees, basking the forest in golden light. Ruby considered the desolate trees, stripped of their leaves and hunkering down for winter.

"How long would it take?" she asked. "How long would you be gone?"

"Maybe a month, depending."

That was a long time to be without him. Besides, so many things could go wrong.

"How does Elliot know the ship captain can be trusted?" she asked.

"Because the captain has no connection here," Chester said. "None at all. For him, it would be about the money. There would be no danger once Elliot and I got the workers on the boat."

"What about before that?" she asked.

He squinted up at the sky. "Yeah, it's a risk." They were both silent. "We'll be stealing the people from the other farm, essentially. That alone is not going to be an easy thing to do, not to mention getting the servants out from here."

"It all sounds dangerous." Ruby couldn't imagine putting Chester in harm's way. "Isn't there another way?"

"I spoke to Elliot about it on the phone, and he's working on a few different plans."

She leaped to her feet. "But Madeline Pierce listens to everything!" The operator who ran the phone lines would have reported it all back to her father, which meant they were already in danger. "Chester, we—"

"It's fine, I promise," he said, stretching his legs out as if he didn't have a care in the world. "Madeline Pierce will tell everyone I'm arranging a large shipment of cattle with my brother. Elliot and I already discussed it in our letters, including a plan for communication. We're speaking in code."

Relief nearly knocked her down. "Code?"

"Yes." He grinned at her. "It's not as clever as pig Latin or anything, but we've replaced a few key words."

"Thank goodness." She admired him so much. "You're really smart, Chester, to think of all that."

He looked at her in surprise. "No one's ever called me 'smart' before."

How could that be? Chester was one of the most intelligent people she'd ever met. He worked hard, was so kind, and had shown her a level of loyalty and friendship far beyond anything she'd ever experienced. She wanted to tell him all of that, but she feared the words would scare him off again.

Instead, she shoved her hands in her coat pockets and leaned back against the log. "So, where can we get the money to manage all this? Your father used his resources on us, and my family doesn't have a thing to spare."

"I have an idea," he said. "But I'd need your permission."

Chester paused, then took her hand once again. This time, he slowly traced her ring finger, then set something cold and hard inside her palm. Gently, he folded her fingers over the top of it.

Ruby gave him a questioning look, then opened her hand.

"Oh . . ." she breathed.

To see the ring again was an answer to a prayer she had not yet made. With fingers that now trembled with cold, she held it up. The evening light caught its dazzling prism, and it lit up in a rainbow of gold, purple, blue, and green. She squeezed it tight.

The feel of it—the cold, hard strength—reminded her of the dark days when the very presence of the ring had kept her going.

The right decision, the right thing to do, would be to return it to her sister. To let Elizabeth make the choice about where to plant this magical seed and see if something good could grow. Yet, Ruby found it impossible to accept the idea that her sister knew their workers were being sold and had done absolutely nothing to stop it.

With a slow nod, she said, "You're sure the captain will accept it?"

"We can't give him the ring," Chester said, looking surprised. "It's too valuable. We'd have to sell it, and you'd have money left over to use as you saw fit."

The idea of turning the ring into money felt worse, somehow, than simply passing it along.

Chester studied her for a moment. Then, in a low voice, he said, "Ruby, can I talk to you about something? It's weighing on my mind."

Still holding the ring tight, she leaned back against the log. Birds called to one another as squirrels rustled from tree to tree. Chester looked upset, suddenly, and she waited for him to speak. It was possible he was about to say that he couldn't separate her from her family and their crimes, and that he'd want to maintain a greater distance as soon as this ordeal was over.

"Ruby, I . . ." His cheeks flushed. "Do you know my father has a long relationship with the Cooks?"

The words dropped like a tree. She'd wondered a few times already if Chester had returned to marry Eleanor Cook. That, once the workers had been returned to their homes, he'd have to focus a little bit more on that part of his life. It was coming; she'd learned it that day in New York City, but that didn't make it hurt any less.

"I do," she managed to say. "Elliot once said you plan to marry Eleanor."

Chester rested his elbows on his knees. "Her father, Wyatt Cook, is like a brother to my father. It's been an expectation for years that I would marry Eleanor."

Heartbreak pounded in her ears. "I've heard as much." The sound of her voice seemed far away, like a bird above the trees. "Eleanor is . . ." She knew she should be able to say "lovely," or "kind," or "a good choice for a wife," but the words wouldn't come. Instead, the trees blurred.

"The thing of it is," Chester said, "I don't want to do that."

She looked at him in surprise. "You don't?"

"No."

Her heart soared, but just as quickly, she reminded herself to remain calm.

Just because he doesn't want to marry her doesn't mean he wants to marry you.

The words had no sooner passed through her mind than Chester Mensley got down on one knee and took her hands. Those warm eyes, the ones that had been as steady as the moon through all of it, gazed at her.

"Ruby, I fall asleep every night thinking of your face," he said, and her heart started to pound. "I wake each day thinking of your smile. You have been a part of my thoughts ever since you jumped on that train with me."

Chester took a deep breath and held her hands tight. Ruby squeezed back as tightly as she could, afraid that if she let go, this moment would fade into a dream.

He cleared his throat. "The thing about my thoughts, Ruby, is that they're pretty simple: I love you."

Love. He'd said it.

Tears pricked at her eyelids. She tried to blink them back, but it was impossible.

"I'm in love with you, Ruby," he said, laughing and wiping her tears away. "I have been for quite some time."

Images of Chester sitting up on the roof in Manhattan, stealing a glance at her while they worked, and bringing her safely home on the train flashed through her mind like a movie.

"I want to spend my life here, with you," he said. "I want to get married to *you*. Do you want that, too?"

"Oh, yes," she whispered. "Of course I do."

He pulled her to him, the scent of the woods rich all around. With his arms tight around her, she finally felt how strong he really was. She marveled at the incredible feeling of being in his arms, hot with desire to be so close to him.

The world stilled as their eyes met. Chester leaned forward and kissed her, the salt of his lips mingling with the softness of hers. It felt like dancing inside the prism of the diamond ring.

"I love you with every breath," he whispered, in between kisses. "I have never in my life met anyone with such a pure heart."

"Not that pure," she said. "You should hear what I was just thinking about Eleanor Cook."

Chester started laughing. Then, he kissed her again.

The heat between them built, and they eased to the ground, kissing until she could no longer think, and her hair was wet with snow. Chester eased back from the kiss, searching her eyes.

"We should take it slow." He traced her lips with his finger before kissing them once again. "Your family can't know we're engaged. Not yet. I need to formally ask your father for your hand, and he still might say no."

"He won't do that." Ruby held tight to his hand. "My father owes your father in more ways than one. It might cause anger that he wasn't the one to orchestrate the engagement himself, but he won't say no."

"There's another issue. Your family is about to get in serious trouble." Chester's tone was apologetic but frank. "They could easily . . ."

"End up in prison," Ruby said. "I know."

Picking up a small stick, she sat up and drew patterns in the light dusting of snow. "I do hope my father will find a way to heed the lesson without doing time. Is that wrong?"

"I understand that." He shrugged. "More than you know."

"How so?" she asked.

Chester looked down. Sometimes, his face closed up in a way she didn't understand. Reaching out, she brushed her fingers along his strong jaw.

"I love you, Chester," she said, quietly. "No matter what. There's no need to hide anything from me."

"I'm not hiding," he said. "I'm just surprised, that's all. I never thought life could turn out so good for someone like me." He pulled her in close. "I love you, Ruby."

"Always?" she said.

"Forever," he said before pulling her into another kiss.

Ruby's relationship with Chester became a delicious secret and a carefully orchestrated introduction of him into her family's lives. She started her plan the next morning at the breakfast table. The entire family was seated, their forks clinking as they ate soft-boiled eggs, toast, and bacon: the type of meal that was no longer abundant but somehow still served each day at Wind Thorne.

Ruby smeared a luxurious pat of butter on a corn biscuit. She was about to take a bite when she stopped, as if something had just occurred to her.

"Mother, have we sent any type of baked good as a thank-you to the Mensleys?" she asked.

Her mother stopped eating and frowned. She glanced at Ruby's father, who remained expressionless.

"No," her mother said, patting the corners of her mouth with a napkin. "It hadn't occurred to me."

"It might be nice, considering what they did," Ruby said.

"There are no secrets at Wind Thorne," her father muttered, then gestured for more coffee.

No secrets, but several injustices that boiled steadily at the surface.

Ruby offered to drop a batch of biscuits off at the Mensley household, and invited Elizabeth to join her.

When they arrived at the small house next to the river, they were greeted with a subtle smile from Chester's father and polite conversation from Chester.

"It's nice to see the two of you," Chester said, once they'd all exchanged pleasantries. "Perhaps I will come to call sometime. Would that be all right?"

Elizabeth fumbled with her words but said, "That would be kind."

On the walk home, she looked back over her shoulder at the house and frowned. "Father will be full of fury at that one. I hope he doesn't come to call."

"Me too." Ruby hated that she had to lie to Elizabeth, but it was the only way. "I will be polite, though, if he does. It's only right, since they've helped us."

"True." Elizabeth shuddered. "I hope, for your sake, he doesn't."

Two days later, Chester knocked on the front door. He presented Ruby with a small bag of chocolates for her family, and one exclusively for her grandmother.

"Did you steal these?" her grandmother demanded, with an accusing glare.

Chester's grin was cocky, the same one Ruby remembered from back when he was a teenager. "I have a few friends at the store two counties over. If you like those, I can get more."

"Was that true?" Ruby asked him as they paraded through the field in sight of everyone at the house. "That you have an endless supply of chocolate?"

"No," he said, laughing. "I had to pay a fortune to get them, but if it makes your father like me, we'll be married five times faster."

"You are full of surprises," she said.

"So are you," Chester said, giving her a look that made her flush down to her toes.

Chester returned several times over the course of the next few weeks. As they walked, they discussed their plan to help the people her family had wronged. At the house, Ruby slowly started to mention how kind Chester was, and how interesting. Eventually, Elizabeth even commented that he was almost handsome.

Every eye was upon them each time they circled the fields, but outside of that time, when no one was watching, she and Chester found several opportunities to slip away together. They stopped going to the forest, because anyone could pass by. Instead, they met in the loft of an abandoned barn on his family's property, finding warmth in the hay and in each other's arms.

Each outing had become more passionate, but Ruby had a burning question that finally, she couldn't help but ask. She pulled back from Chester, breathless.

"What did Eleanor Cook say?" she demanded. "When you told her?"

Ruby had blurted out the words before she could stop herself, when she and Chester were in a state of half undress. In spite of her desire for him, she couldn't give over to the moment because she was overcome with guilt at the idea that she'd stolen him from another woman. Chester, who always seemed to understand what was on her mind, smoothed her hair.

"Have you been worried about that?" he asked.

"Yes," she said. "I feel terrible."

"Well, you don't need to," he said, nestling against her so she could rest her head in the crook of his arm. "Eleanor . . . laughed."

"What?" Ruby gasped. "What do you mean?"

Chester started to chuckle. "Eleanor fell in love with one of her cousin's friends during the summers we were away. When she heard I'd come back, her heart was broken. She was thrilled to learn I didn't intend to hold her to marriage."

"Thrilled?" Ruby echoed.

"Downright gleeful," he said, and the two of them started laughing. "It was damaging for my pride for about two seconds, until I remembered the reason I'd called it off in the first place. You." His expression became serious. "I love you, Ruby. I am truly the luckiest man alive."

Chester gently stroked her face, gazing at her with adoration. Slowly, as he leaned in to kiss her once again, the kiss grew more fierce. This time, she didn't pull back, but pulled him in closer. Her conscience was clear, and Ruby ached to give him her whole heart, to celebrate the life they would soon share, together.

Chapter Thirty

Upstate New York, present day

Lindsey stared at the broken window by the door in disbelief. She triple-checked that her car doors were locked and then called the police. In a shaking voice, she relayed what she was looking at, and hoped that whoever had done this had not paid a visit to Wind Thorne.

"Ma'am, you're at a remote location." The dispatcher's voice was steady. "I need you to go back down to the main road and wait for the police to arrive. Can you do that? They'll escort you back up."

It took every ounce of self-control to follow the directions instead of rushing straight into the house to see if anything had been taken. But at the same time, the thought of someone hiding in there or even waiting in the woods pushed her to drive quickly over the ruts of the driveway and back to the main road.

Two police cars arrived with their lights flashing. One of the officers got out and walked to her car, rain streaming down his coat. He had a steady gaze that made Lindsey feel guilty, even though she hadn't done a thing.

"Did you see anyone up there?" he asked.

"No." Lindsey's hands shook.

Had someone been there? What would have happened if she'd walked in without noticing the door?

"We're going to go on up and take a look."

"Can I follow?" Lindsey asked. The road was dark, and she didn't want to sit there alone in her car.

"That's fine," he said. "Just don't get out of your car."

The other officer had gotten back in his cruiser and pulled past Lindsey. He tore up the gravel drive, lights flashing. Lindsey followed close behind.

Once parked, the first officer walked over and tapped on her window.

"Roll up your windows and lock the doors until we give the all clear." He and his partner approached the house, ducking in the rain, hands on their holsters.

Lindsey sat in silence. She was freezing, either from the cold or fear, and she turned on the heat. It fogged up the glass, and she nearly had a heart attack when one of the officers came out of nowhere and tapped on her side window.

"It's clear."

Lindsey braced herself for an absolute mess, but when she walked in, it was as if nothing had happened. There were no contents from the drawers covering the floor, no books scattered on their spines, not even pictures on the wall tilted to the side. The only thing that was out of place was the open drawer on her aunt's desk in the living room.

Lindsey's heart sank. The drawer had not been open when she left, she was certain of that. The day she'd opened the safe, Lindsey had put the key right back where she'd found it and shut the drawer tight. Chills ran down her arms to see it wide open.

Quickly, she crossed the room to look in the drawer. There was the black stapler, the collection of ballpoint pens and silver paper clips, but no key. Lindsey's knees went weak, and she sat down in the desk chair.

"The key is missing," she said to the officers. "It's the key to a safe at Wind Thorne."

The desk was right by a picture window that looked out over the woods. Anyone could have been hiding out there, watching as she hid it. They could be standing there right now, cloaked in the darkness, and she shuddered.

"My aunt, the owner of this house, also owns the Wind Thorne estate," Lindsey said. "She's turned it into a museum, and I recently discovered a safe there with several valuable pieces."

Mentally, she ran through the items. The gold bars, the necklaces, and, of course, the copy of the ring. She couldn't believe she had stayed in the city for so long without coming back to have them appraised and insured.

"We need someone down at Wind Thorne, right away," she said to the police. "The key goes to that safe, and if someone was watching me here, they could have been watching me there."

"Why do you think someone was watching?" one of the officers asked. "Did anyone else know the location of the key?"

Lindsey squeezed her hands tight. "No."

Otis had helped open the safe, but he hadn't been with her when she put the key away. Either way, he wouldn't have done this. But who had?

She could think of a few possibilities.

Amrita, to start. She had such a sense of entitlement about the property. It wouldn't shock Lindsey to learn that she would stop at nothing to see the items in the safe. That said, Amrita might be a bit mercenary, but she'd never struck Lindsey as a criminal.

It also could have been someone local. Half the women on the cruise with Aunt Petra were from here. Her aunt could have talked about the safe while at dinner on the cruise ship. It would only take one mention in front of an unethical friend or family member to cause this.

Lindsey got to her feet. "We need to go over there. I haven't been here, so I don't know when the break-in happened, but I do know the night watchman doesn't get to Wind Thorne until nine. So, if someone's planning on using the key, now's the time to do it."

Lindsey gripped the steering wheel tight as she followed the police cruiser down the drive. Its red and blue lights flashed in the night, lighting up the woods with an eerie glow. Quickly, she called Aunt Petra, who didn't pick up because it was the middle of the night there. Lindsey was careful to keep her voice calm as she left a detailed message about what had happened.

"I'm headed to Wind Thorne with the police," she said. "Hopefully, the safe wasn't found. I'll keep you posted."

Lindsey hung up, her mouth dry. It had been difficult for Otis and her to track down the safe, so it was unlikely someone could just waltz in and find it. Unless her aunt had said where it was or if she and Otis had been watched.

Her shoulders tensed at the thought.

Lindsey pulled into the parking lot, and one of the police officers signaled for her to stay in the car. She nodded. The rain had let up, and beneath the clear night sky, Wind Thorne looked as silent as a tomb.

The police approached the front of the house first, then scanned the perimeter. Lindsey's windows started to fog again, so she cracked it and hunkered down, waiting. A sudden shout made her jump, and she rolled the window right back up, taking slow breaths and wondering if she needed to drive away. Finally, an officer approached the car.

"The estate has been broken into." His expression was dark. "The window in the library is broken."

Lindsey put her hand to her mouth. "Did you see the safe?"

"We haven't been in," he said. "I need the code and the key to the front door. We'll signal if it's clear for you to come in."

Once again Lindsey waited, her heart heavy. Finally, the officer signaled from the door. She ran across the lot and up the steps, nearly slipping in her haste.

"Was the safe open?" she asked.

"We didn't see a safe, but there's been some damage to the desk."

Lindsey ran past him. The library looked less cozy and inviting than it had the morning she and Otis had been there. The window had been smashed, and shards of glass were scattered across the polished mahogany floors. The part of the desk with the safe had a corner of it completely broken off, but the square that housed the safe was still untouched.

Lindsey knelt down and pulled off its wooden corners. The safe was still there, and it was locked. She studied it, unsure whether or not it had been opened.

"That's something," the officer said. "I never would have known to look in there. Has anything been taken?"

"Without the key, I don't know," she admitted. "We need to get a locksmith over here."

The night watchman arrived, and the police updated him on the situation. They dusted the house for fingerprints and asked for more information, while Lindsey did her best to remain calm and remind herself that it wasn't her fault if anything had happened. She talked to the police about the objects that should be in the safe and tried to explain the importance of the ring.

The officer checked his notebook. "Did anyone other than you know of the location of the safe and the key?"

Lindsey hesitated. Otis had seen the location of the safe, and he knew she had the key. He was also the only one who was an expert on diamonds. She trusted him, but maybe that had been a mistake, especially when money was on the line.

Her father was the perfect example of that. It didn't matter how much her mother's jewelry meant on a sentimental level. The only thing he thought about was how much money he could make from selling it. That betrayal had come from someone she'd known her entire life; Otis, she'd known for about five minutes.

He wouldn't do this, though. No chance.

The officer reviewed his notes. "I understand that you don't want to accuse anyone, but any information you could give us would be helpful."

Otis had arrived in Manhattan after she had. He could have broken into her aunt's house at any time, but not Wind Thorne. He wouldn't have had time, because he was still in the city.

Supposedly.

What proof did she have that he was still there? She hadn't heard from him since he'd called to say he was staying. It was possible, if she wanted to give over to this line of thinking, that he'd left the city before she had, for the very purpose of coming here.

Never trust a gem dealer.

Otis could identify a real diamond a mile away. Lindsey could not. On top of that, she'd never once questioned his assessment, not even when the woman at the jewelry store warned her to get a second opinion.

"Ma'am?" the officer said. "I'm reading my notes. You said this ring was costume jewelry. Let me ask you: Why would someone risk two break-ins to get their hands on a fake?"

The rain was coming down again outside, and its mist chilled her through the broken glass.

"Because"—Lindsey turned away from the window—"I'm starting to think the ring in the safe might not be the fake."

Chapter Thirty-One

Upstate New York, April 1931

Dinner was quiet, as the men of the house had left that morning on their annual fishing trip. Her mother eyed Ruby's plate with disapproval, so Ruby picked up her fork and took a few more delicate bites.

It was important, when looking back on today, that her family would not be able to pinpoint any moment that might indicate Ruby was up to something. Besides, it made sense to try to enjoy the meal, since it might be the last good one she would have for a while.

The braised beef and warm bread smelled decadent, but it was hard to choke it down. There were only five hours to go until the escape that she and Chester had orchestrated. If Ruby held her breath, it felt simple. Like everything was under control. But the moments she forgot the fight to stay steady, her silent panic would begin again.

The ship was at port. The trucks were ready, waiting in the woods, with drivers from New York City. It was unseasonably cold with an unexpected snow, but that wouldn't interfere. Everything had come together so seamlessly, as if the world was pleased with them for doing good. Ruby didn't even have to sell the ring. The ship captain insisted on doing it all for free. It all seemed so simple, but with every moment that passed, her anxiety grew.

Ruby was three weeks late. Such a joyous secret, created in love and reckless abandon as she and Chester rejoiced in their upcoming marriage, but the news about the baby had added a new level of worry.

Chester was certain their plan would be perfectly executed. But what if something happened? Ruby hadn't yet told him about the baby, because each time she considered the idea, she worried Chester would call it off. The memory of that man in the tunnel, with his ankles shackled and fear in his eyes, strengthened her resolve to keep the secret until they were safe.

It was the right thing. They were doing the right thing, and in doing the right thing, surely nothing could go wrong. True or not, it's what she needed to believe.

Sipping her water, she looked up at the clock.

Dinner ended, and her family adjourned to the conservatory. Snow fell outside, and Ruby pulled a blanket close. Her grandmother sat in the corner with a glass of whiskey, her mother embroidering at her side. It was dark outside, and Ruby's hands shook with nerves. She sat with an unread book of love poems in her lap, listening to her sister sing at the piano. Elizabeth was off-key, but her face was bright, her old spirit on display now that Glenn would not be back for several days.

The room was peaceful, and for half a moment, Ruby regretted what she'd set into motion. In her mind, she'd imprisoned the women in this room in a cage of guilt, but they were also her family. They would have been the people she would have relied on for advice about her child, but knowing what they'd done, she could barely look them in the face at all. Still, they were family. Shouldn't there be some grace in that?

Her gaze moved to the back hall. The staircase was out of sight, but the memory of Indira's scream cut through her.

No. What she was doing was right.

Tonight, she and Chester would free the servants at Wind Thorne and the ones they'd found in the tunnel, recently placed in a nearby farm. Once they'd been escorted back to safety, her father, Peter, and the buyers would be brought to justice. Ruby had carefully researched the notes in her sister's folder and built a list of the farms where the servants had been sold. The authorities in each county would be notified. Then, using the evidence Ruby had compiled, the authorities could free the servants and prosecute the men responsible for it all.

Ruby was reluctant to implicate her father, but there was no way around it. She just wanted to get it over with and get these people safely home. Shifting in her seat, she picked up her book. She'd finally managed to focus on the words on the page when the butler, Njaka, appeared.

Elizabeth stopped singing. "Did you need something?"

"Miss Ruby." He stared straight ahead, his face formal and impassive. "Father Aaron has called."

"Why?" Ruby leaped to her feet.

Chester and Elliot would be liberating the servants from the other farm in a few hours. Surely, they had not been found out before they'd even begun. The servants had all agreed that they wanted to leave, but only three servants knew of the plan, and they would not have said a word to anyone.

"I do not know, Miss," Njaka said.

Her grandmother tittered. "Ruby, do you have something you need to confess?"

Everyone in the room looked at her.

Ruby started to sweat. "Wouldn't it be something if I did?"

"It would be high time, actually," Elizabeth sighed, pushing a hair out of her face. "Mother, it's time we start thinking of finding an appropriate match for her before the Mensleys start to have expectations. Is this something you've considered?"

"Mother, is it all right if I speak to Father Aaron?" Ruby asked, sidestepping the conversation.

Her mother waved an impatient hand. "He's probably trying to get his hands on some dinner. Have the servants offer him a plate."

Ruby rushed down the hall at a quick pace. "Please. Is everything all right?" she asked Njaka. He was one of the three who knew what was happening, but his face did not betray a thing.

"No news." His tone was formal. "Father Aaron is waiting in the library. Please let me know if anything is required. Miss, I also want to say . . ." He stopped walking and met her eyes. "Thank you."

Impulsively, she reached out and squeezed his hand before ducking into the room.

"Good evening, Father." She was careful to keep her voice bright. "My mother would like to offer you dinner. Shall we go to the dining room?"

Father Aaron stood by the fire. "Dear child." Turning, he studied her intently. "We must speak in private."

The air felt cold, suddenly, and she shut the door. Taking a seat on the settee, she said, "How can I help you, Father?"

"I believe the question is, How can I help you?"

Her stomach dropped. "I'm not quite sure what you mean."

Father Aaron took a seat on the silk couch. He sat for several moments, then said, "I need to tell you a story."

"Of course." She settled in as if it were a typical night, entertaining one of the locals. "I do love a good yarn. Don't you?"

Father Aaron fiddled with the cuff of his sleeve. "Ruby, there are times in your life where someone pushes you to do something you never would have thought to do on your own. Have you experienced that?"

Chester. He made her laugh, he made her think, and she loved him with her whole heart.

"Yes." She rested her hand on her stomach. "You?"

Father Aaron nodded. "When I served in the war. With Peter."

Even the clock seemed to go silent. Every instinct in her told her to run, to find Chester before it was too late. But she may as well have been in the trenches, terrified to move for fear of what might hit.

There must have been a point when Ruby had heard where Father Aaron had come from, how he had become such an intrinsic part of her family, but she hadn't paid attention.

The priest folded his hands and let out a deep sigh. "Peter was the first person who told me I could change lives. I come from a family with eight brothers and sisters, you see. Much of my life, I was a mouth to feed, not a person. My entertainment was the Bible, which is how I learned to read. My family finally noticed me when I would recite passages. I carried that skill to the trenches, where, often as not, I would also quietly pray.

"Peter was always next to me," he continued. "One day, we got spooked, and I launched into prayer. It calmed everyone. Peter pulled me aside later. Told me I had a gift. Encouraged me to pray for others. To help them get through. That moment changed my life, Ruby. For the first time, I was more than a mouth to feed. I mattered. I had purpose."

Father Aaron fumbled through his pockets and wiped his spectacles with a handkerchief. Ruby smoothed her dress, wondering if she needed to feel as frightened as she did.

"You must be grateful," she said.

"Yes." Father Aaron hesitated, then put his glasses back on. "There's much that you don't know about Peter. Before he was wounded, he had a three-month furlough. He didn't want to waste it on a boat back home, so he stayed in Europe. He found his way to a small town right outside Paris. It was there that Peter fell in love with Indira."

"Indira?" Ruby was shocked.

"Yes. She loved him, too." Father Aaron frowned. "Perhaps the idea of him. A handsome young American soldier." He stared down at his hand, turning a small gold ring on his pinkie. "Peter wanted to impress her, of course, so he painted himself as a man of great wealth. He was, I suppose, compared to the people in her village. Her mother begged Peter to send Indira to the United States, along with several of her cousins, to keep her safe and in good company. Peter convinced your grandfather, who was still alive at the time, to take them on as workers. Two weeks after she arrived in the United States, Peter was badly injured. Nearly lost his leg."

Ruby's eyes filled with tears. "I didn't know it was that bad."

"How can we know the things people do not say?" His brown eyes met hers. "Indira was young, you see. She became bored waiting for Peter to return and admired another young, powerful man of the house." He paused. "If this will be painful for you to hear, I—"

Ruby shook her head. "Tell me."

"Peter's leg healed, but it was horribly disfigured on his upper thigh, with deep scar tissue that caused him great pain. He was in bad form when he returned home. Indira quickly lost interest in him and fell for your father instead."

"My father?" Ruby said, baffled. Then, it slowly clicked into place.

The fight the night of Indira's death. Peter's rage. How her mother had set her jaw and walked away, when she learned Indira had been pregnant.

"Yes, he favored her for years." The priest shook his head. "Peter didn't know at first, but by the time I arrived, he knew. He had written, you see, begging me to accept a job here. I was pleased to follow the man who'd put me on this path, but a broken heart can do funny things to a person. That, coupled with the things Peter had seen in the war and his injury . . . He was no longer the man I knew. Your father betrayed him so deeply. I was not about to betray him, too."

The room was cold, and Ruby blew warm air slowly into her hands, thinking. She looked at the clock. Chester and Elliot would be leaving soon, to wait in the woods by the other farm.

Father Aaron got to his feet. "Ruby, I came here tonight to tell you that Peter never meant to cause anyone harm. Yes, he betrayed her people. In doing so, he betrayed himself."

Ruby looked down at her hands. "Why are you here? Really?"

"Because when I see something that could cause great pain and suffering, it's my duty to stop it," he said. "Running will not be safe for the workers, Ruby. It's too much of a risk."

Her body went cold. "Who told you?"

"Annabelle."

"That's impossible."

Annabelle had been so desperate to help her mother and to return home.

"It's been a burden upon her. She needed to talk." Father Aaron shrugged. "I learn so many things, through no fault of my own. I don't believe she thought it through."

Ruby sat as still as a stone. "What happens now?"

"That's up to you." He stared at the snow falling softly outside the window. "Ruby, when I was put on the front lines, I asked God for a miracle. He brought it to me in the form of Peter. I have made many mistakes, but a lack of loyalty will not be one of them. However, I cannot allow him to hurt others. I suspected what was happening here, but he would not talk to me about it. No one would."

Ruby paced the room, considering the options. The servants had been told the wrong night, in the event that something like this would happen.

"Do you plan to stop it?" she asked.

"In the trenches, I sometimes wondered, 'Would these men push me into the line of fire to save themselves? Would I push them?' I knew the answer with Peter. He would not." Father Aaron's eyes were full of sorrow. "Peter has made many mistakes, but I know his heart. He deserves forgiveness."

He reached into his leather satchel and handed her a telegram.

"I sent this to the hunting lodge last night."

> Servants to run Wednesday night stop Plan in place stop Advise stop

"I have not heard back. I assume they are on their way back home."

The disinformation had worked. He had the wrong day. Ruby's heart pounded with relief.

"These people have been taken from their homes," she told him. "Held against their will. You, out of everyone, should be first in line to help us tomorrow night."

"Ruby, be sensible. The world is falling apart. What will these people do when they return home?" he demanded. "What is there for them? They may have less food and safety than they do here at the farm. The situation is unjust, but it's a form of protection."

"No." Ruby glared at him. "Saying they would be better off in captivity is not true, and it's not right. Slavery has been abolished, and that's what this is, no matter how you want to frame it."

Father Aaron bowed his head. "The church is one of the few places with the resources to make this right. I will talk to your father and Peter, and I will put a stop to what they are doing. But please, do not let it be in the form of a betrayal. Don't go through with this, Ruby. More can be accomplished with diplomacy." He reached into his satchel again and held out a sheaf of papers. "Read these. They were passed on to me by your grandfather, who kept them all. I would like you to get to know the man that was once Peter. To find forgiveness."

Ruby held fast to the letters. "Fine." She squared her shoulders. "I'll read them, but only if you will meet with my father and Peter. If they're unwilling to make this right tomorrow, we'll have no choice but to move forward with the plan."

"Thank you, Ruby." He got to his feet. "I will keep your name in confidence."

Ruby watched in silence as he swept out of the room, then squeezed her eyes tight. By the time Father Aaron met with her father and Peter, this would be over.

Betrayal.

Father Aaron's voice echoed back to her. It was all well and good that he didn't want to betray Peter, but she had bigger things to worry about.

If Ruby failed at helping these people, the true betrayal would be to herself.

Chapter Thirty-Two

Upstate New York, present day

The locksmith arrived just past ten, wet from the rain and escorted by the two officers outside. Lindsey had sat in the library, waiting in silence, her heart quietly breaking.

How could she have been so naive? She should have come back from Manhattan the moment her meeting was finished, pushed for an appraisal, and locked the items into a safe-deposit box. It was a disservice to her aunt and the trust she'd given her, as well as the entire estate.

"This is an old one, eh?" the locksmith said, getting to work.

It only took a minute before the safe clicked open.

Lindsey stood up. "Is it empty?"

The police officer opened the door using the type of stick she'd seen at the airport and concerts to search bags.

"There's a lot in here." The officer gestured at her. "Come take a look."

Lindsey knelt down, heart pounding, as he riffled through the items, not touching anything. For a moment, she felt optimistic. The papers were still there, and even the bars of gold. The more he moved things around, though, the more her hope dissipated.

"Do you see it yet?" the officer asked.

"No. It's . . ." He moved the wand again, and she nearly shouted at the sight of the ring box. "There! It's still there."

He put on gloves and reached in. Her heart pounded. Images of the broken glass in her aunt's front door, coupled with the smashed window on the floor in front of them here, flashed through her mind as he opened the box.

Lindsey nearly collapsed with relief. Steadying herself, she sat down on the floor. The ring was still there, perfectly nestled in the smooth white satin.

"Wait." A disturbing thought had crossed her mind. "I need to see it."

It was still possible the ring or even the stone had been swapped out, and no one would be the wiser. The officer handed her the box, and carefully, she removed the ring. She examined the gold band closely until she found the small dent she'd noticed when they'd found it, and the small scrape on the edge of the diamond. For the first time in hours, she could breathe.

"No one's touched it," she said.

"That ring is something." The officer looked impressed. "Makes sense you were concerned."

Lindsey's eyes smarted. It was such a relief that it hadn't been taken, but she also felt so much shame that she'd jumped to conclusions about the one person she was just starting to trust.

The police began to dust for fingerprints around the safe. She stepped into a corner in the house and held her phone tight. She wanted to call Otis but, to be honest, didn't feel like she had the right. Still, she called and felt relieved when he didn't pick up. After leaving a brief message, she called Aunt Petra again and left an update on her voicemail.

"The security guard will remain on the property," she reported, "and the police plan to patrol the grounds each hour, until the window is replaced in the morning. But everything's here. I'll get the items to a safe-deposit box at the bank first thing in the morning."

"Do you feel comfortable returning to your house tonight, or are you waiting on a friend?" an officer asked once she'd hung up.

"I'll be fine," Lindsey said. "Thank you."

He nodded and then escorted her out to the Land Rover.

It was chilly and wet, and Lindsey stared at the ground as they walked. Her eyes watched the gravel with each step, the old habit of searching for the ring embedded in the ground each time she was on the property.

Lindsey was exhausted, but her heart raced with adrenaline. The rain had stopped, and the sky appeared so vast compared to how it had looked framed by buildings in the city. It was clear, black, and dotted with thousands of stars.

"We'll keep you posted," the officer said.

Once Lindsey was safely in her car, he headed back inside. She checked her phone, still aching to talk to Otis but unable to place the call. She needed time to think, to understand what part of her had been so quick to not trust him. He deserved better.

Someone better than she was.

The thought made her eyes fill with tears.

Lindsey glanced up at the shadow of Wind Thorne, imposing in the dark night. She thought of Ruby, and all that she had been through.

One thing Lindsey admired about Ruby was her strength, her ability to keep going in the face of heartache. Through it all, she had somehow remained strong.

"Help me," Lindsey whispered. "Please, help me to do the same."

The next morning, Lindsey sat on the porch, gripping a cup of coffee. She'd barely slept a wink, due to the worry of it all, not to mention the broken glass next to the front door. To feel secure, she'd locked herself in her aunt's bedroom and pushed the dresser in front of the door, then lain awake listening for most of the night.

Every sound made her think someone was coming back into the house. It was a relief when morning arrived. Since she had barely slept, she was up with the sun.

Now she sat on the porch, dazed. She sipped at her coffee, absently staring at a large pine tree. The tree was tall but thick, with branches that jutted out. Beneath the tree, clusters of pine cones were grouped together, like dried-out clumps of fruit. It was hard to not imagine that someone could be hiding in that tree, or behind it.

Aunt Petra called shortly after seven. "Lindsey. Please tell me you're all right."

"It's fine, I'm fine, everything's fine," she said. "I plan to collect the contents of the safe and take them to the bank as soon as it opens. I'm so sorry for all of this. I should have taken care of everything immediately instead of staying in the city."

"Lindsey, it's not your fault." Aunt Petra's voice was gentle. "I'm just glad you're all right."

The police called shortly after they'd hung up and informed her that they were still waiting on fingerprints and would keep her posted if anything matched in the database.

Lindsey went inside to put her phone on the charger and refill her coffee. She'd just settled in again when she heard gravel crunching on the driveway. Some instinct made her fall back into the shadows. Her shoulders tensed to see Amrita's old car crawling up the drive.

Prickles ran up Lindsey's arms. Amrita had no reason to drop by unannounced at seven thirty in the morning. So far, Lindsey had given her the benefit of the doubt, but now, she quickly made her way toward the door, hoping not to be spotted in the shadows. Lindsey had parked in the garage because she wasn't sure if the storms were done, so Amrita had no way of knowing she was home.

The car door slammed as Amrita got out. She wore a white linen button-up shirt and a pair of khaki slacks, as well as several pieces of jewelry. As she walked to the house at a clipped pace, Lindsey noticed she had an old-fashioned carpetbag slung over her shoulder and carried a small vase of wildflowers.

Lindsey shut the front door and drew back into the living room. She waited, hoping this visit would be as simple as dropping off a gift.

After giving a quick look around, Amrita opened the screen door and then stopped, suddenly, when she spotted Lindsey in the shadows.

"Oh." She sounded startled. "You are here."

Lindsey swallowed hard. It wasn't as if the door could keep her out, so she opened it. "Hi. You didn't think I would be?"

Amrita held up her bag. "Well, it's early. I was going to surprise you with some flowers, but I do admit, I hoped you'd be up. I have more to show you. Some additional pieces my mother had." With the other hand, she held up the flowers. "I brought these to surprise you." She gave her a rueful grin and handed over the vase. It was cold in Lindsey's hands. "It's a thank-you for being so kind to me."

Their eyes met for a flicker of a moment.

Amrita was nervous. Hands shaking slightly, like she'd had too much coffee.

Lindsey took in a slow breath. Had Amrita planned to bring the flowers for this very reason, as an excuse to be on the property, so she could sneak back and return the key? By now, she could have had it copied and might be hoping no one was the wiser.

It might be true that Amrita had objects in the carpetbag to show her. Or that she was hoping for a tour. She hadn't called, though. The fact that she'd driven all the way up the drive, not knowing whether or not Lindsey would be here at all, felt off.

Amrita had never seemed dangerous. They'd bonded over the loss of their mothers, and she'd always been polite, even when she was disappointed in what Lindsey had offered to pay for the diary. Still, there was no getting around the fact that it was seven thirty in the morning, and she had no reason to be there at all.

The woman from the jewelry store jumped to mind once again, her eyes wise and weary.

You can't be too careful.

"Thank you for the flowers." Lindsey's voice was hollow. "These are beautiful."

Amrita glanced down. "Yes. I—" She smoothed her hair with one hand. "Hey, what happened there?" She gestured at the door, and Lindsey froze at the tone in her voice.

High pitched, false.

"Storm damage, I think." Lindsey's mind raced, trying to figure out how to get out of this. "I've been in the city. I just got back late last night. There were branches down, and all the things. Listen, I have to—"

"Do you mind if I come in?" Amrita gave her a bright smile. "I have a lot to show you."

Every instinct told her not to let Amrita in the house, but Lindsey had no idea what else to do. Her car keys were on the counter, but with the Land Rover in the garage and Amrita's car blocking the drive, it wasn't as if she could easily make some quick escape. Worse, Lindsey's phone was back by the bed.

Up until this point, Lindsey had never once thought Amrita would cause her harm, but she knew nothing about her, not really. In fact, Lindsey was willing to bet that if she turned out Amrita's bag, the key to the safe would tumble to the ground.

"Yes, okay," she said, slowly. "Let's sit on the porch. It's so nice out. I have to use the bathroom, but can I grab you a drink or anything while I'm inside? Coffee?"

At the very least, it would give her the opportunity to get her phone and text the security officer from Wind Thorne. The police would take too long, and Lindsey wanted her out of here, now.

"That would be great." Amrita took a seat. "Thank you."

Lindsey forced herself to walk slowly into the kitchen, then rushed to get her phone. When she was back, she peeked out the kitchen window that overlooked the porch. Amrita settled into the chair, then pulled something out of the bag. It was impossible to see what it was, but most likely, it was another artifact she hoped to sell.

Lindsey pressed her hands against the counter. The lack of sleep and the break-in might have been pushing her to jump to conclusions. The odds were good Amrita really had come here to leave some flowers and share some artifacts, and Lindsey had completely misread the situation. She wouldn't text the security guard quite yet, but she would take a minute to talk to Amrita and feel out the situation.

Relieved, Lindsey pulled out an extra coffee cup and started to pour. The sun was coming up and glinted off the metal of the object Amrita was holding. Lindsey squinted, trying to make out what it was. Then, she drew back in horror.

Amrita was not holding an artifact; she was holding a gun. A very modern one. Lindsey watched in shock as she slid it beneath her bag and waited.

Lindsey started to tremble.

Amrita must have broken in and stolen the key, but she'd either been interrupted by the arrival of the police the night before, or she couldn't find the safe. Now she'd most likely come here to force Lindsey to go over to Wind Thorne and show her where it was. Well, that wasn't going to happen.

Lindsey grabbed her phone from the bedroom and darted out the back door that led to the woods. She knew the path that led to Wind Thorne like the back of her hand. Heart thundering in her ears, she crept down the side of the lawn in the shadows and to the woods, then took off running.

Branches scratched her face, and she slipped on the mud from the day before, cutting up her ankle. She kept going, moving quickly and efficiently through the forest. Leaves and branches brushed against her face, and rotted leaves passed beneath her feet.

In the distance, she heard Amrita shouting. She sounded angry, and Lindsey ran faster, trying to call the security guard but unable to get reception. Quickly, she reassessed her plan.

If she made it to Wind Thorne, the security officer could be anywhere. If he was inside, she might not make it there with enough time to pound on the door and get his attention. It was too big of a risk. Instead, she cut to the right and headed toward the upper road, near the old warehouse.

Lindsey raced to the old building and pulled open the door. It was dark and smelled like rotting wood and mold. After waiting for her eyes to adjust to the darkness, she made her way to the old staircase. It was wooden and rickety, and parts of it were broken.

Tears smarted at the corners of her eyes, and she fumbled her way around, trying to find somewhere to hide. Nothing.

Heart pounding, Lindsey went to the stairs. She couldn't see, but she'd been in here often enough to know the stairs went straight down, about twenty-five feet. The structure wasn't sound, but maybe she could grab on to the wood and lower herself down, if it came to that, then run into the tunnels. She'd known them pretty well as a kid. Once her eyes adjusted, she could find her way around.

Gripping the wooden railing tight, Lindsey started down the stairs. They didn't feel solid, but they were steady enough. She moved quickly, then even more quickly when she heard a shout outside. Tears rolling down her cheeks, she clung to the wooden handle and made her way deeper underground.

Then, with a sickening crack, the stairs gave way. Her feet went out from under her, and she fell, crashing to the floor. Her head hit the ground with a teeth-numbing blow, and a warm trickle of blood ran somewhere near her ear.

Lindsey froze, staring up at the blackness, dazed and scared to move for fear of how bad the fall had been. Slowly, she moved her legs and winced. One of the broken boards from the staircase had her pinned.

It was so dark that she couldn't even see her hand. She squeezed her eyes shut. Her head ached, and her leg hurt like something was cutting it every time she tried to move it. She didn't know if any other parts of her body were bleeding.

Reaching around, she dared to touch her hair. Quickly, she drew her hand away, frightened by the feeling of the warm oily substance on it. Her phone was in her pocket, and she pulled it out, but of course, there was no reception in this tomb.

Using all her strength, she focused on trying to lift her knees enough to have the boards fall off. Nothing. Then, propping herself up with one elbow, she reached forward, the sharp pain in her head splintering with the effort. The boards wouldn't move. She was trapped.

Lindsey squeezed her eyes tightly shut, trying not to panic.

One of the things Ruby had talked about in her journal was the peace and solitude she had found in the warehouse and the tunnels. For the first time, Lindsey had a bone to pick with her. This was not peaceful. This was not good. Unfortunately, she might have the opportunity to speak with Ruby sooner than she'd planned.

The wooden door banged, and someone stormed into the warehouse.

"Lindsey! Where are you? I know you're in here."

It was Amrita. Lindsey held perfectly still, scared to move.

It might be smart to let Amrita know she was here instead of remaining trapped and in a place where no one could find her. Amrita most likely wanted to get into the safe, and Lindsey could offer to take her there, if she'd help get her free. Then, she could call for help the second her cell was aboveground. She felt so weak, though, that it might be impossible to fight back if things took a turn.

Amrita's flashlight clicked on, shining down into the dark space. The light swept across the darkness, then clicked off. Lindsey held her breath and stayed still. Moments later, the door banged shut, leaving nothing but silence.

Lindsey blinked at the sudden darkness.

The summer after she'd found her mother dead in the woods, Lindsey had often wondered what it had been like for her mother in those last few moments. Had she lain there for long, hoping someone would find her? Or had she died instantly, like the doctors claimed? Lindsey had always half worried that she, too, might suffer the same fate, dying alone in the woods.

It was frightening to think that, if the cut on her leg was in the wrong place, she might not make it. The gash was bleeding, that she knew, but it was impossible to feel how much or how quickly.

Remembering her phone, she shone her flashlight toward it, wincing at the ghostly sight of the gigantic boards pinning her down. It was hard to see much, but she saw a small pool of blood forming on the ground, and her head went light.

Lindsey used every ounce of energy she had to shrug out of her shirt and wrap it tightly around her leg, a few inches above the wound. Hot tears rolled down her cheeks as she thought of her father and her brother. She'd wasted so much time being angry with them. In the end, they were the ones she was thinking about.

She laid her head against the ground. It was cold and smelled like clay.

"Someone will come," she whispered. "They have to."

Everything felt a little blurry, and exhaustion covered her like a blanket. Finally, Lindsey gave up the fight.

Letting her eyes drift closed, she fell into a deep sleep.

Chapter Thirty-Three

Wind Thorne, April 1931

Ruby lay awake in her bed, listening to the silence and feeling sweat roll off her forehead at each passing moment. More than anything, she wanted to communicate to Chester, to let him know that they would have to run, too, but the news would have to wait. By now, he was at the other farm.

Staring from her window at the cold night sky, she thought about the things Father Aaron had shared about Peter. Life did change people. Good people sometimes broke beneath the weight of the stones piled on top of them. There were moments Ruby had seen that breath of goodness still in Peter, but little was left beyond that.

Ruby had tucked the letters Father Aaron had given her into a new hiding space in the floorboards with her journal. She got up now and pulled out the one on top. She hesitated, then brought the lamp closer, gazing at the neatly rounded cursive handwriting, the same way he still wrote, before reading the words.

> Brother,
>
> There were two moments where I thought it was the end for me last night. I was down in the dirt, my

fingernails digging into the ground. My body shook like one of the animals scared during the booming thunder of a storm. Darkness—sudden light—darkness. The smell of gunfire and sweat. I saw the people that mattered to me the most in those flames. You. Father. Mother.

I know we don't always get on and that we've had more than our fair share of disagreements, but if I don't make it out of this, let them know what I said. You've been a good big brother, strong and sure. I hope I'll see you back, but if I don't, put my words into your heart. If I do, I'll punch you a few times, to get us back to good.

Love you, brother.

Ruby stared at the words, then read them once again. She considered the packet of pages, so many in the stack. She tucked them back into her journal and put everything into a cotton sack.

Ruby did not remember much from the time her uncle returned from the war, as she was quite young, but she did remember the celebration. She was already close with Indira, who had brushed her hair that morning and plaited it in anticipation of his arrival. There had been ice cream and pie, and Ruby thought Peter ungrateful when he walked out to the pasture and stood there, his back turned to the family for hours.

Ruby wondered how many fights between him and her father had had to do with the fact that her father had taken Indira from him. That her father had never gone to war. Peter had often ranted at him, calling him a coward and a glutton. Someone who stole the spoils of war without having earned them.

Ruby's eyes filled with tears. She did not want to feel sorry for Peter; he was a monster. She had seen it in so many ways. But she knew enough to understand that she did not know war. That the people who made it out alive did not always make it out unchanged.

Father Aaron had spoken of betrayal. He didn't want Peter to feel that again. Would the priest betray her, once he learned that she had gone against his plea? Surely, he would.

It was so dark outside. The moon had yet to rise. She could barely see the outline of the trees against the forest, even with the glow of an unseasonable dusting of snow on the ground. The deep darkness chilled her with the reminder that everything could go wrong.

Chester had a place ready for her, three towns over, in a boardinghouse for unwed mothers. How fitting, although he did not yet know she was pregnant. She would fit right in. Wrapping her arms around her body, she considered the clock.

The reality that she wouldn't be coming back here tonight or anytime soon settled in her stomach, and then her heart. She had made a promise to her sister that she would never leave without explanation again. Even though her hands shook so much she might have difficulty forming a sentence, Ruby tore a piece of paper from her notebook and grabbed a pen.

She climbed up into her window seat and began to write. Once the note was finished, she carefully placed it in the envelope.

Earlier that day, Ruby had given the diamond ring to Chester's father, along with instructions to give it to her sister if Ruby didn't come back within six months. When they spoke, Ruby still had every reason to believe she would return to Wind Thorne, that no one would know she had planned the liberation of the workers.

With trembling hands, she left the goodbye note to Elizabeth on her desk.

It was time to face facts—she would never be welcome at Wind Thorne again.

Midnight approached. Ruby had instructed Njaka to have the workers gather in the servants' hall to address an emergency situation, without telling them what it was. There, they would dress in the boots and warm clothing that were waiting.

Ruby crept down the stairs to meet them, the cotton sack close against her body, holding a few underthings, dried meat, and a small flask of water. Her heart hammered in her chest, and the energy in the house seemed to crackle, but she did not hear a sound. For a moment, she expected her father to be waiting, and she steeled herself.

When she walked into the room, several tired eyes turned toward her. There were twenty workers present, including the household staff and the field hands.

Ruby locked the door of the hall behind her and in a low voice addressed the group.

"I'm so glad you're here." Her voice started to tremble, and she forced herself to stand a bit more firmly. "You also need to know that this is a risk."

Njaka translated into Malagasy, for those who could not speak English. Ruby explained the plan, step by step. First, they'd take a truck, followed by two small boats down the river, and a large boat across the ocean.

"We could get caught the moment we step outside," she warned. "My father and Peter know there is a plan to do this, but they don't think it's tonight. I need you to be quick, quiet, and to care for each other."

"What happens if we're caught?" one of the men asked.

She thought of Indira lying on the ground. "Then, God help us all."

There were no protests, no words of complaint. Ruby had been certain that at least one would protest, due to fear of leaving the farm in the dead of winter, in the thick of the Depression. Instead, they were all here, faces full of hope. The shame of that, the fact that these people were so desperate that they would risk their lives without protest, left her blinking back tears.

Standing up a little straighter, she pushed aside a tapestry and showed them the door that led to the tunnel. "We'll leave through here."

When she and Chester had first formulated this plan, they'd considered simply having the group walk as quietly as possible out the back door and run across the lawn to the forest. That idea made Chester nervous, for fear the commotion would wake the women in the household. Ruby's grandmother could not have done much to stop them, but both her mother and sister were dead shots.

Knowing that she would be responsible for leading the people out, Ruby had spent the past few weeks familiarizing herself with the tunnel. She'd drawn up several maps, exploring the different pathways and where they would lead. Now she handed the flashlight to Njaka and gestured that it was time to go in.

"Go in about thirty feet and wait," she instructed.

Njaka nodded and led the group down the narrow slope that would take them into the caverns. Ruby unlocked the door of the servants' hall and took one last look at the main floor of Wind Thorne.

Several moments from her childhood flashed through her eyes, including roller skating in the main hall with Elizabeth, hiding under tables to write in her notebook, and relishing endless moments of laughter. She'd felt heartache, but most of her memories were of a beautiful, safe home that smelled like whiskey, vanilla, and woodsmoke. Wind Thorne was a part of her soul, but she could not remain here, enjoying a livelihood that broke the back of others.

Still, Ruby wished she could have hugged her sister, mother, and grandmother one last time. She hoped that Elizabeth would pass along the messages she'd left in her letter and that, one day, they would forgive her. Until then, it was time to say goodbye.

Wiping away tears, she pushed back the tapestry and walked down the slope to join the others.

The tunnels led to the warehouse back by the road, where Ruby had first discovered the injured man. The group followed quickly and closely behind her. Once they reached the exit, she held up her hand, indicating they should wait.

The wood of the door was rough in her hand as she slowly eased it open. The field was quiet and still. She took a cautious step out, like a rabbit easing out from beneath a bush.

So much relied on that first group, the one at the other farm. If anyone in the house realized their workers were missing, they would look for them right away. It was also possible her father had guards waiting in the woods. It was what he did to protect the whiskey before large shipments, but if he didn't believe anything was happening until tomorrow, he wouldn't have called them. If he had, though, her group would need to move silently to avoid detection.

The snow crunched under Ruby's feet as she signaled for them to follow her out. They moved slowly and silently, with Ruby's heart pounding so loud it seemed to echo in the woods. It took fifteen minutes, but they finally made it across the road and to the clearing, where two large trucks waited, with Chester standing next to one.

He raced forward and held her close, his arms tight around her body. Relief rushed through her, and she found his lips, warm against her cold cheeks, and kissed him. The feeling of being in his arms made her feel safe for the first time all night. She wished they could stay there forever and let everything else fall down around them.

"I'm so glad you're all right," she whispered.

Chester entwined their fingers. "It went without a hitch. The message made it to the right person. Everyone was waiting, silent, in the woods. I almost couldn't believe it."

The happiness in his voice made her heart sing. Chester was so good. He wanted the best for her and for others, regardless of the risk.

He met her eyes and smiled. "Let's finish this." He lifted the flap in the back of one of the trucks, and the people from the tunnel stared at him with frightened eyes. Quietly, Njaka explained to them what was happening, and the man Ruby had found in the tunnel tightly hugged the woman next to him.

With Njaka's help, she and Chester boosted the group from Wind Thorne into the truck. Someone's boots clanged against the metal bottom, and Ruby put her finger to her lips. One of the field hands nodded, his face tight with anticipation.

Once the first truck was full, they helped load the second. Annabelle was the first one on. Ruby gave her a hug, feeling the quickness of the girl's breath, and squeezed her hand.

After everyone was in, Chester tapped the back of the first truck, the signal to start it up. The roar of the engines cut through the silent night.

"I'll be right back," he said.

The headlights flicked on, illuminating the snow that floated through the air. Chester ran to the front of the trucks to signal to the drivers that it was time to move. For the first time that night, there was enough light to see his face.

Ruby relished the freckles, that quick smile, and the eyes that seemed to see into the depths of her soul. He was walking back toward her when the first shot exploded in the night.

Time itself seemed to stop.

Her sister flashed through her mind, their childish games, her languid laugh, and the weight of the ring. Her parents. The farm. The cry of jazz music in the air. The sight of Indira crumpled on the ground.

The hum of the city, the ache of hunger. The dull gaze of Mary with her wide doe eyes. The heat in Chester's arms, and the freedom of a future that had just begun. It all went still.

Then. Her heart froze.

The bullet hit Chester with such force that he was knocked sideways, into the truck. The sickening crack of his head against the metal was louder than the next round of bullets fired, and Ruby slipped in her haste to get to him, before dropping to the ground where he lay, gasping and stunned, onto a pile of snow.

His eyes looked up at her, full of confusion and apology.

"It's okay," she pleaded, falling to her knees. "You're all right. We'll get you to the truck. Come on."

Njaka rushed toward them, followed by one of the field hands. Together, they helped Chester stand. Then she saw it. The snow beneath him was red.

"Chester," she whispered.

His hand pressed against his side. "Ruby, I—"

The next shots fired, and the first truck jerked into action, the back tires sliding in its haste. Ruby choked back a cry, as the men rushed Chester to the second truck with her. They tried to help him climb up into the back, but he groaned, leaning against the metal.

"Leave me," he gasped. "You have to save them."

"I'll never leave you," she cried.

Gunfire popped again from the woods, hitting the metal of the truck.

Two of the field hands, their eyes full of terror, jumped down and helped the other men pull Chester in. Then they lifted up Ruby before banging their feet against the floor to tell the driver to go. The gunfire became louder, closer, and several people screamed.

The truck lurched forward, and Ruby covered Chester's body with hers, holding him tight, as bullets pummeled the truck like rocks. Everyone screamed, dropping to the floor as she had.

The truck jostled her against him. Blood had soaked his shirt, and she searched for the wound with shaking fingertips. The bullet had gone through his arm and lodged in his chest, but he was still breathing. She pressed her hands tightly against the hole, desperate to stop the bleeding. Manda, the cook, tried to help her, but as the tires veered precariously through the slush, Chester gently pushed them away and fumbled for Ruby's hand. The warmth of their skin met, and Chester's eyes held hers.

"Save them," he whispered. "Ruby, I love you. Forever."

He gave her a small smile before his eyes closed, as if drifting into a gentle sleep. His expression was peaceful, and his hand rested with hers.

Ruby stared down at him, the scrape of branches slapping against the truck as it picked up speed and the bullets receded. Her heart started pounding, her body hot with fear.

"Chester," she whispered. *"Chester."* She shook him, but he didn't move. His head lolled back and forth, and she stared at him in disbelief.

He couldn't be gone. Not so easily. Not when there was so much yet to be done. So much of their life yet to live.

Ruby leaned in and listened for his breath, but she couldn't hear it. Manda tried, then drew back, before resting a hand on Ruby's shoulder. Outside, snow rained down and gunfire lit up the forest, too far away to hit. The rest of the people were still down on the floor, trying to escape the bullets, and several of them were crying.

Everyone was so alive. Everything was in motion. The snow, the truck, her tears. She put her head to his chest, desperate to hear his heartbeat.

"Chester, stay with me," she begged. *"Please."*

The truck moved quickly through the slush of the road, trying to make it to the spot at the edge of the river where Elliot would be waiting to load them onto small boats. He would have heard the gunfire and would be prepared to fight. They just had to make it that far.

Ruby held Chester tight, her hand still pressed against the wound. Her mind went back to that morning, so long ago, when he had been beaten up in the forest. Long before she had a future with him. Long before she decided he was her future.

A sob escaped her, and she buried her head in his chest, unable to tell the difference between the warmth of his blood and her tears. Manda patted her back, quietly whispering something that Ruby could not understand.

The brakes squealed as the truck came to a stop. One of the men Elliot had brought opened the back flap, and the terrified group jumped down, talking rapidly in their language. Several looked injured from the rough travel, but no one else had been shot.

Njaka gave her a sympathetic look as he passed, then helped Manda down from the truck.

Ruby stayed where she was, as the snow thundered down. Moments later, Chester's brother was there. He climbed up quickly, as if someone had already told him the news. He felt for a pulse and his face fell. Slowly, he lowered his arm and pulled Ruby in tight.

"He's not dead," she cried. "He's not!"

Ruby wouldn't allow it. Chester's body had moved as the truck rumbled along. His fingers jostled, his face swayed from side to side. It wasn't possible; he wasn't dead.

Elliot's face crumpled. "Yes, I think he is."

The wail that left her body could have been the howl of the wind, a tornado tearing through the forest, or a tree crashing down. Agony ripped through her, and she grabbed at Chester, touching his face, brushing her fingers over the warmth of his lips, determined for it not to be true.

"Chester," she said. "Please, darling. Wake up. Please. I love you."

He lay there, still and unmoving. Without breath. Without warmth.

"No," she whispered. "Please, Chester. *No.*"

It was impossible that this could be the end. Not after everything they'd been through. Not here, in this snowy night at the edge of the woods before she'd even given birth to their child. Before their marriage could be blessed. Before they could visit the city together again. Before the life they were meant to live.

No.

"He's all right," she insisted. "I'll apply pressure. We'll get him to a doctor. We'll—"

"Ruby." Elliot took her hand and held it tight. His gaze was gentle but firm. "We have to get them home." His voice was brusque. "I promised him that."

Ruby wanted to argue, but the words wouldn't come. Instead, her voice came out flat. Numb. "He loved you. He would have done anything for you."

"I know." Elliot stared down at his older brother, then gently touched his hair. "He did everything for me."

Elliot stiffened at a sound down the road. "We have to go. Now."

He jumped back to the ground, reaching in to touch Chester's shoulder one last time. Then, he tapped the truck and ran down the embankment to the river.

The other truck driver started up the motor. The drivers were to go farther down the road in an effort to pull the focus away from the river, then park in an abandoned barn. There, a car would be waiting. Ruby was poised for the truck's sudden motor, but nothing happened. Moments later, the other driver got out. Footsteps crunched in the snow, and Ruby watched as he helped the other driver up into his cab.

"He's wounded," he called. "Let's leave this truck. We have to go."

The sound of gunfire came closer. Leaving the truck wasn't the plan. It would lead them to the exact spot where the workers had escaped onto the boat in the river. Plus, she wouldn't leave Chester here.

"I'll drive," she said.

When she was younger, Ruby's father had insisted she and Elizabeth learn. It was a skill he wanted them to have, in the event they needed it on the farm or to help with the whiskey. How ironic to think this was the first time she'd needed to do it.

Feeling numb, Ruby made her way to the front of the cab and climbed up, the seat cold beneath her, blood on the steering wheel. The truck rumbled to life, and she moved the lever. It lurched forward and she hit the gas, feeling the wheels slide in the snow. She idled as the other truck pulled up the incline with no trouble and headed onto the road.

Snow was coming down fast, and she pulled forward. The truck slid backward. She pushed her foot down harder on the gas, grateful when the truck finally lurched up the incline and onto the road. The snow made it hard to see, and the wheels slipped on the road as she held tightly to the wheel.

Ruby drove as slowly as she dared, following the path of the tires in front of her. No sight, so far, of anyone behind them. The sounds of her heart, her breath, and the rumble of the truck were loud in her ears. Through the snow, she watched the taillights of the other truck pull off the road and into the trees, headed toward the abandoned barn. She followed. Her headlights fell on the barn, where the other driver was sliding back the door. He pulled in, and she followed before cutting the motor.

The inside of the barn felt so still without the onslaught of snow. Ruby rushed to the back of the truck, to Chester's body. She stared at him, in complete disbelief. She had so many things to say to him, so many moments they had yet to live.

"We have to go," the other driver called. "They won't be far behind."

Ruby climbed up and looped her arms beneath Chester. She couldn't lift him on her own.

"Help," she cried. "Help me move him!"

The driver rushed over. "Leave him for now. He's not going anywhere."

Ruby tried to lift him again but couldn't. "Please."

He bent down to try, but then a motor echoed down the road.

He swore. "Come on. Now!"

Tears choked her. What would it matter if she stayed? She couldn't go back home, and the one person she loved with every beat of her heart was gone.

The driver tried to drag her away, but Ruby fought him. Looking anguished, he helped the wounded driver and moved him to the car. He drove out of the barn. Gunfire.

The men were outside the barn.

Ruby stared down at Chester and thought of the child she carried, the small piece of him that was still alive. With every ounce of will she had left in her, she ran for the back of the barn and slipped out through the gaps in the structure. Large boards were lined up against the wall, and she grabbed the one that looked like a door.

Ruby dragged it through the snow to the slope by the river. With each step, she waited for a bullet to slice through her back. The water was loud and rushing as she approached.

Someone shouted from inside the barn. Without taking time to think or talk herself out of it, Ruby launched the makeshift raft into the river, her body on top of it. Water lapped over the edges, freezing her hands and nearly pulling her under. The wet barn door smelled like oak and iron, like blood, but it swept her down the river, keeping her afloat even as it banged against the edges of the shore.

The most welcome sound cut through the air. The honk of the train in the distance. She collapsed onto the wood, face down, resting her cheek against it as if it were Chester. Then, she grasped for a low-hanging tree branch, missing each time and nearly sliding off, until she finally managed to pull herself to the side. She scrambled up onto the snow, clothes frozen solid in the frigid night.

The sharp blast of the train sounded again across the field, and she ran.

Ruby lay on the ground, next to the train tracks, staring up at the pale-gray sky. Her mind was half lost between a dream, the need to stay awake, and the pull to give in to the luxurious feeling of sleep.

A man wearing a black coat and black cap with a gold symbol was shouting something at her, but she couldn't quite hear. With all the energy Ruby had left, she nodded, to let him know that she was still here and that she did want his help. She wasn't afraid. The worst had already happened.

There was no need to be afraid of anything, ever again.

Chapter Thirty-Four

Wind Thorne, present day

Lindsey froze, staring up at the blackness. Her mouth was dry, her mind dazed. The cold ground was next to her face, filled with the smell of dirt. She remembered the crack, the fall, and the sharp pain of hitting her head. Now every part of her body felt light, as if she were floating.

"Lindsey," an unfamiliar voice shouted.

She blinked.

"Lindsey!" called someone else.

It was Otis. Relief cut through her, followed by an instant ache in her head. She wanted to see him so badly, wanted to hold him one last time.

"Help," she tried to say, but the word was barely a whisper. *"Help."*

Tears rolled down her cheeks. She was desperate to call louder but didn't have the strength.

The voices went silent, and her heart pounded. He'd left. They'd moved on. She'd never be found.

Her eyes felt heavy. Then, light shone up above as sunshine came through the open door. *"Lindsey."*

A flashlight clicked on, shining down into the dark space.

"Are you in here?" Otis shouted. "I still don't—oh." The light fell down on her, and she winced, the brightness sending another sharp pain through her head. "Oh, no."

He rushed out of the warehouse, calling, "She's here!"

There was a commotion up at the door, and he ordered, "Call for an ambulance."

"Help," she whispered, tears hot on her cheeks.

The flashlight jostled forward and came to a sudden stop.

"The stairs collapsed," Otis shouted. "We'll need rope."

Immense relief moved through her that someone was here, that he was here, and she fell back asleep. What could have been minutes or hours passed. A sharp pain seared her legs as the weight of the boards eased off them. Several voices were shouting. Then, Otis was there, kissing her face before a hard, cold board slid beneath her.

It felt like a sled, and she thought of her mother and that time at the ski lodge when they'd watched someone get rescued on the snowmobile. They slid the board under him, loaded him up, and raced away. Comforted, she closed her eyes, curious when the board lifted and moved, as if she were flying.

Images of the trees swaying above her felt so peaceful, the wind in her hair.

"Stay with me," Otis said, his voice intent. "I'm not going to let anything happen to you."

Letting her eyes drift closed, she fell into a deep sleep.

When Lindsey woke, everything was white and sterile. She was in the back of an ambulance, where a young paramedic was shining a flashlight into her eyes. "Lindsey."

Otis stood next to her in the small, cramped space. His eyes were red, like he'd been crying.

"How are you doing?" he asked, quietly.

"You tell me," she said.

The paramedic nodded. "That's a good sign."

Lindsey winced. Her head felt stiff and had a piece of what felt like gauze wrapped around it. The most painful part was her leg, though. It throbbed with a dull ache and was covered by a thick bandage.

"What happened?" she asked.

"We're headed to the hospital," the paramedic said. "They have to do your stitches, but we cleaned the wound and packed it. You lost some blood, so we've got to get that figured out. I need you to stay awake, okay?"

Lindsey tried to nod, but it hurt.

Otis squeezed her hand tight. "I got your message this morning and was worried. I tried to call, but you didn't pick up, so I sent my dad over. He couldn't find you, so people started looking. I joined them the second I got here. We found you in the warehouse. The stairs had collapsed on you."

Lindsey stared up at the gray of the ceiling. "I . . ." Her phone rang, and out of habit, she fumbled for it. She recognized the caller ID right away. It was the police, but she didn't have the strength to answer.

"Pick it up," she whispered, and Otis put it on speaker. "Hello?"

"Hello, Lindsey. It's Officer Garcia. I have an update for you. The fingerprints pointed to Tabitha Moraney, the woman you might know as Amrita. We matched her fingerprints to the ones on your aunt's door and picked her up thirty minutes ago."

Otis fumbled for the phone. "Hi, this is Otis Allen. Lindsey's been in an accident and is in an ambulance on speakerphone. What's all this about?"

The officer relayed the information about the break-in and asked what had caused the accident. Lindsey wanted to explain that Amrita had been at her house with a gun, but all she could do was close her eyes. Instantly, a rough touch shook her arm.

"Lindsey, stay awake." The paramedic's voice was firm. "We'll be at the hospital momentarily."

"She came to my house," Lindsey managed to say. "She had a gun."

Otis stared at her. "What?" he whispered.

"I'll need to come and get a statement from you when you're ready," the officer said, and she nodded as if he could hear.

"We appreciate your help," Otis said. "We'll be in touch."

He hung up and held her hand tight.

"She had a gun?" he said, quietly.

"Some things happened when you were gone," she managed to say.

"Update him later," the paramedic said. "He's not going anywhere."

Otis gripped Lindsey's hand tight. "I'll be right here."

It took quite a bit to convince Aunt Petra to not cut her trip short and return home to care for Lindsey, but she seemed a lot more comfortable with the idea when she learned Otis had not left her side.

Every morning the week after Lindsey was cleared from the hospital, she woke to a plate of freshly scrambled eggs and a side of fruit waiting on her bedside table. Otis sat in a chair next to the bed, working away on his phone or computer. Spotting her, he'd smile and then go back to work as she went back to sleep.

It took only a day or two of rest until Lindsey could finally sit up and have coffee along with her food.

"How are you feeling?" Otis asked.

The past few days, she'd only had the strength for surface-level comments, but this time, she told him the truth.

"Haunted," she admitted. "Being alone in that distillery, wondering how anyone would ever find me . . . It was awful. It also did something to me that might be good. While I was lying there, thinking it was the end, I realized I would have had a better time in life if I'd put my time into the things that matter, like you said.

"I've spent too much time focusing on the problems with my father, and instead, I need to focus on rebuilding a relationship with him. I love him. I admire both him and my brother." Her eyes filled with tears. "They might make me mad or make decisions I don't agree with, but what I need to do is keep talking to them, through all of it.

"I also need to speak up. My aunt said it once, that as a woman in this family, we need to talk a little louder to be heard. I haven't talked at all. I've expected them to know how I feel, and that's not fair to any of us. I'm going to speak up a lot more in my life, because it's my life, and I don't want to ever have that feeling again of lying there helpless, thinking it's the end, and I still haven't done my part."

The two sat in silence, the sound of birds chirping outside the window.

"I almost called your father that one day," Otis said, "but I didn't know if I should."

"I'm glad you didn't," Lindsey said. "I want to do that."

He took her hand. "You went through something awful, Linds. But if you can find the good on the other side, it wasn't all wasted time." They sat in silence. Finally, he said, "I have an update on Amrita. Want to hear it?"

The name alone made Lindsey shudder, but she nodded. "Please."

"It's a lot," he warned her. "Tell me if you don't want to hear it. So, the police questioned her. I have a copy of the transcript, but I'll summarize the key points before you read it, mainly because I want to see the expression on your face."

Lindsey was instantly intrigued. "Okay. Go."

"So." He took a long drink of coffee. "You know the police said she had dealt in stolen jewels before? Well, it turns out that her interest in jewels stems from the ties her family had to Madagascar."

"Right, her mother," Lindsey said.

"No. Her *father*. Turns out, Amrita lied about having a mother who worked at Wind Thorne. It was her dad. He met her mother in New York."

Lindsey had started to eat a strawberry but set down her fork with a clatter. "What? Oh, that makes me so mad. She reeled me in with all that stuff about her mother."

"Yep," Otis said. "She knew how to get your attention, because she was doing her research in an effort to find the diamond. She knew about it because her father supposedly worked for the Thornhill family, right? But get this—her father was never at Wind Thorne. He was sold to another farm as farm labor."

"Sold?" Lindsey said, shocked.

"Yes." Otis ran his hand through his hair. "He was tricked, brought to the United States by Peter Thornhill under the ruse that he could save lots of money on his passage, bypass immigration, and start a good life here with a great job."

"Amrita said this?" Lindsey demanded.

"Yes." Otis nodded. "It would explain why the immigration papers didn't have the necessary numbers at the top. Amrita said Peter Thornhill was smuggling workers in through a port north of here and bringing them down the river. From there, the Thornhills sold the workers to the nearby farms. They made a fortune from it."

"That could be the extra money in the logs," she said.

Otis nodded. "Exactly."

She'd also noticed certain phrases from Ruby's diary that hinted at it, things she'd started to say after her return from New York City.

These people have been taken from their homes.

Held against their will.

Lindsey felt sick to her stomach. "I think you might be right."

Otis took another sip of coffee. "It gets worse."

"How?" she said, leaning back against the pillows.

He set down his mug and took her hand. "Well, one night, the workers had some sort of a rebellion, and they escaped. Someone from the Thornhill family helped and managed to get several of them back home to France, where they'd once lived in a community of Madagascan ex-pats. But two of the workers that were left behind, well, they came back for revenge. Amrita's father was one of them. He killed the Thornhills, and they took what they could."

Lindsey's eyes smarted with tears. "So, it wasn't my great-grandfather. I'm so relieved to hear that. It's not exactly the legacy I'd want to carry."

"I know." Otis ran his hand through his hair. "So, you know how there was that whole community of Madagascans that they pulled from for workers? Well, Peter came across that community when he was on furlough from World War I. Get this—he fell in love with one of the women. He planned to marry her, and she came to Wind Thorne to wait for him. Then, he got injured and she fell in love with someone else. That's when Peter lost it and started recruiting people from that group instead."

Lindsey's mouth dropped open. "Do you know who it was?"

"No," Otis said. "She never gave a name."

Lindsey leaned back against the pillow, processing everything he'd said. "You know, right in the beginning, my aunt asked me to avoid anything that would bring scandal to Wind Thorne. Guess I failed on that one. How do we find out for sure that this story is true?"

"The immigration office," Otis said. "If they can't find anybody properly registered from all that paperwork, there's your answer."

"I don't know. My great-grandmother was in that paperwork. I think she actually was listed as Madagascan, but that's wrong, because my genealogy test said . . ." Lindsey sat up straight. "Wait." Her mouth dropped open. "Otis."

"What?" He squinted at her.

Lindsey grasped at a thought just out of reach. It faded, but she fought hard to find it, to pin it down. Then, it clicked. The ring. The inscription.

Otis peered over her shoulder as she scrolled through pictures of her research. Finally, she found the article that recapped the death of the Thornhill family.

"Look." Lindsey's heart was pounding so hard she could barely talk. "The mother, grandmother, and Uncle Peter were shot on the back lawn. Then, the car with the rest of the family—including Ruby—was ambushed. It exploded. No identifiable remains."

Lindsey reread the date on the article and looked at Otis with wide eyes.

"Who helped the servants escape?" she asked.

He shrugged. "I don't know."

"Otis, I think it was her, and then she went into hiding. We need to find two things: the obituary for my great-grandmother and the official report from the night the Thornhill family died."

"Why?" he said.

"Because I don't think Annabelle was my great-grandmother." Lindsey's voice shook with excitement. "I think Ruby was."

Chapter Thirty-Five

Upstate New York, April 1931

The comforting, familiar smell of stew pulled Ruby out of a deep sleep. It was like the heat of the earth in the summer. Rich in onions, carrots, rosemary, and beef.

Her eyes fluttered open, taking in the thin, white curtains with little eyelets above and the hard, lumpy mattress beneath her. The crocheted yellow blanket on her was warm and soft, and moments came back to her where she'd pulled it closer as she rolled over to go back to sleep.

Their voices had been low as she cried. The man and a woman. Slowly, Ruby became alert enough to watch them. They sat by the fire, the man reading a story of some sort to the woman while she knit with a steady click of the needles. It was the sound Ruby had heard as she slept the last few hours or days or however long it had been: a fitful sleep, where that steady clicking was like the movement of a train. It partnered with the crackle of the fire and the low voices discussing her, to let her know she was safe.

Images from that night flashed through her brain. Chester, the moment the bullet hit. The image caused agony to cut through her so deep that she let out a small sound. The man turned his head and, noticing her, rushed to her side. His nose was bulbous, his eyes dark and gentle. His wife was there then, too, resting a cool hand against her forehead.

"The fever is gone," she said.

"Hello," the man said. "I found you near frozen by the tracks when I was driving my route on the freight train a few days back. You've been in and out of fever for four days. What's your name?"

The word formed in her throat, but just as quickly, that fear pushed it back.

"Lily," she lied.

The man glanced at his wife.

The woman took her hands. "Do you remember what happened?"

The loud noise. The smell of smoke. Chester, falling back into the snow.

Hot tears filled her eyes, and she rolled to the side, pulling the blanket close. She flinched at an unfamiliar fabric on her body, a nightgown that was too big.

"Where are my clothes?" she said.

The woman nodded to the fire. The dress was hung up next to it, washed but stained and soiled.

Chester.

"Would you like to eat?" the man asked. "Then we can go about the business of getting you back home." He looked away, scratching his head. "You were near Wind Thorne when I found you. Do you . . . ?"

"No." Ruby pulled the blankets close. Her whole body was shaking. "I can't go back. There is no home."

The man gripped her hands tightly. "Then, you have one here."

"Winston." Her voice was a sharp rebuke.

His gaze was steady as he looked at his wife. "It's her, Imogene. They think she's gone, anyway. I won't send her back there. Not when something like that could happen."

It took a moment for the words to sink in.

"Back where?" Ruby said.

The man looked at his wife. Finally, he said, "Wind Thorne."

Ruby swallowed hard. "Please. What has happened?"
The woman brought her the newspaper.

> Family Gunned Down
>
> On Friday night, in a suspected attack on bootlegger Racine Thornhill, the entire Thornhill family was murdered. Police suspect the activity to be in response to the family's inability to square up several whiskey contracts, due to poorly performing crops, and their involvement in an unnamed crime network.

"No." The word came out as a breath. Then, she buried her head in the pillow, too stunned to make a sound.

This was mere days after the workers had escaped. Days after all the farms involved had been reported to the authorities by an anonymous letter posted in the mail. There would have been raids and arrests, reputations ruined. It hadn't occurred to her that there might be acts of revenge.

It was her fault, all of it. Her family. Chester. Her head went light. Quickly, the man knelt beside her, pressing his hand into her back.

"My sister . . ." Elizabeth had looked so beautiful the night of her engagement party. Joining Ruby under the table in her beads and shiny gloss, completely unaware of the horrors to come. "My . . ." Ruby hated her mother's poisonous words, but Ruby had never wanted this. Chester would not have wanted this.

Chester.

"I . . ." Ruby's stomach went sour, and she gripped the edge of the bed, then was sick all over the floor.

The man's wife pressed a cold cloth to the back of Ruby's neck. "There, there, child."

Ruby squeezed her eyes shut, forcing her mind to something she could manage. Her first notebook. A composition book the older kids used, left over from a boy who'd stayed in school for five pages before leaving again to till the land.

Use this to write about each day, the teacher had told her. *Everything moves by so fast. There might come a time you'll want to see what it once looked like to you, to go back in time.*

Ruby ached to go back. To her father, before she'd let him down. Her grandmother, showing her how to thread a needle. The time with Uncle Peter before the war, so deep in the past, when he swung her up on his shoulders and sang happy songs.

The entire Thornhill family . . .

It was so hard to breathe. Ruby's stomach clenched, and she leaned over once again. The man had a mop, cleaning up Ruby's sorrow with each steady wipe. Hot tears rolled down her cheeks, damp on her neck like a fever.

"I'm sorry," she whispered.

The man stopped cleaning; his white eyebrows knit with worry. "Your sorrow is much too big for apologies. Please. Rest."

The wife stood in the kitchen, slicing brown bread.

"Stay as long as you'd like," she said. "It's safe here."

"No." Ruby could not put these people in danger, too. "I . . ."

"We have guns." The woman set the bread and a bowl of stew on a tray and brought the food to the edge of the bed. "No one will find you here unless you want to be found."

Ruby stared down at the meal, the steam rising like smoke. The sight of the food was confusing, like something from another time. She turned away, drawing the crocheted blanket close.

"You are safe here," the man said. "Weeks, months, years. You tell us if and when you're ready. That's up to you."

"Ready for what?" she whispered.

"To go back home."

Chapter Thirty-Six

Upstate New York, present day

Three weeks had passed since she'd fallen, and Lindsey was finally starting to feel back to normal. She was cooking for a dinner date with Otis when the sudden crunch of tires brought her to the window, expecting to see him. Instead, it was her father, strolling toward the house. It had been weeks since they'd talked and months since she had seen him, but he looked exactly the same. Maybe even more put together and fit than the last time.

Letting out a deep sigh, she limped to the door. "Hi, Dad."

"Lindsey." He stopped short, and bewilderment crossed his face. He actually reached out to steady himself a bit.

"Is everything all right?" she asked, confused by his reaction.

"Fine. You just . . ." He straightened his shoulders. "You look a lot like your mother, that's all."

Lindsey thought about how Otis had once said that perhaps, she reminded her father of her mother. "I'm cooking. You hungry?"

For a second, he looked ready to decline in favor of getting straight to business. Instead, he nodded.

She'd been making whitefish for herself and Otis, with braised asparagus and baby carrots. The sauce was a garlic olive oil, with capers.

Even though it pained her to do so, she sent a quick text to Otis to cancel dinner and requested to meet up later instead.

The food was ready, so Lindsey set down the plates and poured them each a glass of wine, like it was the most natural thing in the world. Then, she took a seat across from her father.

"How are you, Dad?" she asked. "What brings you here?"

When Lindsey had first seen him come to the door, her immediate reaction was that he had traveled all this way for her mother's artwork. Since he'd accepted the invitation to dinner, she wondered what else was on his mind.

"I'm concerned." He didn't bother with niceties but launched right into it. "It's been on my mind what you said, Lindsey. You have hesitations with the licensing deal with your mother's artwork, and in spite of appearances, I do understand those concerns." He had already managed to eat a few bites of the fish while saying it. "This is delicious."

The sauce had turned out a little strong for her taste, but she appreciated the compliment.

Her father went back to talking. "Do you have questions or assumptions as to why I've decided to license your mother's work?" Before she could answer, he said, "I wanted to let you know that I'm happy to try and answer some of them, but when it comes down to it, it would be a lot easier to just explain the reasons I'm doing what I'm doing. It is a financial decision. Which I know is not what you want to hear, but maybe you will want to hear this." He stopped talking and took a long drink of wine. "There were two things your mother loved more than anything in this world. More than me, certainly."

Lindsey expected him to say "metalwork" and "design." Instead, he said, "You and your brother." She took a small bite of asparagus to cover her emotion. "What happened with your mother was completely unexpected. Neither one of us was prepared for everything to end that soon. We were both living busy, full, big lives, and there are many times when I think about how abruptly it all ended, but I wonder how it would have been different if we'd have slowed down, talked more."

He certainly was doing a good job of talking now. It had been so long since she'd spent time with her father that she'd forgotten this. He could ask a question but then talk for fifteen minutes before giving anyone a chance to answer. It was a quality that would have annoyed her only a few months ago, but now, she found it interesting to notice the quirks that made him who he was.

"In spite of all that," he said, spearing a bite of fish, "she and I did have several talks. I knew her well, and I loved her well. We might not have been prepared for her to go, but I knew what she wanted it to look like with her children after she was gone."

Lindsey had to take a long drink of wine herself to keep from saying that the relationship between the two of them was not even close to what her mother would have wanted.

"I recognize my failures with you." His sharp eyes were apologetic. "I want to do better. That's why I'm here. I don't even like asparagus; did you know that? However, I want to explain the reason for those failures. Would that be all right?"

Lindsey was nearly at a loss for words. Not only was her father apologizing to her, but he'd also said he'd failed. The man who never failed at anything.

"Yes," she managed to say. "Please."

"Look." He let out a great sigh and stared out the window for a brief moment. "There's something that you don't know about your brother, something I haven't shared at his request. Considering the damage the secrecy has caused between us, I can't keep quiet about it any longer."

Her strong, self-sufficient father choked up. Then, he took in a deep breath and steadied himself. "Your brother got himself in trouble a couple of years ago, Lindsey. He got into pills. He got behind the wheel of the car and drove it straight into a tree. Totaled the car and nearly totaled his belief in himself." Her father put down the fork. "He got so lucky. Barely a scratch, but everything spiraled from there. He lost his job at the accounting firm and had to open his own practice to survive. Of course, he had a hard time keeping clients because he got back on the pills to deal with the fallout. He finally admitted he had a problem and went to recovery."

Lindsey was so stunned she couldn't move. All these years, she'd been completely wrong about her older brother, the sports star who could do no wrong. She saw him as perfect in the eyes of her father and the preferred choice for companionship and traveling. Not once would she have pictured the lost soul her father had described.

"Jack's a fighter. He's going to keep fighting until he gets past this, and I'm not going to let him give up on himself. Your mother wouldn't want that." He adjusted his watch, then looked her straight in the eye. "I know you've been troubled. Saying that being a parent is hard is not sufficient at this point. However, your brother asked me to keep his struggles confidential, so I did. Until I couldn't anymore."

Lindsey looked down at her uneaten dinner. "I've barely talked to him," she admitted. "I thought he was avoiding me. I thought the both of you were."

"He's avoiding everyone. He's back in rehab." Her father adjusted the collar on his golf shirt. "Lindsey, if it seems like I took a step away from you, you're right. It was because I didn't quite know how to carry this silence. It's a tough decision when it comes to protecting the confidence of someone you love or protecting the heart of someone you love. I should have found a way to do both. I do love you, Lindsey. I apologize that it might have seemed otherwise."

To think that over the past few years, her brother had gone through such a massive struggle, and she knew nothing about it. She'd stopped calling Jack ages ago, mainly because he'd stopped calling her.

"I thought . . ." she started to say, but stopped.

For years, she'd grieved the loss of her mother, followed by what felt like the loss of her father and brother. The hurt and anger had built up over time and then reached a boiling point these past few months. Hearing all this, she had no idea how to feel.

"What?" her father said. "Talk to me."

"I've been so mad at you." She glanced at him, and he gave her a slight nod. "I thought you preferred Jack's company, that you'd rather spend time with him, that you weren't interested in my life. Then, licensing Mom's work . . ."

"Rehab is expensive," her father said.

The comment made her sit up straight. "That's what the money is for?"

"Some of it." Her father folded up his napkin and set it on his plate. "Your brother also works with a sober companion, and he's suffered some health issues. That's all expensive, too."

She started to speak, and he held up his hand. "He's a grown man, yes, who should be able to take care of himself. I get that. But right now, he can't. He needs someone by his side because he can't manage it on his own, and I know your mother wouldn't want him to."

Lindsey closed her eyes. To think she'd assumed her father wanted the money to wine and dine women. She'd given him so little credit.

"I wish I'd handled things differently," he was saying. "Found a way to keep communication open with you, but I failed. Plain and simple. But if I've learned anything in life, it's that failure is not the end. It's a signal to try something new. So, I'm trying. That's why I'm here, but communication is not easy for me, Lindsey, regardless of how much I talk."

The comment made her smile. Her father looked surprised, then gave her a tentative smile back.

"I think Mom would be grateful for what you've done for Jack," she said. "Protecting his confidence. Supporting him. Standing by him."

"I wish I'd been able to do the same for you."

"You are, though. You're here," she said, getting up from the table. "Besides, I have a small confession to make to you, too."

Lindsey took her father out to the barn and pushed open the door. It made a loud rolling sound, as if to announce to the forest that she was about to get to work.

"I just put this together," she said.

A patch of sun from the windows made four squares on the ground, and a swallow called from somewhere up in the loft. Even though the barn hadn't been used in years, it still smelled faintly of hay.

"Lindsey, this is meticulous," he said, taking it all in. "Your mother would have loved being out here. With you."

The words felt like a nod of approval. "I would have loved being out here with her."

Lindsey had spent the last week transforming the old, dusty barn in the back of her aunt's house into a well-lit, perfectly organized station for art and metalwork. Otis had helped her nearly every day, because some days it was slow going with her leg, until the space was just as she would have wanted it.

"I put all of this together for a purpose." Lindsey cleared her throat. "It's complicated, but basically, a friend and I discovered that back in the day, Wind Thorne brought several groups of unpaid workers into the country and sold them to the local farms."

"You're kidding," her father said.

"The thing that's even more interesting is that we think the person who helped them escape was Mom's grandmother," Lindsey said. "Even though her marriage and death certificates have her listed as Annabelle Rakoto, I believe she was actually Ruby Thornhill, the youngest daughter of the Thornhill family."

Her father looked puzzled. "Why?"

Lindsey smiled. "Well, that's what I'm researching. So, I think Ruby helped these workers escape. The boy next door, Chester, lived here in this house at the time. He helped her with that plan but ended up getting killed. Soon after, the Thornhill family was killed. We think she went into hiding after all of that, and later in life, she returned to the area but took on the identity of Annabelle, one of the servants she had liberated, in order to hide from whoever had murdered her family."

Aunt Petra had been captivated by the story. The fact that Wind Thorne had exploited their workers was not a piece of history Lindsey had expected her aunt would want to share, but once she'd heard the full story, Aunt Petra was all in. The two had done some brainstorming, and together they'd decided that Lindsey should build an art installation highlighting the injustice to the people affected by Wind Thorne's trafficking crimes and honoring Ruby, the one who'd put a stop to it.

"I set up this space because I want to start designing again. I'm building my own art installation centered around Wind Thorne's trafficking crimes, highlighting the injustice to the people and village still affected to this day. I plan to donate part of the proceeds to help current victims. I'm hoping the collection will be highly publicized, as it will combine my work with that of a very famous former artist."

It took a moment, and then realization dawned on her father's face. "You have some of your mother's work?"

"Yes," she said, quietly. "I have some of her work, and I'd like to use it for this, if it's okay with you."

Inside, Lindsey was shaking. It was still possible he wouldn't give her his permission. If he didn't, the whole thing would fall apart.

She braced herself. "What do you think?"

"I think your mother would be so proud."

Lindsey's eyes smarted, and she turned away to hide it. "Let me show you what I've got."

She pulled two short wooden stools over to the storage bins. They took a seat, and she lifted one of the lids to reveal part of her mother's final collection.

"So, I've been opening these very slowly," Lindsey said, handing him a gold bracelet with silver wires encircling it like ivy.

"That's beautiful." His voice was quiet. "Your mother saw such refinement in the world. She could capture the smallest details to tell the biggest story."

"Did you know she was basing this collection on Wind Thorne?" Lindsey asked.

"Yes." He held up the bracelet, turning it over in the light. "It's part of the reason I haven't touched it. She talked about it with me quite a bit. Those were some of the last times we ever spoke."

Lindsey considered the idea that this was just as difficult for him as it was for her.

"I found a notebook at the bottom of the bin," she said. "Each item is numbered, and she wrote a little note about each one. I haven't read it all because . . ."

"For the same reason I let it be." He held out his hand. "May I?"

Lindsey passed it to him. They looked through the jewelry together, and he read through each description, voicing his approval several times. Once he'd matched a piece to the number in the notebook and indicated he was ready to move on, she pulled out the next one.

Her father was stunned into silence by one of Lindsey's favorite pieces—a heavy necklace with embellishments that hung like chandeliers. They sparkled with colored Depression-era glass. Her father stared at it for the longest time, then gave a low whistle.

"I remember this one," he said. "It's been a long, long time, but it was my favorite."

He read the description in the notebook, then spoke in detail about the work, explaining some of the elements Lindsey wouldn't have picked up on. In the same fashion, they made their way through the opened items, sharing words and ideas about her mother's art in a way she never would have expected from him.

They continued to sift through, reading her mother's thoughts and sharing their own memories. When the sun set outside and night settled around them, Lindsey turned on the lights of the barn.

"You'll add to all of these?" he asked.

"No." Lindsey stretched, considering the value of the work in front of them. "Only the few that are unfinished. If that's okay."

"If that's what you need, do it."

When they arrived at the final piece, it was pitch black outside, and moths circled below the bulbs above. Lindsey picked up the small package, holding it tight. It was the smallest out of everything, so she'd kept letting it fall to the bottom of the storage bins, wondering all the while what could be inside.

Knowing that the box still contained unseen pieces had been important to her, as if she had more to discuss with her mother. Now, though, the conversation could pick up on a different path, one that no longer held on to the past.

"Last one," she whispered.

Her father nodded, perhaps feeling the same about it.

Letting out a breath, Lindsey unwrapped it. She closed her eyes, sending love to her mother, and full of wonder at what this final thing could be. When she opened her eyes, her heart skipped a beat.

The final work of art was a simple, delicate band that somehow managed to marry the style of Wind Thorne to the style of her aunt's house. The most striking part, however, was the stone in the center.

"Is that a diamond?" her father asked, leaning in. "That's extraordinary."

Lindsey stared down at it, barely able to speak. Its depth, dimension, and sparkle felt like staring into an endless pattern of prisms, stacked with every sort of gem imaginable. It was the sun reflecting on water or the lit, lustrous surface of the moon.

"Can you read the description?" she whispered. "Please."

Lindsey's father found the note.

"Look." He peeled something off the page. "This was attached."

It was a small, sleek satin bag, and when Lindsey opened it, an empty setting tumbled out. With a small gasp, she flipped it over and searched for the inscription.

Sure enough, it read:

2.27.32 R E Forever

"This is the ring." Her voice was quiet. "The lost ring from Wind Thorne. I can't believe she found it. But in some ways, I can."

For so long, Lindsey had believed her mother had missed out on Wind Thorne. As it turned out, her mother had found its greatest treasure long ago and had kept it close to her heart, basking in the glow of the secret.

Lindsey held the setting tight. "What does the note say?"

Her father read it out loud: "'This piece was created from the diamond ring that belonged to the Thornhill family and became a legend after its disappearance. I found it late one night, hidden in plain sight, in a small crevice in the wall of the distillery by the forest. I walked back to the house, a full moon shining a path for me the whole way home. What a remarkable find. Lindsey has always been searching for it. I'll give it to her when I've finished this collection, to remind her that for me, she shines even brighter than the moon.'"

Lindsey's eyes filled with tears.

For so long, she'd believed the loss of her mother meant she was on her own. But the time she'd spent with Ruby had taught her that even in the moments of the greatest loss, love was still all around.

"You do, you know," her father said.

Lindsey looked up at him. "What?"

"Shine."

Her father set down the notebook and opened his arms. She stepped forward and hugged him. It was familiar, and full of forgiveness. She did not want to cry, because her father didn't appreciate that type of weakness. But then, his shoulders started shaking.

"I love you, kiddo," he said, and Lindsey held him tight.

The ring rested on the chair, its presence strong and steady. She'd been looking for it for so long.

To think it had been right there, this entire time.

Chapter Thirty-Seven

Upstate New York, 1931–1932

Ruby spent the months up to the birth of her child with Imogene and Winston. Eating, healing, learning card games, and reading aloud at the fireside. His work as a train conductor took him away often, and when it was only Imogene and her, they listened to radio programs and baked elaborate cakes using as few ingredients as possible. Sugar wasn't widely available, but Imogene could transform molasses into the most tantalizing treat.

Several weeks after her arrival, Ruby and Imogene were sitting out on the front porch, knitting, when a pack of coyotes howled in the distance. The sound alone felt dangerous, and they rushed inside.

"Are they close?" Ruby asked, chewing her lip.

Imogene stood and peered out the window. "It's far from the house. Even if it sounds nearby."

Their home was nearly two hours from Wind Thorne, deep in the Hudson Valley. A small town was a ten-minute walk away, but they were isolated, with the nearest house barely visible across the tree line. The rolling hills were dotted with trees, and some nights Ruby longed for the open space of the farm, for life as she had known it.

One of the coyotes howled again, and she shuddered. "I know they're just protecting their pups, but that sound sets my teeth on edge."

"I hear them a lot, when Winnie's away." Imogene put on a kettle. "I am grateful to have you here, Ruby." Her voice was low. "It can be frightening when he's gone. I've often made friends with the people in the drawings on the calendar so I wouldn't feel so alone. I know our home is modest, but I thank you for staying with us."

"I've worried so many times that I'm a bother," Ruby admitted.

"No." Imogene smiled at her. "The nights alone here are hard. You help me more than you know."

The affirmation gave Ruby permission to settle in and to sleep more deeply in the refuge of this place, to be quick with a greeting for Imogene or an offer to play a game of cards. The days were quiet, but the steady routine made it possible for Ruby to move forward, although grief draped over her like a shroud.

Soon, it warmed outside, and Ruby walked with Imogene into town, where Imogene introduced Ruby as her niece. Most storefronts in town were shuttered up, but a general store and a bed-and-breakfast still served meals. There was no money for that, but Ruby didn't mind. Simply being out with other people proved the sun could keep rising in spite of it all.

Sometimes, Ruby pulled her hat down low, nervous that she could be spotted. It was unlikely but not impossible. One day in late May, her breath caught as she saw someone who looked like Father Aaron. Ruby dropped Imogene's arm and raced to hide behind a nearby building.

Imogene bustled up, her face flushed from concern. "Ruby, what is it? Are you ill?"

Ruby peered out from behind the corner of the building, heart pounding. The man had a much larger nose and at least ten years on him. Ruby fanned herself with her hat.

"I thought I knew someone," she said, and Imogene nodded. "I need to know if people think I'm dead. That way, no one would have reason to try to kill me."

"That wouldn't do, as you need to protect your child," Imogene said.

Ruby flushed and their eyes met. "Yes. I'm sorry I didn't tell you sooner."

"I understand your fear." Imogene took her hands. "We will have Winston find out, the next time he drives a route through."

It took a few weeks, but Winston did some investigating. He reported back to Ruby, over a pungent meal of liver and onions.

"There's not a soul who thinks you're alive," he said, in his authoritative tone. "You need not worry."

Ruby took her plate to the sink, unable to eat. "Will you tell me what happened? That night?"

He hesitated.

"I have to know," Ruby pleaded. "I should know what happened to my family."

Winston bowed his head. "Your mother, grandmother, and your uncle were shot dead on the back lawn. Soon after, a car came racing up the drive, and it was ambushed, too. People assumed you were in there with your father, your sister, and her husband. There were remains that couldn't be identified. Everyone thinks you were there."

Ruby squeezed her eyes shut at the horror. It must have been a family her father did business with. Or perhaps, one of the farms she and Chester had reported, which would make it her fault.

"I have to lie down," she said.

In the days that passed, Winston shared the other news he'd learned, that the Mensleys had taken ownership of Wind Thorne.

"Your father had ten years to repay the debt," Winston explained. "Since that won't happen, the property transferred to the Mensleys. I'm sorry, Ruby. I know that was your home."

It wasn't home. The hayloft with Chester was home. The fire escape in Manhattan. Each breath, each moment, with him.

Ruby sank into a chair. "I don't want a thing to do with Wind Thorne."

Its decay, its deception. Its unrelenting devastation, so much thicker than blood.

"I never want to see that place again."

The light was as bright as a train coming down the tracks. Ruby gripped the edge of the hospital bed, staring up at the ceiling as she screamed.

The women at Imogene's church had put up a collection for a hospital birth, once they'd learned that the father of her child had been killed protecting the persecuted. Imogene had never lied about it; the women had simply assumed Ruby had been married. She was grateful for the gift, as nothing had frightened her more than the idea of giving birth.

"You can do it, love," the nurse said. "Don't give up."

Sweat poured down her face, and her body burned. With one last effort, a small, tinny cry carried through the room.

Ruby used the last of her strength to open her eyes and watch as the doctor took the wriggling mass away, then closed her eyes until someone tapped her shoulder. She woke to see a nurse putting the child on her chest, so warm and as light as a touch. Its skin was the softest thing she'd ever felt.

"It's a girl," the nurse said.

Ruby had thought her child would be a boy, like Chester, but the idea of walking through life with this beautiful girl made tears of joy warm her face.

"Name?" the nurse said.

Ruby stared in awe as the little girl studied her with interest. "Elizabeth Millicent. Millie."

Simply speaking the name brought her back to the home in Manhattan, to that complicated time that had ignited her love for Chester. It was Millie who had pushed them to take trips to the cinema and long walks in Central Park. The conversations they started there often continued late into the night on the platform outside his room and remained in her heart long after.

"Millie." The nurse wrote it down. "Such a beautiful name."

The baby let out a little noise.

"Smart, too," the nurse said, with a chuckle. "Looks like she's going to be something special."

The days with Millie were blissful but exhausting for everyone in the house. She didn't sleep much, often waking every three to four hours to be fed. The bags under Imogene's eyes indicated it was time to leave, even if Imogene disagreed. But it would not be right to stay.

The train conductor and his wife had food on the table but little to spare. They were good, solid people, but they couldn't care for her forever. Only last week, Ruby had asked to take in washing or sewing to help pay room and board, but Imogene had refused.

On a cold night with the fire crackling in the hearth, Ruby sat down with the two of them after dinner and shared her plans. She would contact Chester's father to tell him of his grandchild and ask for assistance, then move into the home for unwedded girls. The deposit Chester had made held her spot for a year, under a name different from her own.

"Is that safe?" Winston said. "Do you trust this man?"

Ruby thought of Chester's father. Steady. Toiling the land from dawn to dusk, caring for his sons without the help of their mother. He'd always had a kind word for Ruby, and in her heart, she knew he wanted the best for her.

"Yes," she said.

Imogene gave a resolute nod. "Then that's what you should do."

That night, she wrote him a note:

Dear Mr. Mensley,
This is my second letter to you ever, and I know you will be surprised to receive it. I ask you for nothing, this time. Not to save my family, but to speak with me quickly. You have more family than you'd expect, now, and I'd like to give you the chance to share in that. Could you meet with me to talk? I can send a time and date in my next letter.
In friendship,
Gale

Chester had once said his name would have been Gale if he'd been a girl. Hopefully, it would help his father figure out who had written to him.

Winston posted it for her, and soon, she had a reply.

Dearest Gale,
It was a shock and celebration to hear from you. Yes, I will meet you.
Regards,
Jeremiah Mensley III

Imogene's eyes welled up. "Well, I'll sure miss you."

Ruby cradled her daughter close. "I'll visit when I'm able."

"What will you do?" Imogene asked, choking back tears.

Ruby kissed her daughter's head. "Survive."

It was an early evening in February, nearly a year since Chester had first declared his love, when Ruby waited in the back office of the train station three towns over from Wind Thorne. Winston had set up the location, and had assured her it would be safe. The trip had been an eighty-mile ride, and she'd spent half of it worried that Chester's father wouldn't come. That he'd forget or decide to let the past be the past. In spite of her worries, a knock on the office door came soon after she'd settled in.

Smoothing her hair, she checked in the bassinet to see Millie still sleeping soundly in the corner before opening the office door. Her eyes filled with tears at the sight of Chester's father and Elliot.

Overcome, she walked to the table without a word and took a seat. The two men sat across from her, and Elliot held out a handkerchief.

Blowing her nose, she said, "I didn't know how it would feel to see the two of you."

The last time she'd seen Elliot, he'd had tears in his eyes and had given her his word that the servants would make it home. Now, he wore a starched button-up shirt, and his hair was so neatly combed that Chester would have teased him for it. "Seeing you again reminds me of so much about him."

Elliot gave her a firm nod. "He loved you, Ruby. There was no question about that."

She looked at Mr. Mensley. "I'm so sorry. If I could change that night, change what happened—"

"It's not up to us," he said. "Life gives what it will, no matter how much we ask for sun or rain. I am sorry, though. For both Chester and your people, Ruby."

"Do you know who did it?" she asked.

Mr. Mensley shook his head. "There's talk that some farmhands were responsible. That, once released, they came back for revenge."

Ruby let out a slow breath. "Have they been caught?"

"No." Mr. Mensley folded his cap. "Do you plan to return? To Wind Thorne?"

"Never," she said.

"There's always a place for you there," Mr. Mensley said. "Chester would have wanted that."

"No," she said. "Too much has happened because of that place. I never want to see it again."

A small cry made the men jump.

"My, oh my," Mr. Mensley whispered.

Ruby bustled over and lifted Millie from the bassinet. "I need to introduce you to your granddaughter." Her hands were shaking, but she held her head high. "Chester would not have wanted me to keep this from you. Millie's twelve weeks old, and already, she has my heart completely."

"Mine, too," Elliot said, getting to his feet. "Hello. You look just like your mama."

Mr. Mensley peered at her with a small smile. "She's a beauty."

"Would you like to hold her?" Ruby asked.

Placing Millie into Mr. Mensley's arms, watching him stare down at her face as he would have if Chester had still been at their side, left Ruby's heart aching but full. She studied his hands, the same as his son's, and the kindness that radiated from his smile. She saw him see Chester for the first time and the wonder that came with the promise of a good life, and her eyes filled with tears.

"He would have been so proud," Mr. Mensley said. "My boy would have been proud of his daughter." Gently, he touched her forehead as if giving a blessing, then handed her back to Ruby.

Clearing his throat, he said, "Elliot needs to speak with you about something in private. I'll take my leave, but I do thank you, Ruby. For seeing all that was good about my Chester."

The door shut. Millie had fallen back to sleep in her arms, and Ruby held her tight.

"I've longed to know what happened that night," she said, breaking the silence. "Did they make it back home?"

Elliot rubbed the back of his hand across his face and took a seat at the wooden table. It reminded her of the day at the boardinghouse, when he'd tearfully shared his enlistment. It felt like a lifetime ago.

"Yes, we made it to the boat," Elliot said, and Ruby listened as he described the trip from the river, to the bus, to the sea. There was illness and doubt, but once they arrived in France, endless celebration. "Do you remember Annabelle?"

Ruby put her hand to her heart. "Of course. She was the one I thought about the most."

"She told me to thank you," he said. "To tell you that you changed her life, and you showed her what kindness and bravery means. She was so happy to be back home."

Ruby bowed her head and brought Millie in close. For all that had been lost, so much had still been gained.

"How did Peter get away with it all?" she asked. "Didn't the people know he was lying after the first time, when they never heard from their friends again and—"

"They had no idea." Elliot glanced over at her with an expression so much like one of Chester's that she had to blink several times before looking at him again. "Each time Peter went back, he brought letters from their loved ones filled with money. Enough to make them believe that more would be on the way or, better yet, that if they came with him, they'd be making all that money, too. In the meantime, he kept the lion's share."

Ruby put her head in her hands. It pained her to think ill of the dead, but the man had done so much wrong. Yes, he'd suffered, but hadn't they all?

"I'm so sorry about your family, Ruby," Elliot said. "In spite of it all."

A cold breeze blew in through the windows, and she put Millie back in the bassinet, pulling the blankets in close. Elliot pulled out the chair when she sat back down; then he let out a breath.

"Ruby, you loved my brother, and he loved you," Elliot said. "He would have wanted his child treated with dignity."

Based on the gentle way Chester's father had treated her, she already suspected what Elliot was about to say.

"I'd like to marry you, Ruby." Elliot studied her with his wide, serious face. "Take responsibility for my brother's child and raise her as my own. Before I can ask you to do me that honor, I need to come clean about something here and now."

Ruby nodded. "Please." She braced herself, for fear the confession would be something about Chester that could cause her pain.

Elliot stared down at the floor. His voice was so low she could barely hear him.

"The night Indira died—"

Dread rushed through her. Ruby could still smell the pine boughs and the smoke from the fire. Still hear the scream, even though her heart had since felt one much louder.

"Do you know what happened that night?" he asked.

She stared out of the woods through the window, not speaking.

"The ring . . ." Elliot cleared his throat. "It didn't belong to your family; did you know that?"

Ruby looked at him in surprise. "Who did it belong to?"

"Indira's mother," he said. "Indira was to marry Peter."

The pieces clicked into place. Ruby's stomach felt sick with the knowledge of what had not yet been said.

"Your father and Peter took that ring from Indira," Elliot said, and Ruby closed her eyes. "She brought it over with her, the only thing of value she had. Your father gave it to your brother-in-law when he asked to marry Elizabeth. Peter thought Indira had taken it that night at the party. That she'd taken it back."

Ruby froze. "No."

Elliot squeezed his hands tight. "Peter wanted to teach her a lesson. He wanted someone to push her down the stairs. Ten dollars. Not to kill her. To teach her a lesson. Ruby, I—"

"Why are you telling me this now?" she whispered.

Tears rolled down Ruby's face as she remembered Chester's bruised and bloodied face, the way he'd run.

"He didn't mean to, Elliot," she said. "He wouldn't have done it. Not if he knew what would happen."

Elliot's face was ashen, and he got to his feet. "Ruby, you don't understand. Chester didn't push her. It was me."

"What?" she whispered.

"I killed her." Elliot's eyes filled with tears. "I didn't mean to. My brother, he . . ." Elliot's shoulders heaved with sobs. "He saw me do it. My brother saw me do that, and he tried to come save me anyway. I joined the navy because I needed to run from what I'd done, from what it had done to her. To him." Elliot closed his eyes. "To me." He opened his eyes, raw with guilt and pain. "I am so sorry, Ruby. I—" His voice broke, and he sank down into a chair.

Ruby knelt in front of him. Her head felt light, and she gripped his hands.

"Elliot, I was the one who took it," she whispered. "The ring."

Elliot stared at her. "What?"

"I stole it from my sister." Ruby's voice trembled, but she kept going. "I took it with me to New York. I was so young, and so selfish. I thought it would cause a fight between her and Glenn, that they wouldn't get married. I didn't know." She put her hand to her mouth. "I didn't know what would happen. Elliot, I had no idea."

He pulled her in close. Sobs shook the both of them, and she held on tight, desperate to keep their shared pain from sweeping them away. Everything had changed with that one careless decision, setting in motion an outcome that could not have been predicted or stopped.

Chester's kind face flashed through her mind. The love he had felt for his brother and the determination to protect him, at all costs.

"Chester wouldn't want this for you," she whispered. "He would not want this for us."

"I know," Elliot said, wiping the back of his hand across his face. His expression was so lost, it mirrored the pain in her heart. "He'd want—"

"Forgiveness," she said. "For the both of us."

For all they had not meant to do.

Slowly, Elliot nodded. His eyes were fierce as they studied hers.

"I will protect you, Ruby," he said. "I will protect his daughter."

"*Our* daughter," she told him. "Chester would have wanted it that way."

Ruby's hand drifted to the bassinet, and she smoothed the blankets. Her mind sifted through the different possibilities, trying to land on the right choice. "I can't live with you," she said. "Whoever killed my family will come back for me."

"We'll protect you," Elliot said. "Me and my father."

"I can't risk it," Ruby said, pressing her lips against the head of her child. "Not with her."

"Then what will you do?" he asked.

Ruby explained her plan to go to the home for unwedded mothers.

"No." Elliot shook his head, wiping his eyes. "I'll take you somewhere safe. We'll raise our daughter together. I don't want you to do this alone."

Elliot pulled out the ring, the one Indira had died for. He stared at it for a long moment. Then, he got down on one knee.

"Love comes in all forms," he said. "Loyalty, protection, and forgiveness. I will honor you, Ruby, in honor of my brother. I will be loyal, and I will protect you. Please, let me help you. Will you be my wife?"

Ruby's hands shook as she accepted the ring. Its weight was heavy, its beauty no longer simple. Her heart ached for all that had been lost, but she was full of gratitude to no longer suffer alone in her grief.

Outside, the train whistle sounded, and Ruby got to her feet. She pulled her daughter close.

"We'll take the train north," Elliot said. "Tonight. I have a friend who can help us. We'll marry tomorrow."

Ruby nodded, and together, they walked outside. Quickly, she ducked into the passenger car that Winston had kept empty. Through the window, she watched as Elliot hugged his father tight.

"We'll be back." His voice was steady. "One day, when the danger has passed."

"No need," he said. "I'll come to you."

The train began to chug, building up steam for the departure. Elliot sat across from her and Millie, his face resolute.

They pulled out of the station, and Ruby turned to watch the outline of the trees passing by, slow as time. The snow had stopped and stars glittered up above.

Life was constantly changing, that much she had learned. The future that faced her was nothing like what she'd planned, but it would be full of love for her daughter and appreciation for the man willing to stand by their side.

Ruby pulled her child in close, the softness of her breath gentle against her cheek.

Elliot watched them for a moment. "Everything will be all right. I can promise you that."

It might be. For the first time in ages, Ruby felt a flash of hope, as steady as the bright light of the moon.

Acknowledgments

I am so thankful to be an author, which is only possible with the love and support of so many of you. First, a huge thank-you to my readers. It's been such a pleasure to hear from you, meet with your book clubs, and read your insightful reviews. I am so grateful for you.

A million thanks to my brilliant editor, Chantelle Aimée Osman. How did I get lucky enough to have you on my team? Your trust, inspiration, and professionalism are a joy. Selena James, thank you so much for bringing this book to the finish line. I'm so excited to work with you, and I feel I have a champion in my corner.

Lake Union, what a joy it is to be one of your authors. You always deliver. Your publicity team goes above and beyond, the cover art is gorgeous, and your ability to connect me with readers is amazing. Huge thanks to everyone who worked on this book, including the experts behind the scenes, crushing it on marketing, sales, and every other shining facet. Thank you to the audio department—Brilliance, you're outstanding.

Charlotte Herscher, thank you for your guidance. You pushed me to dig deeper and write harder each round, maintaining a quiet humor through it all. Bill, thank you for the brilliant copy edits.

Stephanie Parkin, Jennifer Mattox, and Sarah Combs (with an honorable mention to Frankie Wolf), I couldn't ask for a better writers' group. Our Thursdays are so precious to me, as are the croissants and coffee. This book would not be nearly as good without you.

Brent Taylor, superagent . . . you know exactly what to say and when to say it. I'm beyond grateful for the years we've navigated all this together. Thank you, thank you, thank you.

To my big extended family, so much love. I cherish each moment we get to be together, as well as each and every one of you. Kathy and Butch, thank you for the writing retreats. Mom, thank you for all of it.

Finally, many thanks to Ryan, Hudson, and Hazel. You are my everything—your light always shines brighter than the moon. I love you.

About the Author

Photo © 2024 Dana Clark

Cynthia Ellingsen is the Amazon Charts bestselling author of *The Lighthouse Keeper*, *The Winemaker's Secret*, *A Bittersweet Surprise*, and *A Play for Revenge* in the Starlight Cove series as well as several standalone novels, including *The Lost Letters of Aisling*, *Marriage Matters*, and *When We Were Sisters*. She is a Michigan native and currently lives in Lexington, Kentucky, with her family and two Siamese cats. For more information visit www.cynthiaellingsen.com.